Finding

a

Husband

The Lost & Found Series

Kristen Casey

Finding a Husband

www.GallantFoxPress.com

ISBN-13: 978-0-9994045-2-2

Cover Design ©2017, 2021 Tugboat Design

Author Photo ©2016 Kathleen Oristian Photography

EST 2016

GALLANT FOX
PRESS

The Lost & Found Series

About this Book

Everyone has secrets, but theirs could tear them apart.

Molly has learned the hard way that she does *not* need a man. What she does need is a job, and she knows exactly which one she wants. There's a law firm hiring down in North Carolina, and Molly knows she can't go wrong with the reliable paycheck, warm weather, and pristine beaches. Her brother-in-law has even hooked her up with a tour guide in town. It seems perfect—until that guide turns out to be the gorgeous, intriguing son of one of the law partners, and Molly has to concede that she's in way over her head.

Though Jake is just as wrapped up in her as she is in him, he's also holding something back. Their feelings for each other are undeniable. But when the secrets they're keeping threaten not only Molly's chance to land her dream job, but Jake's entire future, the couple must make some hard decisions—and soon. If they don't, their relationship and their hearts might never recover.

Can Molly and Jake overcome the crucial things they've left unsaid? Or will history repeat itself, and force them into lives they can't endure?

Chapter One

MOLLY RAISED HER tray table to its full upright position, then turned to peer down the aisle toward the back of the plane. As she did so, she was careful not to make eye contact with the man across the aisle from her, who'd been driving hard to the hoop pretty much since takeoff. The grim middle-aged woman on her other side had been no help at all—she'd popped a couple motion sickness pills before they even left the ground, and two hours later was still slumped boneless against the shaded window.

Molly had already run through most of her in-flight avoidance repertoire: feigning sleep, then intense interest in the programs on the airplane headphones—but now she had to use the bathroom. There was only about twenty minutes left before they began their descent into Wilmington, so she was going to have to play it exactly right. If she went too soon and the bathrooms were full, "Joe Friendly" over in 14A was only going to follow her back and try to flirt some more. If Molly waited too long, she'd miss her chance—and no one wanted that. It was probably too late to pretend she didn't speak English, given that he'd heard her talking to the flight attendant for the last three hours or so.

Molly checked again and saw a balding, paunchy businessman exit the bathroom on the right. Okay, there was her cue. She flicked open her seatbelt and stood, using the empty headrests for balance as she made her way to the back of the plane. Halfway there, a kid spilled into the aisle in front of her, glasses askew and socks falling off his feet. With jerky, loping steps, he bee-lined for the open bathroom, and locked himself inside. *Damn.*

Molly didn't want to go back and start all over again. Instead, she passed through the short hallway with its two occupied lavatories, then searched the small kitchen area beyond for a flight attendant. If she could strike up a conversation quickly, she might be able to ignore Joe Friendly if he came hunting for her. Molly snorted. *If* was wishful thinking; knowing Joe, he was probably already on his way.

A touch on her arm confirmed her fear. "Hey there," he said. "I think you dropped this!" Molly turned around, frowning. Joe extended a small paperback of Sudoku puzzles toward her.

"Oh, sorry. That's not mine," she told him. She tried to be polite, but this had gotten ridiculous roughly fifteen minutes into the flight. Joe couldn't seem to take a hint and it was wearing thin.

"You sure? I could swear it fell right off your lap when you got up," he insisted.

"Nope. Never seen it before in my life." Molly gave him a vague, noncommittal sort of smile, then let her eyes slide away.

"Huh, that's weird," Joe mused, leaning on the wall across from her and giving Molly an obvious once-over.

The flight attendant in the kitchen finished arranging things in his cabinet and turned to them. Molly sighed, and deflated a bit more. Of *course* it would be the only male attendant on the flight, who seemed to view himself as some kind of high-altitude Casanova.

"I can take that for you," he said briskly. He whisked the little book out of Joe's hands and tossed it in a trash bag hanging from a cart, then shot Molly a conspiratorial smile. Now that he was facing her directly and not looming over her shoulder, she could see that his name tag read "Chad." Molly had already noticed his fake tan and blindingly white teeth—it was the stubble growing between his thick black eyebrows that was the real surprise. *Huh.* Chad apparently waxed his brows—but not often enough, it seemed. That was something new.

Molly kept her pleasant expression pasted on her face, but turned slightly away from them, letting her eyes go unfocused again as she stared off into the distance. Usually that worked quite well to communicate the *not-interested* vibe, but these two were hard cases.

Joe nudged her again. "Get a load of that," he snorted, tilting his head toward the bathroom the kid was locked inside. Horrible heaving noises could be heard within, and Molly grimaced, hoping the other door was the one that opened first.

Chad tossed his head and pushed himself officiously between them. "I'll take care of it," he said, rapping on the door. "Everything okay in there?" he called more loudly.

The kid fell silent, and the water turned on. "I'm okay," the little guy whimpered.

Chad rolled his eyes and smiled at Molly again. "We'll give him another minute or two. If he doesn't come out, I'll walk you up to first class, okay?"

Because…she couldn't find her way up to first class all by herself, Molly thought drily. There was that short, totally straight aisle to navigate, after all—and the daunting blue curtains, closed at the end. She didn't respond like she wanted to, though. She'd learned the hard way that people didn't react well to an attractive woman with a bad attitude.

So, Molly simply rubbed a hand over her face and muttered, "Thanks."

Joe didn't appreciate getting knocked out of position by the other man. He lifted his chin at Chad and blustered, "Hey, guy. You got any beer back here?"

Chad was not in the mood to hydrate the competition, though. He stared Joe down and snapped, "Sorry. We put everything away. Drink service ended ten minutes ago." Molly had no doubt he'd find something for *her*, if she asked—but she wasn't going to hand that minor victory to him.

Joe nodded, looked around one more time—and then seemed to realize that Molly would have to return to her seat eventually. With one last smarmy look her way, he shuffled back up the aisle and collapsed into 14A to wait her out.

Chad elbowed her, a bit too hard. "He bothering you?"

"No, it's all good. Thanks, though," Molly sighed. She absolutely hated being a captive audience. Between the seat belt sign and the inconvenient fact that they were however-many feet up in the air, there was nowhere for her to *flee*.

"No problem," Chad said. "Do you live in Wilmington, or are you just visiting?"

"Oh. Um, just visiting." Molly stared desperately at the bathroom doors. What in God's name was taking these people so long?

"Got some family there?" Chad prodded, unwilling to cede the field when he was so obviously seducing her like a boss.

Molly did actually have family in the area, but admitting it seemed unnecessary. Instead, she droned, "No, I'm heading down for a job interview." Like it was the worst thing in the world, instead of the best.

When she made to look away, Chad ducked down a bit to maintain eye contact. "Yeah? What do you do?"

"I'm an attorney," Molly told him flatly. Chad apparently hadn't been expecting that, because he reared back and had nothing at all to say in response. Not *That's hot*. Not *What are you, some kind of nerd?* Nothing.

At last, the kid emerged from his bathroom, looking wan and shaky. Molly and Chad eyed him as he staggered back up the aisle, then both turned back to the open bathroom door. With a huge intake of air, Chad steeled himself to peek inside—and was already shaking his head when he pulled out again.

"Don't go in there if you can help it," he told her with a wince. He reached into a cabinet for some paper towels and a bright green spray bottle, clearly hating life in that moment. Even Chad was going to have problems making disinfectant look sexy.

Molly blew out her own breath and stared at the other door hopefully. Maybe that person was only changing their clothes, or putting on makeup, or shaving. Something benign, sweet-smelling, and noncommunicable.

"So…" Chad began, setting the green bottle back down again. Molly could tell what was coming by his tone alone. "Why don't I give you my number? We can get together while we're both in town."

Molly shrugged, and held up her empty hands. "Left my phone in the seat pocket." Not that she expected it to work, but it was still worth a try.

Chad scowled at her. "You shouldn't do that," he scolded. "It could get stolen."

"Good to know," Molly retorted. Her phone was jammed in the back pocket of her jeans, pressed safely against the wall behind her. Did he think she was stupid?

"No joke," Chad emphasized. "But here—" He took his own phone out of his pocket, and said, "Give me your number, and I'll hit you up for drinks later."

Molly knew it was pointless—she didn't even bother resisting. She recognized, from long experience, that fighting simply took too much time and energy. Instead she said, "Sure. It's 617…" Molly rattled off the digits she knew by heart, and didn't even feel guilty about it.

The other door opened then, and Molly didn't wait. She spun and ducked in with one smooth motion, then slid the lock home behind her. The atmosphere inside, *naturally*, was a fetid miasma that choked her on her first inhale. Eyes watering, Molly tucked half her face inside her shirt collar, slapped her phone on the sink counter, and wrenched her jeans down. She'd better take care of business as soon as possible or she was liable to suffocate in there.

It seemed that Chad was content to get back to work, now that he had Molly's number in his possession. When she emerged from the bathroom—gasping for fresh air—he'd already left for the front of the aircraft. Molly could see him bending over the first-class passengers, his oily smirk firmly affixed to his face. She still had to contend with Joe in the seat across from her, though—as the plane began its landing sequence, he leaned into the aisle with his best winning pitch.

"I'm only in town for a couple days," he told Molly. "But hey—why don't we grab some dinner later? I know a great place right on the river. They make a mean margarita."

"Sorry, I can't," Molly replied. "I've got a meeting later." It was a date with room service, but how would he know?

"That's all right," Joe assured her. "I can wait. Here's my number. Call me when you're done, and we'll meet for drinks." He handed her his business card—Joe Friendly, it seemed, was actually named "Mike," and worked in software sales.

"Not sure if I can swing that, but thanks," Molly told him. He was watching what she did with the card, so instead of cramming it into the ashtray in her armrest, Molly tucked it into the outer pocket of her leather tote—soon to be joined by her used boarding pass and all the other travel ephemera she planned to throw away later.

"Why don't you give me your number, too?" Joe/Mike said. "You know, to be safe?"

Molly groaned under her breath, then rattled off those ten sweet digits she knew so well. They rolled right off her tongue—like a lullaby, or a prayer. She only hoped that Chad and Mike liked their fast-food burritos delivered.

THE PLANE WOULD probably be on the ground in ten minutes, but Molly retrieved her laptop from her bag anyway. Once she started it up, though, she simply sat there staring blankly at the screen, deep in thought. Her connections—such as they were—appeared to be paying off. When Molly told her sister about this trip, Mina had immediately drafted her husband, Grey, to help.

He had an interesting history, but it was a useful one. After spending three years in the service, Grey took a break from the military to attend college. He'd gone to UNC Chapel Hill, where he'd been the president of the DKE fraternity—despite being both older and a married man at the time. After graduation, Mina's husband rejoined the Marines as an officer, and he remained one to this day.

As it turned out, Grey had a fraternity brother who, conveniently, lived in Wilmington. "Jake" had agreed to look out for Molly while she was in town, after little more than a casual phone call from her brother-in-law. She wasn't entirely sure what that entailed—yet more "drinks" would probably be involved. But given the fact that Molly had rarely known a soul in any position to help her, she was inclined to accept the favor with a grateful heart. Even if Grey could be a bit odd, and any friend of his was probably suspect, too. Though Jake had seemed normal enough when he'd texted to arrange things, Molly knew she should be careful.

At the very least, Molly was looking forward to some warmer southern weather. Winter had been extra cold in Boston this year, and it had been difficult not to get taken in by the fishing photos her dad sometimes emailed her. Out of the two vastly-different locales her parents had landed in,

Molly had fallen hard for her father's current home. And no wonder—those beautiful Carolina beaches were real heartbreakers. Knowing she could live there full-time—if she played her cards right—had made the long, gray winter and abrupt populace of Molly's current town much harder to stomach lately.

Molly had to get her ducks in a row, regardless. First off, she had to land a real job soon, since her part-time gig at the legal aid office wasn't going to hold her for much longer. Molly had student loans from two degrees coming due, now that she'd graduated. She also lived in a sublet room in a group house—whose lease, she'd recently learned, was nearing its end.

Her family, God knew, would be no help whatsoever. Somehow, despite all her careful planning, Molly had ended up in a fix. She needed to find something fast and didn't want to make a rash decision because of it.

In the current hiring climate, Molly would have to make her own luck. She needed to be savvy and clever to land the perfect job. The alumni office at school hadn't come up with many leads, so she'd worked the internet, done her research, and lined up a few interviews for herself.

There was only one position Molly really wanted, however, and that was the junior associate job at *Alexander, Polk & Futch*, in Wilmington, North Carolina. They had taken the unusual step of flying her down and putting her up in a bed and breakfast for two weeks—so she could get to know the firm and attorneys, and submit to a round of interviews to see if she was "a good fit." Molly intended to be more than good—she was aiming to be *perfect*.

It didn't help her frame of mind—her necessary *focus*—that her life had gotten weirdly isolated and lonely for someone so used to being in demand. The people she knew in Boston were beginning to move on from this stage in their lives: leaving town, getting jobs, getting married. Her best friend and roommate from undergraduate school, Meg, was the most glaring case. Molly could only talk about true love so often with her before turning a little green—because Molly knew how fickle and false the emotion could be. True, Meg's fiancé Edward seemed devoted enough, but...you never could tell, could you? Molly knew that for a fact.

She'd keep an eye on Meg. And Molly herself would stick with what had worked for her all this time—when you were pretty and popular, people didn't tend to cross-examine you about your private life. And when you were smart on top of that, good things came your way. Which was fine, because Molly's plans for herself did *not* include following in her parent's footsteps—the less she was judged for their choices, the better.

She wasn't going to be shiftless and disloyal like her father. And she wasn't going to marry for looks or money like her mother. Molly's prime directive for years had involved working hard and avoiding anything or anyone that reminded her of her mom, dad, or a certain young man named Carter. It worked like a charm, too.

Molly shook herself back to the present, glanced across the aisle at Mike, then opened her browser and called up her bookmarked list of favorite websites. In seconds, she was staring at a large photo of a beautiful Victorian house right in the middle of historic Wilmington. It was a confection, really—pastel yellow with gingerbread trim, colorful pots of flowers hanging from the porch ceiling, and dark green shutters. It was exactly the kind of house Molly had always dreamed of living in—someplace she could stay long enough to know the neighbors, and even the neighbors' kids and dogs.

She sighed, eyeing the estimated value of the property. On the one hand, it didn't seem terribly expensive compared to houses in the suburbs of Boston, or even the new condos downtown. But on the other hand, Molly didn't know how much the salary of a bottom-rung attorney would stretch down there. Soon, though, she would know if her life was taking a turn for the better. Soon, she'd know if she could afford a real home like the one in the picture. Molly nodded. One step at a time—she was so close now.

IN THE BAGGAGE claim, Molly found Grey's friend lounging against a wall and holding a hand-lettered sign with her name on it. He was tall and broad-shouldered, with sandy-blond hair and sparkling blue eyes framed by inky lashes. As Molly assessed him, she noted that he was painfully clean-cut—his studied casualness both preppy and reeking of wealth. Molly felt her herself stiffen, already on guard for what was sure to be an arrogant opening statement.

Grey hadn't mentioned that Jake was a looker, but what could she expect? As oblivious as her brother-in-law was, he probably didn't even realize. If not that, he might have assumed Molly would be immune, as she usually was.

She smoothed back her ponytail and stood a little straighter, wishing she'd put on some lipstick in the airplane bathroom. She hadn't wanted to encourage either Chad or Mike, though. If Molly was using her head, she wouldn't want to encourage this guy, either. It was better to view things like clothes and makeup as armor—an essential barrier holding trolls like this one at arm's length, and *not* as invitations to get closer.

Jake might be gorgeous, but Molly knew better than most what could hide behind a handsome face. She wasn't fooled by his crooked, charming smile for one minute. She'd have to be just as wary of this frat brother from the Dekes as she would any other guy—probably even more so. A woman should never underestimate the rot that might harbor inside a shiny, rich shell, after all. Even if that shell was pushing off the wall and heading right toward her, grinning charmingly.

Jake had clearly been supplied with a physical description of Molly, because he was suddenly a man on a mission.

"You must be Molly," he drawled when he reached her side. He was so certain of himself that he crumpled his little sign and dropped it right in a trash can on his way.

"Yup," Molly agreed. She glanced around the area, wishing for a vending machine or a little kiosk where she could buy some water. The air wafting in from the sliding doors smelled of diesel fuel and cigarette smoke—and it was way hotter and more humid than Boston's.

He stuck out his hand. "I'm Jake." her tour guide looked a little taken aback by how terse Molly was. She didn't like being this unfriendly, but the truth was—she'd been surprised by the way Jake's looks affected her. It had thrown her off-balance, and she was scrambling to find her footing.

"Nice to meet you," Molly told him, though she kept her tone chilly. "I told Grey you didn't have to do this, but he kind of insisted." *Good. Now he wouldn't think this was her idea.*

"No worries. I didn't have a lot going on at work this week. I'm happy to show you around a bit." His voice was smooth and deep, with a touch of Southern twang. Molly hated to admit it, but it was a voice absolutely *made* for the bedroom.

She forced herself to look away from the sexy mouth uttering those words, away from Jake's open collar and tanned throat. She wouldn't be anywhere near a bedroom with this guy, because she had learned her lesson far too well the first time she'd met a man like him. Molly was no fool, and never, *ever* made the same mistake twice. Not now. Not ever.

In the knot of other passengers swarming the baggage claim, Molly noted both Chad and Mike hurrying by. Chad caught her eye and gave her a little salute that he probably thought looked spicy, but he didn't pause. Mike waited a moment or two to be sure he had her attention, then raised the slip of paper he'd written her number on in greeting. Had it ever left his hand? Molly wondered—for the umpteenth time in the last few years—if the men would even realize she'd given them the wrong number on purpose, or if they'd assume the mistake was accidental. She sighed heavily.

"What the heck was that all about?" Jake inquired. He strolled after her, then easily grabbed her bags off the carousal when she reached for them.

"They spent half the flight jockeying for position—I had to give them my number just to get rid of them," Molly explained, rolling her eyes. Jake probably thought she sounded like a snot, but she couldn't let herself care. It was probably a good lesson for him, anyway.

"Seriously?" he gaped, turning to check out the other men. "Not your real one, right?"

"Are you nuts? I've been handing out the digits for a 24-hour Taco Bell for six years now." Molly didn't usually like to let guys peek behind the curtain—especially ones she wasn't good friends with—but she was only here for two weeks. She'd be gone before much could come of it, and besides, what was Jake going to do? Rat her out to every guy she'd ever met in a bar?

Instead, he chuckled—a rumbling, erotic sound that warmed Molly's insides. She'd been trying to ignore his sultry voice, but he hadn't laughed like *that* yet. It was probably for the best that he'd kept it under wraps—Molly might have found an excuse not to meet him otherwise, out of sheer self-preservation.

He tried another smile on her. "So. How was your flight?"

"It was fine. Other than those two, obviously." She jerked a thumb at Mike, standing at the information counter. Chad had already jammed a cigarette between his lips and disappeared outside.

"This all you got?" Jake inquired. He hoisted her big bag up on his shoulder and adjusted his grip on her hanging bag.

He was wearing a button-down shirt with the sleeves rolled up, a worn pair of khaki shorts, and boat shoes. Jake was fit and clean and tan, and might have been a model in some trendy, overpriced clothes catalog. Molly repressed a shudder. Jake was everything she tried to avoid if she could help it.

"Yeah," she told him. "That's it." Then she clapped her hands together, forced any thought of how good he smelled from her mind—was that his deodorant, or some insidious new kind of cologne?—and turned toward the sliding doors. "Where to?"

ALEXANDER, POLK & FUTCH was having Molly's rental car delivered to the B&B, but not until early the next morning. Until then, Molly was on her own, and she would have been fine hailing a cab—but Grey and Mina had been adamant.

They'd wanted her to meet up with this friend of theirs right from the get-go, and hadn't budged on the idea despite Molly's initial protests. When they told her Jake was a prosecutor in Brunswick County, Molly had supposed it couldn't hurt to get his take on the legal community there—so eventually she'd agreed. The more she'd thought about it, the more it made sense. But that was before she'd seen for herself what kind of guy Jake was. Now, she was here in Wilmington, at some frat boy's mercy.

Molly groaned to herself. Calling Grey a *complicated* guy was being generous, so having to be shepherded around by a man that had somehow earned her brother-in-law's seal of approval suddenly wasn't sitting all that well. What had she been thinking? Molly should've known better—she'd rubbed shoulders with her share of frat guys during college, and certainly her share of boys who were full of themselves. But when Mina and Grey arranged this whole thing with

Jake, Molly was so staggered at the notion of Grey being helpful, that she hadn't really stopped to consider the ramifications of what she'd agreed to. She felt touchy and irritable about it now, and when Jake waltzed her up to his shiny new Audi out in the short-term lot, well…her bad mood took a bit of a nosedive.

Inside the hot car, Molly caught another whiff of Jake's cologne when he shifted to put on his seatbelt. She cringed. The scent was faint, but crisp and pleasant. If she'd been smelling it in the middle of a department store, for example, she might have even liked it. Ever since the debacle that was Carter, however, Molly had an aversion to men who wore cologne. For the most part, they seemed like preening, effeminate dandies. Except—that characterization might not apply here.

The man sitting beside her was both exactly like Carter…and *nothing* like him. The problematic cologne was light enough to possibly be his deodorant—it *was* really humid out—or maybe even his laundry detergent. Molly only caught a fleeting hint of it when the breeze changed direction or he moved a certain way. Whatever she was smelling, the urge to get closer, to get a nose full of it, was maddening.

By now, Carter might have even managed to tell her what scent he was wearing—and how much it cost. Molly, at age seventeen, would have been suitably impressed. In contrast, Jake looked completely oblivious to the whole entire *thing* going on in Molly's head.

She sat back in her seat and fought a shimmer of confusion, of *doubt*, that whispered down her spine. Damn it, she had her rules for a *reason*, and Molly would be a colossal idiot if she forgot them all now—her career and her future were on the line. No frat guys. No rich guys. No smug bastards, and *definitely* no men wearing cologne. She had never had occasion to question those dictates before now, and today should be no exception.

It would be okay, Molly told herself, trying to stay calm. Jake could drive her to her B&B, and thereby satisfy the agreement he had with Grey. Molly would then go about her business, interviewing at the firm—like a rock star—for the next two weeks like nothing had happened. If Jake tried to see her again, she would simply say she was too busy, and put him off. Easy. Grey and Mina would be content that they'd helped her in their own small way. Jake would be off the hook and could return to his regularly-scheduled life. And Molly would secure her dream job for herself without any good-looking, good-smelling interference.

It was an excellent plan, and it would have worked. It *should* have worked. But then, on the highway heading away from the airport, Jake started shooting her *significant* looks.

"What?" Molly demanded, frowning at him. For a guy getting the arctic treatment, he was awfully cheerful.

Jake smirked, "You think you've got me all figured out, don't ya darlin'?"

Molly pressed her lips together in annoyance, then blurted, "Look, Jake, I'm sure you're a very nice person, but I've met plenty of guys like you before. I've even dated some of them. So, yeah, I can say with confidence that I know exactly what your deal is." She shrugged dismissively. God, she sounded like a shrew, but it had to be done. Better that she not lead him on and give him any untenable ideas about her.

"Is that so?" Jake arched one quizzical brow at her, then looked back to the road. One casual hand was draped across the top of his steering wheel, and the other rested on his gearshift, disconcertingly close to her thigh.

"Mm-hm."

"Lemme guess—I'm a spoiled frat guy raising hell with Daddy's money, leaving a trail of roofies and broken hearts in my self-absorbed wake. That about cover it?"

Whoa. He was good. "Pretty much," Molly agreed, feeling defensive. But given how badly she'd just insulted him, she couldn't quite figure out what he found so entertaining.

"Well, I am also confident that I've got *your* number," Jake told her, glancing over at her again. Could eyes dance? Because his baby-blues appeared to be dancing. At minimum, they were annoyingly sparkly.

"*Please*," Molly scoffed. "You don't know anything about me." She hoped.

"Oh, like you know *me* from Adam? How 'bout this? Everything comes easy for you and now you're frustrated because you can't find a single challenge worth sinking your teeth into. I bet you just flew through school, didn't you?" He paused to eye her, then nodded to himself, satisfied that he was on the right track. "You've been getting too much attention for all the wrong reasons, probably for years. So now, if a guy has the nerve to notice that you're a pretty girl, you write him off from the get-go—because no way in hell is he gonna respect you for your smarts, right? All men want to do is beg, borrow, and steal their way into your bed."

Molly sat there feeling slightly sick. Who the hell *was* this guy?

"Am I right, Miss Molly?" Jake asked again, not letting her off the hook.

She swallowed. "Maybe a tad," she admitted softly.

"Look. I'm not an asshole just because I know Grey, or because I was in a fraternity, or because my family has some money," Jake told her gently. "How about throwing me a bone, and not sentencing me before I've had a fair trial?"

Molly finally had to laugh—because *of course* another attorney would say that.

"All right," she said grudgingly. "I'm sorry I was being a bitch. Truce?"

"Truce," he smiled, and Molly looked away again, blinded by all those white teeth, those blue, blue eyes, that tan skin, and that sun-kissed hair. Geez, he looked like Barbie's boyfriend, "Southern Charm Ken." The more her mind chewed on his words, though, the more she zeroed in on one phrase in particular. It wasn't the one where he'd called her pretty. It *wasn't*.

"Why would I think you were an asshole because you know Grey?" she asked, squinting curiously at him.

"He's *your* brother-in law," Jake retorted, but when his gaze flicked to her, his eyes were wary. "You tell me."

God. *That* was a loaded question. Molly had never liked or trusted her sister's husband—but she'd been keeping that a closely-held secret for more than ten years. As far as she could tell, she was the only person on earth who didn't love the guy. Except, maybe, for this man, who had suddenly turned a lot more intriguing.

"Grey has his moments," she replied vaguely. She'd certainly thrown that comment out before—no reason it wouldn't work again.

Jake turned and raised both eyebrows at her, calling *bullshit*.

"Not all of them stellar," Molly admitted.

"Ya think?" Jake laughed again, but he didn't say more. That was probably for the best. Molly had been lying to her sister Mina for years about how she felt about Grey—it would get even harder to do if Molly was in possession of sordid college tales about him.

"Almost there," Jake murmured, cutting into her thoughts. "How about some lunch before I drop you off?"

"Sounds great," Molly replied absently. It wasn't what she'd intended to do, but absolutely none of her meeting

with Jake was going as she expected. Later, she was going to
have to process what that might mean.

Chapter Two

J AKE'S CELL RANG, then went silent. Rang, shuttled to voicemail, then rang *again*. Molly shot him a look, so Jake reluctantly picked up the stupid thing. A quick glance at the screen confirmed it was Blake, but seriously—who else would call and hang up like that? Jake had become very comfortable ignoring the irritating alerts of his phone in the last few years, and now was no different. Still, when it pinged with an incoming voicemail at the next red light, he tossed a "sorry" Molly's way and cued up the message.

"Damn it, Jake. Pick up. *I need* to ask you about the tent!" Blake's voice said. She'd become a little confused lately about the difference between "need" and "want," and her voice had gone shrill by the time she reached the word *tent,* so…groaning inwardly, Jake hit three to delete the message. He levelled a quick, casual smile at his passenger. *Move along, nothing to see here.*

In the last few weeks, Jake had unwillingly learned everything there was to know about party tents—there were flat roofs and peaked ones, PVC frames and metal ones. Some tents had scalloped edges, like they belonged to a jousting knight. And some weren't quite *white* enough. As

Jake saw it, the reception site folks would provide a perfectly adequate tent—one they knew how to use, and which fit their patio exactly. If it rained on the day of the wedding, the guests would be covered—both literally and figuratively. However, his rather particular fiancée and her mother had taken one look at *that* tent and proclaimed it "common," so they were now on the hunt to find something better. It was enough to drive a man mad, and Jake had only been engaged for a couple of months. He hated to think of what was still in store for him.

Before the light changed, he typed out a quick text to Blake—In a meeting. Can't talk—and was rewarded with an almost instantaneous response: Remember what Mama said!

Did everyone think his memory was deficient? He wasn't a goddamn *child*. It had only been a week since Blake's mother had informed Jake that he was "the devil's own" flirt, and that it was as likely to hurt him in the courtroom as it was to help. At the time, Jake had only been trying to order some iced tea from their harried waitress; a smile had seemed like the least he could do to soften the blow of yet another drink order. But that was Mrs. Sutton for you—she never did like him to talk to anyone but her daughter.

Jake silenced his phone, and dropped it back into the center console. When the light turned green, he drove on, not the least bit sorry for his little white lie. Miss Molly was peering thoughtfully at him, though.

"Anything important?" she inquired.

"Naw, we're good," he assured her. "There's a sushi place right up there. I hope you're hungry." Another flirting smile aimed at his ward for the week. A *devilish* one, Jake thought resentfully.

Molly grinned back at him. "Starved!" she chirped.

Lord. Once the girl decided to drop her dukes and play nice, Jake had realized that she wasn't merely attractive, as he'd first assumed, but drop-dead gorgeous: all long legs and long dark hair and a thousand-watt smile. He had no idea what the hell was going on back at the airport, and he wondered if those other men had even understood what they were missing—what Molly could be like if she chose. It was almost like she was a rosebud—lovely enough on its own, but once it bloomed...well, shoot.

As Jake parked and led her inside the restaurant, he took a moment to examine her more closely. It was no wonder guys came out of the woodwork to gun for her. Molly had naturally pretty looks, an intelligent gaze, and a mostly-cheerful demeanor. The way she smiled at janitors and checkout girls—with a look that was both a little shy and a little hopeful—made her *seem* sweet and approachable as all-get-out. When you paired that with her unconscious sexiness, the entire package became hazardous. But Molly appeared to be deft as hell at blocking and deflecting the male species. She only looked approachable until you actually *tried* to do it—and then some seriously fortified stone walls reared up in your face.

Still, Jake had managed to get past all that with a bit of straight-shooting, and the victory felt sweet. Because once Molly decided to like you, the effect was mind-boggling. Worth the effort. *Not* that any of that mattered to him, he reminded himself. Jake himself was off the market in a big way now, and it wouldn't do to forget it. Perhaps his blushing bride was onto something after all—maybe his memory *did* need some work.

"You know, I just realized that you never told me your last name," Molly mused, studying him over the edge of her menu. They'd settled in at a little corner table near the windows, and Jake had the distinct sense that Molly was trying to figure him out in return—for real this time, not that snap judgement she'd made before. It made sense, he supposed. If he was opposing counsel, she'd want to know what she was up against. And if he wasn't...she'd still want to know what she was up against. Jake shifted in his chair, uncomfortable with the direction *that* sent his thoughts.

"Alexander," he told her, then waited for realization to dawn. All this time, he'd assumed she knew who he was. But her question made it clear she didn't, and Jake wondered how she'd take the news.

Molly laughed a little. "Huh. That's funny, because I'm here to interview with a firm called *Alexander, Polk & Futch.*"

Jake didn't bother responding to the obvious—he merely raised his eyebrows at her, sat, and waited.

When the light came on, she gaped at him. "Omigod," Molly breathed out in a rush. "Are *you* Mr. Alexander? You sounded so much older on the phone! And then…but we texted—and…"

Jake grinned, because how ridiculous was that? The notion that he'd spent the last several years building a prominent, well-respected law firm instead of drinking beer and watching football was pretty hilarious. "No, honey," he laughed, cutting her off. "I'm his son."

Molly sat back in her chair, stunned. She turned it over in her mind, shook her head a couple of times as she toyed with the idea, and then—like he knew she would—scowled.

"Did Grey *know* that?" she demanded.

Not that Jake would put it past Grey Whitney to pull a prank like that, but… "No," he told her. "I don't believe he did."

Molly blinked, taking that in. It *was* a bit of a coincidence, Jake knew. "But *you* knew all this time?" She sounded a little betrayed, poor thing.

"Yeah," Jake admitted. "I guess I assumed you did, too."

Molly grabbed a bit frantically for the little pencil on the table, and began checking off boxes on the paper menu. When she finished, she took a long drink from her sweating water glass, but didn't relinquish that pencil—she was clutching it nearly like she might a shiv. It didn't matter—

Jake always ordered the same thing anyway, and could recite it by heart.

"Does your dad know?" Molly inquired, heading toward full-blown panic now.

Jake nodded and smiled, in what he hoped was a soothing manner.

"And he's *okay* with it?" she cried, seeming appalled.

"Yup," Jake said, then reached across to pry the pencil from her fist before she went and hurt herself—or him. "It's not like I have any say in whether you get hired or not."

In fact, his father had been the one to figure out that the sharp-minded legal recruit he was flying in from Boston was the same person Jake had been asked to show around Wilmington. What was more, Clay Alexander, Esquire, had been overjoyed to discover that his son had a connection, however tenuous, to Molly. Apparently, she had impeccable grades, perfect writing samples, and sterling references. Jake's dad figured that if the firm could manage to snare her, she'd likely make partner inside of five years.

When his father joked that he should "charm the pants off" the new law grad from up north, Jake doubted Clay had meant *literally*. Unfortunately, that was the direction Jake's thoughts seemed intent on taking. Nookie was totally off the table, though—he was, much as he'd like to ignore it, engaged to be married now. This—whatever it was— between him and Molly, would have to remain at a flirting-only level. Jake would keep reminding himself as often as necessary, until the message sunk in.

He looked at her across the table. Jake wasn't quite sure why he'd agreed so readily to show Molly around...and really, he'd rather not deal with the notion that it might be because Blake had been fussing at him the morning Grey Whitney called. Blake was merely being Blake, and it'd be pointless to try to punish her for it. To be fair, when Jake agreed to do this favor for Grey, he hadn't expected the "little sister-in-law" to be quite like *this*. Hell, he barely knew Grey, who'd been a few years ahead of him at Chapel Hill and his mentor in the Dekes for less than six months. Jake barely knew him and even worse, he barely liked him. Grey was mercurial at best, and a moody, brooding asshole at worst. Molly was anything but. If Jake had known that, he might have accepted the case with a few more reservations.

At first, when he picked her up, the issue appeared to be that Molly either had an enormous stick up her ass, or she despised him on sight. So, Jake had laid on the charm in escalating increments, trying to wear her down—and it had the exact *opposite* effect it normally did. He'd had to shift tactics, and thankfully he'd been successful. The going was easier now that they had cleared the air. However, with Molly now responding to him the way she was, Jake was going to have to pull back a bit. He should, anyway. Wasn't that what an unavailable man would do?

Except, being reserved wasn't in his nature, and he was enjoying Molly *liking* him too much to quit. Much more of *this*, and Jake might be in danger of a full-on extracurricular fling. Mentally, he knew he was already reviewing all the ways he could free up his schedule for the next couple weeks, and what he might show her around town. Where he could take her, what they could do, who he could introduce her to…the possibilities were lining up in his brain like toy soldiers. Jake supposed he was thinking like a hound—Blake's mother could probably sense it all the way across town.

Sitting here stewing about his character faults, as it happened, wasn't the best way to keep Molly from getting suspicious of him all over again. Jake was going to have to make some conversation here, and fast. He blurted out the first dang thing that came to mind.

"What's your favorite color?" he asked. God. Like he was five.

She didn't even blink at his absurdity, though. Instantly, Molly pointed through the window and off the back dock, saying, "Green. No! Blue. See? Right there past the foamy white part." She indicated a spot just outside the wake of a passing boat, where the water did indeed straddle the line between blue and green. "Whatever color that is—that's my favorite," she declared.

Well. That had gone better than expected. Kindergarten it was, then. Jake found himself asking, "Alright, then what's your favorite animal?"

"Groundhog," was her succinct response. The waitress arrived with their food, and set down an assortment of colorfully-arranged dishes between them.

"Pardon?" Jake tried again, once the waitress left. Molly was shuffling the plates around, taking what she'd ordered, and shifting his food closer to him.

"Groundhogs," she affirmed. "They're, like, the alpha ZFGs of the natural world. How can you not love them?"

"I'm sorry. Are you talking in code right now? Because I have no clue what you just said."

She snorted, and somehow it was adorable. "ZFG? Never heard that before?"

Jake shook his head, poured some low-sodium soy sauce for himself, and waited to see where this was going.

"Oh, come on." Molly popped a bite of rice into her mouth and chewed eagerly, then snagged the high-octane soy sauce for herself.

"Sorry?" he tried, but mostly he just wanted her to keep talking. Keep spouting whatever crazy-ass…

"*Zero Fucks Given*, Jake. Groundhogs don't give a fuck. They don't eat anyone. No one's trying to eat them. They don't care about being popular or pretty or smart, or even about hanging out in the cool part of town—they just live out there next to whatever road they find, and do what they do. In all their lumpy, snuffling glory. I bet they'd wear sweat pants every day if they could. And shirts with ketchup on them."

Jake opened his mouth… then closed it abruptly, when he found he had no ready answer for that. "Okay—how about your favorite song?" *ZFG*? Was Molly even serious right now? He couldn't remember the last time he'd heard so many curse words exit a woman's mouth at one time. He kind of loved it.

"That's easy—*Super Bon Bon*. Or…maybe *Jump Around*. Depends on how tipsy I am." She grinned, the little tart.

Jake pressed his lips together, trying not to look horrified, because Molly was seriously amazing. Even with her terrible taste in music.

She mistook his silence as more ignorance on his part, though. Molly chanted out a couple lines of the first song— then, when Jake still looked blank, she actually began rapping a whole stanza of the second song. Finally, Molly gave up and shook her head at him in disgust.

"You're hopeless," she smiled, like he was some kind of rare, alien creature. But come *on*—she knew he was in a fraternity in college—of *course* Jake knew those songs. They were probably in the party song hall of fame. That didn't mean he'd ever heard a woman claim them as her favorites, though.

"I like the Brothers Osborne," he offered calmly, nearly certain she wouldn't have heard of them but wanting to participate nonetheless. "*It Ain't My Fault*?" he asked. "You might like them—they're from your neck of the woods."

"I don't have a neck of the woods, dude," Molly scoffed, pushing seaweed salad around her plate with her wooden chopsticks. It smelled good, like sesame. He'd never had it, but rather abruptly Jake wished he'd ordered some, too. Why *did* he always get the same thing, anyway? Would it kill him to try something new once in a while?

"I thought Grey said you were from Maryland—that's where they're from. Here, listen." Jake cued up the song and gave her his phone. When she took it, he reached forward impulsively and snagged a bite of the seaweed from her plate. Doing it felt companionable, the action of a close friend, or even a boyfriend. Molly didn't bat an eyelash, and Jake congratulated himself on yet another victory. The seaweed wasn't half bad, either.

She made all the polite sorts of comments one might expect after listening to the song, but he couldn't decide whether she'd actually enjoyed it or not. They lapsed into an extended silence while they ate the rest of their food, but it felt comfortable rather than awkward. Jake offered Molly some of his spicy tuna roll, and in return she pushed more of the seaweed salad onto his plate. After a while, though, Jake thought he ought to stop staring at her and *say* something again. She beat him to it.

"Hey, so…how far is the beach from here?" Molly inquired, as if she'd been waiting for the right moment to ask him.

Jake frowned. "What do you mean?"

"I mean," Molly said in exasperation, "I have a few days with no interviews while I'm here. One of those days I have to go see my dad, but I'd like to hit the beach on the others."

Jake blinked at her. The primary question in his mind—her *dad?*—was rapidly supplanted by a tidal wave of sordid images of Molly in a swimsuit. Molly laughing in the waves, hair blowing around her face. Molly lying on a towel on the sand, skin tan and gleaming, her long body stretched—Jake coughed, *hard*, to dislodge that dangerous avenue of thought from his skull.

"Molly, there's like a hundred beautiful beaches in spitting distance of here. It's not just one place." When he laughed, it sounded awfully nervous and guilty, but Molly didn't appear to notice.

She bit her lip, weighing what he said. "Well…then what's the *best* one?"

Jake thought about that a minute. "Maybe Carolina beach, but I doubt your rental has four-wheel drive. Kure or Surf City could work, but Wrightsville is probably gonna be too crowded this time of year."

Molly was tapping all that into her phone, not looking at him. Jake wondered if he should offer to take her, or if she'd maybe even *invite* him to go along. But that couldn't possibly be a good idea, right? Blake was proud of her figure and all, and didn't usually feel like other girls were much competition …but if she ever got a good look at Molly, that could change. Molly appeared to be literally *everything* his petite, manicured fiancée was not.

"How do you spell *Kure*?" Molly interjected.

Jake quickly shoved a piece of tuna tataki in his mouth. In the time it took to chew the fish, he tried to get his head on straight. It was no use beating himself up about picturing Molly in a bikini—he was a *dude*, after all—but his mama and daddy had raised a gentleman. Despite his thoughts, Jake knew he'd never actually *act* on any of them.

He had to get a handle on the insidious way his brain kept making comparisons between Blake and Molly, though. It didn't matter whether they were alike or different, because he was *engaged* to only *one* of them. It was a done deal, and Jake was not going to be a dirtbag about it. Jesus.

When he could speak clearly again, he told her, "K—U—R—E."

"Thanks," Molly murmured, finishing up what she was doing and pushing her phone away again. She grabbed her chopsticks and picked up another piece of sushi—eel, he thought—and after a quick perusal, popped it in her mouth.

Jake gave her a moment to chew, then inquired, "Did I hear you say that your father lives around here?" Changing the subject: a tried-and-true tactic for a reason.

"Oh!" Molly squeaked around the food in her mouth, though he couldn't imagine why she'd be surprised. She'd been the one to bring it up, after all. She held up a finger while she finished chewing, swallowed with some effort, and then took an extra moment to sip at her tea. After delaying as long as she possibly could, Molly explained, "He doesn't exactly *live* here. He's just staying with my uncle for a while."

"I see," Jake murmured. But he didn't, not really. There was definitely more to that story. "Where?" It was the simplest in his flurry of questions.

"Holden Beach. That's not too far, right?" Molly shrugged it off. Didn't she *know?*

"No. Maybe forty-five minutes south of here," he guessed. "Easy drive." Jake waited for her to explain, but nothing more seemed to be forthcoming. Molly fussed with the strap of her handbag and the placement of her chopsticks, and *looked* pleasant enough—but she'd stopped meeting his eye. Somehow the question about her father had deep-sixed their entire lunch date.

"You all done?" Jake gestured at her nearly empty plate. "Want anything else?"

Molly heaved a relieved-sounding sigh. "No, I'm good! Totally stuffed. We should probably go find where I'm staying, though. Right? I told the lady I'd be there by four—she's probably wondering what happened to me." Molly uttered those last words with a little self-deprecating sound, as if the notion that someone might care what became of her was downright laughable. *Huh.*

Jake raised a hand to beckon for the check. Five stilted minutes later they were in his car and driving through the shaded streets. In no time at all, they'd found the pretty little bed and breakfast Carla Denson opened after her husband died several years back. Jake smothered a smile at that. His mother *had* to have been responsible for the choice of where to station Molly; she'd always been particularly fond of Mrs.

Denson. Regardless, soon after they rolled up, Molly was ensconced in her large, airy room with her meager amount of luggage, and Jake was...

Jake was sitting in his running car, wondering what the hell had just happened. She'd summarily dismissed him—pleasantly, but still—with no question about when they'd see each other again. After spending the last few hours enjoying Molly's company, it was a little like being hit with a cartoon mallet—Jake was dazed. Maybe even had little bluebirds flying in circles around his head. In order to convince himself to put the Audi in gear and drive away, he had to make deals with himself: it was okay to see Molly again, because he'd promised Grey he would. It was okay to see her again, because he was a gentleman and wouldn't cheat on Blake anyway. It was okay to have all these sudden, crazy, head-spinning feelings about a woman he'd just met because...it was *not* okay to have these feelings. Jake traded in the mallet analogy for one of a shoddily built go-kart, hurtling downhill at full speed. He only hoped he could find the damn brakes before he crashed.

Chapter Three

THE NEXT MORNING, Molly found that her rental car—a nondescript maroon four-door that hopefully sported a powerful A/C system—had been delivered as promised. However, on the way to her first interview at *Alexander, Polk & Futch*, the car began wheezing and shuddering, and Molly had to acknowledge that it wasn't because she was out of practice with the whole driving thing. As if to emphasize the point, the "check engine" light flared front-and-center, emitting a blaring warning tone. Molly pulled to the side of the road, shut off the car, and turned on the hazards—then fished around in the glove compartment for the rental agreement packet.

She found the company number and dialed them on her cell, but as Molly tried to navigate the automated phone system, it started getting warm in the car—really warm. Without the air conditioning running, she may as well have been sitting in a broiling oven, and no amount of pressed powder in the world could counteract the effects of *that*. Molly was wearing a beautiful suit that she'd found on consignment back in Boston, but it was black *and* wool. Even though the dashboard put the outside temperature at a fairly reasonable eighty, the humidity was such that Molly was already sweating through her sleeveless shell.

Her makeup was melting, her hair was wilting, and she had spent far too many nervous minutes getting ready this morning to have this happen right now. Molly checked her mirrors for oncoming traffic, then got out quickly to round the car and stand on the sidewalk. She tried to get a live human on the phone. There was no shade, and no breeze.

Molly soon realized that she was going to make a lousy first impression, regardless. The rental company was closed. She needed to call someone at the firm to help her, but it was seven-thirty in the morning—would anyone even be there yet?

She'd just gotten the "Please call back during normal business hours" message and thrown her hands up in frustration, when life got indescribably worse—a familiar, gleaming silver Audi pulled up on the roadside, two feet behind her rented sedan.

When Jake unfolded himself from the driver's side, there was a flash of surprise across his face when he recognized her.

"Well, howdy," he smirked. "Don't you clean up nice?"

Molly rolled her eyes. Of *course* it would be him: the one white knight in the world she should avoid. Still—beggars couldn't be choosers.

"Of all the gin joints in the world," she muttered to herself. Then, louder, Molly demanded, "Are you following me?"

"*Yes*," Jake hissed ominously. At her incredulous expression, though, he relented. "Stop. I'm kidding. Total coincidence, I swear."

Molly humphed, disgruntled, and kicked her patent leather heel at the pebbles on the sidewalk—then got one stuck in the open toe for her efforts. Why did Jake have to be so cute and charming, anyway? Was it so freaking hard to find a boring, uninteresting tour guide—one that she could blow off and ignore at her leisure? Molly needed romantic complications right now like she needed a sharp stick in the eye.

"What's goin' on, kiddo?" Jake prodded, jerking his chin toward her car. He was wearing a plaid pastel button-down rolled up his forearms, and a perfectly pressed pair of khaki shorts, much like the day before. Molly doubted that something as mundane as a wrinkle would dare settle onto anything he owned—it'd be sacrilege. He inspected the rental and nudged a tire with his boat shoe, then looked back to her.

Molly had spent the last several years riding in cabs and subway cars. She was lucky she even remembered how to drive. Asking her to assess car trouble was a bit of a stretch.

"Battery might be dead," she shrugged, baffled. It seemed plausible enough, anyway.

A smile flirted at the corners of his lips, but it wasn't sexy. It *wasn't*. "Mind if I take a look?" he inquired. Jake was already unbuttoning his shirt, though, and walking back to his car to lay it on his front seat.

"Be my guest," Molly told him, gesturing. "If you have time." In just his white undershirt and shorts, he looked a lot more casual. A lot more laid-back surfer-boy than privileged frat-boy. It was a problem.

"No work today, either?" Molly asked, flustered as Jake leaned in near the steering wheel to pop her hood—and that t-shirt rode up, flashing a sliver of tanned skin. She was trying to find reasons to dislike him, she knew, despite their supposed truce yesterday. It was exactly what she always did.

"Today, I am taking my grandma to the doctor, and then out to lunch," Jake announced, as if he had a date with the queen. He'd told Molly that he would take some time off while she was in town, but she hadn't expected it to be *every* day. That seemed like overkill.

"Aww," she murmured anyway. Because, seriously—
dudes and their grandmas were cute no matter what.
Appreciating that didn't mean she *liked* him or anything.
Molly shifted to the side to watch Jake as he bent over her
engine. His shorts rode a little low on his hips, and without
the button-down, she could see that he was even broader
across the shoulders than she'd realized. His biceps bulged,
his triceps cut up the back of his arm when he braced
himself, and his forearms were tanned and strong. Heck,
even his wrists were...and his hands...Molly swallowed, but
not because her mouth was watering. Her brain, uh...her
brain stuttered to a halt.

Jake straightened from where he'd been poking around
under her hood, and informed her, "At minimum, you're out
of coolant and low on oil." He checked his watch. "What
time's your interview?" His watch band was brown leather,
and he wore the face on the inside of his wrist. His fingers
were long and elegant, but somehow still manly. Molly didn't
want to find that interesting, but she did.

She checked her own watch. "Not for an hour. I was just
going to grab some coffee before I headed over there."

"Oh good. Hang on just one minute more, while I get
this taken care of." Jake sauntered back to his trunk, pulled
something from a case inside, then returned. In moments,
he had secured a red flag to the rental's driver-side window,
handed Molly her purse and laptop bag, then pulled out his
phone.

After a minute of smiling vaguely at his shoes, he spoke:
"Hey Bill, it's Jake Alexander. How're you?" He listened,
then replied, "Just fine. Hey, listen. I have a friend here with
a car that's broken down. Any chance you can tow it to your
shop while we try to reach the rental company?" Jake nodded
to himself. "Yup. It's a maroon four-door. About half a mile
south of Mrs. Denson's on Myrtle." As he spoke, he
unlocked his car, opened the passenger door, and gestured

to Molly. "Sweet. Thanks, buddy," he said, finishing up the call.

"Ma'am? Your chariot awaits," he told her.

Jake held out his hand, so Molly let him help her into the low bucket seat. As she shifted herself to face front, she watched his ultramarine eyes flick over her legs and heels, but he was quick to close the door and walk away. If she hadn't been staring, she might never have seen it—so she couldn't really hold it against him. Jake hadn't been overt, and therefore probably wasn't actively trying to seduce her. Which meant that Molly shouldn't *feel* seduced in the least.

Minutes later, he'd donned his shirt again and started the engine. Blessedly cold air conditioning came blowing from the vents, and from the stereo—out floated a folky ballad. Jake chuckled in embarrassment, stabbing at the stereo icons while he tried to click his seat belt. Molly was faster, though, and tapped the dashboard screen only once or twice before she came to a thumping, bass-heavy dance mix.

Grinning at Jake, feeling relieved and grateful for her sudden rescue, Molly pumped her palms toward the ceiling in a little parody of a dance move. He looked appalled as he pulled onto the street, but after a moment or two of glancing at her out of the corner of his eye, he finally started laughing.

"Are you even *allowed* to act like that in a suit?"

"Well, you know. You can dress me up, but..." Molly's words cut off in her throat when he pulled into a coffee shop drive-through. "*Oh*. My hero," she breathed.

Jake beamed at her, a devastating, blinding smile that she had to look away from. "What can I get you?" he inquired.

"Small caramel latte." She tried not to sound too eager.

"Iced?" Jake asked.

"Duh," Molly retorted, giving him a look. His car said it was 86 degrees out already, and she felt a sting of resentment that her rental was not only a lemon, but a damn liar, too.

Jake inspected her face, then turned to the squawking speaker. "Two large iced caramel lattes," he called.

"No, I said…"

Jake waved her off with another smile. "You can save it and drink it later." He ignored the money Molly offered, handed a twenty to the girl at the window, then accepted his change.

Molly arched an eyebrow at him. "During my first interview, you mean?"

"Ah," Jake blinked. "Shoot, I'm sorry. I wasn't thinking. You can leave it with me when I drop you off, if you want." He looked genuinely sheepish.

"It's okay, don't worry about it. You were just trying to be nice."

He handed her a huge plastic cup with a bunch of napkins and a straw, then accepted his own from the barista. Jake took a long, satisfied pull before setting it in the cup holder beside him. He glanced casually down at her legs once more when he put the car in gear, and Molly tried not to feel triumphant. She'd worn her favorite heels for luck today, and they had never let her down. Even Don Juan over there was not immune.

"Off we go," he muttered to himself. Not immune, and not happy about it, either—Molly preened. At least they were both in the same boat.

As Jake navigated the shady side streets on the way to his father's firm, he seemed distracted. Over and over, he poked at the stereo buttons on his dashboard, surfing between radio stations restlessly. He gave each song only moments before rejecting it, and Molly was left wondering what, exactly, Jake was looking for. The perfect soundtrack for a first interview? Or the perfect song for rescuing a damsel in distress?

Either way, her patience was gone. Molly stared pointedly at the stereo and murmured, "Huh, that's weird."

"What is?" Jake's eyes flicked briefly to her.

"I guess I always assumed a stereo would self-destruct if it was forced to careen wildly between genres like yours is being asked to do." She frowned at the center console with a somewhat-accurate simulation of concern.

"Well, *excuse* me for being well-rounded." Jake's version of indignant was nearly convincing as well.

"Or demented. Because you could also be demented," Molly smiled at him.

He peeked at her again, eyes dancing. "Very funny, Miss Thang."

"Thank you," she said smugly, then proceeded to execute several corny dance moves in mockery of his current song selection.

Jake took his eyes off the road again, squinting at Molly suspiciously a few times before bursting into a full-throated laugh. Molly froze, watching the display and marveling at his deep, erotic voice. She bit her lip and giggled too, garnering another appreciative look from him.

"You're just impertinent, that's what you are," Jake rumbled. He didn't even attempt a semblance of displeasure. Impertinent was clearly how he liked her.

"Bless my Yankee heart," Molly crooned, turning up the stereo and beginning to search for a song she liked.

When she found a hit from the prior summer with decidedly filthy lyrics, she knew she had a winner. "Ah, here we go!" she grinned. It was obvious Jake didn't know it, so Molly started to sing along and dance in her seat.

At first, he leaned forward and patted his car, whispering, "Don't worry, buddy. It'll be okay." But then, Jake began glancing at the stereo with rising alarm. Molly giggled as his mouth opened and closed a few times, kind of like a landed fish.

"Is this…*uh*. Is this song about what I think it is?" he wondered.

"The chorus is *make you melt below the belt*. What do you think?"

"Oh, my sweet Jesus," he mumbled. "Girl, you are trouble with a capital T."

"Something tells me you could use a little trouble," Molly retorted.

Jake looked quickly at her, then back at the road. "Somethin' tells me you might be right."

LESS THAN TEN minutes later, he pulled into the lot of the sprawling brick house that made up the offices of *Alexander, Polk & Futch*. He left the car running, right next to the ramp that angled up to the grand front doors.

"Make sure you give that rental agreement to Maryanne at the front desk," he told Molly. "She'll get it all squared away for you. Who are you talking to first today, anyway?"

"Um," Molly paused, thinking. "Someone named Shannon McCready. Later this afternoon, I'm supposed to see Vijay Singh."

"That's good," Jake nodded, seeming satisfied. "Shannon can seem brusque at first, but it's only because she's one of the younger partners and thinks she still has to prove herself. Don't let her intimidate you."

Molly sighed. "Do you know *everyone* in my life right now?"

"Pretty much," Jake grinned. "It's all good. Don't worry. Now, they're gonna want to break for lunch. Call me when ya'll get done, and I'll swing by and pick you up." He got out and walked around to her door, opening it and handing her out.

Molly smoothed down her skirt and took her bag from him. "You don't have to do that. I'll just walk and grab something." She peered around at the quiet, leafy street and hitched her laptop case higher on her shoulder. "Or…call a cab."

"Don't be silly," he scoffed. "You don't wanna do that."

"But what about your grandmother?" Molly frowned. It *had* to be bad form to crash a guy's date with his *grandma*.

"Shoot. She'll love you," Jake told her serenely.

"*What?*" He could not be serious—he barely knew Molly.

"Woman, will you just call me please?" Jake groaned, exasperated.

Molly checked her watch again. "Fine. But I owe you big time for this." She took one last, lovely mouthful of the cold coffee, then handed him the half-full cup.

Jake's eyes were twinkling as he punched her gently on the arm. "Knock 'em dead," he told her, then strolled over to get back in his car.

Ever the gentleman, he waited until she stepped over the threshold, before pulling away with a subtle growl of that powerful engine. Molly stood in the small foyer and tried not to feel worried. It was okay to like him a little, she thought. He'd been solicitous and helpful, and wasn't acting the least bit skeevy. She could tell that he'd *noticed* her, just like she couldn't help but notice *him*. But Jake seemed fine with keeping things friendly, which meant that everything would almost certainly be okay while Molly was in Wilmington. If Jake wasn't going to get weird, then she wouldn't either. If Molly landed this job and actually moved, then she could put firmer rules and boundaries into place. With that resolved, she licked her lips, smoothed her hair one last time and pasted a wide smile on her face. Molly was a perfect fifteen minutes early, and it was time to rock their world.

Chapter Four

B Y ONE O'CLOCK, though, Molly was both weary of her own "game face" and famished. As Jake predicted, Ms. McCready—a young woman nearly her own age—was reserved but pleasant, and had lobbed mostly softball questions at her all morning. After that, Shannon had taken Molly around to meet a few of the firm's junior associates before finally depositing her back at the front desk with Maryanne.

Molly was thrilled that she wasn't expected to sit through lunch with any of the other lawyers today—she could seriously use a break to gather her thoughts before her second big interview that afternoon. Jake's friendly, light-hearted banter seemed like just the thing to ease her tension. So, despite her earlier reservations, Molly decided to accept his invitation. With a quick smile at the receptionist, she sat on the small divan at the side of the room and pulled out her phone to text him, hoping he wouldn't leave her sitting here too long. His reply came immediately:

Sit tight, we'll be right over.

Molly rose and stepped out the front doors, then looked around for a shady spot to wait. By the time she got to the bottom of the ramp, however, Jake's silver Audi was already pulling into the small lot. He parked nearby, and Molly watched through the windshield, bemused, as his grandmother swatted at him. Grandma threw open the passenger door, pulled herself upright with a wide smug grin, and then quickly resettled herself in the back seat.

Worried, Molly stepped over to the car, but Jake merely snorted and shook his head. She leaned in, anyway. "Ma'am? You didn't have to get in the back. I'm happy to sit there if you want."

"Nonsense. How often does a lady my age get to be chauffeured around by a big strapping man these days?" the woman retorted, chuckling. She clutched her handbag on her lap and looked downright merry about pulling a fast one. Grandma had at least one thing right: Jake *was* "strapping."

Molly looked at Jake for guidance. "May as well get in," he shrugged. "Nice try, though."

Jake opened his door and shoved out of his car, then held the passenger door wide while Molly set her bags on the floorboard and arranged herself in her seat. Once he'd shut her in, she turned around as far as she could, smiled, and held out her hand. "I'm Molly," she told the other woman.

"It's a pleasure to meet you. You can call me Ms. Faye," Jake's grandmother said.

"Thanks for letting me tag along today," Molly continued. "I hope I'm not imposing."

"Not at all, we're happy to have you," the tiny woman assured her, waving Molly off.

Molly faced forward and asked them, "So, everything go okay today?" It seemed like a normal enough question, knowing they'd been to the doctor that morning, but Jake inhaled sharply beside her. Molly hesitated, wondering if she'd been rude to inquire.

Faye was chipper when she replied, "Oh, I'm fine, honey. Just a little checkup, that's all." Jake nodded along, but his jaw was tight as he stared straight out the windshield. So, *not* fine, then. Molly sat back and wondered if *anyone* in the car was actually "fine."

By the time they reached their destination—a casual restaurant right on the river—Jake seemed to have recovered. With an apologetic smile at Molly, he ushered them straight through the cool interior of the restaurant, then outdoors to a table on the covered patio. It was shaded and the fans were whirring full-speed, but the air was still stifling.

Molly was going to have to shed her blazer, she thought, groaning inside. Possibly even order a bucket of ice to set under her chair, or dump over her head. She noticed that Jake's grandmother was also wearing a pressed linen blazer and stockings with her skirt and blouse—but didn't appear affected in the least by the heat. Jake, on the other hand, was already wiping his forehead with his sleeve. Molly hoped this place had something cold to eat, or…more fans stashed in the back.

A quick perusal of the menu showed a collection of mercifully light salads and sandwiches. After ordering their drinks, Molly's companions immediately launched into a debate about what she ought to order. She watched them bicker congenially about it with some amusement—the notion of disagreeing so civilly with anyone in her family was outright laughable. But Jake and Faye were both committed to their ideas and stubborn, it seemed. So much so, that neither noticed when the waitress returned, and Molly placed her order herself.

"She'll have the Cobb salad," Grandma announced, once she'd noticed the girl standing there clearing her throat and tapping her pen on her order pad.

"She's having the soft-shell crabs," the girl replied with a sweet smile. Her name tag read *Alix*.

Faye frowned. "Oh." She peered at Molly as if she was an odd new creature from outer space. "Well, then *I'll* have the...the pimento burger. Medium rare." She examined Molly again. "Are you..." But Faye trailed off, still baffled.

The waitress turned to Jake. "And you, sir?"

Jake looked up from his phone, startled. "Oh, hey! So...*she*—" He pointed at Molly. "—is going to have the fried green tomatoes with pimento. And I'll have the—"

"She's having the soft-shells," the waitress fired back, shooting Molly a *look*. Molly thought she might love Alix, who absolutely deserved a good word put in with her manager, just as soon as Molly could find him or her. And what was up with these two and the pimento cheese, anyway?

"What?" Jake looked stymied, but managed to shake it off reasonably well. "Okay, then..." He thought for a moment. "I'll have the fried green tomato sandwich. The one with goat cheese," he added quickly, when he saw Alix open her mouth to ask. "Also, could you maybe add a little pimento cheese on the side, so my friend can just try it?" Molly watched, fascinated, as he dimpled up at poor Alix, turning on the charm. Alix, young as she was, had obviously not had a chance to build up any immunity to men like Jake, and promptly fumbled her pen right out of her fingers and onto the sticky floorboards. Molly rolled her eyes as Jake promptly leaned down, retrieved the pen and returned it to their waitress, laying another particularly sparkling smile on her in the process.

"Thanks," he told her, and Alix nodded, flustered, before hustling away.

Jake looked at Molly, oblivious. She sighed, shook her head at him, and turned to his grandmother.

"Ms. Faye, I love the color of your jacket," she told the woman.

"Thank you," Faye replied, patting her own sleeve fondly. "And I couldn't help but notice those shoes of yours. They're really something, aren't they?"

"They're my lucky shoes," Molly confided to her, leaning in.

Faye sat back and nodded, impressed, then pivoted to her grandson. "Did you see those pretty shoes she has on, Jake?"

Jake had a faint little smile playing at the edges of his lips. He raised his eyebrows at Molly and dipped his chin. *Oh, he'd seen alright.*

"It was smart to wear them for your interview," Faye barreled on. "Wasn't that smart?" She poked at Jake's arm, nearly causing him to spill water down his chin as he gulped it.

"Genius," Jake sputtered, dabbing at his shirtfront. When Alix set a glass of iced tea in front of each of them, Jake fell on his like a mongrel. Molly took one small sip of hers, wrinkled her nose at the sweetness, and shoved her glass his way, too.

"May I have some unsweetened tea?" she inquired. Alix nodded.

"My Jake here is very smart, too," his grandmother told Molly, as if imparting a critical bit of information. "You should have seen his law school grades."

Molly swiveled and gave Jake a frank once-over. "I can imagine," she commented, making him snort.

The next hour proceeded in much the same way—Jake's grandmother found things about Molly to approve of, and none-too-subtly informed Molly about Jake's finer qualities. Jake wolfed down his food and appeared to make an Olympian effort to stay hydrated. Molly gamely accepted the tidbits of food they both insisted she try, and wished she had more layers she could shed. How the other woman still managed to look so polished in the blanketing humidity, Molly had no clue.

After nearly an hour on the nose, though, Faye's energy started to wane. She'd managed to eat only about half of the large cheeseburger in front of her, and was now only half-heartedly stabbing at a cherry tomato, pushing it around her plate. Molly couldn't fault her for getting tired in the heat, but had to consider the fact that maybe the woman's "checkup" earlier had taken more out of her than she'd let on.

When Faye grew silent, studying the view off the dock, Molly inquired, "Why is the river called the Cape Fear, anyway? Doesn't that seem awfully ominous for such a lazy body of water?"

"You know, I don't rightly know," the little woman said. Her carefully-drawn brows lowered. "Maybe because of the alligators?"

Jake shrugged, then smiled at Molly as she finished scarfing down the remains of the huge fried soft-shell crab sandwich in front of her. She was getting ready to demand he pay more attention to polishing off his own mess of a meal, when he commented, "What is it with all the girls who won't eat these days?"

Molly stopped mid-chew to stare at him, trying to divine if he was teasing her. Her sandwich had been delicious, but perhaps she'd been a tad over-enthusiastic about it.

He looked between her and his grandmother curiously, and explained, "You know—all the salad-pickers."

Molly swallowed her bite of food. Now she knew what he meant. "The dessert-sharers?" she confirmed.

Jake nodded, agreeing. "I know they want to look nice, but don't they get hungry? They're grouchy as all-get-out eating baby carrots all the time."

"Well, I don't think they even look nice," Faye grumbled, stealing one of Jake's french fries and nibbling at it defiantly. "Why do they do that? No man wants to hug a bag of bones."

Jake shook his head soberly at Molly. "No man," he agreed, but his eyes were twinkling.

Molly looked at the disaster on her own plate, and then back at them. She cleared her throat and smiled winningly, trying to be self-deprecating. "Clearly, I don't have that problem."

Grandma Faye, on the other hand, was a tiny thing, barely five feet tall and a hundred pounds soaking wet. The burger order had been a bit of a surprise—Molly doubted she'd *ever* been able to put much food away, but stranger things had happened, she supposed.

"Good for you, honey," Faye murmured, patting Molly's arm. The humidity had been getting thicker somehow as they sat—tied, no doubt, to the bank of dark clouds gathering toward the west. Jake's grandmother was trying to stay cheerful, but even Molly could tell she was losing steam. Hell, Molly had lost steam about five minutes in.

"Indeed," Jake agreed. Molly caught his eye and shot a look toward Faye. Jake nodded, clearly in agreement, and pressed his hands to the wood table beside his plate. "What do you say, Grandma? Ready to head home?"

"Oh, you two don't need to leave on my account," she protested, looking between them unhappily.

Molly made a show of checking her watch. "Actually, I do need to get back soon. I have another meeting this afternoon, and I don't want to be late." Her meeting wasn't until four, but Jake looked grateful for the excuse. He raised a hand to beckon over a server, then handed her his credit card.

His grandmother leaned in close to Molly. "Don't worry, honey," she whispered. "Jake can put in a good word with his daddy, and you'll be all set." She winked comically, pleased as punch that the fix was in.

Molly smiled and turned to Jake, to see if he'd heard. He was busily signing his receipt, and gave no sign that he'd been listening. So, she took a moment to study his profile: the straight nose and square jaw. The long dark lashes, and the way the fine hairs at his temples had turned such a pale blond from the sun.

This server bounced a little on her toes, and seemed as oddly indifferent to him as Alix had been susceptible. As beautiful as Jake was—and as friendly—Molly found it strange that the woman was able to play it so cool. When she reached for the receipt, Molly spotted the tiny diamond ring on her finger and knew: even looks like Jake's couldn't compete with love.

"C'mon women, time to head out," he barked.

Jake stood and helped his grandmother out of her seat, then held her arm while she unsteadily found her balance. Molly slipped her limp blazer off the back of her chair and slung it over her arm, then took the lead—opening and holding doors as their little group made their way through the restaurant. She tried to merely *walk*, but Molly was conscious of every sway of her hips, every brush of her shirt against her spine—and the two pairs of eyes boring into her back, deciding things about her over which she had no control.

They strolled out to Jake's car, deceptively casual. While he got the A/C running and aired out the trapped inferno inside, Faye and Molly launched into another extended discussion of who would sit where. Grandma won out again, and inserted herself into the back of the car with quite a bit less dexterity than she had before. Molly watched her, worrying if she'd be okay and wondering if she'd have someone to help when she got home.

Molly hoped she and Jake would have a chance to swing by Mrs. Denson's for a couple minutes once they dropped off Faye. She could stand to clean up a little before she had to report back to the firm for her afternoon meeting with Mr. Singh. With both that and Faye's welfare on her mind, she was distracted as she got into the car. In her hurry to get cool and get on their way, Molly sort of forgot to be graceful—and promptly lost the shoe right off her foot in the process. When she looked down at the pea gravel of the parking lot, though, her heel wasn't there.

"Where'd my shoe go?"

Jake squatted down to look under the car. "Hang on," he grunted, fishing under there. "Here it is."

But then, instead of just handing it to her, Prince Charming reached over and took hold of Molly's ankle, slipping the shoe expertly onto her foot himself. Like she was freaking *Cinderella*. His warm palm sent an electric jolt shooting straight up her leg, to body parts best left out of the equation. Molly swallowed, fighting back the sensation.

Grandma, clearly rallying with all the frigid air blowing on her, leaned forward. "Well, that was a storybook move, if ever I've seen one," she commented wryly.

Jake slid into the driver's seat and waggled his eyebrows at Molly.

"I'll say," she agreed, blinking stupidly at him and giggling nervously. *Giggling*. Crud.

"All right, settle down ladies," he laughed. He pulled his door shut and checked his mirrors.

Grandma reached forward to grab Molly's arm. "Jake's such a good boy, isn't he?"

"Yes, he is," Molly agreed, eyeing him. "He really saved my bacon today."

Jake shook his head, and turned to back out of his parking spot. "Happy to help," he claimed.

Grandma sat back in her seat, smug and satisfied. "Don't worry dear," she told Molly. "Sometimes these things work both ways."

"NOW, WHERE TO?" Jake asked, preoccupied after they dropped his grandmother off at her swanky retirement home. Faye's apartment had been in a pretty tan-colored building, dripping in bright white trim and planters full of flowers. Molly's concern for her welfare had completely evaporated at the sight.

"If you have time, I would love to run by Mrs. Denson's and clean up a bit before my second meeting," Molly told him reluctantly. She picked at her shirt, sorry she had to truncate this time with him—unexpected in so many ways— but she *really* hated the thought of having to sit through another couple hours of interview questions feeling this sticky.

"Yeah, that suit might've been overkill for Captain Fred's," he teased, pulling out of the home's landscaped circular drive. "But don't worry—we have plenty of time to get you squared away before you have to see Vijay."

Jake's cell buzzed in the center console, startling them. They both looked down, and Molly barely caught the name *Blake* on the illuminated screen before Jake silenced it and slipped it into his chest pocket. He seemed troubled, though.

"Do you need to get that?" Molly asked. The man had been shuttling her all over town for two days now. Surely, he had other commitments to take care of.

"I probably should," Jake conceded. "They were trying to reach me all through lunch." He indicated a little riverside park up ahead and asked, "Do you mind if I pull in there for just a minute so I can call them back?"

"No, of course not," Molly answered, but she couldn't help wondering. Jake had said "them," not "him" or "her." It might be nothing, but it sat oddly in her chest.

With a small smile, Jake parked and rolled the windows down for her, then got out and strolled a little way away before he placed his call.

Molly fidgeted in her seat, watching him when he wasn't looking, and trying to ignore him when he was. It was hot as hell in the car with the sun shining in and no cross-breeze. After sitting through that humid lunch, Molly thought she might end up with heat stroke if she didn't do something soon. She popped her door open and looked around—no benches. Oh well, she could stand; Molly only hoped her thin silk shell wouldn't be too see-through out there in the bright sunlight, damp as it was. She struggled with her seatbelt and the black wool jacket, but once she was out of the car, she was able to lay her blazer across the back of her seat. Jake stood watching her from twenty feet away, making sure she was okay before turning away again.

Molly moved to the shady spot near the Audi's hood and settled back, her shirt stuck to her shoulder blades, and gazed at the trawlers sliding slowly by out on the river. She tried not to be obvious as she studied Jake out of the corner of her eye, but he kept gesturing—short, angry little cuts of his hands—and his smooth deep voice sounded sharp. He glanced back at her once or twice, but mostly stared off at the thunderclouds on the horizon, his jaw set. When Jake finally hung up, he stood and studied those clouds for a moment or two more before trudging back to the car, and Molly. He seemed dejected, but was trying to hide it.

Jake's smile, when he got back behind the wheel, didn't quite meet his eyes. He wouldn't look at her.

"Everything okay?" Molly asked. She told herself not to care, that it was his own business, but...he'd been nice. She couldn't help it.

"Oh. Yeah, it's fine," he lied. "Sorry about that."

Molly shrugged. "No worries. But hey—if you need to just drop me off, I totally get it. I can take a cab, I swear."

"Naw, it's not that," Jake told her. They drove in silence until finally he blurted out, "How long are you here for, again?"

"Two weeks," she told him. "One of the partners is out of town this week, and couldn't see me until next Thursday."

"Shelby?"

"Um..."

"Shelby Polk," Jake explained. "He's got a case in Atlanta at the moment, I believe."

"Right. Yes. Also, your dad said there were a couple events they wanted me to attend, so..." Molly shrugged.

"That's good, though. We'll have plenty of time to get out and see some stuff. I..." he paused, rubbing at the back of his neck. "I had thought I could grab you up for dinner tonight if you weren't busy, but it turns out I can't make it after all. Sorry."

The phone call, Molly thought. But was it work or personal? Jake hadn't mentioned a significant other, but Molly really couldn't imagine a guy like him not being snatched up by some devoted girl or another.

"Oh my God, please don't worry about it! You've done so much already. I'll be fine," she assured him.

Jake just nodded, still lost in thought as he drove. "Actually, there's a seafood festival on the Riverwalk starting tomorrow. Maybe we could hit that for dinner."

Molly smiled, intrigued. "Sounds fun," she agreed. "I finish up early tomorrow, so that should work perfectly."

Suddenly, Jake pointed to the side of the road. "Look, your car's gone now. Bill must've towed it." It took her a minute to remember the rental she'd abandoned hours ago now. She'd have to check in with Maryanne later and find out whether they were going to send her a new one.

Jake was pretending he was fine, but he'd been uncharacteristically curt since they'd left his grandma. Molly was starting to wonder if she'd taken advantage of his good manners. She hadn't intended on intruding on his lunch with his grandma, but they *had* both insisted. Maybe there was some sort of unspoken protocol she was missing—maybe they were merely being polite, and she should've declined the offer more forcefully.

"Your grandma is really sweet," Molly tried.

"Yeah, she really is, isn't she?" Jake replied absently. But then he fell silent again.

This was getting awkward, but they had to be nearing her B&B soon. "Is she your mom's side, or your dad's?" Molly inquired.

He peeked at her, acknowledging her effort with a little smile. "Dad's. My mother's people are more...severe." Molly had the distinct sense that Jake was sugar-coating things, but he didn't continue. After a while, though, he added, "I think Faye really liked you."

"I really liked Ms. Faye," Molly agreed. "I know this probably sounds silly, but I'd love to send her a note thanking her for letting me tag along with you guys. Would you mind writing down her address for me when you drop me off?"

That, at least, got a real grin out of him. "Absolutely," Jake said, perking up. "She'd get a real kick out of that." He turned suddenly down a small side street, and then pulled into the gravel back lot of Mrs. Denson's. Jake pulled Molly's jacket off her seat and handed it to her, then grabbed a small pad of paper from the console and began scribbling.

"Listen, you were so great today. I really appreciate all your help," Molly told him.

Jake made a dismissive sound and kept writing.

"I hope I didn't overstep," Molly attempted with a frown, then accepted the folded slip of paper from him.

Jake made a face. "No, please don't think that," he insisted. "We wanted you to come."

"It's just that—you've seemed a little off since we dropped your grandma at her place," Molly admitted. "I was afraid maybe I did something."

"Oh, God, no. I am so sorry. It's *not* you," Jake insisted, rubbing at his eyes. He stared out his windshield, deep in thought for a minute, then looked over at her. "My Grandma Faye is not well, so…that's hard. And with that phone call, I found out I have something I've got to go to tonight that I did not plan on, and will not enjoy. It all kinda put me in a mood," Jake grimaced.

"Ugh. I'm sorry," Molly commiserated. "That stinks."

"It's not your fault. I'm only sorry I can't take you out again like I meant to." And Jake seemed utterly sincere about that, at least.

Molly gathered her things. "I should probably get my act together here. I'll only be a few minutes—are you sure you have time to drop me off at the firm afterwards?" She got out and leaned in the open window.

"Positive. Take your time—I'll be right here waiting." Jake smirked, eyeing her. "Maybe I'll even get the ball rolling; call Vijay and lay some groundwork for you."

He was making an effort to be cheerful, so Molly rewarded him with a laugh. "I'm not sure that's the best idea in the world." When Jake pouted, she conceded, "But not the worst either. Be right back!"

Chapter Five

WHEN JAKE FIRST met Blake Elizabeth Sutton all those years ago, she'd seemed like a ray of light, reaching down through the darkness to touch his face. Even her nickname was lovely— "Bess," from her initials, was like a kiss or a caress. Impeccably polished at all times, compact, fun-loving—hell, even her hair had seemed holy to him. Pale gold, it had slipped like silk through his unskilled boy fingers.

Jake had never understood, not really, what Bess saw in him. It almost became a game, trying to figure out what he looked like through her eyes. But Bess assured him that she had picked the very best boy in town, and mostly Jake tried to believe her.

It was never an imposition to escort each other to all the requisite social events at that age, since usually their respective families and friends were there, too. It had mostly involved coordinating outfits and being sure to pick her up on time—Bess did love to be on time. Occasionally, they'd run afoul of each other. Jake would drink too much and say what he really thought, or Blake would insult one of Jake's friends and force him to choose between them. They broke up—sometimes for weeks or months at a time—but familiarity was a powerful, insidious thing. Even then, everyone around them already assumed they were a done deal. Forces would inevitably align, and there Jake would be, slinging his arm around Bess at some party or another so everyone could exhale in relief.

Everyone, except Jake. As time wore on, more cracks developed. Bess had certain expectations when he went to college: about how he would conduct himself, how often he'd call and visit, what he'd get her for Christmas...the list was endless. Bess operated according to some inviolable handbook known only to her (and possibly her mother) and Jake discovered that his nineteen-year-old self didn't much care for her rules. His golden angel morphed into something of a tarnished harpy—and it was disillusioning, to say the least. They fought. He drank—too much. And Bess followed him to college a year later.

Jake hadn't wanted her there, had begun to think that he needed some goddamn breathing room. And yet, having Blake at school, telling him what to do all the time, was a known entity, recognizable. Instead of Jake discovering whether he was even listening to music he actually liked, or spending his time with people he found interesting—Bess ushered him through the same sorts of things they had always done together.

Periodically, Jake did something she could not forgive, or Bess caught wind of some richer, more handsome guy she wanted to vie for. By that time, though, they were older, and there were higher stakes. People got hurt. Trampled. People got self-destructive. Sometimes, people even started drowning on dry land, and Jake knew firsthand that there was nothing more surprising than when the person you'd grown to despise was the one who threw the buoy that saved you.

That mess had been years ago, however—and the intensity of emotion that accompanied it had faded to a dull ache on most days.

Not today, though. Today, when Jake had to scuttle more time with Molly to attend a spontaneous dinner with Blake and her folks, he felt that clawing fury in his throat—that sour sting when she emerged the winner as Bess always did. Somehow, in all this time, Jake had never felt *weak* before. He was a grown-ass man, and he ought to be standing up for himself once in a while. How had it come to this?

So, they'd bickered. He and Bess sat on their side of the small table hissing veiled insults at each other in between bites of grilled fish, while her parents politely pretended not to notice. Jake hadn't even *wanted* fish, and that had made him even angrier.

Mrs. Sutton was no rookie, though, and with a deft hand guided them through the meal with the veneer of civility. Towards the end, even Jake sort of believed it hadn't been *that* bad.

Except Bess drank three glasses of wine instead of two and she'd gone and insulted Molly, an innocent bystander in all this. Not...not Molly directly, so much as the whole *concept* of Molly: a geek with a law degree getting ushered around town by Blake's stud.

The word choice had been unfortunate, to say the least. Jake was thick in the middle of telling Bess what she could do with his stud services, when her daddy had interjected.

"Knock it off, you two," he'd intoned, shaking his head. Without turning, he raised one commanding hand in the air and beckoned. Like magic, a server appeared at his side, proffering a little tray with their check.

Mrs. Sutton smiled serenely, the manipulative shrew. "Blake, honey, why don't you ride back with us?" she said. Naturally—because Jake had the temerity to drink a beer, one single beer, with dinner.

Jake had sputtered out some nonsense about promising his mother he'd stop by for dessert—Bess snorted delicately at the lie—and then he was free. Their little spat had the added benefit of getting him out of heading to a snobby wine bar with Bess and her girls, as they'd planned. Conveniently, since she would no doubt have found a moment to apprise her friends of Jake's assholery, and they would've hated him all night, too. What the hell was he *doing?*

He had, in fact, driven to his parents' house, knowing full well that his mother would have pie around at the very least. But he'd ended up sitting there at her kitchen table wondering if it was possible to be two men stuck inside one body. "Outside Jake" made conversation and ate dessert. "Inside Jake" wondered if getting really, really drunk might help. Or perhaps a tattoo—a tattoo would be an excellent middle finger to all of *this* swirling around him. Only problem was, he was liable to get something incredibly inappropriate that he would regret years down the line. Like the words "Fuck It" across his shoulder blades, in ominous, Gothic letters. It seemed a distinct possibility. "Inside Jake" felt like he might want to fight his way out, and fight dirty.

Eventually, Mama left him to stew on his own, and Jake's thoughts drifted around, trying to make sense of the impossible. Molly was no geek, that was just laughable. But so was the notion that she might expect jack shit from him. That girl was like a tomcat someone had stuck a bowtie on: a barely-tamed wild animal dressed up for company. She was smart and beautiful and funny and fierce, and sometimes kind of sweet. Also…vulnerable.

Jake got a feeling sometimes, the faintest whiff, that Molly thought she wasn't a keeper—that all anybody would want from her was to get in her pants. She was independent, but there was a defensive edge to it. Jake wanted to know *why*. He had probably never met such a keeper in his life, but…you couldn't keep what didn't belong to you. He got up, rinsed his plate in the sink, and snagged another beer from his mother's fridge.

With the freakish timing he'd always possessed, Jake's father sauntered in, eyed Jake up and down, and gestured. "Come sit with me a minute, son. Let's talk."

SO, JAKE SAT in his father's study, disillusionment and resignation ping-ponging back and forth in his chest. He gripped his beer bottle in one hand and pressed it against the top of his thigh, and resisted the thought that his whole life was somehow preordained.

Blake's father had "stopped by"—riding up to the back of the house on his golf cart—just as Jake had finished telling his father about the extortion case he'd tried last week. The older men held highball glasses of bourbon in their hands, and acted all casual. But it didn't *feel* casual; Jake had the distinct sense that the whole thing had been planned like a mother. An ambush. And Jake could guess what it was about, too.

"How's work?" Mr. Sutton asked, swiveling in his leather seat to fix his glittering eyes on Jake—like they hadn't just sat through dinner together. *Jesus*. Had the man been listening at the window?

"Pretty good," Jake hedged. "As I said, I wrapped up that extortion case last week. Had a few DUIs. Nothing special." His beer was growing warmer from the heat of his palm. He didn't want to drink it anymore.

His father looked faintly proud, as he always did when Jake talked like a man, about grown man things. Mr. Sutton nodded, too, but Jake could tell he wasn't quite listening. Why would he? Leslie clearly had his own agenda for the gathering. Jake had only to wait to discover what it was.

"That's good, that's good," Sutton hummed, twirling his glass. He glanced quickly at Jake's father, who gave him a short nod. After a careful pause, he queried, "Given much thought to when you'll put in for judge?"

Jake took a deep breath, and let it out slowly. This subject had been talked to death—between him and his own parents, certainly, but also between Jake and that man's daughter. Everyone had an opinion, most firmly in favor, but the only person whose opinion didn't seem to count was Jake. And Jake was a huge vote in the "Nay" column.

"No, sir," he said calmly. It wouldn't be right to rile up Blake's daddy, not after that miserable dinner. It wasn't respectful, for one thing, and Blake herself was liable to give him holy hell for it. *That*, Jake could do without.

His father cleared his throat. "Son. Just hear him out," he instructed. The look he levelled at Jake brooked no argument. Jake swallowed past the knot in his throat and then nodded, knowing what was expected of him. He turned toward Mr. Sutton, and tried to look curious.

It appeared to be what the other man was waiting for. "Here's the thing—we'll have to stage this exactly right. I heard something very interesting today, and your father and I agreed that you ought to know, so you can plan accordingly."

"Okay," Jake muttered, when Mr. Sutton paused for breath.

"People are saying that John Davidson is retiring in two years," he claimed, like he was imparting state secrets.

"It makes sense," Jake's dad agreed. "The man's getting up there in years. Has to be about the right age for it."

"How does this affect me?" Jake asked, though of course he knew.

"Don't you see? The timing will be perfect. You and Blake will have plenty of time to finish up this wedding business and move into your new home, and then we can get you out to some bar association events, meeting the right people. You know." Mr. Sutton looked to Jake's dad again.

"No reason he can't start doing a few things now, though," Clay mused. "As long as he isn't obvious about it. Don't want to get folks *thinking* just yet." He winked.

"Right. We don't want that," Sutton agreed. "Not yet."

Jake gritted his teeth. "*I* think this plan of yours is a bit precipitous, don't you? I've only been a prosecutor for a few years. Hell, even if I could get the governor to look twice at me, I'd probably be the youngest judicial candidate Brunswick County's ever seen." If they wouldn't acknowledge the fact that Jake didn't even *want* to be a judge, surely they would have to listen to reason. *Surely.*

"Well, as to that..." Blake's father looked smug, and shared one more amused look with Jake's dad. Both men chuckled, and Jake knew they found him silly. It rankled. It was his *life* they were arranging so cavalierly.

"What Leslie means to say is—" Jake's father paused, smiling. "The governor happens to be a proud former member of the DKEs." Jake knew that. How could he not, when both he and his own father were also Dekes, as well as Mr. Sutton?

"He was also my roommate for two years at Georgia Tech," Sutton reminded them, smirking into his tipped-up crystal glass.

There it was—the death blow. It didn't matter if Jake wanted this, or even if he was qualified. The powers that be had determined that this was the way his career was going to play out, and so it would. Jake was a show pony, a pawn, and given the way he'd had to claw his way back into everyone's good graces years ago—well, Jake didn't have a leg to stand on now. The only surprising part was how much it stung.

ONCE MR. SUTTON departed like a conquering hero, Jake rejoined his mother in the kitchen. Drunkenness was looking more attractive by the minute, but he still had to drive home—Jake hoped Mama could defuse his black mood enough for him to move along with some shred of dignity intact. She pounced on him as soon as he cleared the doorway.

"What was that all about?" she wanted to know.

"Oh, you know. Just getting my marching orders," Jake said, suddenly weary instead of enraged.

His mother looked thoughtful. "Interesting that Leslie came over without his better half," she mused, folding and refolding a napkin covered in embroidered pineapples. Jake had always hated those particular napkins; the decorative gold thread was pretty, but especially rough and unpleasant to use on your face.

"How so?" Jake wondered.

"Only that his wife clearly doesn't agree with him about what you ought to be doing with your life."

Jake frowned. "You don't mean that nonsense she mentioned about running for States Attorney?"

A hard-to-read smile played about his mother's lips. "She said you were a 'natural born politician,' I believe."

He rubbed his face and dropped into a chair at the kitchen table. "Did she, now?"

"Mm-hm."

"That's hardly a compliment."

Mama was now fussing with an empty wine glass and didn't answer. Instead, she gazed out the French doors to her landscaped, blooming back yard.

"She'd never be satisfied with States Attorney, you know. In five years, she'd probably have me running for governor," Jake complained.

"You are probably correct," his mother agreed.

She seemed like she was about to continue, when they heard the doorbell ring out in the front hall. Reluctantly, Jake heaved himself up to go answer it. He'd only wanted to hear what his mother was going to say, and then he could have left—back to the relative safety of his own condo. But now...

It was Blake, naturally, already chattering a mile a minute like they hadn't been at each other's throats earlier in the evening. And what was she doing here, anyway? Had she actually left her friends to check up on him?

"Was Daddy here? Did he tell you?" She was excited. Breathless. It seemed like centuries ago when Jake had last enjoyed that sound.

"He sure did."

"Isn't it perfect?" she trilled.

"Yeah," he shrugged, unable to muster one ounce of enthusiasm. "Sure."

Mama announced her presence, no doubt to underline Bess's lack of greeting. "Hey there, Blake. How are you, sugar?"

"Great, thanks!" Bess chirped. One might have thought nothing at all had happened between them only hours before. Jake gritted his teeth, wanting to throttle her. How dare she show her face here? How dare she pretend none of it mattered?

"Can I get you something to drink? Some pie?" his mother inquired politely.

Jake snorted, feeling contrary. Bess hadn't touched a dessert that wasn't on his plate in years. Come to think of it, she hadn't eaten anything remotely interesting in his presence since at least sophomore year of college. It bugged him, he realized. A *lot*.

"Just half a glass of whatever you have open," Bess said, parking her butt on one of the bar stools and smiling widely. She made herself at home, and cast an expectant look around.

"You sure you don't want any pie?" Jake asked.

"No thank you," Bess said, frowning slightly.

"But it's pecan. You like pecan," he said.

"I'm sure it's wonderful," she smiled at Mama. To Jake, she said, "But that doesn't mean I want some *now*."

Jake's mother cleared her throat, handed Bess a wineglass, and said to him, "Why don't I go find your father and see if he's ready to take a walk with me?" Jake narrowed his eyes at her. The *traitor*. He couldn't believe she was abandoning him.

The minute Mama left, Bess was all business.

"I just couldn't wait till you got home," she said quickly. "Now that Daddy told you his big surprise, we can finally tackle the house issue. I've been dying to get started!"

Jake rifled through his recollections of their last few conversations, but came up blank.

"I'm sorry?" he inquired.

"You know, the *house*, silly! When do you think your Aunt Ceecee is gonna sign it over to you, anyway?" Jake had never regretted telling Bess that Ceecee intended to bequeath her house to him more than he did in that moment.

"I…" He couldn't come up with anything else.

Bess huffed impatiently. "If we want to put an addition on and gut that old kitchen in time to move in after the wedding, we probably need to get started soon, Jake."

His questions were piling up, making a speed bump at the back of his mouth as they each vied to be the first one out. "How do you know what the kitchen looks like?" He sounded calm, Jake knew. He'd honed that skill for years now.

"*Because*, Mama and I went over for lunch a week or two ago," Bess explained, as if he'd lost his damn mind. She rolled her eyes, and resettled herself on the barstool.

How in God's name had she finagled an invitation out of his crusty old Aunt Ceecee? The thought of the two of them—Bess and her interfering mother—in his beloved *house*, without him there to protect it, made Jake see red. The thought of her laying one manicured hand on that kitchen, where he'd spent so many lazy summer afternoons drinking lemonade and eating Ceecee's cookies, made him crazy.

Jake jumped up and paced to the sink, putting the kitchen island between them so he didn't murder his own fiancée.

"I don't know when or if Ceecee will actually give me that house." He couldn't help the small emphasis on the word *me*. "Since when were we planning on moving in there so fast, anyway? I thought we'd keep my place for a while, take our time to figure out what we want to do."

Bess made an inelegant sound, dismissing him outright. "*Your* place? You've got to be kidding me! How are we supposed to buy any furniture or entertain *there*?"

Jake shrugged again, not sure how to answer that. What was wrong with his place? It was a decent enough size, and in a good part of town. It wasn't like he'd been shacking up in a hovel all this time, and hell—he had a perfect, years-long history of on-time mortgage payments.

Blake's place was definitely out. She still shared a townhouse with two sorority sisters from college, and Saturday mornings could be a bit of a traffic jam with the various boyfriends milling around looking for Tylenol and caffeine.

Jake would be damned, *damned,* if he let either his parents or hers help them out with some other, new place. He was already indebted enough to all of them, and no way in hell did he intend to deepen *that* freaking hole.

But *Bess*, in Ceecee's beautiful, beloved old home—that was a more unbearable thought than all the rest.

Chapter Six

M OLLY SAT, DISGRUNTLED, at her little round table, trying to scan the headlines on a beat-up newspaper that someone had left behind. Her coffee was still too hot to drink. Her "grande half-caff caramel one-pump latte." Or whatever the hell it was. She was still stewing about how the baristas insisted on re-stating her order *every time* she came here, making it eminently clear that Molly was an idiot who could not even order a cup of coffee properly.

Didn't matter what she ordered, or at which location she ordered it—the process was the same. Molly squinted at the menu, flummoxed by the offerings, while the barista fidgeted and eyed the line behind her. Molly made some embarrassed comment about needing glasses, or *needing* coffee so she could *order* coffee—then she launched into her attempt and was promptly corrected by a painfully hip teenager. There were two kinds of those: the over-caffeinated and the hung over—but Molly knew neither type liked her one bit.

Too bad she liked coffee so much. The end result was worth the predictable humiliation, and *almost* worth the five bucks. Molly took her first sip from her cup, no longer able to resist the enticement of the aroma…and promptly burned her tongue. Well, then. One of *those* days.

She gave up on the paper and her coffee, and studied the other customers instead. It was the usual crowd: construction workers, business types late for work or happy to be free of the office for a client meeting. There were students who smelled like they had slept in their clothes, and frazzled moms for whom there was not enough coffee in the world. The retirees would camp out for hours in the best chairs, and finally—there was Molly. Uncategorizable as usual.

In walked two women that instantly made her stiffen. She had rapidly decided that these were some of her least-favorite kinds of people, and Wilmington seemed to have plenty of them. Paragons of Southern virtue. Society girls, debutantes, or whatever a "Georgia Peach" was called in North Carolina—Molly was sure there must be some sort of affectionate term.

Back in Boston, people might find them preposterous, but here…not so much. Molly knew she disliked them, and she was pretty sure why—because God, they were *perfect*. They all had the same gorgeous shade of glossy, light blond hair, perfectly styled despite the oppressive humidity. They looked fresh, feminine, pretty, stylish. Great skin, great tans, perfect nails, perfect *toe*nails.

Molly shifted uncomfortably in her chair. She hated feeling insecure, and no one could make her feel smaller than women like this. They made her feel messy and mean. Dysfunctional. Hopeless. These were the women that belonged with men like Carter.

Molly watched the faces of the baristas, looking for eye-rolling. Strangely, there was none—just polite efficiency. Apparently, even low-paid hipsters thought these girls were something special. The women chatted casually in their sweet, slow drawls, taking the table next to Molly's on a beautifully-scented breeze. They pulled out strange little clips that they attached to the table edge, and then hung their purses from them—their very *expensive* purses, too special to come into contact with the floor of a mere coffee shop. Molly watched as one of them trotted gracefully back up to the counter to retrieve their coffee cups.

"Now *that* is a woman with sorority sisters," Molly muttered. The other woman turned to glance at her, sizing Molly up in moments before she turned away again, dismissive. *Better not make eye contact with someone talking to herself,* Molly thought grouchily. And, God-forbid, someone *dowdy.*

Furious, Molly wondered why she hadn't packed cuter clothes to wear in her off-hours. She wondered, eyeing the other women, whether she even *had* any Wilmington-cute clothes. The temptation to go out and find a new outfit was strong, but Molly couldn't let herself do it. Soon she'd have to move, and would need every cent she had. Sartorial splendor was simply not in the equation right now. Molly peeked again. Maybe just *one* pair of sandals, and a fresh pedicure. That could work wonders.

The woman Molly decided was the alpha of the pair cleared her throat importantly, stopping the easy flow of their conversation. She dug around in her bag, then pointedly draped her hand across her friend's forearm, resting on the table. The friend's face transformed, with a blinding grin that managed to light up the already-bright room.

"Blake Elizabeth Sutton!" her friend squealed, "Are you serious right now?"

Molly peeked up through her lashes to see what the commotion was about, and her heart constricted a little at the enormous diamond on the girl's hand. The friend turned it this way and that to catch the light, examining every facet.

This was obviously a recent acquisition—a very beautiful, very large recent acquisition.

"Oh, Blake, I am *so happy* for you all! When did he do it?" the friend gasped, all atwitter.

Molly noted the look of smug satisfaction on the woman's face. Not giddy at all, or even excited. Instead, she looked rather like the cat that ate the canary. Molly's dislike was rapidly turning into irrational hate—and she decided it might be time to make a break for it. She was beginning to gather her things, when the bride's reply made her pause.

"Jackson gave it to me about two months ago," she said, "But we waited a bit to tell his parents."

"And what did *they* say?"

That was interesting, Molly thought. She sensed a little bit of an edge there from the friend.

Blake Elizabeth Sutton gazed at her ring intently, rather than at her friend. "Oh, they were happy. *Very* happy," she affirmed.

A lie, Molly decided, wondering how she knew it with such conviction.

"You know how Jackson is," Blake murmured conspiratorially. "I have to poke and poke to get him to do *anything* I want him to do. It's exasperating, is what it is." The other woman murmured in agreement.

"To be honest, and I swear—you cannot tell a soul this—at first, I thought he was going to try to split up again. He seemed a little surprised himself to be handing me a diamond." Then, almost as if she realized she'd said too much, Blake smiled widely. "Anyway, that's not important. What matters is that I finally got it. That's what counts in the end, right?"

The friend nodded, agreeing with that outrageous sentiment. "So, did Jake pick out the ring?" she inquired politely.

"Are you kidding? No, Mama and I had this picked out ages ago. I just slipped him a card with all the information a while back, and he knew what to do. It's so much easier that way, don't you think? Otherwise, I would've had to exchange whatever he chose."

On that note, Molly decided it was really time to shut things down. She slung her practical black leather tote over her shoulder, and headed out of the coffee shop. Would it have been so hard to find a purse in a nice summery color before she came here? Maybe Molly could find a cute straw one on sale in a tourist shop, when she looked for some sandals. And a sundress, too. Mrs. Denson, at the B&B, would almost certainly know where Molly could look. She shook her head. Avoiding the inevitable was going to be impossible, clearly. Now she just had to resolve to pay as little as possible for the outfit she wanted.

Molly walked slowly out to the new rental car that had been delivered that morning, her brain gnawing away at what she'd just witnessed. There must be hundreds of men named Jackson around here, she mused, many of them going by the nickname Jake. Such a common name. It could have been any one of them who had proposed to his perfect specimen of a girlfriend two months ago. One who met her in college, where he played football and she was—obviously—a cheerleader. Whose families went way back. A Jake who wouldn't flirt with a strange girl in town for a job interview, because how could someone like Molly possibly compare to his own woman?

This was just a coincidence, nothing more. For all she knew, *her* Jake wasn't even named Jackson. He could be a Jacob, or just Jake alone. Molly only felt that twinge in the pit of her stomach because she was paranoid and suspicious by nature. That was all.

HER OWN FAMILY bore no resemblance whatsoever to what she imagined Miss Sutton's must be like. No mani-pedi's with mom. No expensive gifts from dad. Nothing even approaching stability for the O'Connell brood.

Her parents were mere teenagers when they married each other. Skip and Elaine had moved around a lot when Molly and Mina were young, her dad tending bar and fishing in various waterside towns. They'd been living in Mystic when Molly's dad left them for a new family.

Skip hooked up with an ER nurse who lived nearby. Nurse Brandi had three kids of her own, slightly older than Molly and Mina. They treated the girls civilly—if a bit aloofly—when the sisters visited, but it was hard not to resent the way they acted, from the start, like Skip belonged to *them*. All of them had done it—even her father.

The arrangement hadn't lasted. Now, several years and several women later, Molly's dad still hadn't settled down. In a weird bit of coincidence, though, Skip happened to be crashing with Molly's uncle currently, in a retirement community down near Holden Beach. According to his emails, he spent his days taking fishing photos for the Charlotte Observer, bartending at some sleepy little joint at the beach, and golfing with his older brother and the other retirees. Jake had confirmed for Molly that her dad was less than an hour away—Mina would probably kill her if she didn't find time to visit him while she was in town.

As for Molly's mom, it had taken a while for her to find her footing and get them settled again. Elaine, Mina, and Molly had followed Skip and Brandi to Annapolis and holed up in a crummy motel. Once Elaine realized her marriage was truly over, she got a job waitressing and insisted she was going to land an admiral her second time around the matrimonial block.

But Mina was the one to get married in that town, unexpectedly deserting Molly by running off with Grey—a young Marine—at barely nineteen years old. Given the history, Molly had never been able to understand how Elaine could have approved of it. But her mother was still crazy about Grey, even to this day. Even as touchy as he could get.

However, Mina's *happy event* also led Elaine to declare the Maryland waters "overfished"— so that summer she and Molly returned to Connecticut, and Mystic. Her mother was a woman on a mission, and in short order she managed to marry a divorced dentist who lived in the apartment across the hall. He moved them to New York for Molly's senior year of high school, and Molly had been plunked into a hideously elite prep school where her life had tanked into Shitsville.

Elaine knew a good thing when she saw it, and wasn't about to give up *that* husband without a fight. She held to a rigid routine of exercise and shopping to keep herself occupied, and dressed like a twenty-year-old. Even though Elaine was all about keeping Doctor Rob happy, she still found time to weigh in on Molly's relationship choices—and didn't exactly understand why Molly might need *quite* so much education.

As for Mina, once Molly's only friend, she'd been married for nearly a decade now. Molly didn't much like her brother-in-law Grey—and she didn't like her sister when she was with him—but Mina insisted she was happy. Molly tried to be happy for her, and tried to understand the relationship for Mina's sake. But Mina was no dummy, and knew it for the lie it was.

Molly didn't see much of Mina anymore, and had no idea how to fix that. When Mina and Grey had unexpectedly volunteered their friend Jake to usher Molly around Wilmington, it had been a surprise. A welcome one, that maybe would be the thing to bring them all back together. Maybe.

Molly sighed, slumping down behind the wheel of her rental and feeling dejected. She wasn't going to be like them—any of them. Molly was going to learn from their mistakes, as well as her own, and carve out a better life for herself. Starting now.

She wished she had more to do today, or some idea of where to go. Without any interviews scheduled, she was at a total loss about how to spend her time. And now—after dwelling morosely on her family—she wasn't sure she was even in the mood to explore.

Molly fought back at the black cloud trying to swamp her, though. Some days, it was all too easy to believe that the world was full of people like that woman Blake, and like Molly's ex, Carter. People with whom she would never fit in, never belong. It took real effort sometimes to remember that Molly had value just as she was. That there were *all* kinds of people all around her—in Wilmington, in Boston, and in the wider world—who could appreciate Molly as a person with meaningful thoughts, unique gifts, and valid feelings. People like her friend Meg, and maybe even someone like Jake.

With a start, Molly remembered that Jake had offered to take her to a seafood festival for dinner tonight. If she really intended to find a cute outfit or two to wear while she was here, this was definitely the time. Cute clothes paired quite nicely with cute men, after all. That put a smile on her face, at least. Thankful for the second wind, Molly put the sedan in gear and headed out.

JAKE CHECKED IN with her by midmorning, and they arranged to meet near the festival's main entrance after he got off work. It shouldn't have been a problem at all, since Molly had nothing else to do except eat lunch, sit around for a few hours, then get ready to go. She had no excuse whatsoever for being even one minute late.

There had been the issue of the outfits, though. Once committed to the idea, Molly had become a *teensy* bit obsessed. Despite driving around for literally hours, however, she'd only managed to find a string of overpriced tourist traps, two very high-end boutiques, and one okay pair of flip flops—but no cute clothes within her budget.

Molly had known there must be shops that she was missing, but she'd run out of time. She rushed back to the B&B, showered, and did her hair and makeup. And then, Molly stood in the center of her room in her towel, trying to cool down. The steam from her shower and the heat of her hairdryer had turned the room into a veritable sauna.

What the heck was she going to wear? Molly grudgingly donned a tank top and a pair of shorts, but then the hallway outside her room erupted in a commotion.

There was a lot of dropped luggage and slamming doors. Girly laughter—shrieking, gasping laughter peppered with swearing—and the unmistakable clinking of glasses. Molly squinted through her peephole to spot several women in the hall, loitering and chatting like it was a cocktail party in someone's living room. By the time one of the women knocked distractedly on her door, Molly's curiosity was rampant.

Three things became immediately apparent: one, the ladies now occupying the other rooms on this floor were already staggeringly drunk. Two, they hadn't expected to find a stranger in Molly's room, but were oddly okay with it and determined to make friends. And three—their leader was a petite brunette by the name of Tansy, and Tansy was a bit of a talker.

In short order, Molly learned that the group of older moms were there for a long girls' weekend, that Tansy's sons all attended Wake Forest, and that someday Molly's future children would also be old enough to attend college in the blink of an eye. Once Tansy got around to removing her sunglasses in the dim hallway—to take a closer look at Molly—the group had already plied Molly with a mimosa and learned most of her life story.

They'd discovered how unsuccessfully she had spent her day, but of even more interest was how Molly planned to spend her evening. Rapidly sizing her up, the women whisked Molly into the room of a tall, chatty blonde—and had her outfitted in a swingy printed skirt in no time.

Molly had to tear herself away, and promise to both take pictures and to debrief them on her night when she returned. Then she was free.

Chapter Seven

MOLLY DROVE AS fast as she dared to the intersection Jake texted her that morning, but she was still running several minutes late. She searched for a place to park, and wondered how on earth she'd find him—knots of people were all heading along the sidewalk toward a cordoned-off area up ahead, and the crowd looked even thicker there.

But then, just as Molly saw the entrance to a small outdoor parking lot, she spotted him. Jake was getting out of his sleek silver Audi, parallel-parked in a resident-only spot on the street. He was wearing a suit, and looked as cool and starched as if he hadn't just worked an eight-hour day. Torn between agonizing over her own recently-borrowed outfit, and gaping over how unexpectedly perfect Jake looked in his work clothes, Molly almost missed her turn. She slammed on the brakes, the car behind her honked—and Molly flushed in embarrassment, hoping he hadn't witnessed it.

She circled the packed lot, looking for an open spot and cursing the half-hearted A/C in her rental. She kept one eye on Jake where he stood on the sidewalk next to his car, fussing with his phone. The other eye was trained on the cars looping the lot like vultures.

But, in one of life's small mercies, a rusted pickup backed out of its spot just as Molly rounded the corner of an aisle. She darted into the space—to the fury of at least two other drivers—and didn't dare realign the car to give herself more room, lest she incite them further. Molly cracked the door and squeezed out, trying valiantly not to ding the door of the spanking-new Range Rover next to her. Her rented Kia looked about as elegant as mud next to the gleaming SUV.

For the second time that day, Molly tried to shake off the fog of inadequacy that had clung to her since childhood. The car was *fine. She* was fine. As she wove through the parked vehicles, hurrying to where Jake waited, Molly watched him slip off his suit jacket and lay it in his trunk.

She forced herself to slow down and catch her breath before calling out, "Hey there!" It seemed like a cheerful greeting inside her head, but sadly, it emerged dorky and unbearable from her mouth.

Jake didn't appear to notice. When he turned and caught her eye, time ground to a halt. Molly had the odd sensation of walking a runway as he eyed her from head to toe, keenly aware that each of her elbow, knee, and hip joints suddenly seemed to not work very smoothly.

A lazy smile played about Jake's lips as he undid his collar button and loosened his tie, all while never taking his eyes off her. Molly tried to force a smile, but that tie business was so unbelievably seductive that her throat constricted and her breath lodged in her chest.

Jake slipped the tie over his head and threw it in the trunk with his jacket. He slammed the trunk closed, locked his car with a chirp from the key fob, and began rolling his shirtsleeves up over his elbows as Molly reached him.

"Hey yourself," he drawled. "Don't you look nice?"

She felt herself flush. "Thanks. So do you." Glancing at his clothes, she remarked, "Different look today, huh?"

"These old things?" Jake smiled, plucking at his gray pinstriped trousers. "Yeah, not great for the festival, but I didn't have time to change." He pulled her in for a little half hug—which was probably half more than he wanted, given the humidity. "Mmm. And you smell nice, too," Jake murmured.

Molly felt her face turn a deeper red, and couldn't think for a minute how to reply. She hadn't remembered to wear perfume tonight with all the drama about picking out actual clothes, and wondered if he was smelling the vestiges of Tansy's scent—she *had* been awfully clingy.

Remembering her manners, Molly whispered a weak, "Thank you," before her eyes slid away to the more comfortable territory of the fair. Then a warm wet nose nudged her hand, and Molly finally noticed the adorable dog sitting patiently on the sidewalk next to Jake—sweeping his tail back and forth and watching her expectantly. Molly wondered how she could have missed him.

"Who's this?" she asked, fascinated. She scratched first at the dog's black ears, and then, when he flopped over onto her feet and exposed his black and white speckled stomach, she scratched his belly.

Jake shook his head, eyeing the dog with amused disgust. "This is Duke," he sighed. "He's clearly a total wuss."

"Duke?" Molly asked, glancing back up at Jake. "That's kind of funny, isn't it?"

"Yeah, I know." Jake's face became grim, his mouth tight.

"Because didn't you say that you went to Chapel Hill? Aren't Duke and Chapel Hill bitter rivals or something?" Molly wasn't a sports fan per se, but she'd been on enough dates with jocks over the years to pick up that much.

"Yes," Jake agreed sourly. "Yes, they are."

"So, your dog is named after your alma mater's rival."

"Yeah, I *know*."

Molly blinked and straightened, Duke leaning against her legs. "Why would you do that?"

"I didn't do it!" Jake protested hotly. "My best friend went there—he thought it would be hilarious to give me a damn puppy named Duke as a joke."

"But why didn't you just—"

"I *tried* to rename him Rufus," Jake interjected, anticipating her question. "Didn't take."

"I see," Molly said. She tried to keep a straight face, but really—that was an excellent prank. The work of a pro.

Jake sighed. "It gets worse, though."

She gazed down at the dog, who stared back at her sweetly. "How so?"

Jake jammed his hands in his pockets and watched his pet. "Duke here is a *bluetick* hound."

"Why is that funny?" Duke had gone back to laying on her feet, and was pedaling his tan feet in the air while Molly rubbed his belly. He was obviously in heaven with all the attention he was getting.

"Because the Duke sports teams are called the Blue Devils," Jake grumbled. "I mean, seriously—the name wasn't enough? The bastard had to find a dog breed with 'blue' in the name, too?" Jake studied his dog with a scowl. "Little bugger *acted* like a damn devil when I first got him, I'll say that—pretty much took a leak on everything I owned."

"Stop it," Molly giggled in disbelief, petting Duke's head. "He's the perfect handsome gentleman now. Look at him." Duke stood and wagged his tail, watching her carefully.

Jake looked forlorn, though. "I'm totally serious. My buddy must have paid a freaking fortune for the little guy. And then I paid another fortune trying to train him. We worked hard, didn't we, buddy?"

Duke huffed and tossed his head, looking both rueful and full of disdain as he plopped down on his haunches.

Now Molly was really laughing. "I think I'd like to meet this friend. He sounds ingenious."

"Tim's devious, I'll say that," Jake admitted. He watched his dog a moment longer, then let out a short whistle and patted the side of his thigh. In seconds, Duke was on his feet, alert and ready for anything. "If Duke here weren't the best damn dog I'd ever had, I never would've put up with it." Jake patted the dog's side fondly, stroking down his neck and smoothing his fur.

Molly smiled, all her agitation from earlier melting away. Watching the two of them together was the best thing she'd seen in months. Jake looked up and searched her face, with that same crooked smile tilting up his lips. Finally, he broke the silence.

"Let's go eat!" Jake said gamely, then threw his arm around her shoulders and steered Molly in the direction of the fair.

As they strolled down the main aisle, Molly inhaled the clean scent of Jake's cologne. She noticed his strong, tan forearms when he pointed out the different stalls and booths. While he chatted amiably and made conversation about the food and the people and the town, Molly absorbed the soft edges of Jake's voice, and his deep, sexy laugh. She felt every single brush of his eyes, and every last blinding grin, right down to her toes.

When Jake asked her how hungry she was, Molly had to pause before blurting out the first wicked thing that came to mind. The answer was *very*, but Molly doubted it was the way he meant.

He plied her with samples of shrimp and grits, slices of fried green tomatoes layered with crab dip, and trays of grilled oysters. Jake offered Molly craft beers from local breweries, and cocktails with racy names. Like a little kid, he seemed intent on having her try pretty much every kind of delicacy there was to be had—then watching how she reacted to them. Molly was growing thankful that her borrowed skirt had a little give to it. If Jake kept this up, she'd be straining the seams by the end of the night.

She'd enjoyed the feeling of being spoken-for all evening, even if they were just friends. Sure, Molly had caught a look from a guy here and there—but with Jake at her side, none of them even tried to approach her. She hadn't realized what a welcome thing that was, until the feeling ended.

Molly was standing in a patch of shade with Duke, sipping a weak mojito in a sweating plastic cup—while Jake went in search of some special kind of hush puppy—when life returned to its regularly-scheduled programming.

While Jake wended his way through the clumps of milling people, Molly had been looking around. The stall she and Duke were standing next to looked like some kind of aid station. There were portable tables set up across the entrance, with pamphlets on fire safety and rows of water bottles. A handful of firefighters handed out shiny red plastic hats to the kids, and talked about smoke alarm batteries with their parents. In the back of the tent, two EMTs cared for a flushed pregnant woman and her whining toddler.

Molly's guard was down, after an hour spent shielded by Jake's looming presence. She was relaxed and happy, and when the two men closest to her turned her way, it didn't even occur to her to avoid eye contact. Before Molly knew it, though, the security guard on the left was leveling a knowing smirk at her, and his companion was handing her one of the water bottles.

Molly juggled her drink and Duke's leash, so she could accept it.

"Gotta stay hydrated in this humidity," the man said, smooth as molasses. The patch on the shoulder of his uniform told her he was an EMT. The expression on his face told Molly all she needed to know about how he viewed himself, and his chances with her.

"Good to know," she told him. "Thanks."

Duke shuffled closer to her shins, leaning heavily against her and searching the crowd for his master. Molly searched, too, but the guys kept talking.

They weren't *so* bad. At least they were sober and kind of funny—but Molly was still relieved when Jake finally reappeared. He balanced three square paper trays in his hands, containing the famous hush puppies and a couple other things Molly couldn't immediately identify. He shot a measuring look at the men with her, so she sent him a weak smile that probably read as more pained than anything else. Jake didn't look amused.

He greeted the men first. "Hey guys," he said, lifting his chin in greeting and moving close to her side.

"Hey, Jake," Security said. "How ya doin'?"

"Good," he replied. Molly couldn't tell much from his tone. "Cole," he said, addressing the EMT. "I see you all have met Molly."

The paramedic smiled widely. "We sure did," he told Jake. There was a note in his voice that wasn't quite friendly. "You two having a nice time?"

Molly nodded, looking between them.

Jake agreed, "Yup. But hey, you guys are working. We'll get out of your way, so you can get back to it."

"No problem," Cole demurred, but Jake was already nudging Molly along.

He hung back a step, though, and hissed irritably at the men behind her, "Seriously, dudes? I was only gone for, like, five minutes."

"Didn't think you'd *care*, boss," Security snarked back. Cole caught Molly's eye and winked at her.

Jake grabbed her elbow and turned her away, rolling his eyes and snorting. As they ambled along the main thoroughfare, he was clearly trying to work through his annoyance—apparently, by insisting Molly try some of the fried shrimp he was holding. Finally, she stopped dead, pushed back at the food, and stared pointedly at him.

Their standoff lasted a long minute, but at last, Jake let out a big breath and chuckled, "Damn girl, I can't leave you alone for a hot second before the gnats start swarming, can I?"

There'd been more going on back there than just *that*. Molly knew it, but she couldn't quite unravel what it was. Rather than interrogate Jake, though—and possibly ruin the great time they'd been having—she smiled ruefully and said what he probably expected of her.

"Welcome to my world."

Jake scowled. He wasn't buying it. "Naw, welcome to mine. I'm sorry they were bothering you, Molly."

"I'm used to it," she shrugged. "I think I just give off a 'bother me' sort of vibe."

"Doesn't make it right," Jake grumbled. Then he pointed to an open area up ahead. "C'mon. Let's go take a load off."

They reached the far end of the festival, and stopped at the last booth to buy ice cream cones before breaking free of the mob. Jake directed Molly away from the tents with their humming generators, away from the parked trucks and stray clumps of people, and led her to a relatively empty section of the wooden walkway that stretched the length of the river.

They ducked under a rope cordoning off a short dock, and walked to the end. Jake sat casually on the edge, dangling his legs over the side—suit pants, dress shoes, and all. Duke flopped next to him, panting heavily. Before Molly could slip off her new flip flops, Jake had produced a spare water bottle from a bag and poured it into a plastic bowl for the dog. Molly left her shoes a few feet away, then gingerly sat next to them, trying not to snag her borrowed skirt on the rough wood.

Jake licked his melting ice cream cone and watched Duke slurp up the water. Molly watched Jake, and wondered why he seemed pensive all of a sudden. She'd never really worried before about how a date might interpret the attention she got from random men. It hadn't ever mattered one way or the other. But for the first time, Molly cared, and cared a lot.

"What's wrong, darlin'?" Jake asked softly, absently. He hadn't even had to look up to know she was bothered.

Molly didn't answer his question. Instead, she reflected, "I love your accent."

Jake's head snapped up, and his eyebrows shot skyward.

She blushed again, shrugging self-consciously. "Everything you say comes out sounding so…*nice*." Oh, God. Had she *really* just blurted that out? When had Jake turned her into such a complete doofus? Molly looked down at the ice cream dripping across her knuckles and started lapping at it, trying to clean up the mess and get her cone under control. More control than her mouth, at least.

Jake smiled, though, unruffled as usual. "Thank you. I think." He considered Molly a moment, and then waved his hand toward her. "Your accent is a bit different. I thought you might have that classic Boston accent when you came down, but you don't, do you?"

"Not really, no," she agreed.

"Why not?"

"We moved around a lot when I was a kid," she told him.

But Jake wasn't done. He peered at her curiously, and asked, "How come?"

There was no easy answer to that, not to someone like him. It would be easier to try to explain the weird way she spoke. Her accent had been a matter of discussion before, of course—namely for being impossible to pin down. Even Molly had to admit it could be a moving target, depending on who she was with. It could tend toward Mid-Atlantic or a sort of generalized New England on any given day, and sometimes from word to word. People up north thought she sounded vaguely southern, and people down here knew she didn't. Consequently, it confounded almost anyone who attempted to use it to categorize her.

It was just as well. No matter where she tried to fit in, Molly always ended up feeling like a fraud, anyway. She must have said as much, because Jake immediately frowned.

"*What?*"

"You wouldn't understand," Molly muttered.

"Why do you say that?" he inquired. He didn't even sound offended by her brush-off.

Molly paused for a moment, mulling it over. "Well...you grew up here, right? And your parents, too—your whole life, your whole history, right here in Wilmington?"

Jake nodded, affirming this most unremarkable of facts. "Aside from college? Yeah," he agreed.

Molly continued, "You know everyone, they all know you, they know your...your *kin*, right? And you know theirs."

He nodded some more, though his expression had shifted. Jake looked like Molly was delineating the biggest curse one could possibly endure.

"You never have to explain yourself here," Molly said, "Because this is your *home*. Everyone here understands you and your intentions. They know your people, they know your whole back story—and you know theirs. You never, ever, have to justify being here or being who you are, do you?"

"No, ma'am," Jake laughed ruefully. His eyes shifted away from her to stare out across the murky water, pondering that.

"Me—I don't belong *anywhere*. I don't fit in anywhere and I don't have one group of family all in one place. No one has ever really known me for more than a few years at a time. I have lived all over the place, and have never *once* belonged. And I'll tell you what—the endless explaining of myself and my motives is exhausting." Embarrassed by her outburst,

Molly remembered the ice cream she held, and ran her tongue along the edge of the cone to catch the drips.

Jake's brows were knit together, concern carved into his face. He watched her in silence, so Molly felt compelled to continue.

"You know, sometimes with the bad stuff—the stuff that's harder to explain—it feels okay to be anonymous. It can be nice to not have everyone judge you for what your family members screwed up. When people only know you, you sink or swim on your own merit."

"That *does* sound good," Jake mused.

"Yeah, until you screw up, yourself. Either way, no one ever really trusts a stranger."

Jake pulled one knee up and turned toward her. "Except you're no stranger, Molly."

"Yeah, I kinda am." She kicked her bare feet a little, watched the water rippling below, and studiously avoided looking at him.

Jake reached out and tucked a lock of hair behind her ear. His fingers brushed her neck, faintly, and Molly wondered if he'd done it on purpose. "No...you're one of those magnetic people that everyone wants to be close to," Jake said.

"Hardly," Molly snorted. Jake slid closer to her, mischief in his eyes.

"I'm serious. The way you talk to people—I mean, you meet every new person with this open heart."

At Molly's dubious look, he chuckled. "Okay, every non-threatening, non-skeevy person. You don't see it because you're all wrapped up inside that..." he paused meaningfully, gesturing, "...*very* pretty head of yours. But honestly, there is a *lot* of jockeying for position going on all around you."

"Stop," Molly laughed.

"No, really! Take Duke over there." They both shifted position, sitting knee-to-knee to get a better look at the panting dog. "He's been inching closer and closer all this time, waiting for his opening. He's just itching to muscle me out of the way. You'll see—you'll have a lap full of hound in five minutes flat if you aren't careful." Duke blinked up at them, tongue lolling out the side of his grin, the picture of canine innocence.

"Duke? Is that true?" Molly cooed at him, grateful for the diversion. "Do you want to sit on my lap, boy? Do you?" she coaxed.

With a delighted woof, Duke happily launched himself onto her, knocking Molly backward and licking frantically at her face and her fallen ice cream cone. Molly laughed hysterically, trying to get him off and catch her breath.

Jake just shook his head, and threw his own unfinished cone over his shoulder into the river.

"See? What'd I tell ya? 'Stranger,' my ass. Neither man nor beast can keep away."

THEY SAT QUIETLY for a long time after that, watching the sun go down, listening to bands play at the street fair, and to other couples chatting as they strolled along the Riverwalk. Finally, though, Molly sighed and got to her feet.

"I hate to leave, but I've got another round of interviews tomorrow. I should probably get going."

Jake stood up slowly, then bent down to ruffle the fur on Duke's head, waking him. "No worries," he told her. "If we cut over a block, it'll be easier to get back to the cars."

The next street was quiet, and darker than Molly expected. Even though she had Jake and Duke beside her, it still made her a bit nervous. Molly couldn't help it; after years of living in Boston, she was trained to keep looking over her shoulder, to always be aware of who and what else was around.

"Girl, what are you lookin' for?" Jake finally asked, both amused and perplexed.

"Oh, you know…just looking." Molly replied casually. Maybe she was being a touch paranoid, but she was also a little out-of-practice with the self-defense skills.

He laughed outright. "You been living in the big city too long, you know that?"

"If you say so. Doesn't hurt to be careful, though," Molly retorted.

"I won't let anything happen to you," Jake said. He sounded a little hurt.

"I know," Molly told him, but did she really? After all, if a guy looked like Carter, and talked like Carter, what were the chances he was really a whole lot *different* than Carter? They walked slowly, picking their way over a sidewalk cracked by tree roots and skirting the festival down a residential street—while Molly tried to decide if she had Jake pegged all wrong. He *seemed* nice. But then, so had Carter.

"Why do you want to move all the way down here anyway?" Jake asked quietly.

"Because this is going to be my place. This will be my last move, ever. I'm going to relocate one last time, of my own free will, and then I'm going to put down some monster-sized roots and never leave," Molly informed him.

"But…how can you know you'll be happy in one place forever? Especially someplace you've never lived before? People change all the time—maybe after being here a while, you'll decide that a different place would be better for you."

Molly had the distinct feeling that Jake was playing devil's advocate and didn't really believe that. For some reason, though, it tickled her that he wanted her to take a stand on it. To be sure. "Honestly, I am so tired of being a nomad, in body and soul. It's a condition that was inflicted on me, and it goes against every fiber of my being. Truly. I'm a homebody who seriously needs to have a home."

"But why *here*?"

"I've seen everywhere else. Here works for me. I like *here*. Someday, when I have kids, and those kids want to come home—they're going to know exactly where to find it."

Jake smiled down at her. "Sounds like you have it all figured out."

"I do," Molly said. "I even know which house I want to live in."

"Is that right?" He looked surprised.

"Yes. It's right around here somewhere, too. I found it online," she admitted.

"What's it look like?" Jake asked.

"It's so pretty," Molly gushed. "It has a big front porch with all these little wooden flourishes in the corners, like icing on a cake. There's a ton of big windows, and a live oak right in the side yard."

"That sounds like my aunt's house," he murmured. "Wouldn't that be funny?"

Molly nodded, slipping her hand into the crook of his elbow and leaning her head against his shoulder. In that moment, it was impossible to think of him as another possible Carter. He was only Jake, and he was sweet.

"I wonder—" she said.

"Hmm?"

"What about you? If no one knew you or expected anything particular from you…who would Jake Alexander be?" Molly asked softly.

He didn't even hesitate. "I know that."

"You do?" She looked up, trying to see his face clearly in the dark.

"Yes. I would be an estate attorney." He said it so clearly, so firmly, like it was the pinnacle of impossible dreams.

Molly snorted, because there couldn't possibly be a more sedate practice of law. It was a little like saying he longed to be an actuary, or a statistician. Or a bean counter.

"I'm serious!" Jake protested, jostling her with his arm and chuckling at himself.

Molly giggled, too. So much for her worry that Jake was secretly some flashy hotshot.

Just then, they heard unsteady footsteps and snickering behind them. Loud whispering and louder shushing. Jake looked down at her with a quizzical expression, so Molly shot a surreptitious look over her shoulder. There weren't many streetlights here—despite the row of houses, it was fairly dark and lonely. But rather than someone scary, they were clearly being trailed by a group of tipsy women, so how bad could it be? Duke didn't seem the least bit worried. Jake, though, looked somewhat alarmed.

Molly turned around again, peering back through the trees, not able to make out much. But then, cutting through the night, came the sound of a loud, shrill wolf-whistle. The ladies broke into raucous chortling, and even Molly had to giggle.

"Heeeeey, hot stuff!" sang a gleeful voice that Molly instantly recognized.

"Well, I'll be damned," Molly laughed. "I think that's Tansy."

"Who?" Jake demanded. He turned around and began walking backward, trying to see the shadowy group.

"My new neighbors at the B&B," Molly explained. "Hi ladies!" she called to them, waving grandly.

"Nice skirt!" came one sly voice.

Another hollered, "How's the stud muffin?" More snickering erupted.

"You've got to be kidding me," Jake muttered. "They are so drunk. Come on, Molly. Let's cut down this street."

She shook her head at him, rolling her eyes. "Oh, all right," she said.

"Gotta go! Bye!" she yelled back to her new friends.

"Knock 'im dead!" Tansy belted out from a block away, just before they turned the corner.

"Take pictures!" screamed yet another woman.

Molly eyed Jake, towering next to her in the gloom. She would've bet her last dime that he was beet red. She elbowed him.

"First your friends, and now mine. I guess we're even."

That got a smile. Jake bumped her with his shoulder. "Guess so," he murmured, his voice smooth and slow as honey, right next to her ear.

Chapter Eight

J AKE HAD BEEN thinking about what Molly said on that dock for almost fourteen hours straight—the notion of self-determination, of choosing who you wanted to be and what you wanted to do with your life, sounded both impossible and freaking amazing. He'd never seriously considered living anywhere else except here. But for the first time, Jake wondered what that might be like—to just up and move somewhere else, far away, where not a single soul knew him. What would he do? Wear? Be? The thought was intoxicating; it made him a little breathless and a lot panicked. But also, the cloud of dread that gathered in his ribcage probably indicated something pretty awful about his current state of existence. If Jake was…Jesus, if he was *scared* by a daydream about making his own life choices, there was something really terrible about his life as it was. And things were just going to get worse, too.

He'd spent the morning trying—and winning—an embezzlement case he'd been assigned months ago. A church treasurer had spent the last few years lining her pockets with the funds she was supposed to managing. That particular parish collected a healthy yearly tithe from its worshippers, and as a result boasted things like a full-size gym, a tricked-out game room, and a huge outdoor meeting space—replete with a dining pavilion, and horseshoe and barbecue pits. It had also attracted quite the stupid criminal, who made little effort to cover her tracks and spent her loot like a drunken sailor. Given the damning evidence, Jake had been able to make his case with only two hours of testimony, and the grand jury had quickly found her guilty.

He'd had a meeting with the pastor afterward to explain the embezzler's eventual sentencing, and then had submitted to a short interview by the editor of the church newsletter. But now, Jake was free for the rest of the day.

He'd already called over to Maryanne at *APF* and discovered that Molly was also done for the day. Perhaps that was why Jake was driving this particular route—he'd come across her once before on this road, and maybe he would again. Perhaps this way, it was less intentional of an act, and more spontaneous. Because if Jake didn't spot Molly here, then he'd have to decide if calling her and inviting her along this afternoon fell into the category of "showing her around" or if it constituted an outright date.

His newest coping mechanism seemed to be thoughts of Molly and what she was doing at any given moment, and thoughts of running into her accidentally-on-purpose. Jake had other thoughts too, thoughts best saved for the dark of night and his own guilty conscience.

The thing was, going to that seafood festival last night? By the end it had felt exactly like a perfect first date would. Even though he hadn't kissed Molly, had barely even touched her, that thrill of connection was still there. Jake wondered if Molly felt it too.

The things she said on the dock, and later, when she walked through the dark holding his arm, had burrowed under his skin and sprouted into life. Painlessly, too—how else could he explain the way he had blurted out that confession about himself without even batting an eye? Temporary insanity, maybe, or some kind of Molly-induced sickness.

He'd considered Molly's words from every angle, looking for flaws, but still they felt so natural, so *right*...even that bit about her dream house. It might or might not be Aunt Ceecee's—and Jake waited for the territorial, junkyard-dog feeling he got whenever he tried to picture Blake in his house. With Molly it never came. The thought of Molly in that house, with him, had the exact *opposite* effect.

Jake was torturously aware that she probably didn't know about Bess. How could she? His relationship status had never come up naturally in conversation, and bringing it up out of the blue felt awfully presumptuous—like he was expecting her to want him because he was so dang irresistible. With the way they had started things off, Jake had to work extra hard—against that exact stereotype—to get Molly to trust him. But now...had he messed up and let too much time pass?

Maybe she *did* know, though, and simply found the information unremarkable. Perhaps someone from his dad's firm had mentioned it, or her brother-in-law Grey. Jake didn't think Grey knew about Bess, but it was certainly possible he'd heard the news through some social connection or another. Maybe that was why he'd found Jake such an acceptable tour guide.

So, Molly might know exactly what Jake's relationship status was. Maybe she was merely being herself with Jake, with no expectations whatsoever. She might not care how he felt about her in the least.

That would make Jake the problem. Jake—with his screwed-up life, and his stupid, juvenile compulsion to wish for things he couldn't have. But Jake could manage this, he knew he could, *especially* if his feelings were one-sided. He'd been denying himself all kinds of things that he wanted for years. Molly—beautiful, intriguing Molly—would be no different.

As if on cue, Jake spotted her in nearly the same location as he had before. Like he'd summoned Molly by hope alone, there was her now-familiar frame—walking slowly along the sidewalk in the heat of late morning, when no one else was out but the hard-core runners and the old folks who loved the warmth. This time, there was no rental car in sight, and Molly was dressed casually in gym shorts and a touristy t-shirt. Her hair was wrapped in a sloppy bun on the back of her head, and she had that serious-looking dark handbag of hers slung across her torso. She gripped the leather strap with both hands—to fend off a stray mugging, Jake presumed.

He grinned and sped up, pulling to the curb a safe distance in front of her and lowering his window. The soupy air hit him like a solid thing, and Jake pulled his frayed and faded ball cap low over his eyes while he watched Molly approach in his rearview mirror. It was several long blocks back to her B&B from the coffee shop Molly liked—and between the uneven brick of the sidewalk and the oppressive heat, she looked a little flushed and winded. Probably hadn't eaten more than a muffin or two for breakfast, but damn— even Jake knew Mrs. Denson's muffins were crazy good. He could hardly blame Molly for that.

She was chuckling and shaking her head as she picked her way over to his car.

Jake grinned. "Hey, baby girl. Where ya headed?"

"Oh, just back to my room," she gestured vaguely. "It didn't seem so far away when I was walking *to* the coffee shop."

"Hop in," he offered, jerking his head. He draped his forearm across the steering wheel, and used the other to hit the button that unlocked the car doors. "Let's go for a ride."

Molly squinted up the block at the grand Victorian façade of her hotel. Jake could actually see the waves of heat shimmering up off the road and the sidewalk. She'd have to traverse all that hot air in order to get to her room, with the weak A/C coming from that old window unit. Molly could probably already feel the rivulets of sweat snaking down her spine. Jake blinked away the erotic, and unwelcome, image.

"I have a lot of email to plow through," she sighed. "Probably a few phone calls I should be returning."

"Aw, come on," Jake urged. "You don't have any more interviews today, do you? What else could be so important?"

Molly groaned. "I work at a legal aid center. They don't pay me very much, but they also can't really spare me for long. This was the price I had to pay to take off for two weeks. I promised I would keep checking in."

Jake read her expression—Molly wanted to come, even without knowing where he would take her. "I swear, you can do all that work where we're going," he encouraged her.

"Maybe I should grab my laptop," she hedged, still uncertain.

"You just have emails and phone calls?"

Molly nodded, looking hopeful.

"No need for the laptop. I got you covered. C'mon, girl, let's roll." And somehow, despite his corny down-home lines, she bought it. Molly sighed again, stared off up the street, then gave up the fight. She came around the hood, opened the passenger door wide and climbed in. Jake took her chai, with its half-melted ice, and dropped it into the cup holder. He rolled up the windows, and with one more triumphant grin aimed her way, pulled back onto the road.

A couple quick turns later, they were on the highway and Molly was settled beside him like she could stay there all day. Jake hummed happily along to the radio, but wasn't in any hurry to enlighten her as to their destination. Her trust in him was, frankly, delectable.

Finally, Molly couldn't stand the suspense any longer. "*Where* are we going?"

"It's a surprise," he smiled mysteriously. "But don't worry—it's not far now."

Eventually he took an exit, and a few minutes later, they were pulling into a private little driveway bordered by scrubby bushes and grass on both sides, plus a couple low, twisted sea-grape trees. Molly leaned forward to look around. Everything was covered with a fine layer of sand— even the weathered boards of the little house up on stilts, rising in front of them. Crape myrtles bloomed in vivid pink at the back of the property, and flowers spilled from the window boxes up above their heads. Jake hopped out, grabbed a bag from the back seat, then went to open his trunk. He pulled out a small cooler and set it on the driveway, then went around to open her door.

"Where are we?" Molly asked, breathing deep like she enjoyed the tang in the air. She tilted her head, listening to the waves crashing nearby.

"My aunt and uncle's beach house," Jake explained. "They let all of us use it when they're not here." He hitched the small cooler up in his hand, then walked under the house to the short flight of wooden stairs at the back. Molly trailed behind, and when they reached the top, there was the beach—lined with swaying seagrass and little wooden fences tilting precariously sideways from the wind. A long wooden walkway stretched ahead, crossing over the rolling dunes before ending in the pristine white sand.

"*Oh,*" Molly murmured in amazement. "The beach! Look at that."

Jake looked. The sky was blue. The ocean was bluer. And even though this stretch of beach was lined with other little cottages just like this one, it was quiet and empty on a weekday afternoon. An expanse of protected marshland stretched for a mile across the street, and there wasn't a single public access for blocks in either direction. Except for some sandpipers darting back and forth with the tide, not a soul stirred anywhere on the sand.

Jake chuckled at Molly's low hums of appreciation, and started across the walkway. At the end, he picked up a beach chair leaning against the railing, then set off across the sand. About halfway to the water, he dropped the cooler, set up the low-slung chair, and slipped the bag off his shoulder. He pulled a towel from the canvas tote, draped it across the back of the chair, and pointed.

"Sit here," he instructed her.

Molly stood near him, gaping at the view up and down the shoreline. When she turned back to him, her brown eyes were alight. She walked closer, hung her purse primly on the corner of the chair and sat, slipping off her sandals and digging her feet into the powdery sand.

She leaned back with a blissed-out sigh. It was still hot, but here on the beach a strong breeze was blowing off the water, cooling things down to a bearable level. Jake cracked the cooler, pressed a cold soda into Molly's hand, then reached around her other shoulder to hand her his tablet.

"Okay, darlin'," he said, feeling downright cheerful, all of a sudden. "Get to work. I'm gonna run up to the house to grab another chair and a towel and I'll be right back."

Boston, this was not, Jake mused. His chest was just about bursting with pride that he got to call this beautiful place home. Molly twisted around to get a look at his face, but he slipped his sunglasses over his eyes so she couldn't read his expression. In that moment, Jake didn't feel the least bit confident that she wouldn't be able to see every one of his deepest thoughts on his face.

"What are you going to do while I work?" Molly asked, not a little amazed.

"Dunno. Maybe make some calls. Maybe nap," Jake shrugged. "I haven't quite decided."

"Do you just…cut out of work and pick up chicks on the side of the road a lot, or…what? Cause it seems like you planned this." Always so suspicious, that city girl.

Jake grinned and looked up at the sky, lacing his hands behind his head. "I was already playing hooky from work this afternoon, so in that respect, yes, I had planned to come out here. Bringing *you* along was a spontaneous, late-game decision, however." *Sort of.*

"I see," Molly said, though he imagined she didn't, not quite.

"You looked like you could use a break," Jake added, ruffling her hair a little, and turning her back toward the sea. "Now stop trying to look a gift horse in the mouth."

Right. Somehow Jake suspected Molly didn't have a lot of gift horses to worry about. She blinked at the waves, at the wheeling seagulls, and at the fishing boats dotting the horizon. Then she took a deep breath, tapped open the browser on his iPad, and got to work.

As Jake turned away, she murmured to herself, "I wish I had a bathing suit."

"Here—I'll put your purse up in the house, so your things don't melt, and I'll see what I can find." Hiking up the sand and the flight of weathered wood stairs at the back of the house, Jake warred with himself. Chances were, either his sister or one of his cousins had left a bathing suit behind that would fit Molly. He knew exactly what kind of suits those would be, too. What Jake had to decide was whether he could stand sitting beside Miss Molly in a string bikini for more than two seconds or not. Whether it would be *appropriate* for him to do that, or not.

In the end, it really was no contest. Jake stood on the back porch of the house, dangled his sister's black swimsuit from numb fingers and stared down at Molly's hunched form, talking on her cell phone out there on the beach. The longing in her voice had been palpable, and he had no idea if she'd have the time or the ability to get back to the ocean again on her own. He owed it to her to lend her this suit. Molly should have the chance to swim—to feel the heat and the sun and the salt water on her skin, just like Jake intended to. Swallowing hard, he put one foot in front of the other, until he stood beside her.

"You're in luck," Jake said when Molly looked up. "My sister left this. It might fit you, right?" Healey was shorter than Molly, and about as slim—but what did Jake know? Maybe fate would smile on him and take the choice out of his hands. Maybe the bikini wouldn't fit, and Molly would be confined to her running shorts all day.

She looked at the tag on the bottoms, then back up at Jake. "Looks like it might!" she chirped, excited. Popping up out of her chair, she handed Jake her cell and his tablet, and shuffled into her shoes. "Can I go change inside?"

"Of course," Jake said, feigning a nonchalance he did not feel. "Door's open. Oh, and there's a basket of sunscreen and stuff on the floor near the back door." Then he dropped into his own beach chair, stared at the ocean, and waited. Molly seemed to take forever, and then some.

He didn't hear her coming, and somehow—despite sitting there like it was his own execution—Jake wasn't prepared. When Molly stepped up next to her chair and cleared her throat, he jumped to his feet and stared. *Shit.* The woman was all long limbs and a flat expanse of incredibly bare stomach. Quickly, his eyes noted much lusher curves in between those things. Hips. *Breasts.* Panicking, Jake forced his eyes away, but like a magnet Molly's gloriously half-nude form drew them right back again.

She didn't see; she was too busy staring at his chest and wetting her bottom lip with the tip of her tongue. Jake looked down, confused, and realized—Molly hadn't seen him with his shirt off, either. Once again, they were even. He chuckled, and her eyes flicked up to catch his.

Just like that, Molly's expression shuttered and she hunched her shoulders, slinking into her chair as modestly as she possibly could. Jake stood there feeling like a prize ass, while he realized—getting ogled was exactly what she was used to. Being treated like an object, like something to be acquired regardless of her feelings on the topic, was something Molly probably dealt with every day of her adult life. She folded her arms across her stomach and peeked at him, her face begging him not to be weird.

Jake sank into his chair and darted a look or two her way. He had a sister, and a few girl cousins around his own age. He knew Molly was likely expecting some skeevy comment, maybe a flirting come-on from him. And he also knew only one way to fix this.

So, Jake whistled, long and low. "Daaaaaamn," he began, praying it would work.

Molly hugged herself tighter, and looked a little betrayed.

Jake continued, "Have you been living in a meat locker for the last three years? Good Lord, girl, you're as pale as something Duke pulled out from under a *log*."

As he'd hoped, he shocked her. "I—*what?*" Molly protested, affronted.

"I mean, seriously," Jake laughed. "Do you all even *have* a sun up there in Boston? Self-tanners? *Anything?*"

Molly sat there, gaping at him like a fish for a full minute. And then, miraculously, she laughed. Throwing back her head, she barked out the most surprised, infectious guffaw he'd ever heard, and as hard as he laughed in return, Jake didn't dare close his eyes for fear of missing a single second of it. When she finally petered out, Molly slouched down in her chair, grinning from ear to ear at the waves, all signs of tension gone.

Jake watched her as surreptitiously as he was able, for as long as he could bear it. Then, he stood carefully and gestured behind him.

"Need anything from the house? Cup of ice or something?"

"Nope, I'm good," Molly replied, smiling up at him.

He took off, like the coward he was. In the bathroom, Jake splashed cold water on his face, then reapplied some more sunscreen to his nose. In the kitchen, he fussed around rinsing cups and wiping the counter. And when he thought he had regained some semblance of composure—when he was fairly sure he wouldn't embarrass both himself and Molly with an obvious, uninvited guest in his swim trunks—Jake dragged his ass back down to the sand.

"You know, I was thinking," Molly said, once he sat down again.

"That can't be good."

Behind her sunglasses, her eyebrows shot up. "I'm serious. Why—if you want to be an estate attorney—are you working as a prosecutor?"

Jake took a deep breath. The simplest, most logical of questions. And for him, also the most complicated. How did a man who was nearly thirty years old explain something like that?

"Would you believe," he started, and then paused. Could he just…tell her? Could he simply blurt out the truth he'd kept to himself all this time, to a woman that he barely knew?

"Because…" he paused. No, he couldn't tell Molly that. He hadn't even told his own mother. His own fiancée.

"I feel like I owe my father. It's what he wanted for me, so…" Apparently, Jake *could* tell her. Go figure. He traced a pattern in the sand with the sole of his foot, over and over, and didn't look at her. He waited for Molly to sneer. To argue with him. She didn't.

"Do you think you'll ever switch?" was all she wondered.

"Maybe someday," Jake answered, not knowing if it was true. The thought of a lifetime of getting Stepford wives out of their DUIs and former frat brothers out of their weed charges made him want to stick a fork in his eye.

"What do you like most about estate law?" Molly wanted to know.

Jake had never tried to articulate that before—but with Molly, it seemed easy. "I really enjoy older folks, for one thing. I'd like to help them protect what they've spent their lives working so hard for. And also…I think I'd enjoy seeing all the sweet things that people wanted to pass on. Not the trust funds and family silver, necessarily, but the small ephemera that gain so much meaning in a family. Like someone's great-great-grandmother's embroidery sampler, or their dad's handmade hatchet. Wedding rings, bibles, you know—the special heirlooms." Jake pressed his lips together to keep from saying more, and checked to see what she thought.

Molly had pushed her sunglasses up on her head and was watching him, a wistful look on her face. Jake shifted, feeling uncomfortably exposed, but she just shook her head.

"I hope you get the chance, someday," Molly said softly, smiling gently at him.

He tore his gaze away, so he didn't do something asinine like lean over and kiss her, and looked back out at the water—far out, to where it just touched the bottom of the sky in a sharp navy-blue line.

"Me too," he admitted. "Me too."

LATER, THEY RAIDED the cooler, and ate the sandwiches he'd bought on the way. Jake pretended not to watch Molly happily bobbing in the waves for a full forty-five minutes—then finally caved and joined her in the water for another hour or more.

When they returned to the chairs to dry off, her cheeks were starting to get pink—so Jake lent her his beat-up Tar

Heels ballcap. He kicked back in his chair and had mostly fallen asleep…to heated visions of grabbing hold of Molly in the surf and wrapping her long legs around his waist—so he could feel all her gleaming, slick skin against his.

He jerked unpleasantly awake at the sudden, uncertain sound of her voice, though.

"Hey, Jake?"

"Yeah?" he sat up—quickly checked his shorts to make sure he wasn't about to embarrass the hell out of himself with one hard-to-hide *statement*—and passed an unsteady hand over his skull. His head was bare, and he remembered…turning to look, he confirmed that Molly was still sporting his hat, and still looking adorable as could be in it.

"What are you doing the day after tomorrow?" she asked nervously.

"Not much. Why?"

"Well, yesterday at the firm, Maryanne told me that there's some Brunswick bar association cocktail party. Apparently, the partners think I should go."

Jake waited, holding his breath.

"Are you going?" she inquired.

"I am now," he smiled back.

But it seemed that wasn't only what she was angling for. "Okay. Good. Because I thought that morning I might try and run down to see my dad. I figured if I had something definite scheduled for that evening, he wouldn't expect me to stay too long."

"Ah," Jake hedged. He'd forgotten about her father, and the weird way she apparently felt about him.

"I don't suppose you'd be up for riding shotgun?"

Jake thought of her rented Kia and hesitated. Shotgun would suck in that thing.

"It's going to be totally awkward, I realize that," Molly barreled on. "But, I thought if there was a neutral third party there, maybe it wouldn't be so bad." Jake watched her throat as she chugged down what had to be the world's flattest, warmest soda.

"Do you even know where you're going?" he wondered.

"Not exactly. But I'm sure I can figure it out," Molly replied—hopeful, but careful not to outright beg him.

Jake chuckled. Damn, she was cute. "No need," he assured her. "I'll drive."

"Oh my God, thank you so much," she exhaled, relieved. "I owe you big time. Let me buy you dinner tonight." She was grinning from ear-to-ear.

Jake, however, wanted to choke. "Uh, I can't do it tonight, but totally some other time, all right?"

Molly didn't seem to notice a thing. "Yeah. Sure, whenever. And *thank* you. Thank you, thank you, thank you."

Chapter Nine

AFTER JAKE DROPPED her off and she showered, Molly hit the internet. She wanted to find somewhere fun to take him, since he was going to be cool enough to visit her dad with her. But looking at all the offerings merely made Molly hungry right then—so she put aside her laptop and set out in the Kia to wine and dine herself.

Molly didn't expect to find both dinner *and* a show. She'd ended up at a funky bistro with an interesting, mostly-healthy menu—and had somehow snagged the small two-person table nestled right in the front bay window. Molly sipped her watermelon margarita and people-watched for a while. It was a little like doing it from inside an aquarium—but sometimes her whole life kind of felt like that, so that was no great revelation. Between the glare on the glass, and the dim lights of the bistro's interior, she doubted passersby could make out much, anyway. Besides, everything interesting was happening across the street.

Molly had ordered one of the oven-fired pizzas. When all the excitement began, she was busy picking the charred dough bubbles off the crust and popping them into her mouth. But across the street and a few doors down, a beautiful young woman was sweeping out of a swanky restaurant in one heck of a snit. She stood on the sidewalk whacking at the skirt of her maxi dress like it offended her, and she wasn't alone for long.

Soon after, a tall, nattily-dressed man emerged. His head was bowed, his stance diffident, but Molly had never seen anyone so close to completely losing their shit. The woman adjusted the halter neck of her dress, and tucked her sleek blond bob behind one ear. The man smoothed his broad palms up and down his thighs, his blazer straining across his shoulders. Until that moment, Molly hadn't been aware that men actually *wore* seersucker jackets anymore—it seemed like an affectation straight out of a long-forgotten era.

The eruption came suddenly. The man had his back to Molly, but she could still hear the faint rumble of his shout through the glass of the bistro's window. His shoulders bunched when he yelled, like a chained dog lunging at a squirrel. Unafraid, the blonde woman screeched something right back at her companion. Molly heard the peal of that, too. The woman's face looked vaguely familiar.

Molly's waitress sidled up, asking if she needed anything. She ordered an unsweetened iced tea, then turned back to the unfolding scene.

By now, the angry woman had stalked off down the street. When two older couples slipped out of the restaurant, one of the men immediately peeled off to follow her. His date, another flawless blonde, glanced between everyone, looking worried. The last couple appeared concerned as well, though their attention was entirely focused on the man in the blazer.

That woman bent to pick something up off the sidewalk near his feet, and Molly strained, unsuccessfully, to see. Whatever it was, the woman handed it to the older blonde after only a brief, fraught exchange—then Blondie hustled down the sidewalk after her companions.

Blazer Guy was now speaking testily to the dignified couple who remained. As angry as he appeared, his posture was also somehow deferential. His parents, Molly guessed. The two men were built the same, tall and long-limbed, with the same sandy blonde hair. Sort of like Jake's, come to think of it. But that wasn't Jake, was it? It couldn't be. What were the odds?

Molly tried to remember if he'd said what he was doing tonight, but couldn't. Jake had been busy, that was all she knew. Still—if he was the type to brawl with women on street corners, it probably would've been obvious by now. Molly couldn't picture him willingly wearing that ridiculous blazer, anyway.

In moments, Blazer Guy had turned to leave—slipping down a narrow alley between the buildings, presumably to a parking lot in the rear. Molly watched a little longer, catching glimpses as they were obscured and revealed between cars driving down the road, and people walking on the sidewalks. The last couple was deep in conversation, their faces grim.

Someone was having a very bad night. But not her. Molly was comfortably buzzed from the margarita, her pizza was delicious, and she had spent the day ogling one very hot man's chest. No worries there, that was for sure.

She thought about that irate woman's face, her bright floral dress, and expensive-looking handbag. Money didn't buy happiness, that was for damn sure. Molly peeked down at her utilitarian black leather purse on the floor. Shoving it a little further under the table with her foot, she got back to eating.

It wasn't until later—when she was wandering down the street in search of the ice cream parlor selling the cones everyone seemed to be eating—that Molly remembered where she'd seen that woman's face. Sleek, pale blonde hair. Clear, fair skin, and a fancy purse. Molly thought she might have just witnessed Blake Elizabeth Sutton, of coffee shop notoriety, dump her man. Her man, who—Molly recalled with an unpleasant jolt—went by "Jake."

THE JAKE THAT Molly knew called her out of the blue, later that evening. He seemed like he wanted to talk, but he sounded rough. Tired.

"Hey." His voice was rusty and deep, and Molly felt it hit her, low in her gut.

"Hey, yourself. What's going on?" She glanced at the clock on the nightstand—it was after ten. That wasn't like him. Come to think of it, had Jake ever actually called her outright, or had he only texted before now?

"Nothing. Listen—I'm sorry to call so late, but I, uh…I got to thinking. I realized I have most of the day off tomorrow, and I just wondered if you wanted to get together again. I know this plantation nearby that we could take tour of. There's a big house and some nice gardens. It's a real…Carolina history kind of thing." His voice was trailing in and out of normal volume, and Molly wondered what Jake was doing. Undressing? Lying in bed, like her?

"Well, I have a meeting at the firm first thing in the morning," she said, uncertain.

"That's all right. I have a quick bond docket I have to do, but I'll be done by noon. We could try to hit that place for the two o'clock tour, if you wanted. I could swing by the B&B and pick you up around one thirty."

Molly hesitated a moment too long, thinking. Had it been *him* earlier, or someone else? Impossible to know.

"Or not," Jake mumbled, disconcerted.

"No, it's only that I've been taking up a lot of your time this week," Molly hurried to say. "I'm not going to get you fired, or—" she paused, working up her nerve, "in the doghouse with your girlfriend, am I?"

"No, Molly," Jake assured her. "I already took the time off work."

She pressed him again, because that was a non-answer. "So, you're not seeing anyone?"

Jake chuckled under his breath, but it wasn't exactly a happy sound. "Nope. I am currently as single as the day is long."

Molly could say one thing—he was awfully definite about it. "How is that even possible?" she wondered.

Now Jake really laughed. "By the grace of God, I guess." A muffled rustling, and then, "What about you?"

"What do you mean, *what about me*?" Molly stalled.

"Are you. Dating. Someone," Jake enunciated crisply.

Molly thought back to her last semi-regular relationship: a bartender in Boston who switched jobs as often as other people bought milk. That must have been six...no, eight months ago now? The question was, did she want to see where things went with *Jake*, or not? Molly's answer came easily.

"I'm as free as a bird," she murmured.

"Good," Jake replied. "Then come out with me tomorrow. *Please*."

"All right. Sure."

A satisfied grunt rumbled in her ear, but then there was nothing but the hum of the open phone line for several long moments.

"Jake?" Molly asked.

"Hmm."

"Are you really okay?"

"Yeah." His voice drawled low and slow, hitting her midsection with a wave of warmth.

"You sure?" Molly curled onto her side, wanting him to talk. Wanting to listen.

"I...might've had a drink too many. But don't worry, it's all good. I never do this."

"Uh, get drunk? Or drunk-dial chicks?"

"Either." His laugh was deep and sexy. Molly wished she was with him right then, in his bed, making him laugh like that again. What would it take?

"If you say so," she said, lost in the maze of sordid images flooding her brain.

"I do." Jake seemed content to just listen to her breathe, but she *did* have to get some sleep sometime.

"Good night, Jake," Molly said, hating that ever-present feeling of responsibility that always clung to her. She'd been foolish once, and it had nearly destroyed her life. She'd never let that happen again, even for a man that sounded like Jake.

Her words roused him. Clear and alert, Jake told her, "Night, Miss Molly. See you tomorrow."

After he'd hung up, Molly remembered what she'd meant to ask him. "Where were you earlier?" she muttered, turning off her light and laying down to sleep.

Chapter Ten

S ON?"
        Jake didn't answer his father. He couldn't. Instead, he took another couple steps away.

"*Son.*"

He froze in place, his back still turned. He knew that tone.

"Correct me if I'm wrong, but you just got that ring on Blake's finger. What in the world did you do to get her to take it off again?"

"Not a damn thing," Jake growled, wishing he had in fact, taken the opportunity to do something to merit this. Instead, he'd only been himself—apparently that was bad enough all on its own.

There was a deadly kind of silence brewing behind him. He turned to find his mother's eyes wide and his father's narrowed in irritation.

"Not a damn thing, *sir*," Jake gritted out. There was nothing in the world his mother hated more than a scene, and there was nothing his dad hated worse than his wife unhappy.

Jake's mom leaned over to retrieve the engagement ring from the ground. He supposed that made sense, given what he'd paid for it, but Jake didn't want to touch the thing. Ms. Sutton danced closer, looking distraught, not wanting to ask…Jake's mother hesitated, but then, horribly, handed over the diamond to her longtime friend.

Blake's mama slunk away after only a few disjointed words of apology. She could hardly be *surprised* that her daughter was a spoiled brat—she'd essentially raised her to be that way. But Jake would probably regret the small handoff between the mothers later. Every minute without that godforsaken ring in his possession was another moment in which Bess could start wearing it again, could snare him in her net even more permanently. Now that Jake was actually free of her, that suddenly seemed a fate worse than death.

HE WENT HOME and grabbed a glass from the kitchen— and after barely any consideration, the bottle of bourbon he kept for when his parents came over. Visits were a rare event—and Jake mostly drank beer—so naturally the bottle was pretty dusty. It left gray smears on the sleeve of his seersucker blazer, where he had Mr. Beam cradled in the crook of his arm. Jake didn't give a crap. The damn jacket was a birthday gift from Bess that cost nearly the same as his monthly mortgage payment, and he hated it.

In his bedroom, he placed the glass and bottle on the night table, and stripped to his boxers. He kicked his clothes into the corner. Jake turned off the lights, flicked on the fan, and propped himself up in bed. The drywall was cool and smooth against his upper back, his down pillows too soft to bolster him much. He poured the first glass by feel, sloshing a little onto his thigh, and didn't bother replacing the cap. As he drank, that conversation over dinner came back to him.

"Where the hell have you been?" Blake demanded.

"What are you talking about?" Jake tried to stay calm. Tried not to set her off worse.

"You've been ignoring my texts, ducking my calls, and you said you couldn't go to the cake tasting because you had to work."

Had he said that? He supposed he had, but it must have been three weeks ago or more.

"I did have to work," he affirmed.

"That's bullshit!" Bess hissed at him.

Jake glanced around the table at their two sets of parents. "Shh," he told her.

When her mother cleared her throat across the table, Bess shot a blinding smile at Jake's parents.

"What do you all think you're going to order tonight?" she inquired politely. "I have my eye on the grouper."

After a moment or two, once conversation resumed on the other side of the table, she'd spat at Jake, "Don't you tell me to shush."

"What is your problem, Bess?" Jake muttered then. "Chill out. Geez." Even as he'd said it, he'd known it was the wrong thing to do, like throwing gas on a fire.

Blake swiveled in her chair toward him, tilting her chin toward her shoulder so their parents wouldn't hear. "My problem is that I went to your goddamn office today, so you could take me to lunch. Except then, that Maryanne woman informed me you were on vacation. How is that the same as working?"

Good Lord, she'd been spitting mad. Realization had dawned on him. Jake originally thought the embezzlement case would take at least two days, maybe three. When it hadn't, he'd grabbed the chance to spend some extra time with Molly—and never thought once about tasting cake for a party eighteen months in the future.

"My case wrapped up early," he'd murmured back. *"I spontaneously decided to take a few hours off. What's the big deal?"*

From across the table, Blake's mama asked her whether she planned to get a salad. From there, they ordered a bottle of wine for the table, and Jake's dad asked the waiter if his father had ever played football. Familiar face, and so forth. Jake thought he'd run across the waiter himself in some courtroom or another, but that was a different story.

"Where were you?" Blake wanted to know.

"At my aunt and uncle's house," Jake said in a normal tone. No secret there.

She'd examined him, disgusted. *"The* beach. *I might have guessed. Your face is as red as a lobster."*

He'd shrugged. So what. Jake's dad called across to him, triumphant to have been right—the waiter's father *had* been a ball player for UNC, and a pretty good one, from the sound of it.

"Why didn't you tell me where you were going to be, Jackson?" Bess *persisted. Because* of course *she did.*

Fury had unfurled in Jake's chest, both at her inquisition, and at the fact that she chose to hash it out there, in public, *again.* As the waiter slid their salad plates in front of them, Jake had glared at her.

"I don't owe you a 24/7 play-by-play on my whereabouts, Bess."

Her voice had turned even more poisonous, if that was possible. "Oh, don't you? I can't believe you'd say that, given what you owe me. And Daddy. We wouldn't even be having this conversation if you were the least bit reliable."

She couldn't possibly have been alluding to his trouble in college. "I'm sorry, what did you just say?" Jake inquired, still civil and calm.

"I said, if any of us could trust you, we wouldn't have to keep tabs on you all the time!" Bess belted out, full-volume.

Jake had whispered, "We?" before meeting the eyes of each of their parents across the table, not to mention the stares of quite a few of the other patrons. At last, his gaze landed back on Blake. The parents had abandoned any pretense of having a separate conversation, and merely watched.

"If you don't trust me, why the hell would you want to marry me, Blake?" he asked.

Her face flushed a vivid hot pink, and Bess had suddenly seemed to realize that her temper had gotten the best of her. She glanced haughtily around, noted all the people staring at them, and shot to her feet. Grabbing her precious monogrammed Hermes bag, she made a break for the front door of the restaurant.

Jake had followed on autopilot. As he did so, he couldn't help reflecting how frequently he found himself swimming in that woman's wake. He'd felt the eyes of all four parents on his back as he walked away, and heard them calling for the check back at the table.

Out on the street, Bess had quivered with rage. She was literally sweating with it, the silk of her orange and pink flowered dress sticking to her chest.

"Blake?" Jake had asked again, unwilling to back down. She smacked him, hard, on his arm. Jake felt the sting of it through every layer of linen and seersucker between her palm and his skin. "Why the hell are you marrying me, if you freaking hate me so much?" he'd bellowed. And how could he have missed such a crucial detail about her?

"I'm not!" Bess had shrieked, ripping his diamond off her finger and lobbing it straight at his face. She was a bad shot, and missed. The ring bounced off his shoulder and fell to the sidewalk, while Jake stood there wondering if this was really, truly happening.

Their parents edged carefully through the doors of the restaurant, faces wary.

Restaurants and shops lined that street, and all of their patrons—behind those big plate-glass windows—witnessed the performance. A collection of drunken hipsters had sauntered by, slyly needling him. One of the mothers, either his or Blake's, bent and retrieved the ring—he could no longer remember which. Jake was so *done*, though. He'd essentially run away, mind reeling. They couldn't possibly expect him to marry her now, could they? No one could possibly expect him to marry Bess now.

And that meant, at least where hearts were concerned, that Jake was *free*. The fact that he did not currently have the ring in his possession was a technicality, nothing more. His mind firmly back in the present, Jake snagged the bottle of Jim Beam for a refill, only to discover with some confusion that it was mostly empty. No matter—if Jake was a free man, there was one and only one person he wanted to talk to right now.

He slid to the floor, felt around for his pants, and found his phone. He needed to hear Molly's voice, but while the phone rang, Jake tried to think of a reason for calling that didn't include the words *come over*.

LAST NIGHT'S SEMI-DRUNK phone call—while somewhat embarrassing—had led to a meeting with Molly today. Jake couldn't say that he minded. After knocking out a quick bond docket at the courthouse that morning, he'd run home and changed, then swung by Mrs. Denson's to pick up Molly.

She looked fresh and pretty in her tank top and shorts, and Jake's fingers itched with the need to touch every inch of her. Instead, he gripped their tour tickets and the information pamphlet like life preservers, and tried to breathe.

They had already strolled along the path leading up to the house, admiring the effusive displays of blooming azaleas in the garden. Occasionally their arms would brush, but otherwise not touching Molly seemed maddeningly proper. Jake felt like he was courting her—and maybe it was the heat, but the languid pace was beginning to feel excruciating.

The crowd of fragrant old ladies surged forward, jostling Molly into Jake's back as they pushed to enter the main house. She pressed against him, warming his skin through his button-down shirt. The day was oppressive again, and he hoped he smelled like starch and soap instead of the sweat trickling down his spine. Molly smelled perfect, he noted, enticing and delicious. Her face brushed the back of his shirt as she was herded into him, and Jake thought about breathing in the light, fresh scent on her neck instead.

Inside the house, it was even more crowded, and Jake worried that they'd get separated. He let his hand drift back to clasp Molly's, then he pulled her gently around in front of him. Jake tried to use his size to make a more comfortable pocket of space for Molly in the logjam of people feeding through the foyer. She had taken her little sweater off in the blazing sun of the garden and stuffed it into her purse. When Jake rested his hands on her bare shoulders to anchor her, an electric jolt crackled up through his arms—and was echoed by a shiver running down through Molly. He fought the urge to pull her back against him, and his bones seemed to melt within him.

Once he'd touched Molly's skin, Jake couldn't seem to stop. The air conditioning in the house was icy, and the damp back of her tank top sent goosebumps racing across her skin—but Molly didn't put her sweater back on. Jake kept finding excuses to caress her arms and shoulders with his hands. On Molly, Jake's hands seemed big, and hot. He discovered that he liked to hold her smaller hands and warm her fingers as they wove through the rooms. Jake wanted to use Molly's hands to pull her close in the stuffy upstairs rooms, and even in the claustrophobic stairwells. He was reasonably certain that neither of them listened to a word the tour guide said.

Finally, the tour spit them out of the manor house's back door, and they could be alone again. Splitting off from the other visitors, Jake and Molly made their own way across the lawn, the sun warm on their faces. The terraced back garden dropped away from the house in a gentle slope toward the river, and pea gravel paths weaved a maze through the high boxwoods, rhododendrons, and crape myrtles. They strolled downward, lagging farther and farther behind their tour group. The ground leveled out about halfway down the slope, in a secluded camellia garden crisscrossed with herringbone brick pathways.

At its center, the paths converged on a round enclave surrounded by high blooming shrubs—a private sea of azaleas, and other sweet-smelling flowers Jake didn't recognize. Little stone benches lined the edges. Jake strolled behind Molly, then reached forward to grab her hand. She stopped and turned to face him. He took Molly's other hand too, squinted off into the shrubbery, then looked down at her face again.

"Yes?" Molly asked. She was smiling, but her voice caught a little in her throat when she saw his expression.

"I'm finding your perfume incredibly distracting," Jake murmured.

"Oh really? And here I thought you were busy memorizing all that fascinating historical information," Molly grinned.

"I'm also having trouble keeping my hands to myself," he commented.

"Just for the sake of argument, why would you want to?"

"Oh, I dunno. Maybe because I'm supposed to be escorting you around town relatively unmolested?"

"What if you were to hurt my feelings by not coming on to me?" she winked, goading him.

"Now that would be an even bigger crime." He tucked a piece of hair that had escaped her clip behind her ear.

Molly shifted slightly, out of snarky quips for the moment. There was a heck of a lot of cute and sexy smiling up at him—Jake took a minute to process it all.

"Miss Molly," he said then, "I believe I'd like to give you a kiss." A small smile played at the edges of his mouth, and he settled his hands on her tempting hips.

"Is that so? And if I refuse?" she inquired. Her eyes danced, and she moved slightly closer to him.

"Well, I *am* a gentleman, of course," Jake mused. "But between your perfume and that sweet little outfit of yours, I might have to take some liberties anyway." He watched his fingers trail lightly up her bare arm before looking into Molly's eyes again. She shivered, even in the heat, so Jake pressed her lightly to him.

Molly peered over his shoulder, though, trying to see if any of the other knots of visitors were getting close.

"No one's gonna see," he murmured, amused as usual by her wariness. "Why are you worried?"

Molly shrugged. "I don't know—in Boston, I doubt anyone would even notice us. But here it seems like people might care. What would they say?" Her brown eyes sparkled. Maybe she was wondering what story a stranger might spin about them.

Jake snorted. He could answer her question, no problem. "Oh, let's see—they'd say my father was certainly some kind of rogue. My mother would be a good girl who fell under the influence of a bad seed, a victim of the inescapable lure of vice and debauchery."

"Good God, that seems a bit lurid. What the heck would they say about *me*?" Molly frowned, her nose wrinkling adorably.

"That you were overcome by the majesty of this fair plantation, and that the romantic fragrance of the flowers made a nice girl do inadvisable things," Jake recited.

Molly looked dubious, naturally. She was too smart to swallow that whopper whole.

"All right, maybe not. You'll be like Eve in the Garden, leading a sweet Southern boy astray with your evil little apple," Jake laughed. For emphasis, he let one hand drift down to squeeze her rear, and used his grip to yank her closer against him.

Molly squeaked. "I think they might have our roles backwards."

"Who cares? Can I kiss you now, or what?"

"By all means," she breathed.

Jake's mouth came down on hers. Any thought of propriety flew out the window when her arm snaked up around his neck, holding him close despite the heat. He clutched Molly's waist with one hand and her ass with the other, her skin blazing hot through the thin material of her clothes. Jake's tongue was even hotter as he invaded Molly's mouth. There wasn't a shred of courtliness in his kiss, but there was a lot of desperation. She melted against him, her neck arching back as he bent over her.

Suddenly they heard voices, and Jake wrenched his mouth away. He had a little more difficulty getting his hands to obey the cease-and-desist, though—they were perfectly happy right where they were.

Molly opened her eyes and blinked at the sudden, glaring sunlight. "What...?"

"Well, *that's* something!" A bevy of impeccably turned-out, very elderly women emerged from one of the paths leading to the enclave. They spotted Jake and Molly and recoiled, as if faced with a nest of venomous snakes.

"That is just...*vulgar*," the second lady added, clutching her handbag to her chest. "Appalling behavior!"

That seemed a bit much. Jake rolled his eyes.

A third lady was literally *tsk*-ing as they all hurried past. The flock progressed down one of the other paths leading downhill, their assorted canes flying. A short distance away, though, the little group paused for a debriefing. Jake stared down at Molly, blinking slowly while they listened to the conference.

"I always thought he was such a nice boy," the first woman lamented.

"Not once he went to college. It just goes to show you," the second said. "All the breeding in the world can't make up for plain wildness." At least they were taking care not to insult Jake's relations, he supposed.

"It is a lovely garden, though—isn't it? You almost can't blame them." That one had some sense, at least. Jake flexed his fingers on Molly's luscious bottom in implicit agreement.

The last woman had more pragmatic matters in mind. "Who is she?" she wondered. When there was no answer, she mused, "She looks to be about his age. That would mean that she came out around the same time as your Sara, right?"

The first old biddy drawled, "Well, I've never seen that girl before in my life." At that they moved along, and their scandalized voices faded away.

"That's because she's *Yankee*," Jake whispered dramatically, widening his eyes at Molly.

Molly giggled, and he smiled back—but then Jake sobered. One of those ladies had known him. He let go of Molly and looked away uncomfortably, not feeling like laughing anymore.

"Sorry," she smiled, squeezing his arm to get him to look back at her. She shouldn't have apologized—kissing her was his idea, after all.

Jake cleared his throat, trying to think of what to say. He wasn't normally the kind of guy that was embarrassed by something like that, but the current circumstances *were* a tad unusual. Molly looked confused about what exactly was the issue, though.

"Are you okay?" she prodded.

"Well, shoot," Jake sighed, resigned to the truth. "The thing is, this will probably get back to my parents before long. My mother ought to be calling me about it by Saturday at the latest," he explained.

"But why?" Molly asked, baffled. "You're a grown man. They can't possibly expect you to be celibate." In Molly's world, it likely didn't matter if she chose to kiss someone on a date. This probably seemed like a whole lot of fuss over something very ordinary to her.

But Molly wasn't Jake, and hadn't split up with a fiancé less than twenty-four hours ago. Jake scrubbed at his face, feeling pained. Had he needed to be *quite* so impatient?

Molly peered at the path that the old ladies had disappeared down. "Did you *know* those ladies?" she asked, trying to make sense of the shift he'd undergone.

Molly was only in town for two weeks. So yes, Jake had good reason to be impatient, he decided. "No, I didn't" he answered. "But they obviously knew me. I guarantee you, one of them has a sister in our church choir, or a cousin who was my third-grade teacher—or some other weird connection." Jake's eyes drifted over Molly's beautiful upturned face, and he leaned down carefully, tracing his nose and his lips one last time lightly along the line of her neck.

"Oh, come on. What are they gonna do? Get you in trouble?" Molly laughed. Whether it was from uncertainty at what he was telling her, or a ticklish response to him nuzzling her, wasn't quite clear.

"You might say that," he muttered, taking her hand and leading her along a different path. "Wilmington is a small, small town when it wants to be, honey."

"That's ridiculous. There's like, more than a hundred thousand people living here!" Molly sounded sure about that. She'd probably looked it up when she'd landed the interview.

"And you can be *sure* that every one of those people is all up in each other's business," Jake told her morosely.

Whatever delicious spell they'd been under before had clearly dissipated now. While they walked, each lost in their own thoughts, Jake considered the situation. Duty and decorum had their place, sure—but Jake was twenty-seven, for crying out loud. They'd been enthusiastically kissing, but it wasn't like they'd been dry-humping each other in a flowerbed or anything. *Not* that he'd done anything like that…recently.

Jake fought back against the smog of uncertainty that was poised to envelop him. Maybe he should have waited longer before he kissed her, or possibly made sure they were somewhere more private before grabbing her ass. But the fact remained that they were both consenting adults, and hadn't technically done anything wrong.

Jake had spent a lot of time recently letting other people tell him what to do, how to be, what to want. Right now, deep in his soul, he wanted Molly. And if her response to his kiss was anything to go by, she wanted him right back. Jake refused to feel one iota of guilt about that.

Chapter Eleven

J AKE CLAIMED HE was famished, so Molly figured it was as good a time as any to buy him some dinner. After all, he'd willingly agreed to act as her wingman when she went to see her father, and it only seemed fair to repay him. She stayed quiet as he drove them to a Tex-Mex restaurant he liked, though. That scorching kiss he'd just laid on her was banging around in her brain—as was his odd reaction to someone seeing it.

Molly didn't quite understand what had changed between them—leading Jake to swerve into more physical territory. Molly did know that he'd been as affected by the kiss as she was. She had felt Jake's heart pounding against her chest. Had heard his quick, shallow breaths. She wanted to recapture that feeling of connection.

Once Molly was seated across a chunky wooden table from him, she tried to wheedle Jake out of his funk. It worked, mostly—by the time their meals hit the table, she was able to start flirting without it seeming weird.

It felt good to do it. Molly realized that it had been a long time since she made the *choice* to flirt, and wasn't merely reacting to the advances of someone else. Jake was fun to tease, too. He got flustered and blushed far more than she would have expected from someone as handsome and confident as he was.

Perhaps he wasn't as discombobulated as she'd thought, though. Jake still managed to snag the check before Molly got a chance.

"But I was supposed to buy," she complained, watching him sign the credit slip in a firm, commanding scrawl.

"You snooze, you lose," Jake told her, smiling smugly.

"You know the firm is giving me a meal stipend, right? Your dad would essentially be buying us dinner."

"Good to know," Jake nodded. "But it's done now."

"But why did you do that? I thought we agreed!"

Another amused shrug, but no actual explanation from him. Molly studied his face.

"You aren't *ever* going to let me buy you a meal, are you?" Molly inquired.

"Honestly?"

"Of course."

"It's doubtful," he admitted. Molly hmphed and slouched in her seat, not sure if she was impressed or annoyed with him.

He cleared that question up when he dropped her off at the B&B. Jake threw the Audi into park, wound a hand around Molly's neck and pulled her close for a goodbye kiss, not bothering with small talk. He tasted of salt and lime, and something uniquely *Jake*, and he kissed like he couldn't get enough of her. When he broke away, Molly sighed. This kiss was both shorter and hotter than Jake's first one, and Molly was *impressed*. Definitely impressed—she tossed and turned half the night dwelling on how damn impressed she was, and wondered when she'd get a chance to be impressed again.

As THEY'D AGREED, Jake ambled into Mrs. Denson's dining room bright and early the next morning. The ends of his hair were still damp from his shower and he smelled fantastic, even from two feet away. Jake smiled widely, leaned across Molly to snag a muffin from the basket on the table, and bit into it. Guiltily, she tried not to look like she'd been fantasizing about him for the last several hours.

"Hey," Molly greeted him. "You're early. I was just finishing up."

"Take your time," Jake replied. "I just wanted to pilfer one of these babies before we left." Laughing, she offered him the basket and he grabbed another.

Out in his car, Jake kept smiling. He peppered Molly's face with quick, sweet pecks and licked at her lips—then pulled back to consider her.

"You taste like cranberries. And oranges, and…sugar," he claimed, moving in for another, deeper kiss.

Molly giggled, holding Jake off and peeking around the lot, to be sure no one was watching them. "No, I don't! I just ate a *blueberry* muffin," she laughed.

"That's weird. Let me try again," he said, pulling her toward him. Two experiments later, Jake had shared his second muffin with Molly just so he could taste the grains of sugar on her lips, and Molly had finally convinced him to get going.

The light mood didn't last, though. She fell silent once Jake pulled onto the highway, and couldn't have helped it if she tried.

Jake glanced at her. "Why do I feel like I'm driving you to your doom right now?"

Molly shrugged, a cop-out. "No reason."

"Okay, that wasn't even kind of convincing," he chuckled.

"Look—my dad isn't the most reliable guy on the planet, okay? He's personable and funny and you'll probably love him. But you can't count on him for anything worth a damn," Molly blurted out.

Jake thought about that. "So…why are we going to see him?"

"I don't know. Because he's my dad. Because if I don't, I probably won't see him again for five more years." Molly shrugged again, feeling stupid. Her father would probably gush to Jake about how proud he was of her. For two hours Molly would pretend—even after all this time—that he meant it. That she was actually worth something to her dad. That Molly wasn't the kind of woman men had no trouble leaving behind.

After a while, Jake asked, "What'd he do, anyway?" His voice was carefully neutral, and Molly supposed that was fair. Her father might've been cruel, like too many other fathers out there. He might've been an abuser, instead of just *gone*.

"He left us for an ER nurse when I was thirteen," she told him. "We were in Mystic at the time. He was tending bar back then, and said they hit it off because they were both night owls. She probably lasted the longest of any of them— five years—but even Brandi couldn't tie Skip O'Connell down for long."

"So, there were others?" Jake confirmed.

"Oh yes. Legions," Molly agreed.

"What about your mom? What did she do?"

"Mom wasn't going to fall for a handsome face twice," Molly grimaced, remembering all the terrible, jaded, pragmatic *advice*. Her mother had always tried to get the girls to cut off their hair, for instance, to wear it more like she did. But they had known the truth, even back then. Boys preferred women with long, unruly locks. They must— wasn't that what their dad had traded their mother in for? Someone earthier. More untamed. So, the girls refused to cut their hair short, just like they refused her suggestions about clothes and dating and everything else.

Molly and Mina had suspected, even then, that Elaine didn't want to compete with her pretty daughters. So many of her suggestions involved them suppressing themselves for the greater goal. Molly shook off the memory, and continued her story.

"We followed Dad and Brandi to Annapolis, just to make sure it was serious, you know." There had been the months and months of privation, in which they'd lived in a seedy motel while their mother struggled to feed the three of them on her waitress's salary. Elaine had cried every night while she scoured the dating websites. Molly was the one to remind them all that she and Mina were supposed to be in school— to actually *force* her parents to enroll them.

"After Mina and Grey got married, Mom and I went back to Mystic. She met a guy named Rob who lived across the hall, married him, and he moved us all back to his hometown in New York. I was a sophomore in high school by then."

"How was he?" Jake asked.

"Disinterested," Molly said. "They parked me in a fancy prep school where I didn't belong, and tried to dine out and go on trips as much as possible so they could pretend I wasn't there."

"Shit, honey." Jake stole another concerned look at her. "That doesn't sound very fun."

If he only knew the half of it. It was all so much worse than it sounded, especially once her step-father learned exactly what kind of kid he had living in his house. An upstart. A social-climber. A conniving piece of trash.

Molly shrugged yet again, and gave Jake a sardonic grin. "It wasn't," she chirped. "But it's all over now." *Thank the Lord.* "Now I get to hear about how Rob's kids think my mother broke up their parent's marriage, even though she didn't. And I get to hear about how a lady must always dress like she's hunting a man, even when she's already hooked one." *And* Molly got to hear about how *most* people were classier than she was, and would never dream of following the path she had.

Jake accepted that, and didn't press Molly.

She looked at him. All that old pain was in the past. Now she was in a fast car with a gorgeous guy. The weather was glorious, the windows rolled down, and they were headed toward what was bound to be a beautiful beach-front town. Molly could almost, *almost* forget who they were going to see when they got there.

THE BUILDING HER dad had directed her to was tucked under a sweeping bridge that spanned the canal and connected Holden Beach to the mainland. Her father's hair was longer than the last time she'd seen him—feathered and scraggly where it covered his neck, and wet at the temples where sweat stuck it to his head. Despite the fact that Molly had warned him she was bringing a friend, he still looked startled to see Jake.

He'd been leaning against a pylon waiting for them, but now her father strode forward and greeted Molly.

"Hey there, Commander!" he called happily, then enfolded her in a tight hug. He smelled of aftershave and deodorant and sweat and beer, and it was both painfully familiar and oddly upsetting. His bulky camera bag banged Molly on the hip when it swung forward during the hug, and—as with many things related to her dad—she tried to pretend it didn't hurt.

"Dad, this is my friend Jake. He's been showing me around Wilmington this week."

The two men shook hands, and Molly's father said brusquely, "Hey, what's up."

Jake smiled politely. "It's a pleasure to meet you, sir. Molly's told me all about you." As soon as the words exited his mouth, he seemed to realize that it was not the best thing to say.

Skip looked at her quickly, and she trilled, "Only the good things!" Molly could tell from his expression that he didn't quite believe her, but he gamely played along.

"Where'd you find the time?" her dad chuckled. Then he gestured behind them to a low-slung, brightly-painted building. "The marina canteen does some great seafood. What do you say we grab some lunch there?"

"Great," Molly agreed brightly, feeling as fake as a college freshman's ID. She wondered if Jake could tell, and if so— what he'd think of her.

Jake slowed his steps behind Molly's dad and murmured in an aside, "Commander?"

Molly muttered back, "Apparently, I looked like the commander of my grandfather's Navy ship when I was a baby. Dad's called me that ever since."

"Aw, that's cute," Jake smiled.

"Cute? He thought his baby girl looked like a sixty-year-old career Navy officer!" Molly protested.

"Hey now," Jake laughed, holding up his hands. "It'd be worse if he thought you looked like some weathered old man *now*."

"Do I?" Molly pleaded under her breath. "Because he *just* called me Commander."

Jakes eyes got hot as he looked her over. "Naw. Honey you look nothing like a man, old or otherwise." He set the palm of his hand lightly on the small of Molly's back to guide her through the doors of the restaurant, and it seared her like a brand.

Inside, it was dim after the bright summer sunshine, but there were three flat screen televisions mounted over the bar broadcasting a baseball game and lending extra light. Brightly-painted oars hung from the ceiling in haphazard groups.

Molly's father seemed jumpy and nervous as they waited for their table, bouncing on his toes and asking them twice how their drive down was. He was distracted—his eyes roving restlessly over the interior of the place, as if he was looking for someone in particular. Other than three desultory groups of diners, two waitresses, and a bored-looking bartender, there was no one else, though. The air conditioning was blasting, instantly chilling the sweat Molly didn't even realize she had between her shoulder blades. She rubbed her hands up and down her arms, trying to warm up.

The skin on the back of her thighs stuck uncomfortably to her cold metal chair once they were all seated. Molly decided to launch a conversational offensive instead of waiting to see what her dad might come up with.

"So, Dad, what's new? What have you been up to?" she asked. There was nothing Skip liked better than to tell a good story about himself—surely in the three years since she'd seen him, he'd managed to save up a tale or two.

"Well, I've been shacking up with your uncle for the last six months or so," he said. Peeking at Jake, he added, "It's kind of on the down low. The minimum age over there is fifty-eight, so technically I'm too young to live there."

"Oh, that's—" Molly began.

"It's great," her dad claimed. "I'm like the development's jailbait. The ladies can't stop eyeing the fresh meat." He laughed, an obnoxious, over-loud braying that raised the hairs on Molly's neck.

Jake arched an amused eyebrow at her, and she couldn't help but wince. What had she been thinking, bringing him here?

Mercifully, assistance arrived. One of the waitresses marched up, a smile blooming on her face when she recognized Skip. He was clearly one of her favorite customers, if not her *most* favorite.

"Well look what washed up," she purred. Her expression was open, friendly. Expectant.

"Hey, Felice," Skip boomed. He jumped up to give the woman a long hug. She was tall and strong, with dark brown skin, slightly Asian features, and a head full of tiny shoulder-length braids. Some of them had little metal beads affixed at varying heights, and they caught the eye whenever Felice moved her head. Molly realized—this woman was beautiful, seemed sweet, and only had eyes for Skip. *Uh oh.*

"Who are your friends?" the waitress wondered, her gaze lingering on Molly's face.

Her dad glanced at her, but ignored Jake. "This is my youngest daughter, Molly. She was in town, so naturally she came to see her old man."

"Isn't she pretty," Felice mused, a slight island accent coloring her voice. To Molly, she commented, "Your dad loves a good visit. He talks about you and your sister all the time."

For some reason that irritated her, and Molly felt an overwhelming need to clarify. "I came for a job interview. Up in Wilmington." Then, when it became obvious that her father had no intention of ever acknowledging Jake, Molly added, "This is my friend Jake."

Jake rose half out of his chair to shake the waitress's hand. "Pleasure," he said, smiling.

Felice examined Jake now, assessing him. Deciding something, she asked, "You from around here?"

"Yeah, from Wilmington. Is it that obvious?" Jake chuckled.

Felice nodded, laughing along. "Yes, it is."

Skip didn't like having the focus off him—no surprise there. He grinned and said a little too loudly, "What's good today, sweetheart?"

Felice got right down to business. Looking at her order pad, she told them, "There's some blackened grouper that's not bad. But we got some good-looking shrimp in this morning that the cook is barbecuing. I suggest those."

Skip nodded at her, not even glancing at his companions. "Sounds good. We'll all have the shrimp, right guys?"

Felice scribbled something on her pad, and asked Molly and Jake, "What can I get you two to drink? Any salads or appetizers?"

Molly ordered an Arnold Palmer: half iced-tea, half lemonade. Mrs. Denson had only introduced it to her this week, but it was already Molly's new favorite drink. She had no idea how she'd lived through all her other summers without it.

Jake and her father ordered beers with names she'd never heard of, and Skip asked for a basket of bread. When the busboy dropped it off, it contained an assortment of French bread, hush puppies, and small cornbread muffins that Molly discovered were stuffed with cheddar and jalapenos. The one she popped in her mouth was delicious, but there were only three. Jake took the second, and when he saw that Molly was keeping a greedy eye on the third, he snagged it from the basket and set it on her bread plate. Skip didn't notice, too busy bragging that the focaccia he had uncovered was ordered all the way from a bakery in New Jersey. Looking around the tired little restaurant, Molly doubted it.

Her dad called across the room to ask Felice who was working the grill that day, then poked at the remaining offerings in the bread basket, claiming the hush puppies for himself. Felice approached with a tray, set their drinks in front of them, then lingered for a moment with her hand on Skip's shoulder. When he didn't offer her even the slightest sign that he noticed, she moved on to another table.

Skip raised his beer bottle for a toast. Molly braced herself—she never knew what one of her father's toasts might entail, and she didn't like the feral glint in his eye whenever he looked at Jake.

Her dad inhaled importantly, then intoned, *"May those who love us, love us. And for those who don't love us, may God turn their hearts. And if He doesn't turn their hearts, may He turn their ankles, so we'll know them by their limping."*

As parental threats went, that hadn't been the worst, Molly supposed.

Jake chuckled, unaware of any ill will aimed his way. "Amen to that," he agreed, then took a large swig of his beer.

Molly watched her father glare at Jake when he spoke, and had the sudden realization that he *must* know about Carter. She hadn't actually ever told him herself, but…he and her mother did stay in touch over the years, through semi-regular phone calls. Molly could almost picture how Elaine would have framed the tale: Skip's probable culpability. Her new husband Rob's valiant rescue of Molly.

Her father had never done or said a thing about the whole situation, except now—when he was staring down her new friend. Molly didn't know whether to hug Skip for his first protective impulse (however faint) in years—or to smack him for the world's worst case of too-little, too-late.

After a stilted lunch, Molly's dad asked them to take a walk with him along the marina. There were shrimp boats docked, as well as a couple charter boats. There were a handful of sailboats, too, their metal fittings clanking against the masts in the stiff breeze barreling up the Intracoastal. Wherever Molly had lived, all up and down the eastern seaboard, that sound was always the same. In Mystic, Annapolis—even near Boston Harbor—that sound set off a wariness in Molly's soul. A fear that if it began to feel too much like home, it would all be ripped away from her again. Shaking off the feeling, Molly remembered: her nomadic existence was coming to an end. Soon, if she could convince *Alexander, Polk & Futch* that she was the best woman for the job, Molly would be home forever.

Jake ended up talking with some guys coming in from one of the morning's fishing charters, so Molly nudged her father and his clicking camera farther down the dock. It wasn't easy to get him alone—Skip seemed to think his glares would have more power if he levelled them at Jake up-close-and-personal. But it was time to get to the bottom of his uncharacteristic reaction to her friend.

"Dad." She paused, swallowing hard. "He's not Carter, you know. Jake is nice." It was a test, and she waited to see what he'd say.

"From what I've heard, he seems about the same to me," Skip growled.

"So, you *know* about Carter, then?"

Her father nodded, but didn't quite meet her eye.

"How long have you known?" He'd never mentioned it. Never offered a single word of advice or comfort, in all this time.

Skip snapped a few frames of the marlin the charter guys were holding up and posing with. "That's a big'un," he commented, zooming in with his telephoto lens.

Molly didn't want to let this go. It seemed too important. "How *long* have you known, Dad?"

"About six months," he replied. Not that long, then. Actually, he'd found out right around the time Molly's stepdad had sent a check to pay off her lawyer, once and for all. Molly bristled, wanting to wring her interfering mother's skinny little neck.

"How'd you meet this character?" Skip wanted to know. He jerked his chin at Jake, standing over with the fishermen, being friendly. Politely giving Molly and her father some space.

"He knows Grey," she snipped. Molly pressed on, "Did *Mom* tell you about Carter? Is that how you know?"

"Uh huh." Wow, so, any loquacity Skip had been inclined toward during lunch was apparently out the window now.

But who was really surprised, given that this was actually a conversation that mattered, and didn't come pre-loaded with a gullible audience?

Molly was frustrated, maybe even more than her father was. "*Why* would she do that?" she griped.

Skip was unmoved. "I dunno. She was awfully proud of her new husband's contribution," he muttered. *New*, he said, despite the fact that Elaine and Rob had been married for several years now. And never mind the fact that her stepdad's supposed generosity had taken five long years to rear its ugly head—or that Molly had declined to accept it.

Her dad cast another baleful look in Jake's direction. Jake, who was still chatting happily with the other men, hands shoved in his shorts pockets and sunglasses pushed up on his forehead. He looked friendly. Guileless. When her father wasn't watching him, he kept checking on Molly, making sure she was okay.

"You know, I was serious. Jake's not like Carter. Besides, you never even *met* Carter. What do you care?" It came out sharper than she'd intended, and it clearly hit the mark. Skip turned his scowl on Molly, and he was not pleased.

"I care because you're my *daughter*—and that kid over there seems like the same damn song on a different record. If you ask me."

Her dad, for all his shiftlessness, had seen a fair bit of life. He was many things, some of them unsavory, but he was usually an accurate judge of character. So, Molly looked at Jake. *Really* looked. She thought about everything he had done and said since she met him.

Then she told her father, "No, you're wrong. Jake is actually completely different." And Molly believed it, too.

LATER, ON THE drive home, she couldn't quite bring herself to act cheerful. Her father had given her a quick, casual hug goodbye—like they saw each other twice a week, instead of twice a decade. Molly was relieved to have the visit over with, but seeing her dad had a way of making her feel depressed. Emotionally drained.

Eventually Jake said, "So, your dad's a trip." His voice was light but his eyes, when Molly met them, were concerned.

"Hm," she agreed. "He is that."

"Think that woman in the canteen will ever catch his eye?"

"No," Molly mused, remembering Felice. That poor woman was setting herself up for heartbreak, no question. "But even if she does, it won't matter. He'll be gone again, long before it can turn into anything real."

"You think?" Jake asked, looking between her face and the road. He seemed surprised, but of course he didn't know Skip O'Connell like she did.

"I *know*," she said, staring morosely out the window. Trying to throw off her melancholy mood, Molly reached for a joke. "You probably shouldn't have told him what you do for a living," she teased. "I think he really believed you might prosecute him for age fraud."

Jake snorted. "Oh, hell yeah. I'm totally launching an investigation into retirement home meat markets. Are you kidding? It's probably gonna make my career."

"Assuming you even wanted to stay a prosecutor," Molly reminded him with a smile.

"Well, sure," he agreed. "But it's good to know I have a slam dunk in my pocket, just in case people stop making money and dying."

And then, Jake did the damnedest thing. He reached over the gearshift and took Molly's hand, holding it easily and confidently like it was the most natural thing in the world. A small thing, but also—in that second—huge.

"You did real good, honey," he murmured, catching her eye.

"Thanks," Molly whispered, choking on the tears backing up in her throat. She gripped his hand back, and hung on.

Chapter Twelve

L UCKILY, JAKE HAD already agreed to bring Molly to
the bar association party that evening. If he hadn't, she
might've been reduced to begging him. As it was, he'd left
her side for less than half an hour and she'd already been hit
on twice.

She'd also been informed, by no fewer than four or five
"well-meaning" parties, that moving all the way down to
Wilmington to work for Clay Alexander was a fool's errand.
It seemed that "everyone knew" he'd be retiring any day, and
when he did—heads would be rolling at the venerable firm
bearing his name.

Molly tried not to feel worried. The people letting her in
on the supposed secret seemed gossipy at best—and at
worst, paranoid over-reactors. It was hard not to notice how
they all waited for Jake to amble away before seeking Molly
out, or how they seemed disappointed when they didn't get
a reaction at the news. Maybe they were testing her. Or
maybe this was some kind of arcane hazing ritual. Either
way, they'd have to work a lot harder than that to get Molly
to give up her chance at the job.

She was busy wondering how many of them might be vying for the same position when Jake sidled up to her from across the party. He'd been stuck in conversation with two disheveled and sweaty young men—but when he saw Molly alone with a frown on her face, he'd bee-lined over.

Jake leaned over the bottles on the bar, looking for his favorite. She'd been lingering, trying to look busy while surreptitiously watching him, but Jake's expression made her think she wasn't as smooth as she thought. He poured himself two fingers of Kentucky bourbon.

"Are you making eyes at me, Miss Molly?" he murmured under his breath.

"I beg your pardon?" God, was she that obvious? She was trying to make a good impression here. Who knew how all these people were connected to *Alexander, Polk & Futch*? One wrong move—lusting after a partner's son, say—could lose her the job.

"Oh, I think you heard me just fine," Jake smirked.

"Well, I am doing no such thing," Molly huffed, trying desperately to hold the line.

"I beg to differ. The question is, how far are you willing to go with it?"

"What on earth are you talking about? You're crazy."

"Not hardly," he claimed, leaning one shoulder against the wall. "I could drag you off into a corner right now and kiss you senseless, for example. Or you could keep sending looks my way for a while more, until I get desperate enough to find an empty janitor's closet to pull you into."

Molly groaned. "Get a grip," she told him. "Drink your bourbon and don't move from this spot. I'm going to go to the ladies' room and you better be here when I get back."

"That bad already?" he squawked in disbelief.

"You have no idea."

When Molly returned from the ladies' room, Jake handed her the wine he'd poured for her. He intercepted the predatory gazes of two young attorneys checking her out, then turned to raise a quizzical eyebrow at her.

"Holy buckets, it is a meat market in here," she breathed. "It may as well be my uncle's retirement community!"

Jake laughed. "I imagine you have that problem a lot. And just think—these could be your future coworkers. The late nights working on cases...the office happy hours..."

"No, seriously, *stop*." Molly quickly averted her eyes from yet a third circling shark. "I think I'd better stick close to you from now on. These guys are hitting the booze pretty hard."

"I have no problem whatsoever with that," Jake said, pivoting his body to shield her from the gaze of the middle-aged men sitting nearby. "For a number of reasons." He smirked when he realized she'd heard the last part.

"Okay, I'll bite," Molly smiled, enjoying the game. "Give me the top three reasons."

Jake moved closer and hunched down so she could hear him over the blaring music—at some point, it had switched over from the Sinatra tunes favored by their parents' generation to the thumping dance selections geared toward the younger attorneys.

"One: I will *look* like a total stud with a woman like you on my arm." He nodded at her convincingly.

"I'm sure you are a total stud," Molly agreed, "But— 'a woman like me?' What's that supposed to mean?"

"Let's see. One part Ingrid Bergman," He ran a thumb lightly over her lower lip and then her cheekbone. Molly's glass tipped, spilling red wine onto the toe of his shoe. Jake cleared his throat and wiped it discreetly on the carpet—and Molly giggled like a teenager.

"One part Meg Ryan," Jake added, touching a finger lightly to one of her dimples. "And one part....um...Penelope Cruz." He picked up a lock of her hair and ran it through his fingers, then peered down to examine the length of her leg from ankle to hip.

Molly's breath hitched in her throat, but she made a supreme effort to appear unaffected. She cocked her hip and groaned, "That's just bizarre. We'd better come back to that. What's the second reason?"

"Uh, Two," Jake rested a hand on her hip as couples pushed past them to reach the dance floor, then gently guided her toward the tables arranged around the perimeter of the room. "You wanting to stick close to me makes me *feel* like a total stud, because I get to be the tough guy protecting the damsel in distress."

"Well, you *are* pretty big. But—not very scary. Hmm. Let's try Three."

A smile played at the corner of Jake's mouth. "Ah, Three—Three is good. You wanting to be near me gives me hope that my feelings for you might get returned one of these days." The tables they had been heading toward filled up quickly when the music switched suddenly to more slow ballads.

"Hmm. Nicely done," Molly grinned. She took their glasses and set them on the tray of a passing caterer, then took Jake's hand and led him back toward the dance floor. Young attorneys who had sweated through their dress shirts only moments before had somehow managed to procure partners to drift across the parquet with them.

Molly and Jake found a spot near the edge and began dancing slowly. Jake scanned her face, then chuckled a little to himself as he gazed off over her shoulder. His hand engulfed hers, and his other palm scalded Molly's back through the thin material of her cocktail dress.

"What's so funny?" she asked in consternation. "Please don't say my dancing—everyone always tells me I try to lead."

"No, no—your dancing is fine." Jake spun her around, and Molly realized that she seemed to be able to follow *his* lead just fine. "I'm just laughing about the secret Fourth

Reason. I like hanging out with you, but I wouldn't be much of a gentleman if I enlightened you on it just yet." Jake squeezed her hand.

"You really are a terrific flirt, you know that?" Molly said in amazement. "But of course, now that you have mentioned the mysterious fourth reason you'll *have* to tell me."

"No can do, sugar," he drawled, expertly turning her again.

"If you didn't *really* want to tell me, you wouldn't have mentioned it," she reasoned.

Jake eyed her. "My lips are sealed," he replied, pressing those lips together. Even making such a comical face, Jake had a great mouth. Knowing what that mouth could do only made it better.

Molly tightened her fingers on his shoulder in what she hoped was a threatening manner.

He laughed, though, and pulled her a little closer. "Number Four is dangerous, you see."

She tried to look superior. Unimpressed.

"Totally treacherous," Jake confirmed.

"Do go on," Molly urged, smirking.

Her examined her shoulder and when he spoke, his voice was gruff and sexy. "Number Four involves the ridiculous degree to which I am attracted to you. So, you sticking close to me here in the dark, would clearly make *all* of me quite happy," he murmured near her ear.

Molly's eyes had inexplicably drifted shut, so she pried them open. It seemed like the room had grown darker.

"I see," she replied, arching into Jake as a far as she dared. "And that is perilous...why, exactly?"

"Because there's a gray area—where you are close to me, but not quite close enough," he breathed against her ear, "That can feel excruciating." He drew out the last word to emphasize his point.

"Ah." Molly held herself warily against him, afraid to let herself melt into Jake's embrace like she was dying to do. She had to remind herself this was a *work* function, and she had not been offered a job yet. Though to be fair, the prevalent culture of this association appeared to be very...*social*. No one would likely even notice them.

Jake glanced at her face briefly before looking resolutely away again. Molly wondered how clearly her thoughts were broadcasting, because he seemed to be reading her mind. His hand on her back pressed her closer still.

"This is pure torture," he whispered, shaking his head.

Chapter Thirteen

JAKE STAYED LONGER than expected at that bar association party, holding Molly in his arms and swaying to the music. After that, he'd *tried* to drop her off at the B&B, but ended up making out with her in his car—like a teenager—instead. They went at it again on the back porch of the inn, and didn't quit until nearly one in the morning.

That meant he was late getting his dog from his sister Healey's house. By the time Jake got there, she was sound asleep on her couch, and poor Duke was whining for a patch of grass to do his business on.

The dog was hyper when they got home: jumping around and knocking stuff over right and left. He was needy, too. Whenever Jake had finished cleaning up the dog's latest disaster long enough to sit his butt down, Duke struggled onto Jake's lap, whining in apology. Jake couldn't help but feel bad for the pup—he had been cooped up and by himself way more than usual since Molly had hit town.

Jake was too wound up to sleep, and his dog seemed to feel the same way. It got Jake to thinking, though—nothing fixed the crazy mutt's behavior better than a nice long day gamboling around in some high grass. He knew just the place to take him. Come to think of it, it might be the perfect place to take Molly, too—nostalgic, peaceful, beautiful…and way-the-hell out in the country, away from prying eyes and ears.

Jake leaned back on his couch and smiled, thinking of all the ways he could kiss her, where they were sure to be alone. Maybe even *more* than kiss her.

He reached for his phone right as Duke darted between the couch and the coffee table. The dog knocked into Jake's arm, his glass of sweet tea splashed onto the rug, and Jake groaned. At this rate he was going to have to make a run to the twenty-four-hour market *tonight*, just for paper towels—and some doggie Xanax.

Pausing before he mopped up Duke's newest mess, Jake sent a text to Molly. They could spend tomorrow at his family's farm, and no way would she be busy—on Saturday, almost no one at the firm would be working.

Want to take a drive out in the country tomorrow? he typed.
If you want, we could go to my family's old farm.

Molly's response was gratifyingly immediate. Jake felt downright cheerful that she hadn't fallen asleep yet either.

Yes! she wrote. What time?

Jake thought about that. It was going on two a.m., and they both needed time to get some rest.

Let's say eleven. Wear jeans.

As he tried to get ready for bed and get his dog settled down, Jake tried really, really hard not to think about all the places a tick might get to, if Molly didn't wear pants.

THE FAMILY'S "HOME farm," as his father always called it, had once been used for growing tobacco. These days, some of Jake's cousins made a half-hearted effort to grow soy—when they could be bothered to plant and harvest on time.

The main house was kept in decent enough condition, if a bit dusty. And Granddaddy's old barn—where Jake and his sister used to play when they were kids—was still standing tall. It was one of Jake's favorite places on earth, so he took Molly there first.

She'd worn jeans as he instructed, but clearly hadn't thought through the why of it—Molly was also wearing a shiny pair of flip-flops on her feet. So, inside the barn Jake rooted around in the cabinet beside the door, trying to find a pair of tall boots that might fit her. He did, but they were old and scuffed and probably left over from some cousin's teenage years. Jake had to knock the spiders out of them a couple times before Molly would agree to put her bare feet in them. But when she did, *Lord have mercy*—the woman was every country boy's fantasy come to life. Long hair, long legs, and all woman in between.

Quickly, Jake redirected her attention to the architecture of the barn—no use letting Molly think that he had dragged her all the way out here with only one thing on his mind. They walked around inside for a bit, while Molly ogled the soaring ceiling with its crisscrossed beams, and Jake ogled her fine little butt in those tight jeans.

The hunting boots did not help matters, in his opinion. The grubby, shapeless rubber just seemed to highlight the shapeliness of her thighs—and for some reason, made the rest of her look that much more feminine. And every damn time Molly bent down to peek at an ancient farming implement on the floor, her t-shirt rode up in the back and Jake got a good view of at least three inches of smooth-looking skin.

After a while, his vision was growing hazy with repressed desire. Duke had caught some small critter with a long tail, so he shooed the dog outside before Molly saw it. Then, Jake casually herded her toward one of the filled stalls and—when he judged her position to be close enough—he hooked her ankle with his foot and took her down to the hay.

Daylight filtered softly into the building through the louvered windows set up high on the walls. Dust motes drifted lazily through the warm air, caught in the angled sunbeams slanting through the space. And Molly gasped in surprise to find herself flat on her back with Jake pinning her. She recovered nicely, though. Once her eyes warmed up for him and she snaked an ankle around his knee, Jake pressed his hips against hers and gave her a nice long kiss.

Molly's tongue tangled with his, and her hands drifted up his back to grip his head tight. Jake didn't think he'd ever wanted a woman as much as this. The way she tasted was extraordinary—intoxicating. He couldn't get enough, didn't care one whit for stupid things like breathing, and as long as Molly kept kissing him back, Jake was content to lay right there until the sun went down and the crickets started chirping. But Molly pulled away far too soon, murmuring something against his lips.

"Hmm?" he managed, gazing down at her and brushing her mahogany hair back off her forehead.

"Hay is pretty itchy, isn't it?" Molly repeated. And then—as if to emphasize the point—she sneezed violently right into his neck.

Jake groaned and wiped at his throat with the collar of his shirt. In seconds, Molly began poking him between the ribs, trying to dislodge him from her body. Jake got to his feet laughing, not bothering to hide his reluctance, then gave Molly a hand so she could get to hers.

He waited until her back was turned and she'd started for the door to readjust himself in his jeans, and wondered what the hell he'd gotten himself into. Molly was, no joke, hotter than beach sand on a ninety-degree day—and now that he'd kissed her a few times, Jake was beginning to worry for his sanity.

Molly sauntered outside and grinned at him. "Your tours are beginning to develop a certain theme," she joked.

She had no idea. If she knew the half of what Jake's dreams were like, that theme would be even more noticeable. He just smiled and picked some bits of hay out of her hair, then said, "Come on."

He walked her through the woods to the old pond where they used to go fishing, and sometimes—on really hot days when they were older—swimming. Duke galloped ahead, his prize from the barn still clamped in his jaws, while he went nosing around the shoreline. Jake hadn't fished there in forever. Naturally, once he'd said that out loud, Molly immediately wanted to. He hadn't brought any poles though, and weirdly—more words came skipping out of his mouth. Jake stood there, promising Molly he'd bring poles next time even as he wondered if there ever *would* be a next time. Lord knew he wanted there to be.

But sometimes Jake felt like a lowdown piece of dirt, not knowing if he'd ever have the balls to stand up to his parents, to Blake's parents—to Bess herself—once and for all. He'd made a start, at least. Now he only had to hold the line. But what kind of loser would Jake be, if providence handed him *this* beautiful woman, and he ruined any chance to keep her through simple cowardice?

They turned back up the dirt track through the woods, and eventually came to a rough ladder nailed to the trunk of a tree.

Jake gave Molly a little smile. "Wanna see my treehouse?" he asked.

"Are you serious?" She peered up into the branches, trying to make out the frame of rough boards they could see up there in the leaves.

"C'mon, this is a big honor. Usually it's strictly no-girls-allowed."

Molly rolled her eyes and began climbing. Jake stuck close behind her in case of loose boards, but being eye-level with that ass of hers was too damn distracting. He could have had an entire bough drop on his head, and he probably wouldn't have noticed. He might have been a stag in mating season with the way he was acting. Heck, even his own mutt was better-behaved, and after last night that was really saying something.

Up top, they reached the large wooden platform with its haphazard, ineffectual walls. The whole thing blended into the branches and leaves, and had a great view of the farmhouse and barn—closer than anyone ever expected them to be. Jake had loved to perch up here when he was a kid, far enough away from his family to feel brave, but still close enough to feel safe. He could watch them moving around between the house and the barn like he was watching a television show about home.

"What is this place?" Molly breathed, fascinated. Jake wondered if she'd ever seen anything like it. When would she have had the chance?

Jake sat carefully, then scooted back against the main tree trunk. His legs stretched farther across the floor than they used to. Without thinking, he grabbed Molly's hands and pulled her from her crouch toward him—spreading his thighs so she could nestle between them and lean back against his chest. Jake wrapped his arms loosely around her and buried his nose in her hair. As usual, she smelled amazing—like lemons maybe, or orange blossoms. Tart and sweet and edible.

"Calling it a treehouse might be a bit ambitious," he admitted. "I think it was actually supposed to be a deer blind."

"Oh no. Poor deer," Molly murmured sadly.

"Don't worry—it didn't get much use that way," Jake told her. Too close to the house, for one thing. Any gun shots would've scared the animals, and God forbid one of the bullets ever went astray near the people.

"Are you a hunter, though?" Molly asked.

"Not really. My Dad let me pick the tree and helped me build this when I was younger—back when we used to come out here all the time. I never quite developed a taste for the hunting part. Mostly I just sat up here and spied on my family. Read some comics. You know, the usual."

"Oh."

Molly was a warm bundle in his arms. Jake wished he'd had her here with him for years, instead of only moments. He searched for something else to say.

"My sister used it more. She's pretty handy with a bow, if you can believe it."

Molly made a little sound of amazement, and then they fell silent, just watching and listening to the woods around them. Duke reappeared down below, without the critter from the barn—but now in possession of an oversized branch. He plopped on the ground and began chewing industriously on it.

"No need to worry," Jake whispered eventually. "Look." He indicated a doe and her two spotted fawns picking their way across the path and into the underbrush, back in the direction of the pond. "See? Safe as can be."

Molly made yet another sweet little sound. Jake bent and nuzzled the perfect, delicate shell of her ear, and planted tiny kisses along the side of her neck.

"We should all be so lucky," she teased quietly. But she tilted her head to the side to give him better access.

"I beg your pardon," Jake laughed, then nipped at her earlobe. "You are not in a lick of danger from me, Miss Molly."

"Yeah, well—we'll see about that," she muttered.

Maybe Molly could feel how very real and very present the "danger" actually was. Jake raised his hands and trailed his fingertips lightly across the tops of her breasts, tracing lines and circles right over the spot she was fullest. Her breasts rose and fell with each heavy breath. Over her shoulder, he watched himself touch her, watched the way her body reacted, and knew if he couldn't touch her skin—soon—he might just die.

Jake twisted around and tried to put the moves on her, to get Molly flat under him, to get her shirt up or even her boots off—but the blind was just too freaking small. Molly tried to shift down to help him, but ended up cracking her head on the wall hard enough to put tears in her eyes. Jake reared back to give her some space, but only managed to bang one knee on the wall, and get the other foot stuck in a loose board near the doorway. Molly sprang forward to help extricate him but sat back almost instantly, wincing and pulling a long sliver from her palm.

Jake could empathize—he was pretty sure he had one or two of those bastards stuck in his hide himself. Trying to maneuver himself onto his knees in front of Molly was a comical disaster. The floorboards creaked ominously beneath them and suddenly his cozy hideaway seemed more like a confining box, not fit for man nor beast. Two grown-ass, amorous adults had no business whatsoever playing up there. Jake wasn't sure whether to laugh or hit something.

Molly had no such problem. With a tremendous, gasping inhale of air she began howling—so hard that tears streamed down her cheeks and words would not emerge whole from her lips. Jake watched her, amazed, as she snorted and laughed, gasped and cried—and thought he'd never seen such a beautiful thing in his entire life. The joy of it filled his chest until he thought he'd burst. Down below, Duke leaped to his feet and barked, pawing at the trunk and wanting to join in.

THEY WERE BOTH pretty grimy by the time they switched out Molly's shoes in the barn and made it back up to the house. Jake dug the back-door key out of its hiding place beneath a flower pot, and let them into the kitchen. The air was warm and still, and smelled faintly of dust and lemon floor polish. No one had been out here in quite a while, it seemed. But Molly was thirsty, and Jake had been in too much of a rush that morning to plan properly. He made his way over to the fridge, hoping for the best.

The "best" yielded nothing more than a single water bottle of indeterminate age in the fridge. The pantry contained only two dusty cans of beer and a stale bag of chips. Jake set those on the counter to toss out, and handed Molly the water. She looked flushed and hot and disheveled—and somehow even sexier than if she'd been fresh as a daisy.

She drank half the water, made a face, then handed the bottle back—insisting he finish it. Jake eyed her as he chugged it, trying to come up with a way to extend the day. For one hot second, he thought about pulling Molly upstairs to one of the bedrooms, but he could tell the house hadn't been aired recently. He shuddered to think about what the sheets on the beds might look like—if there even were any. Finally, Jake had it.

"Hey, I just had a thought. How'd you like to go swimming before I bring you back?" Oh yeah—that perked Molly up right quick.

"Really? Where?"

"My parents are down in South Carolina visiting my mom's aunt right now, but they have a nice pool in their back yard that is calling our names," Jake said. "And, it's on our way back to town."

Molly bit her lip, considering. "Damn. Once again, I didn't bring my bathing suit. I'm beginning to think you plan it this way."

Jake grinned. It wasn't the worst idea in the world. "I didn't. I swear. But don't worry, no one's home. We could just swim in our skivvies, if you want." He was sure he had some trunks stuck in a drawer at his folks' house, and guessed his sister probably kept a suit or two there, too. But swimming in their underwear suddenly held quite a bit of illicit appeal. *God*, he was a hound.

"Are you sure they won't mind?" Molly asked, beginning to smile.

"Naw, they won't care," Jake assured her. At least, his dad wouldn't. Mama was a whole other story. "Let's do it."

Molly shrugged and looked game. "Okay. Sounds good!"

JAKE HAULED ASS down the little country road that led away from the farm, heading for the highway that would bring them to his folks' house. He couldn't stop stealing glances at Molly's sweet profile, looking out her window at the patches of passing farmland interspersed with scrubby overgrown lots no one cared about. Maybe she felt his eyes on her.

Sitting straighter, she asked, "Hey, are those cantaloupes growing out there?"

Jake squinted at where she was pointing. "Looks like it. They have a little tobacco growing back there, too. You see it?" He gestured to a darker green patch further back from the road.

When Molly stayed silent, Jake glanced back at her face. Her expression was equal parts puzzled and amused.

"What?" he wondered. "Something funny?"

"No." Molly shook her head and shrugged one shoulder. "But…would you look at me?" She grinned then, but it didn't *quite* reach her eyes. "Here I am, flying along some rural road, handsome southern boy at the wheel—"

"Why, thank you, ma'am," Jake drawled, interjecting.

"You're welcome," Molly fired back, but she seemed distracted. "Windows down, country music on the radio…" she trailed off again, seeming flummoxed. "If you'd told me six months ago that I'd be sitting *here*, like this—I never would have believed you."

"Are you happy, though?" Jake inquired. It had to be a bit of a culture shock for her. As far as he knew, she'd spent most of her life in New England port towns. Wilmington was one thing, but he imagined that Carolina farmland looked—and felt—a bit different.

Molly nodded again, but she'd gone mute—with shyness, maybe, or perhaps something more vulnerable. Jake couldn't decide, but something seemed off. He wanted to prod her back into her usual effervescence.

"Well now, if you're really going to play the part, girl—I'm gonna need a real good rebel yell out of you," he laughed, deepening his accent to caricature levels.

"You…what? You don't mean Billy Idol, do you?" Molly's nose wrinkled up, and Jake wanted to lean right over and kiss it.

He suspected if he *had* meant Billy, Molly would be up to the task. He peeked at her again, and pasted his best curled-lip impression from the Eighties on his face. Jake had no idea if he looked more like Elvis than Idol, and he didn't much care.

When Molly giggled again—just like back in the treehouse—Jake admitted, "No, not Billy Idol, you doofus. I meant you gotta really let out a big redneck holler to show your appreciation of…all this." He gestured, encompassing the two lanes winding like a ribbon through the baking fields, the wilting pines and trees gathered around the edges of each plot, and the hot, cerulean blue sky. If Molly thought she wanted a southern boy, then a southern boy she was going to get.

"Um, I might regret asking this, but may I please have a demonstration?" she inquired politely, folding her hands in her lap and examining him like a convoluted case file. As sexy attorneys went, Molly had the look down pat. Jake wondered if she ever wore cute chunky glasses with her high heels.

His grin grew wider, stretching his face. Without giving her any warning, he let out an unholy howl at top volume—loud enough to set some crows in the field next to them flapping into the air, and his dog woofing happily in the back seat. Molly looked stunned, like she hadn't thought him capable of it. Well, he'd showed her. Jake chuckled a little as she contemplated him, her eyes a little wide and her knuckles white where she clutched them together in her lap.

After a moment of stillness, she asked hesitantly, "You sure you want me to do that?"

Jake nodded. "Oh, *hell* yes," he replied, taking his eyes off the road to glance at her again. "It's required," he added solemnly. Jake held his breath, waiting to see what Molly would do.

She inhaled deeply. "Okay," she muttered. She edged the volume on the radio a little louder, gazed out the windshield, and gathered herself. Then, at the top of her lungs, she emitted a window-rattling whoop that mimicked his perfectly. Jake hadn't been prepared for it, even though he'd been goading her. He ducked a little behind the wheel in reflex.

Laughing at himself—and her—he told her, "There it is! Good girl. You're gonna do just fine, aren't you?"

Molly flushed an adorable shade of pink. When they locked eyes, she barked out a full-throated laugh that Jake had never heard from her before. There was nothing restrained about it, and he immediately wanted to hear it again. Something to shoot for, he guessed, along with all the rest.

Chapter Fourteen

J AKE GOT THEM there in record time. Instead of tracking their grime through his mama's pristine house, though, he let Molly and Duke in through the side gate and walked them around to the back yard. The dog made for the shade under the porch and sprawled in the mulch, panting happily.

The pool sparkled in its frame of white pavers—a gleaming blue rectangle beckoning from the lawn. Molly was nearly running, she was walking toward it so fast. He chuckled. This might've been the best idea he'd had all week.

And that impression went double once she started stripping. She didn't even wait for him—just toed off her sandals and shucked her jeans, dropping them on a chaise lounge angled toward the afternoon sun. In a minute more, her shirt was up and over her head—Jake caught the briefest glimpse of a demure set of pale pink lingerie—and then Molly was airborne, jumping feet-first into the deep end. She swam underwater like a mermaid, finally coming up for air near the center of the pool. Her hair was slicked back on her skull, as shining and dark as melted chocolate. Jake was frozen to the spot by So. *Much*. Molly. All on display for him. God—she was really, really wet.

She grinned up at him, splashing some water his way. "Come on, what are you waiting for? You big chicken!"

Jake's lungs rediscovered that great thing called *air*. He stalked closer, sat on the chaise, and pulled off his t-shirt and boots. Molly tried like hell to maintain her teasing expression but her eyes betrayed her, settling on his chest and staying there. Jake stood slowly, undid his jeans with shaking fingers, and dropped them to the ground. He walked to the edge and looked down at her, knowing Molly would see exactly what she was doing to him—*wanting* her to see. Jake was hard as a boat mast, and his boxer briefs didn't hide a thing.

Molly's face went blank and he watched her swallow, the tendons in her neck shifting and catching the light. She paddled her arms back and forth in the water—once. Twice. Jake flexed his toes and leaped, tucking into a cannonball and landing three feet behind her. He heard the beginning of Molly's scream half a second before he went under.

Two seconds later, Jake was sucking in air and lunging for her. Molly was too busy swiping the water from her face to see him coming, so he had the advantage. He wrapped her wet, delectable body in his arms and dropped his mouth straight to hers.

Molly met him eagerly, opening her lips and granting him entry. Jake's tongue dove hard and deep, dancing with hers in the hottest kiss they'd shared yet—and that was really saying something. Her bra and panties had gone mostly sheer now that they were soaked, and the combination of that peekaboo effect and all of her wet, glorious skin sliding against his was driving Jake wild. He pulled her legs around his waist and kissed and kissed her. Never, ever wanting it to end. Molly hung on tight, her ankles locked together at his lower back and her arms snug around his neck. Somehow, instead of feeling caged, it made Jake feel free. Like he'd made it out of prison and into the great wide world beyond.

He walked them over to the side of the pool, ready, and aching for more of her. Lifting Molly by her waist, he set her on the tiled edge, then pushed her legs wide so he could stand between them. Molly ran her fingers through his wet hair and down over his shoulders while Jake cupped her breasts in his hands, and kissed the tops of them. His lips were wet from the droplets of water on her skin, and from the water dripping off the ends of her hair. Jake didn't even mind the faint taste of chlorine, not when it was overlaid with something so elementally Molly.

Why did just a touch from her make him feel so strong? Like he could protect her from anything by willpower alone? Jake looked up at her gorgeous face then, and saw something truly amazing: Molly was gazing down at him with desire in her eyes, but mostly she looked at him with *trust*. The woman in front of him wasn't waiting for him to screw it all up. She didn't think him inadequate, or incapable, or not enough. Frankly, she looked pretty confident Jake had the goods she needed. He couldn't remember the last time he'd seen something so astounding, and it made him pause. Take a step back—take stock of what he was doing.

He'd gotten carried away and lost track of time, as he tended to do around Molly. For one thing, he should have gotten them something more to drink, so she didn't wind up dehydrated. And for another—Molly must be starving. Neither of them had eaten a thing since he'd gone through a burger drive-through on the way to the farm, and that had been hours ago.

"What do you say we get cleaned up and I make us some dinner?" Jake asked, his voice coming out gravelly. "I can throw our clothes in the wash while we shower, and by the time we're done eating they ought to be finished."

"Mmm," she moaned, weakening his resolve. "That sounds good. Lead the way."

And damn if that wasn't the sexiest thing he'd heard all year.

THEY GATHERED THEIR things and headed in through the mud room. Duke trotted off for the kitchen, to find the water bowl and food Jake's parents kept for him there. Jake disarmed the security system, and tossed Molly a pool towel when he noticed her shivering in the air conditioning. Wrapping one around himself, he peeled his briefs off under the towel and threw them in the washer with the rest of their clothes. Jake cued up an express cycle while Molly wriggled around trying to get her soaked lingerie off without losing her towel—and he tried not to hope *too* hard that she'd fail. Then he led her through the kitchen and up the back stairs.

He hadn't grown up in this house—it was his parents' version of downsizing once he and his sister had gone off to college. Jake supposed it was slightly smaller than their first home, and it was nestled in the heart of a golfing community replete with walking trails and community gatherings. Their bedroom was in a large suite on the ground floor, just off the family room. They'd assigned the upstairs bedrooms to their children, to use as needed. Jake led Molly up to his room now, her presence by his side warming him inside and out.

He followed her into his bathroom and peeked in the shower, relieved to find that his mother's housekeeper had restocked it with soap, shampoo, and conditioner. He cranked the spigot to let the water warm up, then turned away. Jake had intended to let Molly have at it while he tried not to listen from the other room like a creep—but Molly had other ideas.

Instead, she stood in front of the wide marble counter without a stitch on, the towel puddled on the tile at her feet. Over her shoulder, the back view was on equally spectacular display—the furrow of her spine and her tight, round derriere reflected crystal-clear in the huge mirror over the sink.

Jake moved forward carefully, suddenly afraid to spook her. But Molly wasn't worried—she reached out with both hands, tucked her thumbs under the towel at Jake's waist, and pulled. There was no hiding it now, no disguising his need for her. And blissfully, Molly didn't seem to mind.

Their hands landed on each other's skin, sliding and grasping. Over the rushing of the shower spray, Jake almost missed the sound of Molly's gasp against his mouth. But he swallowed it and drove his tongue deep, trying to elicit another. The air grew warmer and filled with steam, and Jake wallowed in glorious sensation of kissing Molly with nothing between them.

He wanted her skin wet again, like it was out in the pool. Jake backed her toward the shower, holding the door wide so they could get under the hot spray. Reverently, he lathered Molly's long hair with shampoo, rinsed it, and smoothed through a handful of conditioner. She leaned her shoulders back against the marble tile and watched, eyes dark, while Jake set about soaping her skin, worshiping every inch of her from top to bottom.

When he peeked up at her face Molly's eyes were shut tight, her head was tipped back against the wall, and her breasts rose and fell with each deep breath she sucked in and out. Jake stood and pressed his body against hers, then dropped his hand between her legs—stroking her slick folds gently apart until a shaky sigh whispered out of her throat.

He couldn't stop tasting her mouth as he worked his hand against her—and within her, where Molly was even hotter. Her mouth, her breasts, her neck, her earlobes: Molly was the best damn thing he'd ever had on his tongue, and Jake was going to feast until he couldn't do it a second longer.

It didn't last, though—Molly came lightning-fast and hard around Jake's fingers. Other than a huge, desperate gulp of air that she held in her lungs when it hit her, Molly didn't make a sound. Not a squeak or a cry or a moan. To Jake, that was more erotic than anything else might have been, standing there under the rushing water. He, of all people, knew what it was like to try to hold something in and not be able to. When Jake pulled his hand away and curled Molly into his arms, he could feel her heart pounding against his chest.

He kissed her softly one more time, pressing his lips to hers. Molly's mouth was soft and pliant against his. She hummed in her throat, and pried her eyes open to gaze dreamily at him. Her lashes were wet and spiky with water— Jake watched one droplet fall to her cheekbone then darted his tongue out to lick it off.

"Let me run downstairs and put our stuff in the dryer," he told her. "You stay here and finish up, and I'll be right back." Molly blinked, still dazed, and nodded.

Jake ducked his head under the spray and washed quickly, then stepped out. He grabbed a towel from the rack to dry off, and slung it tightly around himself for his foray down to the mud room. As hard as he was, he essentially had to pin his dick to his stomach with the damn terry cloth. It wasn't the most comfortable of arrangements, but he consoled himself with the thought that if he hurried, he'd be back in Molly's delectable wake in no time.

Stopping in his room to pull a t-shirt and gym shorts out of the closet for Molly, Jake then made his way down the back stairs again. He could hear the washer beeping, signaling the end of the cycle. He could also hear his cell vibrating across the granite island in the kitchen.

Jake grabbed it as he passed, and without looking at the screen pressed it to his ear.

"Hello?" He yanked open the washer door, and began moving their clothes to the dryer. Jake's eyes lingered on the sight of his big male clothes mingled with Molly's pretty, delicate ones—and he loved that they'd been swimming in there, all tangled up together just like their owners upstairs.

Blake's voice squawked in his ear, making Jake jump. "Oh *nice*. Now, you finally answer. I bet you can't wait to hear how it went."

He froze and looked around, wondering if she could *see* him. But that was nonsense—the only people in this house were him and Molly. "I have no idea what you're talking about and I don't have time for this, Bess. What do you want?" Jake growled, his effervescent mood turning black.

"Well, to *talk* to you, for starters," she complained.

"I have nothing to say, and you've certainly said more than enough. But hell—if you want, we can talk about the fact that you still have something that belongs to me." An assortment of clothes, probably a key to his place, and definitely an expensive rock. Jake wanted it all back.

That pissed Blake off, though. "You mean like the case of *Raging Bitch* beer you left on my front porch? Is that what you want back?" she screeched, losing her marbles yet again. "Way to keep it classy, Jackson."

Jake smiled. "Wasn't me," he told her, though he wished it had been. He could guess who was probably responsible, though—that move had his buddy Tim's name written all over it. Maybe with a dash of his sister Healey thrown in there, too—she never could stand Bess.

Bess was still going, but in a moment of total clarity, Jake realized—she wasn't his fiancée anymore. She wasn't even his girlfriend, and Jake was not obligated to listen to a single word of what she was saying. Especially not now, when he had much better things to concern himself with.

He held out his phone and stared at it, then tapped the big red icon to disconnect the call. Blake's voice cut out just like that, and the only sound left was that of the dryer drum—rotating when he pressed the Start button. Jake leaned down to wipe up some drips of water on the floor, and walked out. He dropped his phone back on the kitchen counter next to his car keys, and heard the faint sound of Molly blow-drying her hair upstairs.

He took the front stairs slowly, enamored with the thought of laying Molly out in the center of his big king bed. He'd unwrap the towel from her body like she was a present, then ditch his own. Jake was nearly to the top when he heard the sound of the garage door going up. *Damn it*. His parents had come home early.

He sprinted up the remaining stairs two at a time, made a break for his room, and threw on some clothes. Jake scrubbed his hair dry with the towel, combed it with his fingers, and dashed into Healey's room. Rifling through drawers and her closet, he cobbled together a reasonable-looking outfit for Molly as fast as he could, then booked it back to his bathroom. Jake hadn't heard the chime of the security system yet, indicating that his parents had come in the house, but he knew it was coming any moment.

"What's going on?" Molly asked, searching what Jake knew must be his panicked face. He tried to rearrange his expression into some semblance of calm.

"Shoot, honey—I'm pretty sure my parents just got home early."

"*What?*" Now Molly was the one panicking. She looked around the room a little desperately, so Jake shoved the bundle of borrowed clothes at her.

"Listen, it's going to be okay. Take your time, finish getting dressed—whatever you need to do. I'll go down and make sure they know we're here."

"Son of a…*biscuit*," Molly muttered, struggling into his sister's jeans.

He had to laugh. Jake *had* to. Their entire relationship to date had felt like one week-long comedy of errors. Molly glared back at him, taking offense.

"Hey," Jake told her, pulling her close. The chime he'd been waiting for sounded downstairs. He pressed a hard kiss against Molly's lips, then released her and backed toward the door. "It's gonna be fine." At least, he hoped so.

He'd barely made it to the top of the stairs, when his mother reached the tiled front hall. She squinted up at him.

"Jake? Is that you? We *thought* that was your car."

"Hey, Mama," he replied, trotting down the steps. He bent to hug her. "You're home early."

"Susie wasn't feeling quite up to dinner tonight, so we thought we'd leave early. What are you doing here?" She set her purse on the hall table, then checked her hair in the round mirror on the wall.

Jake had no idea how much time he might have to explain. Molly could come down the steps at any moment, so rather than dance around, he launched right in.

"Well, I took that girl Molly out to the farm this afternoon, and we were pretty hot and sticky from trooping around the woods and the barn. I figured ya'll wouldn't mind if we took a quick dip in the pool on our way back to town," he said. Jake tried to act natural—to look relaxed—even though he felt anything but.

His mother's eyebrows climbed up her forehead, her eyes wide with shock. His father ambled in, but had obviously already caught the gist of Jake's explanation.

"You mean the woman interviewing this week at the firm?" he inquired, dropping his car keys next to his wife's purse. She picked them up and placed them carefully in the little bowl reserved for the purpose.

"Yeah," Jake affirmed. "Remember? I've been showing her around a bit. I thought she might like to get out of town for a couple hours today."

A small smile lurked at the edges of his dad's mouth. "Oh, I remember all right," he said.

Jake's mother wasn't fooled either, but she also wasn't nearly as impressed. "So?" Stella inquired tartly. "What are we doing? Does she get the *cold Southern gentility* or the *down-home reunion* welcome?" She looked from Jake to his father.

The issue might pertain to her husband's firm, but it'd also been only days since Bess had given Jake the heave-ho. His mother was not going to take Jake's abrupt appearance—in her *home*—with this new woman very lightly. There was moving on, and then there was *moving on*. Jake might have felt annoyed if he couldn't see the real worry lurking in the back of her eyes.

"Neither," he said gently. Abruptly, he realized how important it was to him that this meeting go well—that his mama actually *like* Molly. Somehow, he had to find a way to explain.

"Oh?" his mother replied, her eyebrows twitching once faintly. "What's left?"

Jake wanted to suggest that she try to act normal, with no subtext—overt or otherwise. Since that would be like suggesting she breathe underwater, he simply told her, "Mama. Treat her like family. How 'bout that?" Too late, Jake realized how neatly he'd let slip exactly where his head was at.

His mother scowled mightily. "Not letting any grass grow under your feet, are you?" she scolded.

"No, ma'am," Jake answered. "Frankly I didn't see the need." Jake's father appeared even more amused by that, and chuckled softly. As for Molly, Jake expected that she was eavesdropping on the whole exchange at that open guest room door.

Stella stared at Jake, clearly taken aback by this development. "Really?" she demanded.

Jake nodded. "Really."

"*Well,*" his mother huffed, emphatic and stunned. Then she spun on her heel and walked away, in search of something more tractable that she'd be able to set right.

He called out, "Duke is here, too. He's probably sacked out on his bed in the kitchen."

"Oh good," his mother shot back. "At least *he's* predictable."

Jake wasn't worried, though—his mama didn't do well with sudden changes in direction, but she loved her babies fiercely. If Jake decided that Molly was the one for him, Stella Alexander would move heaven and earth to get him what he wanted. She just needed a teensy bit of time to get used to the idea.

His father smacked him on the back of the shoulder, but otherwise didn't address the issue. Instead he said, "We brought some crabs back with us. Why don't I get your mama a drink and help her cook them up for dinner? Have ya'll eaten yet?"

"Not yet. We were just getting ready to when you guys got home."

"Fair enough. Bring her in when you're ready." And then his father left, trailing after his wife with a speculative expression on his face.

Jake turned and looked up the sweeping curve of the staircase. It had been silent as a stone up there the whole time he'd been speaking to his parents—not a hairdryer or a footstep to be heard. Sure enough, after a moment Molly poked her head out of the guest room door, looking guilty as sin.

Jake laughed. "Hear anything interesting?" he asked her, jamming his hands in his pockets to quiet his nerves.

Molly looked a little shaky herself, and he couldn't exactly blame her. God only knew how much his parents suspected. Jake hadn't exactly been keeping his paws to himself in that swimming pool—or the shower. Though it felt like hours,

Jake had been making this woman come only minutes before. As far as he knew, they both looked like that's exactly what they'd been doing.

Molly drifted down the stairs. When she hit the last step, Jake caught her around the waist to anchor her to him. His sister's pants fit her snugly and were short enough to look cropped on her. As he smoothed his palms over her rear, it occurred to him that Molly must be commando under the denim—her only panties were currently circling his mother's dryer in an express cycle. She wasn't wearing Healey's shirt— maybe it hadn't fit. Molly had exchanged it for one of his button-downs that Jake hadn't worn in years, rolling up the sleeves and tying it loosely at her waist. He pulled her close and looked straight down the unbuttoned neck—no bra in there, either. Molly resisted him, staying rigid and holding Jake off with her palms on his chest. Her eyes, when she looked up at him, were warm, though.

"Thanks for setting me up to succeed," she whispered softly.

"Happy to oblige," Jake smiled back, then dropped a quick, chaste kiss on her trembling lips. "You ready for this?"

"Not even a little bit," she snorted. "What is your dad going to think?"

"That I'm irresistible?" Jake tried.

"Or that I'm unprofessional!"

"Please don't worry," he begged, then kissed her again. He could not get enough of her lips, of her taste—fresh and sweet and soft. Molly pulled back harder, and reluctantly, Jake let her go. "Come on. We'll stay for a quick dinner and then I'll get you out of here."

"Famous last words," she grumbled sulkily, starting for the family room.

Jake couldn't help it. He smacked her hard, right on that gorgeous ass, eliciting a squeak and a jump that made him grin from ear to ear.

STELLA KEPT SHOOTING them looks as she finished cooking dinner, and by the time they all sat down to eat his mother had busted Jake and Molly being affectionate one too many times. Jake suspected that, at minimum, his mother was lining up a few tests for their guest.

He had warned Molly that his mother's grandfather was a Baptist preacher, though Mama didn't practice the faith much herself. She did, however, tend to want to pin down what religion new people were—presumably to slot them into some internal categories that she carried around in her head. After a spate of polite small talk, Stella got started.

"So, Jake tells me that you are not a Baptist, do I have that right?" Jake had told her no such thing, and he raised an eyebrow at his mother, calling her bluff.

"Actually, I'm Catholic," Molly answered easily. Jake eyed her in interest; he hadn't known that.

"Ah," Mama murmured faintly, shifting her eyes to Jake in a significant way. She may as well have been shouting, *A papist! In my own home!* He rolled his eyes, then ripped a leg off one of his crabs and crammed it into his mouth. The soft-shell season would be ending soon—he was happy to have another chance to eat them.

"But, certainly you have found Jesus?" Mama pressed, her voice betraying only the tiniest hint of distress. Jake snorted. His mother was laying it on a tad thick, even for her.

"Mama, come on," he said, annoyed with the performance.

At the same time, Jake's father warned, "Stella."

"We were introduced when I was a baby," Molly smiled serenely. "I don't believe I've misplaced him since then."

Jake grinned at her, delighted. Then he turned triumphantly to his mother, who cleared her throat—seemingly unperturbed by Molly's flash of sass. She studied Molly like a rare bird had alit in her dining room, her eyes narrowing dangerously the longer she looked.

"Is that my son's shirt?" she asked at last.

Jake quickly tried to swallow the bite he'd taken, wanting to head off trouble. Instead, he ended up choking, coughing and sputtering while his dad thumped him on the back.

"Mind like a steel trap," his father muttered behind his napkin.

"Yes, it is!" Molly chirped happily. "My clothes were pretty gross from the farm, so Jake let me borrow it. I love the colors, don't you?"

Jake marveled at Molly's complete refusal to be cowed. She was incredible, and he was smitten—a little more each time she opened her mouth. Even his mother looked a tiny bit impressed.

"I better like those colors. I'm the one who bought it for him," his mama grumbled.

"Oh, that's nice," Molly smiled. "You have wonderful taste."

Well that was an excellent salvo, Jake mused. One could never go wrong complimenting his mother's taste. Instead of thanking Molly, though, Stella turned on him.

"Jake, why don't you wear it anymore? It used to look so nice on you."

"Mama," he laughed. "Look at her. That shirt hasn't fit me in years."

Stella looked, flushing a pale rose across her cheekbones. After a quick, pained glance at her husband, she rose and asked brightly, "Well! Who'd like some more iced tea?"

Chapter Fifteen

MOLLY INSISTED ON clearing the table and washing the dinner dishes, so Jake shooed his mother out to the back patio with a cup of tea, intending to help in the kitchen himself. But Jake's dad had different plans, and took the opportunity to drag Jake into his home office for a talk.

The door had barely closed behind them when Clay groaned, "Son, *tell* me you know what you're doing right now."

"Dad, I do. But it's complicated." Jake slumped into an armchair.

"Because, if you are playing two women at the same time, that's not *complicated*. That's just foolishness," his father said. He leaned against the edge of his big polished desk and watched Jake carefully.

"I *know*, Dad," Jake protested, feeling about fourteen years old.

"Do you? I'm not so sure." His dad glared at him, demanding more of an explanation.

"I know what I'm doing," Jake tried again. "I just—"

His father raised an unconvinced eyebrow, unmoved by Jake's equivocating.

"I just have to work out the details of how to get from point A to point B."

"Let me guess," his father drawled. "Miss O'Connell out there is point B?"

"Essentially. Yes."

"You do realize, not four weeks ago, you had that smug little Blake Sutton up in here, telling us every little thing about how you all were going to tie the knot." His father's disgust was plain.

"I am *painfully* aware of that fact," Jake muttered.

"Son, you'll forgive me, but—how in *God's* name did you manage to give a diamond ring to the wrong damn woman?"

"Dad, I…" Jake froze, startled. "Wait—you thought Bess was the wrong girl?"

"Of course, I did. I thought you wanted her, though, so I kept my mouth shut. But you two are terrible together—a train wreck that just keeps happening, over and over again. No good could possibly come of that." His dad crossed his arms over his chest and shook his head, as if to clear the image from his brain.

"And were you ever planning on *saying* anything to me about that?" Jake probed, incredulous.

"Well I certainly might have, if I'd known you were going to do something as asinine as propose to her!" his father retorted. But then, relenting, he added softly, "I don't think I would've let you actually go through with it."

"Damn, damn, damn." Jake muttered. "I thought you and Mama *wanted* us together."

"Well, you all were a cute enough couple, but…" His father shrugged and peered at him. "She's not pregnant, is she?"

"Who?" Jake burst out, rattled.

"Either of them, I suppose." He was remarkably calm, considering.

"Dad, seriously? What do you take me for?" Jake jumped up and took a few paces toward the French doors.

"Well, I *assumed* you had some sense, but right now that's debatable."

"Bess can be very… manipulative," Jake tried to explain. "Somehow she made the ring thing seem like my idea. And anyway, I thought you all *liked* her!"

"Don't you feed me that mess," his father scoffed. "You're a grown man, and you've never been weak before now."

Jake swallowed, wondering when exactly, he had *become* weak. Sometime during the stretch when he'd been trying not to disappoint his parents. Or Bess. Or Bess's parents, he imagined.

Things had been fine in high school, as Jake recalled it. It was when he got to college that the wheels had really fallen off the wagon. He'd rushed DKE and begun drinking hard, Bess had shown up and taken over, and Jake's grades had tanked. Halfway through his sophomore year Jake had found himself sitting in this very study, trying to explain how he was on the verge of getting kicked out of school. How he was on the verge of developing a real drinking problem. How he hadn't even *been there* for that hazing thing, even though someone said he was.

He hated the entitled bastard he'd been back then, and Jake had been trying *not* to be him ever since. Because if there was one truth in his whole fucked-up world, it was that he loved his folks like crazy and he never wanted to disappoint them that way again. He'd had nightmares about the looks on their faces for years afterward.

The stupid, unformed things Jake might want did not matter—making his mistake up to his parents did. Being a grown-ass adult who did what he was supposed to do, *that* mattered.

He'd fixed things though. He'd moved out of the frat house and cleaned up his act. Jake had barely touched a beer for a quite a few years there, just to make sure he was okay. Blake had helped, too—like a cruise director, she had cleaned up his act even more and kept him on the straight and narrow.

Jake's parents had been so, so relieved. With Mr. Sutton's help, Jake got into law school, and after, Jake settled more fully into the idea of shacking up permanently with the Suttons' daughter. He hadn't raised a complaint or a single bit of hell in years, and he was proud of that fact.

There was a problem, though—Jake had gone and overcompensated, and it had taken Molly blowing into town to make him see it. As he sat there, he wondered absently how many women like Molly he'd had a shot at in the last eight years or so. How many chances at happiness had he stupidly passed up? Jake didn't intend to pass up this one, that was for damn sure. Not for the Suttons, and not for his own parents either. At some point, Jake was going to have to live his own life, on his own merits—and that time might as well be *now*. Even if it meant pissing off the whole dang town.

"Is that what you think? That I'm weak?" he inquired.

"Of course not," his father relented. "But I cannot fathom how you are in this fix right now."

How could Jake explain? The absolute power of that relentless pressure—and the deep, gnawing debt to everyone that Jake felt?

His dad said, "Just tell me one thing. Did you start sleeping with that girl out there in my kitchen before or after you and Blake broke it off?" Clay stared, refusing to give an inch.

"I haven't slept with Molly, Dad. Come on." But if Molly wanted it, Jake would—he *would*. "And for the record, Bess dumped *me*," Jake reminded him. "Not very amicably, if you'll recall."

"That's neither here nor there," his father scoffed. "I'm trying to *hire* Molly. When I found out you were going to show her around, I didn't think—"

Jake interrupted. "Dad. Do you really think I *planned* for this happen? Molly was a huge surprise, believe me."

His dad tried a different track. "How many people *know* you and Blake called off the engagement, do you think?"

"Are you kidding? You know Bess *and* her mama. She's probably still meeting with the florists, even as we speak. We may need arbitration before they comprehend that I took Bess at her word. I know I have to talk to her—and I will—but…"

His father swore feelingly, then sat on his desk, contemplating the situation with steepled fingers under his chin.

Jake kept checking the door, hoping no one was out in the hallway listening in. He wondered how Molly was faring, and whether his mother had sidled back inside to give her the third degree.

"You've only known Molly for a week, son. How sure are you that this isn't some temporary infatuation that's going to run its course?" And there it was—the question that Jake had been dreading, the one that he had been wrestling with himself for days.

Jake inhaled. "Let me ask you this," he said calmly, since this part of it was easy enough. "How long did it take for you to know that Mama was the one for you?"

His dad eyed him speculatively. "About two minutes."

"There you go," Jake said. In the end, there just wasn't anything else to say but that. It defied comprehension, but that didn't make it any less real. Father and son just sat there, looking at each other for a time.

At last, his dad leaned back and folded his hands in his lap. "Does she know?"

"Which one?" Jake sighed, dejected. "Bess knows I agreed to show the sister-in-law of a friend around town. To my knowledge, Molly doesn't know anything about Bess."

"I meant, does Molly know how you feel about her? But Jake, you act like you've never been to this town before. Something like this is going to get around right quick. And I think we both understand it will only get messier the longer you take to figure it out."

"Don't I know it," Jake groused.

"All I can say is, Bess might have done your dirty work for you, but you're going to have to be the one to make it stick," his dad said. God, Jake hated how much sense *that* made. "And Miss Molly better hear about Bess from you first, if you ever expect her to get past it."

For the first time, Jake felt a shiver of real alarm. Before he could dwell on it, though, his mother let herself in through the hall door. She still balanced her dainty china cup and saucer in her hand, so maybe she hadn't been harassing Molly, after all.

"Come on back, gentlemen. You've been gone long enough," she commented.

"Alright sugar, we're coming," his father assured her. He stood, then turned back to Jake. "Mark my words, boy. You better fix this mess sooner rather than later, or you're not gonna like the way it turns out."

"I will. Somehow," Jake said.

"Kinda makes me wonder, though…" his father drawled, cuing up one last parting shot.

"What's that?" Jake looked up, confused by his dad's tone.

"What else don't we know about you?" His father asked it smoothly enough, but Jake still halted, his butt halfway out of that tufted leather club chair.

"Pardon?" he choked out.

His dad waved him away, though. "Never mind. Go on, get," he said. "Your mother will never let us live it down if we ruin the dessert. She brought a pie back from Aunt Susie's."

AFTER THEY SAT in the kitchen and scarfed down honking big slabs of Susie's strawberry-rhubarb pie, after Jake had roused his dog, gathered their laundry from the dryer, and shoved it all into a stray grocery bag—they'd finally been able to make a break for it. Molly *seemed* fine, it was true—but Jake wasn't taking any chances. He apologized nearly the whole drive back to the B&B.

She shut him up good, though. He put the car in park, took in air to tell her…something—and just like that, Molly twisted sideways and planted a scorching open-mouthed kiss on him.

Jake tried to stay the course, he really did. He had to make some mention of what happened in the shower earlier, after all. And he really, *really* had to arrange another time for that to happen again. Also, he had to…but Molly reached down and cupped him firmly through his shorts, and all the air left his lungs. All thoughts left his head, too—the one up top, anyway.

"Girl…" he breathed, trying to warn her. And also, not.

Molly threaded her free hand into his hair and gripped tight. Jake shifted his hips, not wanting to push himself harder into her hand, but not exactly able to help it, either. A weird, deep sound rumbled out of his throat, and against Jake's lips—Molly smiled.

"I'd invite you up, but I'm pretty sure Mrs. Denson would frown on that sort of thing."

"Are you kidding?" Jake managed. "She'd kill me. Besides, I'm not sure I'm in any shape to run into those other ladies staying there, either."

"Oh yeah, Tansy and her girls would have a field day with you up close," Molly nodded, grinning. She gave him one more stroke, then leaned back and opened her door. "Night, Jake," she said sweetly.

With her lips and her hands gone, Jake's brain stuttered back online. "Wait! I'm supposed to, uh…" he tried to think. Jake squeezed his eyes shut and shook his head, trying to clear out the haze of lust clouding everything. "My dad collared me on our way out—he wanted me to invite you to their house tomorrow night. They're having a cocktail party for some friends and a few colleagues."

Molly looked surprised, so Jake rushed to explain. "It's no big deal, seriously. If you don't want to go, I can—"

"No! It's fine," she interjected, regaining her composure. "I can, um…" she hesitated. "Do you even *want* me there? Are you sure he's not just being polite? This is awkward. Maybe I shouldn't go." Her brow furrowed as she tried to sort it out.

Jake laughed. "They aren't doing it to be polite. They wouldn't have invited you if they didn't want you to come— but more than that, *I* want you to come." The devil on his shoulder snorted. *Boy, did he ever.*

And there was that sweet expression in her eyes again. Molly's face cleared, open and trusting him. "Okay. Text me what time and everything."

Jake nodded and kissed Molly one more time, and then she was gone.

DUKE HOPPED INTO the front seat, and then Jake drove away. When they got home, they took a long walk around his apartment complex, listening to the frogs in the man-made pond and startling a bird or two. It calmed Jake down enough that he thought he'd have a chance of sleeping. That was before his mother called for a debriefing.

"So, Mama, what did you think of Molly?" Jake inquired, once the preliminaries were out of the way. He checked his watch—his mother had made it a whole two hours before her curiosity got the best of her.

A pause, then: "Well, she's very fastidious." Her voice was measured, giving nothing away.

"What?" Jake blurted. That was about the last thing he'd expected to come out of her mouth.

"I said," Stella reiterated, "She's very clean. When I went up to straighten your room, there was almost nothing to do." His mother was maybe the only woman on the planet who cleaned up before her housekeeper arrived—Jake knew Meryl would be there all the next day, preparing for the party.

"Did you expect her to trash the place?" Jake paused, taking a deep a breath. "Mama, that woman cleaned up your kitchen, and sat there talking to you and Daddy all evening. And the best you can say is that she's *neat*? Did you really like her so little?" He was incredulous. Molly, in his opinion, had been her usual, sparkling self. Jake couldn't imagine *anyone* not liking her. He'd barely been able to tell she was nervous, and he knew Molly a hell of a lot better than his mother did.

Stella thought a moment, and Jake could almost see her pursing her lips through the phone. She let out a heavy sigh. "I don't know, baby. I'm not sure she's our sort of people." It was an old, meaningless jab, and even his mother couldn't give it the necessary heat.

"Why?" Jake demanded. "Because she doesn't tart herself up like a peacock? Or isn't she rich enough for you?" No one in their right mind could claim Molly wasn't smart or pretty, and luckily his mama didn't even try.

She murmured, "Like I said, sugar, I can't put my finger on it." A demurral. Great.

"She's not Southern, obviously," Jake observed, offering up another silly excuse for his mother to claim.

"No, she isn't," Stella confirmed—definite on that, at least.

"It doesn't matter to me," Jake explained. "And it shouldn't matter to you, either."

She diverted down another avenue. "Will she be joining us tomorrow evening?" Always *she*, never actually calling Molly by name. Jake scowled.

"Yes, *Molly* will be coming," he told her.

There was a heavy pause. Jake's mother put her hand over the receiver, muffling what he knew must be a conference between her and his father. When her voice returned, it was suddenly brisk.

"Well, to the surprise of no one, your father wants a snack before bed. We'll have to take this up another time," she said, dismissing him.

"Can't wait," Jake told her before disconnecting. He flopped back on his bed and stared up at the fan, rotating lazily around its axis. He *had* to figure out a way to make this work.

Chapter Sixteen

W HEN JAKE PICKED Molly up the following evening, he didn't wait out front, like he normally did. He didn't go into the B&B's tiny sitting room to lounge in an armchair. No, this time Jake waltzed straight upstairs to her room, like he owned the place. When he knocked Molly threw open the door, expecting one of the ladies from down the hall. Her shoes were on the bed, her black lace cocktail dress was gaping wide down her back, and Molly had a mouth full of foaming toothpaste.

Jake laughed and leaned insolently against the door jamb, taking in the chaos.

"Oh, crap," Molly mumbled around her toothbrush. "Hang on, I'll be right back."

The fan blew chilled air down her exposed spine as Molly bolted for the bathroom. Jake stepped in without a word, kicked her door shut behind him, and followed on her heels. He watched Molly rinse out her mouth, then—when she straightened and met his eyes in the mirror over the sink— he crowded close, pinning her against the marble counter.

Jake looked handsome in his light tan suit and navy striped tie, but his expression shifted into something hotter when he looked down at Molly's bare back. Watching his hand with laser-focus, he trailed feather-light fingers all the way from the nape of her neck to the waistband of her panties. His nostrils flared when Molly shivered, and Jake gripped her hips in strong, broad hands.

He leaned down and murmured in her ear, "Hey, darlin'." His breath blew hot against her neck.

Molly licked her lips. "You're early," she squeaked out, watching him watch her.

"Lucky me," Jake agreed. He blinked slowly, considering her. Then, he carefully unhooked the neckline of her dress and pushed it wide. Jake ran his fingers up her arms, then outlined the lacy back of Molly's bra. He slipped his big, warm hands inside her dress, smoothed them over her stomach, and moved up to cup her breasts. Jake's mouth captured her earlobe and sucked, *hard*.

Molly gasped at the way that one action rocketed through her veins on a slash of wicked lightning. Jake lifted his head and met her eyes in the mirror, then spun her around and yanked her tight against him.

"What do you say we show up late?" he asked, his voice deep and sultry.

Molly opened her lips to answer, but Jake was already there, invading her mouth with his tongue. Seeking her out, toying with her, Jake delved deeper and harder, igniting something explosive inside her.

Carter—Carter had never been this way with Molly. He'd never been anything but utterly aware of himself and the way he affected her. Molly had never cared enough about any other man since to *let* them affect her. But Jake, heaven help her, was unleashing one raging storm of sensation, and Molly wasn't going to refuse that.

"Late's good," she gasped, breathless.

With urgent hands, he pushed the hem of her dress up over her hips, then lifted Molly to sit on the counter in front of him. She braced herself on her arms, trying to keep up with his kiss and tasting mint on his tongue. In short order, Jake peeled her dress down her to her waist, too—so he could caress her shoulders, her stomach, her collarbones and her neck. He ran his hands up and down Molly's thighs and never once released her mouth. Molly concentrated on the way his thumbs kept drifting achingly close to her panties, and tilted her head back to give Jake better access to her neck.

He broke off the kiss reluctantly, sucking at her bottom lip before dropping his head lower. Releasing the front clasp of her favorite bra with deft fingers, Jake set his hot and questing mouth to her breast. He growled—deep and sexy in his throat—and the end of his tie drifted across her legs, tickling her.

Molly threaded her fingers through his sandy-blond hair and squeezed her eyes closed, concentrating on the feel of his hands framing her ribcage and his lips working their magic on her breasts. When a moan escaped her lips, Jake's fingers flexed, pressing into her skin as he nipped at her.

Jake released her abruptly and dropped to his knees in his beautiful suit. She worried for him—that his knees might get wet or his pants wrinkled. But Molly's scattered focus soon narrowed to one very small, very-sensitive crux of space and time, waiting for his touch. Jake worked her panties down over her hips and legs, slipped them off and tossed them over his shoulder. She kept her eyes on his face, so she wouldn't miss the moment when his mouth met her body, and Jake didn't disappoint. He touched his tongue to the yearning heart of her right at the moment his wild blue eyes flicked up to meet hers. His gaze flared hotter, and Molly swallowed shakily at the sight.

Jake seemed satisfied with just those three seconds of connection, because his eyes drifted closed when he tasted her, tongue limning her cleft with long, careful strokes. His lashes were soot black and fanned against his skin, outrageously long for a man. Molly noted the hectic flush painted across the top of his cheekbones—just before she stopped noticing much of anything—except the way Jake seemed to know her body like the back of his hand.

He was masterful and efficient with his tongue, wasting no time. Much like in the shower the day before, Jake had Molly panting in a heartbeat. She tried to hold in her sobbing breaths, not wanting any of her neighbors to hear. But when Jake's fingers dug into the meat of her hips, urging her on, Molly couldn't resist any longer.

"Come on, honey," Jake demanded, working her harder and faster, sensing she was close. Molly toppled over the cliff with a cry to wake the dead, and felt Jake's appreciative hum vibrate straight through the core of her.

His hands were tender as he soothed Molly back down to earth. He stroked her calves and peppered her thighs with soft, hot kisses that percolated across her skin like spilled champagne. Jake set her on her feet and put Molly back together again—straightening lingerie, snapping clasps, and zipping her up like she was precious treasure wrapped in black lace. He scooped up her earrings from the counter and handed them to her—then watched avidly as she put them on.

Molly turned back to the mirror to reapply her lipstick, studying her reflection while Jake went to retrieve her heels from the bedroom. Oddly, not a hair was out of place. Her cheeks were pink and her lips were swollen, but otherwise, she merely looked like a more-sultry version of her usual self. Not at all like she felt—like she might be coming apart at the seams, unravelling from the inside out in a messy jumble of parts. Jake smiled at her while she leaned heavily against the counter to slip on her heels, and then broke the loaded silence between them.

"Damn, Molly," he said tranquilly, like he hadn't been rocking her world moments before. "You look so darn pretty tonight."

"You don't say." She forced it through sensitized lips. Jake had just *shown* her how pretty he thought she looked, but why did he have to keep doing it at the worst possible times?

"I do. And you taste pretty great, too. Ready to roll now?"

The cold wash of reality crashed over her. Molly would have to go show her face for the second time in two days at his parents' house—one of whom was considering hiring her for a job. And for the second time, Molly would have to pretend that their son hadn't just had her sobbing with pleasure moments before. She felt the need to turn things around on him for once.

So, with a pointed look at the bulge marring the tailoring of his pants, Molly said, "Packing some heat there, aren't you Officer?"

Jake looked down and yanked on the hem of his blazer. "Don't you worry about that, miss," he chuckled. "That's for later." He pecked her on the cheek and steered her toward the door.

"We have *got* to stop meeting like this," Molly grumbled, irritated by his nonchalance. Her legs felt like jelly, and she tottered on her heels, making her even more annoyed.

Jake steadied her—of course he did. "Really?" he asked, the soul of civility. He snagged her beaded clutch from a side table and handed it to her. "I disagree."

IF THE ROWS of cars parked along both sides of the street were any indication, they were the last to arrive at the party. Her knees felt disjointed and her heels were giving her trouble on the uneven terrain, so Jake led Molly slowly down the curving road, and then helped her up the cobblestone driveway. They slipped in the mudroom door at the side of the house.

Molly was positive that she must be broadcasting sex-crazed pheromones like a nuclear cloud around her. She figured it all would have been a lot easier if Jake had tucked her into a bed instead of into his car—but she *had* agreed to come here. She probably shouldn't whine about it.

He pulled her by the hand through the dining room, skirting a couple of caterers laying down platters of hors d'oeuvres on the long table. In the foyer, Jake glanced quickly around—but they seemed to be alone for the moment.

"Before we go in there…" he whispered, gazing down at Molly. He let his voice trail off, though, and didn't finish. Instead, he squeezed her hand where it was wrapped in his, and raised his other to touch her gently.

Jake watched his fingertips graze the base of her neck, then drift down the skin of her breastbone, exposed by the deep vee of her neckline. He had reached the top edge of Molly's dress, perilously close to her cleavage, when they heard his mother's heels briskly clacking toward them. Jake drew his hand back quickly, frustration flooding his gaze.

"Later," he whispered to Molly. "*Again.*"

His mother appeared suddenly, inserting herself neatly between them and straightening Jake's tie a little too sharply. "Jackson, do attempt to look like you belong here," she huffed. "And Molly—thank you for joining us on such short notice."

"Of course," Molly said. "Thank you for having me."

"You're late, Jake," Mrs. Alexander continued acerbically. She beckoned them to follow her. "I believe your father is just getting ready to say a few words, but he wanted to wait for you."

With that, she melted back into the crowd of guests standing in pairs and trios throughout her living room. When she resurfaced at the other side, Stella stood to the side of her husband—the perfect image of a poised society wife. Jake's father kissed her briefly on the cheek, then stepped up onto the wide stone hearth.

"Some of you may have heard a rumor that I'm going to retire," he projected into the room. He was charismatic, and his voice reached the far corners effortlessly. Molly was impressed—he must be unstoppable in front of a jury. She wondered whether Jake was the same.

The crowd chuckled knowingly, and the entire room seemed to hold its breath, waiting for his next words.

"Well, folks…" A laden pause, a merry grin as he looked from guest to guest. "I'm here to tell you that's flat-out wrong. I plan to stay on at *Alexander, Polk & Futch* a good long while yet. Wouldn't want them to have to change the sign, right?" He raised his tumbler of bourbon and called out, "Here's to many more years of fighting the good fight."

His guests wolf-whistled and roared their approval. Beside him, his wife's smile turned brittle, her eyes arctic.

Molly had heard the rumors at the bar association get-together, of course. Person after person had insinuated that Mr. Alexander was either retiring outright, or planning to go with a different firm. She'd assumed at the time that it was sour grapes—other attorneys either trying to dissuade her from vying for the open position, or testing her in some way. Now though, looking at Jake's mother's face, Molly wondered if there was more to it than that. Maybe the rumors had more truth to them than she'd believed— because no one in that room had been more blindsided by Clay Alexander's announcement than his own wife.

With a rueful shake of his head, Jake left to get Molly a drink. She snagged a tiny quiche from the tray of a passing caterer, and plastered a polite smile on her face. She hated to stand still in the corner, though—it felt awkward. So, Molly slowly moved through the guests, meandering along the perimeter of the party looking at family photos on end tables and expensive-looking oil paintings on the walls. She headed in the direction she'd last seen Jake, and listened to the cultured voices around her.

There was the expected chatter about Mr. Alexander's announcement, naturally. Speculation about what prompted it, and whether it truly needed to be done. Molly heard conversations about shoes and boats and family vacations. And she heard quite a few women wondering where *Blake* was. As Molly neared Jake's position at the makeshift bar on the far side of the room, one of the women came out and queried Stella directly.

"Now how is Blake doing, honey?" the woman wondered. "I thought we might see her here tonight."

Molly paused, listening.

Stella laughed. "Oh, you know how she is," Jake's mom scoffed. "She's been planning a long girls' weekend for ages." Her eyes moved around the room, looking for something. "No way was she going to reschedule for this little party."

The other woman seemed dubious. "Is that right? Where did they go?"

Stella re-focused on the woman, searching her face. Then she scrunched up her forehead and stared at the ceiling, thinking. "You know, I'm not positive, but I think it might have been Charleston." Looking back down at the room, Jake's mother made eye contact with a caterer poking his head out of the kitchen door. "Excuse me for one moment," she said to her companion. "I've got to go check on something." And then Stella hurried away, as fast as propriety allowed.

Molly peeked at the woman left behind, joined shortly by a friend. They watched Stella depart like a pair of housecats confronted with a baby bird—then turned to gaze at each other, brows raised. Molly forced her feet forward and considered precisely what she'd heard, trying not to jump to any conclusions. Jake's mother had a relationship with a woman named Blake, such that other people would expect her to know details about Blake's life. That could encompass a lot of different situations.

The "Blake" Molly had come across resembled Jake's mother in many ways, but primarily in the way she held herself. It was possible, certainly, that one of the older couples on that street corner had been the Alexanders—but if so, what had been their role? Were they there to support their son, Jake? Or could they have been advocating for Blake herself, intervening on her behalf with her jilted man?

Molly ran all the different possible scenarios in her head, testing how they felt in her gut. It could all be a coincidence. Blake could be a cousin, or a goddaughter, or a sorority acquaintance. Or—Molly remembered—Blake could be Jake's *sister*. He'd said he had a sister, and Molly didn't think he'd ever mentioned her name. She certainly hadn't met a sister tonight.

Of *course*, that must be it. If their daughter had some personal problems, it would explain so much: Stella's discomfort with people questioning where her daughter was. Blake not wanting to socialize with her parents' friends. It might even explain *Jake* being on that street corner the other night—siblings certainly had spats all the time where they yelled at each other. The different last name hardly seemed to signify. Blake could've been a family member's baby adopted as an infant, or even a child from a previous marriage.

Molly could envision it all: the fight inside the restaurant, the other couple trying to smooth things over…Jake following his sister outside to stick up for his friend, maybe. His friend, Blake's man, who was named…Jackson. *Jake*. Wait. Had that been what those women in the coffee shop said? Or was Molly remembering that part wrong?

Jake popped up in front of her, filling her field of vision with his large frame.

"Hey, I've been looking for you," he said, handing her a glass of red wine. "Come on. Let's grab a couple plates and get some grub."

"Jake?" Molly began. "I was—"

"Jake! There you are," a rotund man hollered. He had a thick shock of white hair and florid cheeks, and grabbed Jake's arm with a death grip. "Come on over here and meet my partner. I was just telling him about how we might be seeing your ugly mug up on the bench one of these days…"

Jake trailed after the man, tossing an apologetic look over his shoulder. Molly gave him a little wave then scanned the room, trying to decide on a game plan. Near the fireplace, she spotted Shannon McCready and Vijay Singh from the firm—one conversational possibility. And she saw Jake's mother a few feet away, looking positively breakable. Molly tilted her head, watching her. Stella wasn't okay.

Mrs. Alexander placed her wine glass on an end table a little too precisely, glanced around, then swept through the swinging doors into the kitchen. Molly followed casually behind her, certain no one was paying her the least bit of attention. Mr. Alexander was swamped with friends, and Jake was entrenched—he was being handed off from group to group of blustering older men like a golfing trophy.

Molly found Stella standing at the huge granite island—pouring herself a much stiffer drink than her original rosé, while the caterers swirled around her.

She cleared her throat. "Mrs. Alexander?" It chafed her a bit, that she had not been invited to call this woman by her first name—the pointed formality stung. But still, it didn't mean she wished her ill. "Are you okay?"

Stella's head snapped up and she frowned. "Do I *look* okay?"

Molly guessed, "He didn't tell you what he was going to say, did he?"

"No. He did not," Stella shot back. "*Not* that it is any of *your* business." Her voice was infused with all kinds of scorn. Molly began to wonder why she had followed the woman in here at all.

"No, I suppose it isn't my business," she agreed. "I just thought maybe I could help."

"I truly thought this time he'd retire. What a fool I am. I mean, honestly," Mrs. Alexander continued, "Am I so appalling to him that he can't *bear* to be around me anymore?"

Molly was pretty sure that was a rhetorical question of the highest order, but she answered anyway. "Of course not. The way your husband looks at you—it's obvious he adores you."

"Is that *so*?" Stella retorted, before bursting into angry tears. She swiped at her cheeks and looked away, struggling to compose herself. She and Molly heard a woman just outside the kitchen door, asking for her, then heard the murmured responses of others nearby. Jake's mother looked frantic.

"If you want to make a break for it," Molly told her, "I'll cover for you."

"What? I don't need—" The kitchen door began to swing inward.

"I'm serious. Go," Molly said quietly. "*Quick*."

Jake's mother gathered herself together, snatched her drink, and made purposely for the back stairs just as another woman barreled in.

Molly had been introduced to this woman earlier—Mrs. Peggy Haywood from across the street, she believed.

The neighbor clomped across the kitchen in her perilous heels calling, "Was that Stella? Where is she going?" She grabbed for a caterer's arm, who sidestepped her neatly. "Stella? Is that you?"

"No, that wasn't her," Molly interjected. "I was just looking for the, uh..." She searched her brain for what this woman might call it. "The powder room. I haven't seen Stella at all."

Mrs. Haywood fixed her with a gimlet-eyed glare. "Are you *quite* sure? I am certain I saw her come in here."

"Really? I didn't," Molly looked around pointedly. "I don't suppose *you* know where the powder room is?"

"Well, it's not here in the kitchen," Mrs. Haywood huffed, as if Molly were an idiot. "It's out in the hallway there." She gestured vaguely, but her restless eyes continued to move around, returning repeatedly to the shadow of the back staircase.

Molly pasted her best look of confusion on her face, and tried to keep the other woman's attention. "I must be *totally* turned around," she said, "Which way?" She hoped she'd put the proper note of desperation into that last bit.

Finally, Mrs. Haywood seemed to really see her. Rolling her eyes, she let out an exasperated breath. "Oh, come on, sugar, it's right out here." Diverted for now, she delicately led Molly from the kitchen.

Molly took her time in the bathroom, smoothing her dress, touching up her makeup, and studying her hair. The exacting standard of beauty presented by these refined women was exhausting her. They were impeccable—*always*. Molly felt like a troll around them, and at the moment just wanted to slouch on a sofa eating nachos for spite. She crammed her swollen feet back into the heels she'd shed as soon as she locked the door, and vowed to collar Jake as soon as she could find him. Surely, she'd be allowed to go home by now. It felt like she'd been there for hours already.

When Molly finally exited the bathroom—having delayed the inevitable as long as she could—she crashed headlong into Mr. Alexander.

"*There* you are, darlin'," he exclaimed, his smooth drawl exaggerated by high spirits and probably a healthy dose of bourbon. "Jake was looking for you." In a conspiratorial undertone, he added, "I don't suppose you've seen my lovely wife? Because *I* am lookin' for *her.*"

Molly smiled at him. Jake was so much like his charming father. "You know, I did—a little while ago. I think she wasn't feeling well and maybe went upstairs." Molly scanned his handsome face to see how that affected him.

He smiled knowingly. "Laid out by the shock, I expect." He waited expectantly for Molly's response, eyes dancing.

Molly considered her options. Finally, she offered, "Possibly."

Mr. Alexander slung an arm around her shoulders before turning her firmly toward the party. "All right, you sweet thing. You and I will catch up at the firm this week. For now, why don't you go find my son, and I will take care of the missus." With that assurance, Molly would have believed him capable of taking care of nearly anything.

She nodded and set off, determined to find Jake and get out of there.

Chapter Seventeen

J AKE HADN'T EXPECTED his parents' party to be quite
that stressful. He'd considered it as more of a necessary
evil, a couple hours to endure until he could get Molly alone
again. But Lord, by the time they'd broken free—he'd been
a basket case. Every woman there had found a way to ask
where Bess was, and every man had been slyly calling him
Your Honor.

Jake had been afraid to even *look* at poor Molly, much less
lay a finger on her. There seemed to be over-curious eyes
around every corner. He'd ended up leaving her on her own
for almost the entire evening—a total dick move, after pretty
much mauling her on her bathroom counter only an hour
before.

It was no wonder she noticed him acting weird. Molly was
quiet in his car afterwards, and seemed tired. She hadn't
invited him up, and Jake didn't even attempt to bring her to
his place. He'd been too worn out to pretend he was fine,
too overwhelmed to figure out the words to explain why.

The whole night might have been a complete wash, if not
for that scorching pregame show. Jake kind of resented that
the party had been too much of a mess—he'd intended to

tease Molly with the memory of what they'd done. He'd wanted to revel in the taste of her on his lips for a while, before begging for more.

However, even *in extremis* at the end of the night, Jake still managed to invite Molly out for drinks Tuesday after work. There was sulking like a wuss, and then there was just being a flat-out idiot. Jake was no idiot—he knew he had to fix what had gone wrong, especially if he wanted there to be more fun and games between them.

Tuesday afternoon, though, he was summoned to his great-aunt's house after work, and instructed to pick up his grandmother on the way. It didn't bode well—normally Aunt Ceecee liked to see Jake on the weekend, when she could count on him doing handyman stuff for her around that big old house of hers. After he changed out lightbulbs and oiled hinges, Ceecee plied Jake with baked goods and wanted to play cards on the back porch. Duke would race around the yard in crazy zig-zags before flopping down to pass out in a patch of sun. Jake loved it. But to be called over like this? It made him worry.

DUKE WAS BARKING at a squirrel in the yard. Inside the kitchen, the plate of oatmeal cookies was still warm from the oven. Jake checked, and sure enough they had chocolate chips—and not raisins—in them.

It must be twenty-five years now that Ceecee, Faye, and Mama had been making cookies that way—ever since his great-aunt babysat him one afternoon, and Jake had shyly suggested the change. The result incorporated both the chips and some extra cinnamon that he'd spilled into the batter, and was so good that the women changed the recipe permanently. The only problem that Jake could see was this: if they had specifically asked him to come *and* there were fresh cookies—his favorite—on the table when he arrived, then something was almost certainly up.

Jake took in the loaded looks his grandmother and her sister were giving each other, and stalled for time. He shoved the largest cookie on the plate into his mouth, and tried to forestall the inevitable.

"Wanna play rummy?" he asked around the crumbs. Faye snorted, an uncharacteristically indelicate sound. Ceecee just shook her head at him, obviously ready to get down to the business at hand.

She opened with, "Tell me, honey. How's work?"

"Fine. I won my case last week. Lady was embezzling from her church, if you can believe it." That was met with silence. Jake's eyebrows took a hike skyward. Normally the two of them would at least *pretend* to be gushingly proud of him. Today? Not so much.

"What?" he asked, looking between them.

Ceecee turned abruptly toward her older sister. "You know what I've never understood?" she asked her.

"Bridge?" Grandma Faye inquired tartly.

"Charming," Ceecee retorted, with equal acid in her voice. "*No*—what I have yet to unravel is what exactly you think you owe your daddy, Jackson." Her eyes were back on him, boring into his like steely blue lasers. He grabbed another cookie.

Jake hadn't been prepared for that question, and darted a worried look at Grandma Faye.

"Don't look at me, sugar," she said. "I don't know the answer."

He swallowed down the remains of the second cookie, though it had turned into a lump of sawdust in his mouth. "I had some trouble at school," he told them. "Sophomore year."

"So?" his great-aunt demanded, unimpressed in the extreme.

"*So*—they were going to kick me out, Ceecee. It was bad," Jake tried to explain.

"How bad?" Faye wanted to know. She seemed dubious, but that was because she was as loyal as a grandmother could possibly be.

Jake shrugged. "I was screwing around a lot. Drinking too much. I, uh...I stopped going to classes, mostly." In retrospect, it sounded so stupid, but even after all this time, he still hated to admit his foolishness to them. Just like back then, neither thought to ask him *why*. He wondered if he could even explain it if they did.

They sat watching him silently, longer than he could bear. Jake continued, and wondered if they already knew all this. "And there was a whole hazing thing with some freshman." Grandma Faye narrowed her watery blue eyes at him, and Jake rushed to explain, "I wasn't there. I swear. But they thought I was. Anyway...Dad had to come to school and convince them to let me stay."

After an interminable while, Ceecee commented, "You must have been mortified."

Jake toyed with some crumbs on his plate. "Yeah, I think that's fair to say."

Faye told her sister, "They tell me that little Blake Sutton was a great help to him after all that."

Ceecee raised a dubious eyebrow at him. "Is that right?"

Jake nodded. That, at least, was somewhat true.

"And what about *her* daddy? How did he get involved?" Ceecee wanted to know.

"You know that?" Jake asked, surprised. When they both nodded, he enlightened them. "Well, Dad wanted me to go to Wake Forest for law school, remember? My LSAT scores were okay, but my GPA wasn't quite high enough after what I did." This was probably the part he regretted the most.

Ceecee placed another cookie on his plate and prompted, "And?"

He took a breath. "And Blake's daddy knew someone at the school. Either she or Dad got him to call over there or something, and next thing I knew I was in."

"I bet he never lets you forget it, either," Ceecee muttered. That was interesting. For all the years that his folks had been friends with Blake's parents, he had never heard anyone speak ill of them. His aunt's words were true though—Mr. Sutton brought up his "help" all the dang time.

Faye placed her hands on the table, bracketing her own empty plate. "You do realize—don't you Jackson—that *you* are the one who went to all those classes and did all that work? *You* are the one who studied so hard to pass that bar?"

"Yes, ma'am," he whispered. It wasn't enough, though. It would never be enough. He was a royal fuck-up then, and with all his relationship drama, he was heading right back that way again.

Faye said, "You earned your job—your career. All by yourself. No one else did that for you. And you deserve to be happy."

"But—" Jake began.

Ceecee interjected, "Do you even *want* to be a judge?"

Ah. Somehow, they knew *that*, too. "No, ma'am," he said.

"How about the States Attorney?" Ceecee pressed. Jake began to wonder if she'd allowed Bess and her mama to come over for lunch that day solely to grill them for information. It seemed likely at the moment.

"Not in the least," he confessed.

Grandma Faye was truly irritated by that one. "Have you ever *told* your daddy that you don't want those things?" Jake stared at her. He didn't think she had ever taken such a tone with him.

"I told him I wasn't qualified, Grandma." Jake swiveled to plead his case with Ceecee. "He didn't listen."

"That's a lot different than telling him you don't want to," Faye snapped.

"I—"

"It's different, Jackson," Ceecee agreed.

"Okay," he muttered. What did they want from him? Just to add their voices to the cacophony already swirling around in his brain? More looks shot back and forth between the two women, and Jake figured sullenly that at this point, the cookies weren't even worth the trouble.

Ceecee asked him, "What's this I hear about a new girl you're escorting around, hmm?"

Oh, that just topped things off. "She's just someone interviewing at Dad's firm. I went to school with her brother-in-law, and I told him I'd look out for her while she was here."

His grandmother stared at him with her lips pressed into a flat, unforgiving line. Jake swallowed, uncomfortable with the way his answer was both the truth, and a total lie. Grandma Faye turned suddenly to her sister.

"Cee, you should see the way he looks at her. Like a starving man presented with a dressed-up Christmas goose," she said.

"Gramma!" Jake blurted, horrified.

"It's *true*," she insisted. "And the way she looks at him— *well*. Bess Sutton has never *once* looked at Jake like that, I can assure you."

Ceecee looked at Jake, shaking her head and clucking her tongue like he was the most disappointing man on the planet. "Well, well, well, son. You have gotten yourself into one heck of a pickle, haven't you?"

"Aw, come on women," Jake complained. "Let me up off the mat, would you?"

"No," his aunt barked. "That would be the wrong thing to do." She reached over to the counter to retrieve a packet of papers and said, "Either way, you'd better sign this now."

"What is it?" Asking a lawyer to sign something without reading every word was a little like asking a pianist to chop off their own hand. Jake shuffled the papers into alignment and started at page one. He had time.

"I've decided to move into River's Bend with Faye. We're going to take one of the big two-bedrooms that came open," Ceecee informed Jake.

"Mr. Duncan passed," Faye explained matter-of-factly.

"And…" Jake drawled, looking up. Ceecee had resisted moving for years. Maybe she had decided to go now because her sister had been ill—perhaps she wanted to be closer, so she could help Faye if the woman took a turn for the worse. Still, it was quite an announcement.

"And sooo," his aunt said, like he had cotton for brains, "The time came for me to visit my attorney."

"Who? Dad?"

"*No*," Ceecee fired back. "If you must know, I visited Jeff Futch."

One of the other partners at the firm, then. But— "Ceecee, this looks like…"

"Yes. Those are the papers signing my house over to you." She was blinking quickly, and even Faye's eyes were welling up. "You can see right there that you'll have to pay me one whole dollar for it."

Jake's fingers seemed to be trembling, so he set the stack carefully in front of him and gripped his knees under the table. For something he'd always dreamed about, it suddenly felt too soon.

"Are you sure about this? This is a big deal."

"Don't be ridiculous. Of course I'm sure. Besides—no one else loves this old place like you and I do. What else am I supposed to do with it?"

"I don't know? Keep living in it?"

"The stairs are a pain in my patootie, you know that. It's time."

Jake wondered about that. It hadn't been time when he graduated college—or law school, for that matter. He'd clerked for a judge and gotten a full-time job as a county prosecutor, but that hadn't been adequate, either. Heck, even him putting a ring on Bess's finger hadn't swayed his aunt. But now, when his carefully-constructed life was displaying all kinds of hairline fractures—like a dam about blow wide open—*now* Ceecee gave him the house?

"I don't...I don't know what to say," he whispered, stumbling over the words. Hell, Jake might as well be a little old lady himself, the way he was starting to tear up.

"*Thank you* works just fine," Grandma Faye instructed him, patting him gently on the back.

"And Jake?" Ceecee asked, making him look up and meet her eyes. "You don't owe me a dang thing after this, you hear? Not one goddamn thing."

"Yes, ma'am," Jake said, feeling the tears run down his cheeks, drop off his chin, and hit the back of his hands. His aunt gripped his arm in her arthritic fingers and squeezed.

Grandma Faye cleared her throat. "Do you need me to lend you the dollar, Bubba?" she inquired.

Jake gasped out a startled laugh. "No, Grandma, I think I got it." He leaned back and fished his billfold out of his suit jacket—he'd hung it on the back of his chair earlier, when he realized that Ceecee's A/C unit was on the fritz again. He slipped the single free and tucked it under the large paper clip holding the papers together. Then, without reading a damn word, Jake flipped to each sticky-note and just signed his name.

HE LEFT HIS grandmother at her sister's house, where the two women were settling in to watch some reality television in the tiny back parlor. Someday, Jake thought he might make that room into a home office. While that day had inched much closer suddenly, for now he had more exciting fish to fry. He swung by home to drop off Duke and change, and then he headed out again.

He'd texted Molly that he was on his way, and to dress for a casual dinner near the river. Jake drove over, noticed a spot right in front of the B&B, and parallel-parked the Audi. He rolled down the windows and turned off the engine. Mrs. Denson's was a large old brick house, casting the whole sidewalk in front of it into shade. There was a nice breeze tonight, and it wasn't too humid—if Molly wanted, maybe they could even sit outside somewhere.

He'd just gotten out of the car and was coming around the hood to go meet her, when Jake saw Molly exit the front door. She flipped her hair over her shoulder as she crossed the front porch, and started down the wide front stairs like some kind of supermodel. He'd been fixing to apologize for not arriving sooner, but at the sight of her somehow the words just died in his throat. He blinked slowly as she caught sight of him halfway down, a wide grin lighting up her face. Jake leaned against the side of his car, crossed his arms over his chest, and watched the vision that was Molly O'Connell come toward him.

It didn't *feel* like he had run right to her like some kind of hound, the minute he was free of Bess. This didn't feel like spite or a rebound, or anything else like that. The truth was, when it came to Molly Jake just couldn't keep the hell away. Not for decency, or propriety, or any other damn thing people might cook up. Molly drew him like a magnet and Jake was powerless to resist the pull, the way she fit him like a glove.

God, she was sexy. Jake was suddenly thrilled that he'd washed and polished the Audi recently, because she was going to look absolutely stunning in it—sleek and tough and gorgeous in his shiny silver sportscar. He was one lucky, lucky dude.

"Hey there!" she smiled as she reached him. "Right on time, I see."

Jake took in her outfit with a lingering gaze. A girl like Bess might have worn a flowery pastel sundress for dinner and drinks with him. Probably would have her hair shellacked into submission against the humidity, and be carrying an insanely expensive purse that her mama had gotten her. She would have waited inside her house, done a little twirl for him when he rang the bell, and expected Jake to make the requisite compliments on her appearance. He would then have to endure a fifteen-minute discourse on where and when Bess had come across the dress, say, or the shoes—but his mind would almost always be elsewhere by then.

But the thought of Bess gained no traction in his brain whatsoever. Instead, Jake admired Molly's long, slim legs in her tight, dark jeans. She was wearing seriously-high black heels, and a sleeveless, lacy black top. His gaze hitched on her lovely toned arms, all the exposed skin seeming pale and vulnerable next to that dark clothing. A woman's arm was certainly something he'd seen a million times before—so why was the sight of Molly's anything but routine? Jake wondered. As she hitched her purse on her shoulder, he caught a flash of the tender underside of her bicep, and that skin—white as a pearl and even softer-looking—was painfully erotic.

Molly was clearing her throat to catch his attention. When Jake lifted his gaze to her face, she eyed him with one hip cocked and brows raised.

"We ready?" she inquired archly. Oh, Molly knew she had him hooked, that was for sure. He'd stared too long, damn it.

Jake smiled, slow and sexy, at her. He had his own bag of tricks, and if he expected to hold his own he'd better dust them off and start using them.

"Got a little bit of a rock-and-roll thing going on there, don't ya, darlin'?" There'd be no mistaking his tone—he approved and then some. Jake swept his eyes down, and up, once more. Slower this time. Lingering.

Molly paused, but recovered quickly. "And let me guess—you're a little bit country, right?" She laughed it off, smirking as she reached for the passenger door, but Jake knew he'd given her something to think about. "Come on, let's go, you big stud," she urged. "I'm starving!"

Before she could sit, though, Jake hooked an arm around her waist and pulled her against him, hip to hip. Molly tilted her face up to his, still smiling, still trusting, still beautiful as the sunrise over the ocean. Jake brushed his lips against hers, once, twice…reveling in the feel of her lips and her breath against his mouth. But when Molly opened her lips and invited him in, well—who was he to refuse? Jake and his tongue marched right in and made themselves comfortable.

Not only was Molly *not* fishing for compliments, she was amused as hell at his efforts to flirt. When he could manage to pull away, Jake pushed himself off his car and turned to hold Molly's door for her, mentally re-evaluating where he wanted to bring her. He'd made reservations at a very safe, reliable little place that his parents favored, but now he reconsidered. He thought he knew of a better place—a cooler one—and he could not *wait* to see what Molly thought of it.

THEY HAD TO wait a while, standing crammed into a corner beside the bar, but eventually Jake and Molly were seated in the tiny new pizza place that had been garnering rave reviews in all the papers. The décor was fairly industrial, and the open kitchen and enormous wood-fired pizza oven dominated the space. Jake inhaled the warm yeasty air, looked around at the plates littering the tables next to them, then met Molly's wide eyes across their little table.

"Am I drooling? I think I might be drooling," he told her.

She shook her menu at him. "No shit," she agreed. "I want *everything* on this menu."

Jake felt his eyes crinkle at the corners. He'd loved pizza from the moment he'd first tasted it, but he hadn't eaten it much lately. Blake, of course, wouldn't touch that many carbs with a ten-foot pole—and especially not within twenty months of a wedding and a honeymoon. She wasn't shy about keeping them away from Jake, either. Molly, on the other hand, looked like she might be ready to gnaw off her own arm if someone didn't put some dough in front of her, fast.

The staff was efficient and professional, thankfully. After a short negotiation, he and Molly worked out an array of appetizers and pizzas that they both wanted to try. The waiter suggested a couple craft beers to go along with everything, and minutes later they were stuffing their faces. The reviews hadn't lied—Jake thought he could happily eat there every day for the rest of his natural life, and still die a happy man.

Conversation with Molly flowed easily, as it always did. Flirting, witty banter, fun as hell. Jake didn't have to explain much of anything about work or himself—Molly seemed to just get him. She didn't dig too deep for now. That was a relief, but Jake knew he wouldn't keep anything from her if the topic of Bess were to arise. He'd tackle it, and then—hopefully—move on.

Conversely, he wanted to know every dang thing about her. Molly was sharp as a tack, quick and tart and funny, and he loved it. Loved parrying words back and forth with her. Loved watching her, too—Jake was having the devil's own time trying to rip his gaze away from her mouth as she ate.

Molly really enjoyed her food, digging in and actually eating it with undisguised appetite—not just pushing a salad around her plate and then stealing half his dessert. It thrilled him. Aroused him to an irrational degree. He was in so, so deep, and Jake didn't have the slightest urge to save himself. He only wanted to swim deeper.

Chapter Eighteen

S HANNON MCCREADY MET Molly at the front desk of the firm at eight-thirty sharp. The prior week, Shannon had worn her hair smoothed back into a tight bun at the nape of her neck, but today her hair fell in crimped, glossy black waves that hit her chin in a short bob. Her suit was an immaculate off-white—gorgeous against her dark skin—and her spicy perfume drifted after her as she led Molly deeper into the building.

Molly tried not to feel intimidated. Shannon was a few years older than she was—smart and polished and professional—and Molly could do a lot worse than look up to someone like her. Luckily, Shannon seemed inclined to mentor Molly while she was there. Whether she was doing it to be kind or had merely been assigned to, remained to be seen.

"I hope you don't mind—we rescheduled some of your meetings with the newer associates today," Shannon said. "Jeff thought it might be better if you shadowed him instead."

"Jeff?" Molly asked, wracking her brain to place a face with the name.

"Futch," Shannon said. "One of the partners." She smiled, though, seeming to understand that Molly had heard an awful lot of names in the last week and a half.

Molly squeezed her eyes closed and grimaced. "*Right*. Of course."

Shannon said, "I'm going to cover his sentencing this morning, so he has more time to spend with you."

"Okay." Molly followed along behind the other woman, then flattened herself against the wall when a secretary pushing a cart full of files rounded the corner and edged by.

Just then, Mr. Alexander popped his head out of his door, startling them both. He looked cheerful. "Morning, ladies! How goes it?" He looked back and forth between them expectantly. The secretary smiled genially, but hurried on her way.

Shannon said, "Good. Jeff's going to have Molly shadow him today."

"That's great!"

Shannon smiled and nodded, clearly amused by his enthusiasm.

Mr. Alexander turned to Molly and laid a hand on her arm. "Hey—stop in before you take off later and let me know how it went."

"Will do," Molly agreed. "Thank you."

"Don't worry now, all right? Between Shannon and Jeff, you'll be in good hands," he told her.

"Okay," Molly said yet again. His friendliness had clearly ticked up a notch since she'd been to his house. *Twice*. Molly wondered what Jake might have said about her.

Shannon shooed Clay back into his office with impatient hands. "That's enough. We're busy. Back in your cage now, Mr. A."

He laughed. "You know—I brought you into this firm, Ms. McCready…"

"…and you'll kick me right out of it. Yeah, yeah. You don't scare me, old man," Shannon snarked, smacking him lightly on the arm.

Clay winked at Molly. "You see that? That right there is why you don't hire your children's friends. When they've known you since they were in diapers, they have no respect whatsoever for your authority."

"*Goodbye*, Clay." Shannon rolled her eyes and motioned to Molly.

"Fine. I see how it is." He strolled back in his office and plopped down behind his desk, then gave Molly a jaunty salute.

Molly blinked. Her interviews were taking on more of a "first week" vibe now, rather than a "convince us to hire you" feel. Did everyone at *Alexander, Polk & Futch* just assume that she wouldn't dare turn them down? Based on the chatter around that bar association party, the job opening here was a coveted position—but Molly had not seen or heard about a single other contender since she'd been here. True, if she was offered a job, she wouldn't say no…but couldn't they at least *pretend* she wasn't easy? At this rate, Molly was beginning to wonder if they'd even let her return to Boston to pick up her stuff.

AFTER A FULL day of trailing around behind Jeff Futch—from the firm to the courthouse and back again—Molly had a mere ten minutes to change out of her skirt and blouse before her date that night. There was no time for flourishes. She released her hair from its clip and finger-combed it, threw on her favorite going-out outfit, and touched up her lipstick. She locked her door and walked to the window at the end of the hall, then looked down on the street. Empty.

And then, like magic, Jake was there—parking, rolling down his windows, lounging in his car like some kind of male model. Molly hurried down the B&B's stairs, dove for the front door, and felt a gentle hand on her arm. Mrs. Denson?

"Hey," Molly said a little breathlessly. "I'm heading out for a little bit." She almost added *I'll be back later*, but if all went well…maybe she wouldn't. Molly took in a big lungful of air and tried not to hope, just in case.

"I know, sugar, just…" Mrs. Denson smiled and patted Molly's arm. "Make him work for it."

Molly felt herself flush. Oh God. Was she that easy to read? She forced herself to slow down and relax. The B&B's proprietor nodded at her, seeming to approve. Mrs. Denson stepped to the side and held the beautiful glazed door wide.

When Molly emerged from the old Victorian's entrance, Jake's face lit up in appreciation. He crossed his arms and settled in for the show, so Molly took her time on the stairs. Put a little swing in her hips. He liked *that*, too—she could see it.

It was a good thing he did, because Tansy and the crew had checked out yesterday. For the rest of her trip, Molly was back to wearing her own clothes: dark New England colors. Thick, heavy fabrics. Not a floral print in sight.

Jake inspected Molly from stem to stern, and she tried not to preen from the attention. She could flirt shamelessly with the guy later—but for now, she *had* to get something to eat. Mr. Futch had taken her to a sandwich place near the courthouse hours ago, but she'd been too nervous to eat much of her chicken salad. She was regretting that now.

Molly had never been one of those girls who could go days eating only baby carrots. She got hungry—really hungry—at least three times a day, and often more than that. Jake was messing with fire if he thought she wanted to stand around making out for an hour on an empty stomach. He wound an arm around her and dipped his head.

Scratch that. Making out with Jake might work out totally fine. He held her against his tall, strong body, letting her feel every inch of his muscular frame. Jake savored Molly's mouth slowly, lingering over her, tasting her with his lips and tongue like he had all night. His arm was heavy at her waist, drifting low like he was trying not to grab her ass—like he was struggling against his own restraint.

Jake was trying not to yank Molly against his groin. Or…maybe he wasn't. Maybe that was only what Molly *wanted* him to do. No sooner did she have the thought than he pulled away, and she was fighting the urge to protest. Looking sexy as sin, Jake tucked her into his fancy silver car and strolled to his door like nothing much had happened. Damn it—Molly was doomed. She had no weapons to fight an infatuation like this one.

HE MADE GOOD on his promise to feed her something amazing. Not that she begged or anything, but within an hour he had them seated in the most amazing gourmet pizza joint Molly had ever laid eyes on. They stuffed their faces like mongrels, and managed to maintain a conversation— somehow—around all that chewing.

Once she was full and happy, Molly had the bandwidth to start thinking about the kisses Jake had been laying on her. She started thinking about how to drag out the night longer, and how to secure for herself more of what he'd been dishing out.

"Do you have an early morning tomorrow?" she asked him. *Just a quick exploratory foray—nothing to see here, folks.*

He wiped his mouth, then reached across the table to brush a crumb from her cheek. "Not particularly," he said. "I have a bond hearing at eleven, but not much else. What about you?"

"I'm having lunch with your dad at one. That's it, as far as I know. I'm not sure if Mr. Polk is back from Atlanta yet or not, but he's basically the only person at the firm I haven't met yet."

Jake frowned, thinking. "Hmm. I don't know if he's back yet, either."

"Anyway—you want to get a drink after this?" Molly tried to read his face, suddenly nervous. "Or...I don't know. What's fun around here?"

Jake perked right up, though, like he'd been thinking the same thing. Molly's confidence soared. "A drink...yeah, let's do that," he said. "We can leave my car where it is and walk a block or two over. There's a ton of stuff to do over there."

A *ton of stuff* sounded like it might take a while to accomplish, and that was perfect. It would give Molly plenty of time to figure out how in the world she was going to get Jake into a real bed with her. He'd kissed her senseless—and then some—for days now, in all kinds of non-bed locations. It seemed like some crazy thing always happened to keep them from going much farther. Molly was fed up with laying around the B&B at night, her nerves thrumming through her while she wondered what it would be like to sleep with Jake. It was time to take matters into her own hands and find out.

Chapter Nineteen

ON THE RIDE over to dinner, there'd been country music on the radio. Molly claimed to have never heard the song before, but after only a few choruses Jake noticed she was humming along. He supposed that meant Molly liked it, but that didn't necessarily mean she'd want to cozy up to a bar and listen to two or three more hours of it. So, as they walked down the street, Jake bypassed a few places he knew well, looking for a bar that offered rock or top-40 as an option.

Molly's steps slowed in front of a place that Jake had never set foot in, though. It was a little too dark, too scruffy, too edgy and smoky. He'd seen it before, and always thought it looked interesting—but had never bothered asking Bess to go. What would have been the point? He knew what her reaction would be. As for going with the guys, that had never really transpired either. For one thing, Jake spent more time than he cared to admit with the boyfriends and spouses of Bess's friends—and as a unit they were…what was the word he wanted? Oh, yes. *Pompous.*

Cutting up with his own friends on stag nights had always seemed just a shade juvenile—just a touch too close to the way he'd been in college. It would have felt like Jake was too much of a wuss to stand up to his woman when he was with her, and therefore had to overcompensate when he wasn't.

He didn't think he was like *that*, but Jake had definitely entered some kind of numbed-out twilight zone where he didn't even consider stuff at all. He had, he realized, actually given up on seizing anything resembling his own happiness—instead allowing other individuals (some of them well-meaning) to hand him what they thought he needed. Right now, that pissed him off.

But Jake wasn't *with* Bess anymore, was he? He wasn't with anyone who knew her, either. He wasn't with his parents or his fraternity brothers or his coworkers or his friends. He was standing on the street with a gorgeous woman who basically didn't know him from Adam, and the freedom to be whatever he chose in that moment was *intoxicating*. Jake turned to Molly to find her laughing, craning her neck to see inside the bar.

"What on earth is going on in there?" she giggled, trying to get a look past the bodies moving around in the darkness within. There did appear to be some caterwauling going on, competing with the popular music on the stereo system. On other occasions, Jake knew he'd heard a gritty blues band playing in there—and wondered if they might be hitting the stage later.

He grinned at Molly. Now or never. "I dunno—but you wanna find out?" He held his breath and hoped she would answer the way he expected.

"You know I do," she drawled, in her odd, neither-North-nor-South accent.

Jake paid their cover charges and they got their hands stamped, something he could say in all certainty he hadn't done in at least ten, maybe fifteen years. He moved in front of Molly and grabbed her hand, then plowed a path through the people standing around watching the makeshift stage set up across the back of the bar.

Jake felt a thrill, anticipating some live music. Something cool, he hoped—something rowdy, something…*hmm*. A random guy took the mic, nodded at the man sitting at a large table off to the side, and began singing awkwardly along to an instrumental track.

Huh. Not what Jake expected, but opening acts weren't always the best. Still, all these people on a weeknight had to mean something decent was in store. The bar was a mob scene, and the only place he could find for him and Molly to sit was right near that man and his folding table. Jake parked Molly in a chair, got her drink order, and headed for the bar.

It took a while. By the time he was making his way back to her with a couple shots and a couple beers, vivacious Molly was deep in conversation with the table guy—and flipping through a huge binder he was holding. The dude at the mic had relinquished the stage to a young woman. She was slightly better, but not exactly what Jake would consider a professional performer.

And then, as Jake slid into the chair next to her, Molly grinned hugely. She grabbed one of the beers he'd brought, knocked back half of it, and tried to tell him something. It was loud in the bar, but it finally dawned on him what she was saying.

"Oh my God! It's karaoke night!" she laughed.

"Oh shoot, I'm sorry," Jake told her, feeling vaguely embarrassed. His sexy blues bar was apparently anything but. "I had no idea. Don't worry, we'll just drink these and then we can…take…off." Jake frowned when Molly rose and made for the stage.

She waved back at him as he trailed off—then skipped up the steps to an approving roar from the crowd. Just like that, the music to one of the songs she'd been teasing him about in his car started blaring over the speakers—a very raunchy, very dirty country song. Jake was frozen to his chair, equal parts terrified and fascinated.

Molly had the mic. She watched the large teleprompter screen for her lyrics, then began singing in a rich, throaty alto. Of course, she did—because apparently this woman was his former fiancée's exact opposite. She didn't get the words exactly right, but no one cared a lick, especially him. Molly was all long legs in tight denim up there, tossing her brown hair and laying on the sass. A person would have to be dead not to love her—and Jake wasn't dead, not by a long shot. He couldn't take his lusting eyes *off* her.

Molly caught his eye, gave him a heart-stopping shimmy of her hips, and pointed—beckoning Jake up to the stage beside her. He definitely knew the words to that song backwards and forwards—certainly better than she did, since she'd only heard it for the first time about an hour ago—but no way was he getting up on that stage. Jake shook his head, giving Molly the thumbs down.

Not to be denied, she smiled her thousand-watt smile, made a face at the crowd—then crooked her finger at him again, sexy and begging. Next thing Jake knew, the people standing around him were all up in his personal space, shoving and yelling for him to not be stupid, to get up there. Jesus—if he continued to turn Molly down, the crowd was going to mutiny.

Jake dragged ass as long as he could, letting the song wind mostly down before he finally heaved himself out of his chair and climbed the steps of the stage. The rest of the bar fell away. Molly winked, sultry as a screen siren, when Jake walked toward her. She extended the microphone, and he realized it was the final line of the song. The crowd held its collective breath, Jake leaned in and paused—then sang in his best baritone,

"Ride me like you stole me."

Molly threw back her head and absolutely died laughing. The crowd howled and cheered, and she threw her arms around Jake's neck, looking proud as a peacock. Before he did something incredibly dumb—like kiss her brains out right up there on that wobbly stage—Jake lifted Molly against his chest with one arm and hauled her back down the steps, placating the crowd with one victorious fist pump. He felt like a rock star. On karaoke night. Lord.

Someone had commandeered one of their chairs, but the DJ had managed to preserve the other one, as well as their drinks. He chucked Jake on the shoulder and gave him an approving nod before turning to his next victim. Jake held the remaining seat for Molly, then stood beside her to take a long swallow of his beer. The things this girl made him to do.

Leaning forward, he put his lips perilously close to the delicate shell of her ear and murmured, "Baby girl, you are a bad seed."

Molly just shook her head and rolled her eyes at him. "Oh stop. You need to get out more. You had fun and you know it."

The thing was, she was right. She knew it, Jake knew it, the American people knew it. He never wanted the night to end.

MERCIFULLY, THE KARAOKE program didn't last forever. About an hour after Jake and Molly arrived, the blues band that he had hoped for took the stage. The crowd thinned out, so he was able to get a better look around. The bar was done up in lots of exposed brick and thick wood beams—rustic and dark and bleeding sin. Molly's face was alight with happiness.

"This place is great," she enthused, grabbing his arm. "You must come here a lot!"

"No, never. This is my first time," he admitted. What a crying shame that was.

Jake noticed that both their beers were empty, so he pulled her to her feet and led her back over to the long copper bar. He waved to get the bartender's attention, Molly watching him curiously the entire time.

"What would you like?" Jake asked her, speaking loudly near her ear to be heard over the music. He found himself dying to know what Molly would say, and really wanting it to be *right*. Jake didn't know what "right" would be, precisely—only that it certainly wouldn't take the form of white wine, Blake's usual order. Jake didn't think "right" would be something colorful, or with a cheesy little umbrella in it, either. So, what would it be?

"Hmm, I don't know," Molly hedged, glancing around. "This place…" She clicked her tongue, making a show of thinking. "This place seems to require something special. What are you going to have?"

Jake's gaze passed over the wall of bottles behind the bartender's head, and he opened his mouth. What emerged surprised the hell out of him. "I am going to have a shot of *Ryemageddon* whiskey," he stated to the barkeep, and to her. "Maybe even two." Whiskey was hardly an outré order, but Jake liked the name of it, and felt defiant nonetheless. Naturally, it was something Bess would not have approved of. God only knew why. Come on—*Ryemageddon*. How could you not love that? It was genius. And if it was as wonderful as it sounded, maybe it would even make Jake forget his former fiancée's name—instead of her creeping into his thoughts every few minutes like a bad rash.

Molly's naughty grin illuminated her face. It made Jake reach for her and slip his arm around her waist, staking his claim for all and sundry to see.

"Me too," she chirped at the bartender. Jake gave her a little squeeze and they turned to watch the band. *End-of-the-*

world whiskey. Yep, that would do it—a drink order that was right as rain.

THEY FOUND A spot to stand, off to the side. Within the relative safety of the dim lighting, Jake stole some surreptitious glances at Molly. He studied the line of her throat—glimpsed in flashes when she turned her head—and her shiny brown hair as it moved across her back and shoulders. It wasn't the dyed platinum blond so favored by Bess and her peers; Jake would put money on the fact that Molly's hair grew out of her head that indescribable color, and that those caramel streaks near the ends were from the sun and not a bottle. He'd also bet that she didn't put a thing in it—it looked so soft and smooth and natural the way it swished when she moved her head. Jake wanted to brush aside the long bangs that fell across her forehead, to get a better look at her eyes. He wanted to touch a finger to the tiny, delicate sliver chain glinting at Molly's neck, and to the little disk that hung from it.

Jake took advantage of the fact that her attention was on the stage, and let his gaze drift lower. He shouldn't even allow himself to glance at her ass in those diabolical jeans of hers, not if he expected to survive this night in one piece. But it was there, right next to him, fine as could be—and Jake was a red-blooded man like any other. Molly's backside was taut and round and inspiring a thousand filthy thoughts.

A small motion even lower down caught his eye, though, and Jake noticed that she was rolling her ankle a little bit. As he watched, Molly tried to take her weight off each foot in turn, suffering for the sake of beauty like every other dang woman he'd ever known. Not that he didn't appreciate the effort, but still.

"Aw hell, honey, I'm sorry," Jake said into her ear. "Those shoes must be killing you, standing here like this."

He'd noticed them earlier, certainly—the way they shaped her calves and put a little giddy-up in her stride. Jake enjoyed the height they lent Molly, too, bringing her face nearly level with his. It wouldn't take but the smallest motion to lean down and catch her lips with his own. But despite all that, he'd forgotten that those heels must be bothering her by now.

"Oh, that's okay," Molly demurred, her breath warming his own ear in an exceedingly appealing way. "It's my own fault for wearing them." She looked a little sheepish, but not terribly repentant; if she had even half a clue about what those shoes did to him, Jake could see why.

He searched the crowd anyway, and found what he was looking for close behind them. Slipping his hand around hers and ignoring the electric charge it gave him to touch her, Jake tugged on Molly and inclined his head. When they reached the small table set against the wall, vacated moments earlier, Jake gave the devil the reins.

He might've been dumped by his fiancée on a public street only last weekend, and Bess would likely try crawling back to him any day now. Jake might have no idea what the future would bring, like so many times before. But what he did know was that he was right here, right now, with an incredible woman who made his knees weak. He was a single, unencumbered man by the barest of margins, and he'd been denying every wish of his for years. Watching Molly's uncertain face, Jake sank into the lone chair and reached for her.

Chapter Twenty

MOLLY WATCHED JAKE sprawl his long-limbed frame in the only chair. He gave her a slow, devilish smile—like a sultan on a throne—then took his hands from his splayed knees and beckoned.

"C'mere," he told her.

She exhaled carefully. Her heart began to thump alarmingly in her chest. Somehow, Molly managed to take one step toward him, then two. Jake reached out and grasped her hips, pulled her between his knees, and then—before Molly even saw it coming—he hooked her behind the knees and sat her on his lap.

"There now." Jake brushed her hair back behind her shoulder, and murmured hotly against her ear. "That's better, isn't it?"

"Much," she agreed, a little faint from the feel of his warm breath on the side of her neck. Jake's scent was as enticing as always—clean and heady and drifting around her.

Her feet were overjoyed to be off-duty however, so rather than think too hard about the implications of sitting on Jake's lap, Molly let herself relax a bit. It really had been sheer vanity to wear five-inch heels anyway, and she was sort of embarrassed that Jake had noticed her discomfort. Just because she could walk in them, didn't mean she *should*. Her ankles were going to be killing her in the morning.

Molly turned toward the stage and wiggled her butt a little, trying to distribute her weight better on her enticing new chair. Next to her ear, Jake emitted a strangled sound, then turned his face stoically away when she shifted again to glance back at him. It seemed her efforts at seduction were taking a toll on the poor thing. She smirked. Good, let him be the one simmering in his own desire for once.

Jake wasn't entirely at her mercy, though—for every move she made tonight, he came up with one to lob right back at her. Molly wasn't quite sure how she'd ended up on his lap, for example. She couldn't deny how much she *liked* her current location, but still. Jake was the son of her possibly-future boss—and a former fraternity guy, to boot. She *had* to try to keep her head clear while she angled for what she wanted.

Each minute Molly spent with Jake, this electric thing between them took another step farther away from "showing her around town" and another step toward showing her around something else altogether. Molly was rooting for that outcome, but only to a point.

She wouldn't mind a roll in the proverbial hay—not the real hay, that had been way too scratchy—as long as no one's heart got involved. *That* was the part that was beginning to worry her. Jake was hot and sexy and downright bitable…but he was also sweet and funny and intriguing. Dangerous to her heart.

Jake's muscular arms caged her loosely. Molly still tried to sit mostly upright, in an effort to maintain some small shred of dignity.

"Molly," he began, warning in his tone.

"I'm sorry," she blurted out. "Are you okay? I'm too heavy, aren't I?" Drat—this was why grownups didn't sit on each other. Molly rearranged herself on Jake's lap again, all at once conscious of every bite she'd eaten at dinner. Was it *really* necessary to get an appetizer *and* dessert? Suddenly, she didn't think so. She tried to find a little leverage so she could stand up again, but Jake just held on tighter. Molly peered at him, mortified. Maybe she'd inadvertently taken the game too far.

Jake's face looked pained while he made an obvious effort to compose himself. Still, his arms stayed locked around her waist when he finally croaked out, "No, darlin', you're not too heavy. For crying out loud, you can't weigh much more than a buck ten or so."

"More than that," Molly corrected automatically.

Again, Jake looked like he was struggling to rein himself in. "Regardless, it might help if you just…relaxed a bit. Keep still. Stop moving around like that."

"Okay," Molly agreed meekly. It dawned on her that she wasn't flirting any longer—she was grinding her ass against a very delicate place on Jake in an effort to get comfortable. There was teasing a man, and then there was *that*. Geez, you'd think she'd never been out with a guy before.

The waitress brought them a couple more shots of *Ryemageddon*. Now that Molly was off her feet, she noticed the booze sneaking up on her a little faster. They'd been having such a great time, that she sort of lost track of how much she'd had.

It was beginning to show: Jake's embrace and suggestive little comments had somehow evolved into his lips on her neck and his teeth—so help her God—on her ear. Jake's stubble was rough on her skin, and Molly wanted to feel it *everywhere*.

THE BAND FINISHED up—but she and Jake sat for a while more, letting the alcohol wear off and acting like they didn't want to jump each other in the middle of a dingy bar. It was getting late, and Molly was beginning to wonder if that was going to be all there was.

But finally, Jake leaned forward and murmured in her ear, "Come home with me."

Like she would even think of refusing. Jake had her wound up tighter than a spring—tighter than any man had in years. Molly grabbed his hand and pulled him outside, so they could walk the several blocks back to his car. Halfway there, she admitted defeat, and slipped off her heels. They dangled from one hand while Jake held the other. He stopped every ten yards to kiss her again. Molly tried to pretend she was breathless from the uphill walk, and not because Jake made her deranged with lust.

There was a hot little interlude in the front seat of his car, and then another at a red light five minutes later. The drive to his condo took too long—despite Molly's sterling intention to not act *too* loose she still found herself up against the wall of Jake's foyer, with her leg wrapped around his hip and his hands up her shirt.

Jake explored her mouth with his hot tongue—and what a masterful tongue it was, too. They might have stayed there all night, but when Duke nudged his leg, Jake broke away with a gasp. Molly could feel his heart pounding against her chest, and loved that she could affect him so. Loved that Jake was as desperate as she was.

He left her alone so he could walk his dog outside, whispering apologies and dropping kisses on her cheeks as he went. When the door swung shut behind him, Molly blew out a breath and looked around, trying to get her bearings. She dropped her purse on the kitchen counter and her shoes in a corner, then switched on a lamp and wandered around examining his home.

There was the requisite leather couch—staple of bachelors everywhere—and the huge flat-screen television.

Jake had a comfortable-looking recliner and a fleece dog bed for Duke, covered in bones.

While she waited for him to return, Molly tried to steady her breathing and calm her galloping heartbeat—but she was *here*, at last, in Jake's home. It was night and they were alone, and Molly hoped that soon, she'd get to see Jake with his shirt off again. This time, she wasn't going to lose the chance to run her fingers all over those tan, defined abs of his—or any of his other riveting manly parts.

In moments, Jake was back, looping his arms around Molly with a satisfied groan and inhaling the air near her neck.

"God, Molly. I can't believe you're really here," he whispered. "I've been imagining this so much."

In fits and starts, he herded Molly toward his bedroom—stopping to kiss her and press her against furniture and walls with his body, as if to mark his home with her presence. In the hall, he laced his fingers through hers and brought her hand to his mouth, tasting Molly from the tips of her fingers to the inside of her elbow, then on to the curve of her shoulder. Jake furrowed his hands into her hair and cupped Molly's skull. Staring intently at her mouth, he brought her close so he could kiss her again.

Deeper. A tiny bit rough. With a whimper, Molly melted against Jake, trying not to beg.

"A bed, Jake," she muttered. "Please find a damn bed."

He groaned again, fumbled behind her for the doorframe, then backed Molly into his room. She needed to become better acquainted with Jake's own special brand of Southern hospitality, and soon. Her chest was heaving with how bad she wanted him.

It was dark in the bedroom. Jake stood her in the center of the room and stripped Molly carefully—searching out snaps and buttons and zippers and undoing each with precise, deft fingers. As desperate he'd seemed before, Jake didn't yank or tug—he removed each piece of Molly's clothing and set it aside like she was an intricate puzzle to be solved. He was measured. Methodical. Jake forced her to be patient and wait while he did things his way, and it drove her *crazy*.

Molly dropped her head back and watched the ceiling fan spin lazily overhead, around and around, and concentrated on each soft brush of his hands on her skin. She tried to calm down, to focus as each inch of her was exposed to the air, and to Jake's gaze.

She was down to her panties when he finally hesitated. Jake stepped back and studied Molly's body, running his palms from her shoulders to her hands. She caught his eye while she slipped off the last piece of her clothing, and listened to his breath hitch.

"You're so beautiful," he murmured. "Even more than I imagined."

Jake pulled Molly against him. He draped her arms around his neck, cupped her rear in his broad, hot palms, and kissed Molly once more. It had been only minutes since the last one, but Jake was like a man too long denied—pressing harder, demanding more, bending Molly's head back so he could *take*. And she wanted him to—she wanted to give and give and give to him, until nothing stood between them any longer.

Molly nibbled and sucked and tangled her tongue with his, tugging at Jake's shirt and the waist of his jeans. His clothes had to *go*. But in her need to feel all of him, her fingers were clumsy, too hurried. Molly couldn't get anything to open, to *work*, and Jake struggling to help her and grope her at the same time was no help at all. Finally, he pushed her away.

"*Stop*," Jake laughed, breathless as he whipped his shirt over his head and tossed it aside. "Crazy woman." His jeans dropped next, and then Jake was stepping out of his pants, his shoes—everything, all in one motion.

She didn't get much of a view, though, because in seconds, he had backed Molly toward his bed. Their knees hit the side of the mattress. Molly sat down and scooched back, Jake crawled after her, and then they were *there*, at last, stretched out across his white starched sheets.

"Is this what you want, baby girl?" he asked, nuzzling her neck.

She nodded, and tried to pull him closer.

"I want to hear you say it," Jake murmured, holding himself off her.

Molly swallowed, touched that he'd make sure, even now. "I want this," she told him. "I want everything."

Jake stared down at her face, his eyes intense, and Molly wondered what exactly she'd just set herself up for. But he kissed her again, and his desire—his palpable need for her—burned away her worry, like always.

They'd hit the bed sideways. Molly didn't notice it at first. Jake had left her mouth to lick a scorching trail down to her breasts, and then sometime after he was kissing her stomach—his searching lips raising a trail of goosebumps across her skin in the chilly air conditioning. She curved into his mouth and slid further across the bed.

In total command, Jake positioned Molly the way he wanted her. He pulled her knees up, set her feet beside his broad shoulders, and spread her legs wide with a growl of appreciation. His dominance made her pant harder.

His mouth was blazing—when Jake set it to her aching core, Molly moaned, long and loud. She arched her back and stretched her arms high overhead…where they dangled out in open space. Still, it didn't worry her—she had much better things to concentrate on as Jake's tongue and fingers tied her up in delicious, quivering knots.

Her thighs were trembling and Molly was begging him incoherently for *more*, when Jake finally relented. Leaning to the side, he rummaged in his nightstand drawer and finally pulled out a condom. Jake knelt and held Molly in place with one proprietary hand on her hip. He ripped open the little packet with his teeth and rolled it over himself, staring intently down at the silken place his mouth had just been. Molly had never seen an expression quite like his—such hunger and determination, all aimed at her.

Jake met her eyes. "You're the most delectable thing I've ever seen," he rumbled.

When he loomed forward to cover her body with his own, Molly's precarious position became even more obvious. She slid back another few inches, and clutched at him. Jake braced himself on one muscular arm, grasped his erection, and guided himself to her entrance. Molly held her breath and waited while he dragged himself through her folds, teasing her.

At last, Jake entered her sensitive flesh in one smooth, firm thrust, pushing her across the bed. Then he paused, dropped his head, and shook it like he couldn't believe what he was feeling. Molly could understand—the sensation of puzzle pieces snapping together in perfect alignment was a strong one. So was the feeling of falling. In love, off the bed—in that moment, it all felt the same.

"Feels so good," Jake muttered.

"Yes," Molly agreed softly. "Let's have more of that."

Molly stroked Jake's ribs, and reached up to touch his face. There was the faintest dew across his lip and once more, she could feel the drumming of his heart against her chest. Jake exhaled in a short burst of air, raised his stormy blue eyes to hers, and leaned down to kiss her again.

"You got it, sweetheart," he said.

Lowering himself to his elbows, he pressed his torso to her breasts, gathered himself, and thrust again. Hard. Molly shifted back on the cold white sheets, and held Jake closer—wrapping her arms and legs around his body to anchor herself to him. Her neck arched, her head dropped back, and the vulnerability was a visceral little thrill to add to all the others. Jake was big, and he was strong. His urgency was overwhelming. Heady.

He withdrew slowly, pulling nearly all the way out before pushing hard into her again. Molly's head angled back even more over the edge of the bed, and she felt air hit the back of her shoulders. Jake gripped her closer, keeping her pinned beneath him. With his muscular thighs pressing hers wide and his arms grasping her close, they found a desperate, frantic rhythm.

Like it belonged to someone else, Molly heard her voice echoing off the walls, pleading with Jake. *Please, please, please,* she gasped, incoherent with want. He swallowed her cries hungrily and sped headlong toward the finish—ripping his mouth from hers only when he felt her muscles contract suddenly around him.

Jake paused and squeezed his eyes shut, seeming to absorb the feeling of Molly's climax. Then he was in motion again, speeding up his thrusts, hitching her legs higher and pushing deeper. At last, with an agonized groan that sounded like it had been ripped from his throat, Jake froze in place, dropped his head back and let the bliss of his own completion wash over him.

"Jake," Molly whispered, touching his hair where it was damp against his forehead—unable to stop caressing him. He collapsed on her, pressing Molly into the mattress with his welcome weight while they caught their breath. A rush of affection washed through her. She traced the nape of his neck and the length of his spine with shaking fingers.

They lay there, tangled up and half off the side of the bed, while the spinning fan clicked the passing seconds above them. Molly's hair cascaded down to the floor like a waterfall, and Jake tangled his fingers in it, cupping her head to support it. He pressed hot, gentle kisses against her neck, then withdrew and carefully shifted to the side—suddenly aware, it appeared, that his weight was probably the only thing keeping Molly from sliding headfirst off the side of the bed.

"What the heck," he laughed, when she squeaked and clutched at him, still breathless and dazed. "Where do you think you're going, sweet thing?" Jake steadied her shoulders and helped Molly move back onto the bed, then reoriented them both in the right direction. He laid his head on a pillow and turned on his side to face Molly, trailing trembling fingers through her hair like he couldn't stop petting it.

Molly smiled at the incandescent joy on his face. "Never a dull moment," she giggled.

"Nope," Jake agreed. He slid out of bed and stepped into his bathroom for a moment, and then he was back, pulling the covers up and over them. "But I'd follow you anywhere for fun like that."

Chapter Twenty-One

J AKE FELT LIKE a junkie, there was no other word for it.
He was hooked on a woman, and every moment he was
forced to spend apart from her was a complete pain in his
ass. Jake knew he was a grown up, but someone might've
thought he was a teenager the way he resented every
obligation that demanded his time. Job—*sucked*.
Car…condo…parents—*snore*. Probably the only reason he
still loved his dog was because the mutt adored Molly almost
as much as Jake did.

Jake was jumpy and restless and jonesing for his next fix.
And Molly—lovely delicious Molly—was sweeter-smelling
and better-tasting than any drug even Jake's fevered
imagination could have conjured. Last night, he'd nearly
fucked her right off the side of his bed, and then barely let
her catch her breath before he was trying to do it again—
before he was trying to line up another date for tonight.

If Molly hadn't reminded him of her lunch meeting with
his father, Jake might never have let her leave. Laying with
her head on his chest, skin to skin, had felt like the greatest
thing he'd ever done with his life. As it was, Molly had to
sneak into Mrs. Denson's way later than was proper, slinking

in the back door like a dang thief in the night. What they'd done hadn't felt criminal, though—it had been a restoration. A regeneration.

Jake felt like he'd been broken open and exposed to the sun for the first time in years. Molly had done that—uncovered all the parts of him that had been withering in the dark, like fresh air and sunshine for the soul.

After he dropped her off last night, Jake sat in his car, and in his head counted her steps inside that B&B. Across the kitchen, up the staircase, into her room. Her light upstairs went on, and he timed her probable movements—changing into pajamas, brushing teeth. Jake sat and watched that window until the light went out again, then sat some more, unable to make himself leave. Eventually, Molly texted him.

Time to head home, Tex.

Mortified that she knew he was still there, Jake had put the car in gear and driven off. He lay in bed the rest of the night, wide-awake and longing for her—because Jake was a lovesick child, and Molly was suddenly, inexplicably, his world.

NOW THAT HE had her in his clutches again, he couldn't stop staring—couldn't stop touching her. Couldn't stop wanting her, with an ache even deeper than he'd been nursing all day. Molly had yet another pair of devastating jeans on, though this time she'd gone with a sensible pair of flats, instead. Her hair was twisted up in a large tortoiseshell clip that Jake wanted to release and toss away. Molly picked at her pasta dish while she regaled him with stories from her lunch with his dad.

"Jake?" Molly laughed, exasperated.

He dragged his eyes up from the neckline of her blouse—every time she leaned over to take a bite, it gaped a bit, giving him a flash of her lacy tan-colored bra underneath.

"Are you even listening to me?"

"Sure," he said. But it dawned on him—Molly had gone to lunch today with his *father*. Jake didn't even want to think about how hard it must have been to smile and make conversation, knowing Clay's own son had been invading every private nook and cranny Molly had the night before. He had no idea how she'd accomplished that—but if anyone could do it, Molly could. She was amazing.

She also appeared to be mostly done with her dinner.

"You ready to roll?" Jake asked. He tried to play it cool, act natural. But Molly's twinkling eyes let him know she was onto him. So much for subtlety.

"Ready when you are," she grinned.

Jake threw his arm in the air and practically begged their waiter for the check.

As he was guiding Molly toward the door, though, a large man in a navy blue EMT uniform pushed in. It figured they'd run into him, right when Jake was in such a hurry. His best and oldest friend—and the one least likely to ignore the fact that Jake had a new woman draped on his arm. Jake swore, low and profane, under his breath.

Tim's gaze snapped right to Jake and Molly like a goddamn magnet, and he eyed them both with sardonic amusement. When the paramedic sauntered directly over, Jake watched Molly's eyes grow wide.

He shook his head. He'd known Tim a long time, and the dude always made quite an impression. Even when they were seventeen, he'd looked like some kind of superhero—like a good-looking, ripped, African-American GI Joe—and not much had changed since then. Jake figured probably half of the guy's distress calls must be from women fainting at the sight of him.

They did that slap, slap, grasp thing with their hands, like buddies do.

"Hey, brother," Tim greeted him.

Jake let go of Molly and leaned in, giving Tim one of those dude half-hugs. Tim was tall—even bigger and broader than Jake—with hair cropped close to his skull and black tribal tattoos circling one bicep. His dark brown skin and chocolate-colored eyes were the exact opposite of Jake's coloring, and had made for years of people joking that they were photo-negatives of each other. The loyalty to each other and grins on their faces, though—those were always the same. Jake loved him Tim like he was blood, but *why* did he have to show up now?

"Hey, bud," he said. Jake looked longingly over Tim's shoulder—outside, to freedom.

Over Jake's head, Tim was searching the inside of the restaurant. "Is Healey here?" he inquired. Like Jake had just left his sister behind, inside the restaurant.

Jake frowned at the non-sequitur. "Not to my knowledge. Why?"

Tim brushed it off. "No reason. How *you* doin', Hoss?" he asked, bumping Jake's shoulder and smirking. Molly's eyes ping-ponged back and forth between them, missing nothing.

"Just fine, thanks," said Jake. Could he try to leave without an introduction, or might that offend Molly? He set a hand on her shoulder and kind of... *nudged* her along.

Tim, the bastard, stuck his hand out to block her path. "Hey there, I'm Tim."

"Nice to meet you, Tim," she replied sweetly. "I'm Molly." She turned to look at Jake in inquiry. He shook his head. He could explain to her later, but for now, Jake had to make a break for it before Tim acquired any more ammunition. God—his friend was going to give him hell about this, Jake just knew it.

"I believe the pleasure is all mine," Tim drawled. "*Molly*, did you say?"

"Mm-hmm." She stumbled a little on the edge of the rug, so Jake shot out a hand to steady her. Tim's eyes followed the motion, gazing curiously at the way Molly laced her fingers with Jake's.

He turned to Jake and examined his face, still neutrally pleasant. "Did ya'll just meet here?" he inquired. So casual. So polite. Oh, Jake was going to catch a rash of shit, that was for damn sure.

Jake squeezed his eyes shut, pained at the notion. When he reopened them, he feigned resignation. "No, Tim, we did not just meet. This is *Molly*, Grey Whitney's sister-in-law."

Comprehension dawned across the other man's face and his mouth gaped open. "*Ohhhh*," he said, blinking quickly. With effort, he clamped his mouth closed again, then nodded slowly—at a loss for what else to say. His intelligent brown eyes darted back and forth between their faces, and then he plastered another friendly smile on his face.

"You must have met my sister by now," Tim told Molly. "Shannon McCready? At the firm?"

Molly brightened. "Of course! Shannon's great—she's been helping me all week."

Before this spun even farther into the unreal, Jake clapped Tim on the shoulder, and squeezed hard. "Anyway, we're heading out, so..." He released his friend and steered Molly bodily toward the door.

"Okay, I guess I'll catch you later," Tim called after them. Asshole had the nerve to look disappointed. Jake was seriously going to kill him if he said one word about this to anyone.

"Like hell you will," Jake muttered.

He and Molly walked toward his car in silence. Finally, Molly asked, "You don't like that guy very much, do you?" When Jake's head snapped up and he stared at her in confusion, she smiled uncertainly. "It seemed like you kind of hated him, actually."

Jake blew out a breath. "Naw, it's not like that," he said, shaking his head. "Tim's been my best dang friend since the third grade."

"Then what was *that?*" Molly laughed. "Holy awkwardness, Batman. You'd think he busted you with the preacher's wife."

Jake rolled his eyes. Trust Molly to both hit the nail on the head, and have it completely wrong at the same time. "It's no big thing," he explained. "Tim's weird. Don't even worry about it."

But as they reached his car, Jake *was* worried. He was a damn fool if he thought he could go gallivanting around town without someone, somewhere, seeing him with Molly and asking questions. And like a twisted game of *Telephone*, one of them was bound to tell his erstwhile fiancée exactly how Jake had been spending his time apart from her. Maybe not Tim, or even Shannon. But someone would. Resentment flooded Jake, fast and vicious.

He might not care too much about *Blake's* reaction, but if she whined to her parents, and then *his* folks caught wind of it…he was a dead man. He'd promised his father he would fix this situation, and he would. But Jake deserved to live, and Molly was only here for a little while longer. He didn't want to waste a single moment of it arguing with the likes of the Suttons. Jake just needed a little more time to figure this out. He needed a little more time with Molly—just the two of them—before all the shit from his past intruded.

When Molly leaned back against his car in the dark parking lot and gave him the sexiest little grin he'd ever seen in his life, all those thoughts dissolved and melted away. Hell, Jake wasn't going to say no to her, not when he'd been aching for her all day. He kissed Molly's lips, hard and hungry, and vowed not to let thoughts of what he had to do tomorrow, or even next week, intrude on this evening with her. If Jake was going down, it was going to be in fucking *flames*.

Molly gasped, coming up for air with a sudden realization. "Wait—did you say *Tim*? Was *that* the guy who gave you Duke?"

Jake had to laugh. Girl was sharp as a tack. "Yup. That's him, alright."

"Oh man," Molly complained. "I wish I would've known."

"Why?"

"I don't know. So, I could hero-worship him a little better, probably," Molly snarked.

The thing was, if Jake had his way and made Molly his, she'd likely get to know Tim really well over the years. They'd probably get on like peas in a pod, too—ganging up on Jake and needling him for all eternity together.

Jake took a chance and tempted fate. "I'm sure you'll get your chance," he said, hoping. Praying it was true.

IN THE CAR on the way to his house, Jake wasn't drunk—he'd never risk his or Molly's safety that way—but he may as well have been. He couldn't remember the last time he'd felt such a glorious, soaring feeling of possibility. The drive was smooth, the car's sound system was sweet, and the hot woman beside him wanted him in her bed.

Jake felt like a total stud. Optimistic. Cocky, in all senses of the word. When that dirty country tune came on the radio, it didn't even feel weird at all to start singing it to her—and references to muddy boots aside, Molly seemed to appreciate the *lovin'-up-on-you* sentiment.

They tumbled into his dark condo, trailing clothing and bumping into furniture, and barely made it to Jake's living room. Molly had her wicked way with him on his couch, but almost as good was how it felt after, with Molly cradled against his chest. Jake propped his feet on the arm of the sofa, and stroked her satiny hair with one hand. Duke appeared, wedging himself into the narrow space between the couch and the coffee table, so Jake dropped his other hand to rest on the hound's head.

He drifted, hazy images of him and Molly flitting across his brain as her chest rose and fell against his. Her long, long leg was thrown across his thigh, and her pulse beat faintly beneath her skin. He couldn't tell if she'd fallen asleep, but he could hardly blame her if she had—she'd worn Jake out like a goddess of the first order.

Still, something gnawed at him. A big old elephant in the room, though not the biggest. "Molly?"

"Hmm?" Her voice was rusty. Mostly asleep, then.

"When's your flight on Saturday?" Jake asked, ripping off the bandage—hating its existence in the first place.

Molly's whole frame tensed. "I don't know? Four-thirty, I think?" she murmured.

Jake thought for a while, but the words spilled out on their own, not to be contained. "Got a lot going on at home next week?" he wondered.

"Not really. I have to start packing up my place, but school's done. I'm trying to phase out at the legal aid center…" she paused a while, then picked up the thread again. "I'm going to hold off on taking the bar exam until I know where I'm going to be," she finished, almost to herself.

Jake nodded. "So—just getting ready to move?" Would she come here, even if she didn't land the job with his dad? The possibility thrilled him. Molly could even move in with *him* if she wanted—Jake could give her his guest room, if she felt like they needed to move forward more gradually.

"Yeah. I sublet a room in a group house, but apparently the lease is up, so…I have to find somewhere else to stay for a bit." She kept it vague, but Jake understood the subtext easily enough. Until she was offered the position at *Alexander, Polk & Futch*—or not—her life would be in limbo.

"Where will you go?"

"I think I can crash with my friend Meg," she said easily. "She and her fiancé have a pretty big place. I'll have to see."

A beat passed, then two. Jake worked up his nerve. "Molly?"

"Yes, Jake," she smiled, her breath hot against his shoulder.

"What do you think about staying on for another week? If Mrs. Denson doesn't have room, you could crash here with me." He held his breath, and waited a long time for her reply. "If you want."

At last, the words he hoped so badly for came. "I think I can swing that," Molly agreed, hugging him tight and kissing his neck. Jake relaxed. It was going to be okay. It was all really going to be okay.

Chapter Twenty-Two

J AKE WANTED HER to stay longer. Molly could hardly believe it. The feeling of being wanted—the right way— was amazing, delicious. A sensation that she could roll around on her tongue like a cinnamon bun fresh out of the oven. She let the warmth flood through her, coating all her jagged edges and soothing her soul.

The "want" that Molly was used to was so different than this one. Since the time she'd hit puberty, men had seen Molly's face and her body, and wanted her physically. At first the catcalls and wolf whistles had horrified her, making her want to crawl in a shell and never come out. Didn't they know how young she was? Didn't they care that she was a real person with real feelings? She'd gone out of her way not to court attention, skipping makeup, wearing baggy sweatshirts, avoiding eye contact. But then Carter had appeared—had seen right through her façade—and liked Molly anyway.

For weeks and weeks, he'd seemed like the only person at that horrible prep school (or anywhere else) who could really *see* her, the real her. Molly had dropped a small piece of her guard each time he sought her out, each time he remembered something she said or smiled in the hallway just for her. She hadn't wanted *him* to think she was plain or boring. Carter had been meticulous and patient, laying the foundation for what he wanted.

He was good at what he did, Molly could admit that now—she'd fallen for him like a ton of bricks and never thought twice about it. Soon, she was back to styling her hair, and wearing makeup and flattering clothes. The other kids had hated her even more for it, but Carter loved it—had wanted Molly more than ever. In the end, none of it had been enough. Molly's heart had never mattered, and Carter was just like all the rest.

But everything about Jake felt different than that. He seemed just as enamored of her mind and her heart as he was of her body. As handsome and cocky as Jake appeared, his character was sound. Jake hid a gentle and sweet soul inside that flashy outer shell. A compassionate and intuitive heart beat in his chest—and every time he kissed her, Molly felt her own heart stretch and reach out for him.

She'd been guarding and protecting herself for so long, she'd forgotten that connections like this with another person could even exist. Flaring up out of nowhere, in the unlikeliest of places. It seemed inconceivable, but maybe, just maybe, she was being given another shot at love.

MOLLY WOKE UP with a streak of sunshine warming her back. It felt late—the sun was streaming through the cracks in the blinds with enough sultry brightness to counteract both the A/C and the fan whirring overhead. Her front was even warmer, pressed against Jake's side.

Molly took a moment to marvel at the amount of heat the man gave off—he was like a blast furnace half the time, his skin burning hot from within rather than from the humid summer air swirling around them. She loved it, but right now—with the side of her face pillowed on his shoulder—Molly could use a little air. For one thing, her cheek felt damp from sweat, and that seemed like it might gross him out. For another, she wanted the chance to hit the bathroom and brush her teeth before he woke up.

But Jake's heavy arm was draped across her back, and his large warm palm was curled firmly across the curve of her hip. One of Molly's arms was smooshed between them, but her other was resting on Jake's chest. He had it pinned there against his heart with his free hand, his breathing deep and regular. She tried to devise a way to extricate herself without disturbing him. First, she peeled her face off his shoulder and craned her neck, looking around for Duke—the dog should be nosing around soon, shouldn't he? Didn't all pets want to be fed and walked first thing in the morning?

Jake's breath hitched and he moved his arm to the pillow next to his head. Molly took a moment to admire the way his bicep flexed and carved a valley down the inside of his upper arm. His skin was paler there, and softer—kissable.

Before she went too far down that slippery slope, Molly shifted, using her buried arm to brace herself against the mattress. The hand that rested on Jake's chest slipped lower, and grazed the tanned muscles of his stomach. That must have been some sensitive skin, because Jake wrenched awake with a jolt—blinking, then quickly turning to peer at her.

"You okay?" he mumbled, his voice gravelly with sleep.

Molly slumped back down in defeat. "Fine," she told him. "I'm sorry—I was trying not to wake you."

He looked around. "What time is it?"

"I don't know. It seems late. Did we oversleep?"

Jake twisted his torso to push a shirt off his night table, uncovering the alarm clock buried beneath. "It's only six," he mumbled. "There's plenty of time. Go back to sleep." He slumped flat on the mattress, closed his eyes and went slack again.

Molly smiled, charmed by his grogginess. They hadn't gotten a ton of sleep the night before—he was probably exhausted. But then, she watched as Jake's hand drifted across his chest and headed south, lazily gripping his half-erect member through the sheet and readjusting it. Her eyebrows shot up, watching his large hand rest there on his groin while Jake slumbered. Scrambling backward and off the other side of the mattress, Molly darted quickly for the bathroom. If that gorgeous hunk of a man decided to wake up, she was damn well going to be ready.

THE FIRST THING Molly noticed when she woke up again was the absence of Jake's warmth. When she'd climbed back into bed earlier, he'd immediately cuddled up tight behind her and held her close. His steady breathing and strong heartbeat had lulled her soundly back to sleep. Now, Molly was the groggy one, and Jake was gone.

Stretching like a cat, she felt the rapidly cooling sheets on his side of the bed, and the air conditioning blowing from the vent overhead. She could hear Duke's nails clicking on the hardwood floor in the hallway outside the bedroom. Molly recognized the sound of the shower coming from the bathroom, and she dozed again—her mind drifting around images of Jake soaping himself under the spray.

She woke again to the feel of a warm fingertip trailing down her arm, and warmer lips against her shoulder. Cracking an eye open, Molly was startled to see that Jake—impeccable and elegant in a suit and tie—was clearly ready to leave for work. She sat bolt upright, suddenly very conscious of the fact that she was wearing only his old worn t-shirt and her panties from the night before. The... night before. *Oh.*

"You're all ready to go," she murmured, standing up hurriedly. "I'm sorry. Why did you let me oversleep?" Molly clung to the sheet and glanced around, searching for her clothes.

A smile tugged at Jake's lips as he reached for her and pulled her closer. "I hated to wake you. You looked awfully cute all curled up in my bed." His hands stroked down her arms and back, over and over, in blazing streaks of fire.

"You look so nice," Molly marveled. "So handsome." She breathed his crisp cologne in deeply. "And you smell incredible, too."

Jake's hands settled on her lower back, pressing her closer as he nuzzled her hair.

"Stop, Jake! You'll mess up your suit," she protested. "You're all fresh and clean, and I am...*not*." Molly pushed ineffectually at his chest, keeping her mouth turned away. No way was her breath as minty-fresh as his right now, even with that crack-of-dawn brushing.

"Screw the suit," Jake announced, pulling back to shrug quickly out of his jacket and throw it over a chair. "As for the way *you* smell..." His hands dropped to trace feather-light strokes up the back of her thighs, catching at the hem of the t-shirt and lifting it higher. "You smell like me. Like you *and* me, and if I could bottle that scent and carry it with me everywhere, I totally would." His long, adept fingers were tracing the lower curve of Molly's rear now, dipping under the lacy edge of her panties to stroke her softly. "That way," he murmured in her ear, "Whenever I was thinking of you, and missing you, I could pull the bottle out and smell you, too."

Moving Jake's tie aside, Molly pressed her face into his chest to hide her blush. Missing her? He *missed* her when they were apart?

"On the other hand, the way I get just *thinking* about you—maybe that's not a very smart idea," he drawled idly. He caught her hand at his waist and moved it to press the front of his suit pants, in vivid illustration. Oh, Jake was ready for her, all right.

Molly gave a strangled laugh and pulled her hand away, albeit a little reluctantly. He was packing a virtual flagpole in his trousers, but the guy was about to *leave*. Probably better not to get him worked up more than he already was.

"Jake, *stop* it. You have to go to work!" she scolded.

He didn't like that at all. Growling low in his throat, he grabbed the bottom of her t-shirt and pulled it over her head in one smooth, economical motion. His was gaze scorching—Molly folded her arms across her chest, startled and embarrassed to be so suddenly exposed. Jake's eyes narrowed, disliking the denial. His long arm reached out blindly for the top of his dresser, and he grabbed his cell phone without once taking his eyes from Molly's face. His thumb dialed quickly, apparently knowing the number by feel.

"Amy?" Jake barked after the call connected, "It's me. I need you to reschedule my nine o'clock. Something's come up," he said.

"I'll say," Molly murmured, eyeing the front of his pants. In response, Jake parked one broad palm gently, but firmly, over her mouth. He walked her toward the bed as he listened to his assistant talk quickly in his ear. The cool metal of his belt buckle, the slide of his silk tie across her skin, Jake's warm fingers on her face—each detail of him all ran together and left Molly's heart skittering erratically in her chest.

Whatever Jake heard on his phone must have satisfied him, because finally he said, "That's fine," in an uncharacteristically curt voice. Then he was pressing the red icon to disconnect the call and tossing his phone carelessly behind him. Molly shivered. Desire was carved into every masculine plane of his face.

Jake cornered Molly between him and the foot of bed with his large frame. He took his hand from her mouth and the other from her waist, and when he reached up and began tugging viciously at his tie, Molly knew her morning had just turned vastly more interesting.

Chapter Twenty-Three

JAKE HAD REACHED his collar buttons and begun undoing them, when Molly finally smiled and began to look less alarmed. When he started in on his cuff links, she reached out to tug his shirt from his trousers. Jake swallowed, impressions from the night before beginning to flash in his head. In the dark of night, drunk on Molly and tightly-wound from the anticipation, their every move had seemed desperately erotic. It hadn't seemed possible that things would feel the same in the light of day.

They did. Jake had just spent the last few hours dozing with Molly nestled perfectly in his arms, with the silk of her hair—staggeringly, fragrantly, *female*—against his chin. Jake had woken up ages ago, and just watched her breathe as the day arrived. The sunshine slanting into his bedroom had moved gradually across the wall, shifting bit by bit until it was angled in polygons across her skin.

Molly had only gotten prettier with each passing moment—sexier, even in sleep. Pulling away from her to go shower for work had been a Herculean endeavor, requiring more willpower than he'd thought he possessed.

Last night, she told him she wanted everything. Jake wondered if Molly even realized what that meant. She'd already claimed more of him than nearly anyone else in his life. Seemingly effortlessly, she'd managed to elicit the truth of Jake from within him—his honest thoughts and feelings and desires.

Nearly everyone else he knew was stuck with the façade he'd created, and it was amazing how refreshing it felt to just *be himself*. No artifice. No compromise. Just Jake. And Molly even liked him that way. She wanted *more*. She wanted *everything*. Jake wanted to give it to her, too—everything he was and everything he had, all on a platter for Molly O'Connell.

Today, seeing her skin and hair and expressions through the golden prism of late morning was doing odd and uncomfortable things to his chest. Jake was having more trouble than usual getting sufficient air into his lungs—his every breath required more effort than it should, and he hadn't even gone running that morning. Instead of worrying him, though, the odd feeling acted more like a riding crop—driving him forward toward the enticing reward that was Molly.

Now that he knew what she felt like when her body was tight around his, Jake may as well have been a dog in heat for all the restraint he had.

Between them, they'd gotten the buttons of his shirt undone, and he dropped it to the floor somewhere behind him, forgotten. Jake watched Molly sit on the bed and slither backward, her graceful, feminine limbs sliding across the rumpled sheets. *His* messy sheets, he thought with a stab of territoriality, his and no one else's. Molly was *his*. Jake unbuckled his belt and took in the vision of her dainty little underwear, not missing the primitive charge that simple action gave him.

This woman—practical and capable and smart, and somehow both outgoing and insecure at once—was wholly different than any woman he'd ever known. She'd turned Jake into a veritable beast in little more than a week. With a few well-placed eye rolls and incisive questions, Molly had shattered nearly thirty years of bred-in-the-bone gentility and obedience. With her, Jake wasn't a man who wanted to please his parents or avoid social censure—or even a man who had broken up with his fiancée only days before. He was only a solitary, ravenous man, who was born to adore Molly.

In short order, Jake pulled off his shoes and socks, shed his pants, and tossed aside his undershirt. He knelt on the end of the bed and prowled slowly up her body, stalking her like a marauding animal. Molly giggled a little, tugging at the waist of his boxers.

"I think you missed something," she teased breathlessly.

It struck Jake—he felt good. No, not just good—that was too anemic for what this was. Jake felt... *free*. And a bit wild, truth be told. He couldn't remember ever getting off on a woman like he did this one. This one, who seemed tailor-made for him alone.

"You do it," he said in Molly's ear, his voice coming out huskier than normal. He laid kisses along the side of her beautiful neck, trying to slow himself down so he wouldn't ravish her like some kind of caveman. Like he'd done the last two nights, come to think of it—but best not to go *there* at the moment.

Jake brushed his lips across her throat while she worked to get his boxers off him, along her collarbone as he kicked them away, then against her jaw once he was rid of them. Such impossibly soft skin, delicate and feminine, and whole expanses of it for Jake to investigate all morning long if Molly would let him. Like that, possessiveness took hold— it gripped Jake around the throat with an iron fist and he knew, he *knew* he wouldn't give her up. Not now, not next week, not *ever*. He would burn his carefully constructed existence to the God-forsaken ground if he had to, but he was going to selfishly keep this one damn thing for himself if it killed him.

With that realization, Jake lowered his mouth to hers, and there was nothing sweet or slow about it. The sound Molly made in response was so perfect that good intentions—if he'd ever had any—went out the window. Ravishment it was, then. Again.

MUCH LATER, JAKE awoke, jumpy and restless. He had to find some way to bring up the issue of Bess with Molly soon. Each day brought with it new, unanticipated pitfalls, and each person Molly met was one more who might tell her about the engagement. The way gossip and rumor snaked its path around his parents' social circles, Jake had no confidence that anyone would tell Molly the whole truth. They probably wouldn't even know what that was.

But memories were long around here. Most likely, some shrew would paint Jake as an asshole trying to have his cake and eat it too. For some people, Jake might never leave behind the things he'd once done.

Leaving Molly sacked out on his pillow, Jake grabbed some shorts and headed into the kitchen. He poured more kibble into Duke's big metal bowl and slipped out the front door to take a run. If he could burn off some of this creeping anxiety, he'd be able to think better. Come up with the magic combination of words that would make Molly understand what she meant to him.

Forty minutes later, Jake was no closer to a solution. He slipped quietly into the bedroom, nerves jumping, but still felt the same thrill he always got to see Molly asleep in his bed. He'd pushed it hard the last leg of his run, afraid that maybe she'd be gone by the time he returned. Now he was hot and sweaty and probably smelled like a farmyard—but he couldn't tear his eyes away.

Jake grinned to himself at the image Molly presented: sleeping on her stomach, head and arms curled half under the pillow, wanton and uninhibited. The sheet still covered some of her back and one of her legs. Her other long, toned leg stretched down the side of the bed, bare and perfectly formed. Her delicate foot hung off the edge—the pale, tender underside seeming oddly vulnerable to Jake, exposed as it was. He knew now how ticklish Molly was there, and he was sorely tempted to wake her up with one light swipe of his finger right across the arch of her foot. Jake loved the thought of the squeal she'd probably let out.

His eyes wandered higher. She was hardly a statue while she slept—Jake had discovered that the hard way. Molly slept more like a cuddly, aggravated gator than anything else. At any given moment, she might be sprawled across his chest, or have her sweet ass pressed tight against his groin. Either way, Jake had grown pretty darn comfortable having that butt of hers on display and within easy reach. It was probably one of his favorite things about Molly's body.

Problem was, when Jake was busy hanging on to it, that usually meant he couldn't *see* it—and her ass was definitely something to see. He hadn't gotten a good look at those panties of hers last night, but he had a great view right now: stark white with little black dots, and a wide edging of black lace along her thighs and waist. They were adorable and feisty, sexy and cute, all at the same time. Just like all her skivvies were turning out to be. Pretty much like Molly was turning out to be.

The vision of her tight, rounded little derriere stalled Jake in his sneakers—he didn't want to wake her quite yet. Molly was wearing one of his old UNC t-shirts, and in all her shifting around, it had ridden up high around her ribcage—

which was why he had such a perfect view of her caboose. Jake smiled wider. He'd bet his last hundred dollars that the woman didn't own a single plain pair of underwear and he wouldn't want it any other way. The contrast of Molly's beauty, amidst all the trappings of Jake's utter maleness, made him giddy.

He tried to imagine what it might be like, living with her. Having Molly's intimate things strewn all around, taking up space in his drawers and closets. Seeing her sky-high heels on the floor next to his dress shoes. Finding her lipstick on a coffee mug in his sink. Jake stood there, watched Molly sleep, and yearned for all of it. He wanted to take his life and hers, and mix them up together until she couldn't tell where one ended and the other began. He wanted to nail together all their days and years and build something amazing from them.

With Molly by his side, Jake felt like he could do anything. He wouldn't have to worry about owing someone—for a favor done years earlier, and paid for several times over. He wouldn't have to think about spending his life doing only what others expected of him. With Molly in his corner, Jake could finally be himself. He could love a woman who knew him as he really was, and loved him back for it. Jake could have a family and a career that he actually cared about.

Now that Molly had agreed to stay in Carolina another week, Jake had more time to prove to her that he was worth the trouble. He was nearly certain she'd get the job at *Alexander, Polk & Futch*—his father would never invest so much time in wooing her if he didn't think she was the perfect candidate. Now Jake just had to show Molly why Wilmington should be her home, and why Jake should be her man. And why he'd never, ever let her down.

For now, though, he ought to get cleaned up, and then roust his woman. Watching her sleep was all well and good, but Molly was twice as fun when she was awake—and Jake was eager to see her smile again.

A gentleman would at least have some coffee made for her (and her cute little butt) once he woke her. Molly would be hungry, too—so lunch in bed was probably a good idea. If Jake wanted to surprise her with all that, he'd have to shower fast.

He kept his hands to himself and stepped reluctantly away. With one last peek at Molly, Jake slipped back out to his kitchen to start the coffee maker, so it could brew while he got cleaned up. Duke padded over to the bedroom door and sprawled across the opening, watching Molly sleep inside the room with adoring eyes. Like owner, like dog— Jake leaned down and ruffled his fur, then stepped over his mutt. He hadn't felt this eager for a woman to wake up in God knew how long, and the rest of Jake's day seemed promising as hell.

Chapter Twenty-Four

THE MYSTERIOUS MR. Polk had finally returned from Atlanta. Molly had shaken off the lazy delirium of the prior day in bed with Jake to get herself up and dressed, then she'd driven to the firm early that morning to meet him.

No one had told her much about the illustrious third partner yet, but Molly found Polk to be solicitous, funny, and courtly. He clearly had a razor-sharp mind, though he seemed disinclined to make a point of it—after three hours of chatting with him in his posh office, Molly knew more about the chickens on the farm he'd grown up on than about his legal career.

Mr. Polk was shorter than she was, round and red-cheeked. He mopped at his forehead occasionally with a rumpled handkerchief, and insisted that she call him Shelby. Molly wondered what kind of information he was could gather about her from merely shooting the breeze. At some point, however, he'd leaned back in satisfaction, told her "You'll do fine," and invited Molly out to lunch.

Lunch with Shelby Polk took another two hours. He lingered over his pasta and regaled her with comic stories from his forty years of practicing law. Shelby made frequent references to his beautiful wife Sarah, and to his new grandchild. He wanted to try a bite of Molly's risotto. She felt like she'd spent the day hanging out with a favorite uncle instead of a prospective employer.

When he'd finally deposited Molly back at Maryanne's desk at the firm, there'd been nothing else for her to do, and no one left for her to meet. The firm's office manager had shooed Molly out the front door with a big smile, and told her to enjoy the rest of the afternoon. She said she'd "be in touch."

In her car, Molly pulled a printout of real estate listings from her purse and drove around for a while, trying to familiarize herself with neighborhoods and price points. She found her favorite house and parked across the street, then watched the way the sun filtered through the branches of the live oak in the yard. Molly studied the low wooden fence, and the ferns planted around the base of the raised porch. When a little white-haired woman stepped out the front door with her watering can and peered at her, Molly started her car again. The woman watered her potted flowers, and watched curiously as she drove away.

For dinner, Molly grabbed a burrito from a drive-through. She ate it sitting on her bed, flipping through news broadcasts on her small television. She hadn't heard from Jake today. Maybe he was sick of her, after spending nearly twenty-four hours with her yesterday. Maybe he'd gotten what he wanted, and didn't need her anymore. The thought was depressing. Molly threw the last half of her dinner in the trash, and went to take a shower.

She was standing in her pajamas, towel-drying her hair, when her phone finally dinged. Molly leaped for her bed, and sure enough, it was Jake.

Sorry I was MIA. In court all day.

She typed back:

No worries. I finally got to meet Shelby Polk!

She'd barely hit "send" before Jake's response popped up.

Can't wait to hear. Can I come get you?

Molly reached up to touch her dripping hair, but who was she kidding?

Sure! When?

Jake wrote:

Be there in fifteen.

Molly tossed her cell aside and grabbed her hairdryer.

THEY TOOK A winding route, but finally Jake turned onto a deserted-looking, sandy little lane. He drove to the end—nosed his car right up to a rope slung between two wooden posts—then shut off the engine.

"Let's go," he told her, blue eyes shining.

Jake pulled an old soft quilt from his trunk, and holding Molly's hand tight in his, he led her around the rope and onto a lonely stretch of beach. The sky arched wide and inky over them, dusted with a million stars. Molly craned her neck and looked, trying to pick out constellations. A slight breeze tickled her skin, the surf advanced and retreated in front of them, and Jake stood tall and strong beside her. It seemed like a dream.

He shook the quilt out and spread it on the sand, then beckoned to her. They sat side-by-side, but Jake pulled Molly down to lie flat, her head cradled on his chest.

He held her close. "Close your eyes," he whispered. "Listen."

Molly heard the waves crashing. Birds, too—not the cawing seagulls of daytime, but other, sleepier-sounding ones. The breeze rustled through the bushes and seagrass growing nearby. Jake's heart beat under her cheek, slow, steady, strong. Would it be so wrong to fall in love with a heart like that? Jake was an amazing man. If Molly got the job at his dad's firm like she hoped, she would have time to get used to the idea that he was special. Time to trust him. Time for Jake to assuage her misgivings about how fast she was losing her heart, and time to believe that there was no sordid underbelly lurking beneath the surface, waiting to ambush her.

"Now look," he murmured, and Molly did. Up at the huge orange moon hanging low in the sky, and reflected in a wavering stripe across the ocean's surface. At the pinpoints of stars winking in the vast, black velvet of space. And at the length of Jake's muscled arm pointing up.

Molly watched for a long while, and Jake seemed perfectly content to keep things as they were. But his scent and warmth, combined with the beautiful scenery, were working their magic on her. She propped herself up on an elbow and leaned down to kiss him. His lips were soft and eager against hers. Molly trailed her hand down and toyed with the button at his waistband. Jake liked that too—at first.

But then his body went stiff and he laid a hand on Molly's arm, shaking his head. Denying her small effort to take things further. Molly was confused, sort of mortified…until she noticed the sweeping beam of light heading across the sand toward them. In moments, it landed square on her face, blinding her. She reared back and covered her eyes with a pained exclamation.

"Hey, Bobby," Jake said calmly, sitting up and brushing off his shorts.

"Hey, Jake. What're ya'll doing out here?" a voice inquired, as if the answer weren't patently obvious.

Molly blinked through the glare of the flashlight, and caught sight of the patch on the other man's sleeve. Crud— *a cop.* It was like high school all over again.

"Just talking, Bobby," Jake replied, his voice heavy with fatalism. He scratched at his neck.

"Oh, is *that* all," the officer said drolly. "Not supposed to be here, you know." Molly looked around and spotted his cruiser sitting at the entrance to the little lane, blocking Jake's car.

How Bobby had drifted into that spot without Molly hearing him was something of a mystery, though she supposed she'd had other things on her mind. But Jake had heard, hadn't he? Maybe he had some practice with this sort of thing. This exact thing, in this exact spot—with *all* the ladies. Molly stifled a groan. How did he keep getting around her better judgement? It was like Jake's superpower.

"Yeah, well," Jake responded, his voice flat. "I guess you caught us." Molly tried to decipher his tone—was he attempting to mask the annoyance he was feeling? Because Officer Bobby was definitely irritating as hell. Bobby had finally, mercifully, deflected his flashlight from her face, but he was still examining her carefully.

"I don't know you," he told Molly. Turning to Jake, he demanded, "Who's this?" As if this incident could be all her fault, for being a stranger.

"This is Molly," Jake replied. "She's in town visiting while she interviews for a job." It was a simple answer, and strictly factual. But Molly wondered at the big chunks Jake had managed to leave out of the equation.

"Molly." Bobby turned that information over in his mind, studying her, and them.

"Yes sir," she murmured. She felt beyond stupid, since this man was a police officer to her, but only *Bobby* to Jake. There was clearly a bit more going on here than she understood.

Finally, the officer spoke again. "Blake know ya'll are out here?" he asked pointedly. His mouth had curved up mockingly, smug that he'd delivered a blow.

Jake reared up now, anger etching the lines of his face in the peculiar half-light of the moon and the flashlight.

"No, she does not, Bobby," he answered hotly. "And it isn't her business anyway. Besides, Molly and I were just talking," he spat out, furious.

Molly cringed. They hadn't been just talking, and she was pretty sure that was obvious to all concerned. Why Jake would deny the truth so vehemently was an interesting question, though. Maybe he was trying to avoid breaking some local ordinance about necking in public, but it also seemed possible that Molly herself was the issue.

Molly, who was not from around here, not rich, not precious in the way Jake was probably used to. Maybe the problem was that Jake hated to be caught dead with her—though why his sister would be concerned didn't make sense. Still, this felt so much like something Carter might have pulled that Molly felt paralyzed. Something warm inside her chest cowered and shook.

Jake hadn't yet managed to meet her eyes, the dog. He was probably mortified that his little romantic interlude had veered so far off course. What was a man like him doing, bringing a woman he'd just met *here,* anyway? He hadn't made the first move—unless you counted bringing Molly to the most seductive and sense-scattering location in town—but that had to count for something, right? Either way, Molly knew what she'd been about to do. She wondered, if they hadn't been interrupted, if Jake would have let her.

Officer Bobby snorted and shook his head, looking down on them in scorn. He jerked his chin toward his cruiser, and clipped his flashlight back on his belt.

"Alright, pack it up. Ya'll need to leave now," he said. He strolled over and waited near Jake's car while they stood and shook the sand off the quilt. With that accomplished, he got behind the wheel of his patrol car and trained his headlights on them. Jake handed Molly into the passenger seat and tucked the quilt back into his trunk. Once Jake started up his car, Bobby pulled clear of the lane, then sat idling until Jake backed out and drove away. The cop followed them for at least four blocks—his high-beams bright in Jake's rearview mirror—before he finally turned off and left them in peace.

"What the hell was that?" Molly asked, breaking the silence. She wasn't sure whether to laugh or cry.

Jake pulled to the side of the road and turned to her. "Molly, I am so, so sorry. That was *not* the way I thought that was gonna go."

"God, I hope not," she retorted. "If it was, we might need to talk about some things."

Jake's cell lit up in the center console, dinging several times in quick succession. Exhaling hard, he picked it up and glanced at the screen, scanning the incoming texts.

"Shit. Sorry," he said. He took another breath and stared out the windshield, thinking. Finally, Jake twisted back to face Molly and told her, "Listen, this is totally going to be even weirder, but do you mind if we swing by town and pick up my sister? Apparently, her date had to ditch her and she needs a ride home."

"Nice date," Molly frowned, wondering what on earth could be so important that a date would leave a girl high-and-dry, with no ride home.

"Yeah, I know, right?" Jake agreed. "So, what do you say? Wanna meet her?"

The chance to finally meet his sister face-to-face was too enticing to resist, especially after Bobby's little dig. "Sure," Molly said. "Love to."

DOWNTOWN, THE STREETS were packed, so once again Jake headed a couple streets over into the surrounding neighborhood of historic homes. When he turned into a driveway, pulled up behind an ancient brown Buick and shut off his car, Molly was baffled. It wasn't until they'd gotten out and stepped onto the sidewalk that she really got a good look at the place.

She stood there stupefied, blinking up at the home she'd been stalking on the internet for months—and in person earlier today. Jake began walking up the block, not realizing Molly wasn't behind him.

He stopped when she called, "Jake? Whose house is this?"

His whole face lit up, even in the darkness. "It's my Aunt Ceecee's. Well, actually...now it's going to be mine." His chest puffed out, proud as could be, and Molly gaped.

"You've got to be kidding me!" she blurted. It couldn't be true. She turned and gazed up at the adorable Victorian, with its gingerbread trim and deep front porch. It looked different at night. In the day, it was homey and welcoming. Now, it looked safe. Sheltering. She couldn't wrap her mind around the fact that it was *his*.

"*This* is your aunt's house? I mean—she sold it to you? *You* are going to live *here?*" Molly sputtered.

Jake walked back to her, shoved his hands deep in his pockets, and rocked on his toes. He turned his face up to the home looming over them and grinned.

"For the rest of my days," he boasted. He peered down at Molly, and seemed to notice for the first time that she was rooted to the spot. "Why? Don't you like it?" he asked.

"Is this St. Anne Street?" Molly inquired, needing to be sure.

Jake nodded.

"Jake, *this* is the house I told you about! The one I found online, that I said I wanted so badly. I can't believe it's yours!" The fact was both incredible, and awful, too.

"What are the odds, right?" he chuckled. "It's a small world."

"Yeah, except…" Molly fought down the surge of defeat welling inside her. She should have *known* it was out of her reach.

"Wait. What's wrong?" Jake pushed her hair back over her shoulder and cupped her cheek, searching her face.

"Well, if it's *yours*, then that means it's never going to be *mine*," Molly admitted.

Jake just smiled, though, and leaned down to drop a lingering kiss on Molly's lips. Moving back only an inch, he murmured, "I wouldn't go that far."

Slinging his arm around her shoulders, he steered her down the street—back toward all the bars and restaurants. "I'll take you by before you leave, so you can see the inside," he told her.

Molly nodded, but she was a little freaked out by the coincidence. So many coincidences, all swirling around this one man. It was unsettling—the way it felt like fate was leading her by the hand, down a path she couldn't see the end of.

She was nervous and off-balance the whole way to the bar where they were meeting his sister, but Jake didn't seem to notice. Maybe he was nervous too, introducing Molly to yet another family member. Maybe he already knew how she would react to a woman like Blake.

"After that mess with Bobby, I could use a beer," Jake smiled, uncertain as they showed their IDs and got their hands stamped at the door. "Do you want to sit and visit for a minute before we take her home?"

"Sure," Molly said. She scanned the bustling room for a familiar blonde head, but didn't see the woman she knew as Blake. She did see several colorful liquid concoctions crossing the bar, though, and the time seemed right to try one. Or four.

"There she is," Jake muttered, pointing toward the back. Molly didn't see who he was gesturing to, but then he did have several inches on her. She followed blindly behind as they wound through the throng, until Jake stopped next to a small table near the wall. A sheepish-looking brunette sat there nursing her beer. She jumped up when she saw him.

"Oh my God," she cried, hugging him. "I didn't know you were out with someone! Why didn't you tell me? I could've called a cab or something!" The woman smiled at Molly over Jake's shoulder.

Molly couldn't hear Jake's reply, but when he stepped back and gestured her forward, he said, "Healey, this is Molly." He gave Molly a tentative smile of his own. "Molly— my little sister, Healey."

Molly was both startled and confused, but she hoped it wasn't as obvious as it felt. She stuck out her hand and said, "Nice to meet you."

Jake pulled out one of the empty chairs at his sister's table, and Molly sank into it, trying to understand. His sister was a petite brown-haired woman named Healey? Not a blonde named Blake? That was bad news.

Healey was apologizing profusely again, and kept shooting inquisitive looks Molly's way. Molly wondered if Jake had mentioned her to his sister already, or if Healey was merely trying to deflect attention from the fact that her own date had basically just ditched her.

Jake didn't sit with them. "How about a margarita?" he asked her. When Molly nodded, he squeezed her shoulder, then headed to the bar.

Healey watched him go, then turned back to Molly with a friendly expression.

"So…" Molly began, unsure of how to proceed.

Healey noted her expression and launched in. "I know— I have an unusual name. It was my grandma's maiden name, if that makes any sense."

"No, it's not that," Molly explained. "I guess I just thought…" Again, she trailed off. What *had* she thought?

And why? In retrospect, none of the pieces lined up as neatly as she'd thought.

"What?"

"Well, I guess I thought your name was going to be something different," she confessed. "Are there only the two of you?"

"Yup." Healey finished off her beer, then stood and got Jake's attention across the room. She shook her empty bottle at him, and he nodded. "Wait—what did you think my name was going to be?" she asked, frowning.

"Oh, don't worry. I'm sure it's nothing. I must have misunderstood something I heard, that's all."

"Something about me? Where?" Now Healey looked as confused as Molly felt.

"At your parent's party, a few days ago. I kept hearing people ask your parents where Blake was, so I guess I just assumed that was you." Molly figured it was better to leave out the whole thing with Bobby for the time being.

"*Oh,*" Jake's sister winced and immediately looked uncomfortable.

"What?" Molly asked. "Who's Blake?"

Healey looked back toward the bar, searching for her brother. "Well…if you don't know, it's not really my place to say. You'd better ask Jake that," she said.

Suddenly, Molly felt a little ill. "Okay," she replied. "But—did I say something wrong?"

Healey saw Jake coming back and waved a little frantically at him. "Nope! Don't worry about it—but you *definitely* ought to ask him."

Naturally, when Jake sat down and looked inquisitively between them, Molly found herself blurting out, "Who is Blake?"

His face went stiff with shock, and he looked to Healey for an explanation. Molly felt even sicker.

Jake tried to laugh it off. He said, "I guess this is not the part where I say she's my sister."

"Especially since I've just met your actual sister," Molly fired back. Jake glanced at Healey again, questioning.

"She heard people mentioning her at Daddy's party," Healey explained, like she was talking to an imbecile. Molly accepted the margarita Jake offered her, and watched chunks of salt slide down the side of the sweating glass.

Jake blinked a few times and gripped the table, gathering himself. "Blake is…" he swallowed, then soldiered on, "She's a woman I used to be in a relationship with."

Healey's eyebrows flew up and she shot Jake a look of warning that Molly tried not to notice.

"We, uh…we were engaged. For a bit," he added, looking a little green himself.

"Okay," Molly hedged, watching his nervous hands, and his sister's. "Are you—still in love with her or something?" She had no idea what else to ask, but something was off here. Big time. The looks passing between brother and sister communicated so much, but not nearly enough.

"*No.* Definitely not." Jake was firm on that, but still looked around semi-desperately. "Hey, uh—I'm gonna hit the head. I'll be back in a minute." And then he bolted, zeroing in on the bathrooms at the back of the bar like a guided missile.

Molly turned to Healey. "What just happened?" she asked, trying not to completely freak out. Jake was engaged? To *Blake?* That was one scenario she hadn't let herself consider. Suddenly, she could see Blake's face in her head, clear as day, telling her friend about her fiancée Jackson.

"It's okay," Healey soothed. "Don't worry, you just caught him off-guard, that's all."

Now that the information was out in the open, Jake's sister seemed more inclined to talk about it. Molly figured it was as good a time as any to try to get some more information.

"Were they together very long?" she wondered.

Healey explained that she and Blake had gone to a private girl's school together, and that her brother had dated Bess off and on during high school. When Blake graduated and ended up at UNC with Jake, they dated casually some more. That might have been the extent of it, if their parents weren't good friends and always urging on the relationship.

Molly admitted, "I met your folks a couple times over the weekend, but they didn't say anything." As an afterthought, she added, "I'm here interviewing at your dad's firm."

Healey nodded—she'd known that part.

"I hope they don't think I'm interfering or something," Molly said.

Healey brushed that thought away. "Don't worry about that—Blake's parents are close family friends, like I said. If anything, I'm sure Mama would just be annoyed that all her and Ms. Sutton's arranging wasn't going to work this time."

"But—" Molly knew Jake would be back any minute. "Are you still friends with her?"

"For me, Blake is totally that friend that you can't shake because you've known them so long," Healey declared. "She's a pain in the ass, though."

"Were they good together?" Molly hated how masochistic that sounded, spilling from her lips.

"God, no. They were the world's worst mismatch. Personally, I was relieved when it was over. I could never understand what he saw in her, but sometimes Jake's just too damn nice." They saw Jake emerge from the small hallway that the restrooms were in, but he stopped on his way to chat with a couple of guys he seemed to know. Healey rushed on, "I always felt like my brother was getting railroaded into that mess. They would have been miserable long-term."

"How long were they engaged, exactly?" Molly prodded, studying Jake and weighing what she'd heard.

"I dunno—a few months, give or take," Healey stated vaguely. "Why, you want the job?" Her eyes twinkled, and she poked Molly in the arm.

Molly had been caught staring. "Um, not sure yet," she smiled back, trying to figure out where all this was going—and what it meant for her and Jake as a couple.

"If you do, I say go for it!" Healey enthused. "He needs someone like you."

"Thanks, I think," Molly answered. "Hey, why weren't *you* at that party, anyway?"

"Hot date," Healey smirked, swinging her foot back and forth. "Totally on the down low, though, so don't tell my brother. He thinks I had to work."

Jake wandered back over to their table, watching the two women warily. "Ladies," he said. "I thought I'd run and get the car, so you two don't have to hike back over to Ceecee's. You okay waiting here until I get back?" Molly blinked. Jake hadn't even touched the beer he'd gotten for himself—the one he'd specifically said he wanted.

Healey shrugged and slid his bottle in front of herself. "We're cool. Right, Molly?"

Molly nodded, Jake nodded back, and then he was striding away. She grimaced, then turned back to Jake's sister. Molly wanted to avoid the Blake topic until she decided how she felt about it.

She said, "So…that hot date—same guy who ditched you tonight?"

"Yes, but it's not as bad as it looks," Healey explained. "He got called away for a work emergency."

"Why not just tell Jake that?" Molly wondered.

Healey's mouth twisted to the side. "Well…"

"Is it someone he knows?"

She nodded, looking guilty.

Molly's eyebrows shot up. "One of his friends?"

"Please don't say anything to him," Healey begged. "It's still new. If Jake gets involved it will be *way* weirder than it already is."

Molly shook her head. Weirdness was rapidly becoming an Alexander family trait.

LATER, IN THE car, Jake sat beside Molly—holding her hand and shooting her questioning looks. This man, who she had allowed herself to fall for, had been in a relationship—a *serious* relationship where rings changed hands—with that crazy woman Blake. Molly was kidding herself if she thought that wasn't a big deal.

There was no use pretending it could have been anyone other than the woman she kept seeing. For one, Healey had mentioned the Suttons by name. Plus, they'd been running into people all over town who knew Jake's former fiancée, Molly realized. People who were accustomed to them being together, and maybe even liked that woman better than Jake. No wonder Molly had gotten an odd reception from some of them.

What on earth was Jake doing with Molly, then? Well— she could answer that question easily enough. She was the perfect material for a rebound fling, wasn't she? He could get his rocks off, exorcise his former fiancée from his system, and then Molly would be gone again—back to Boston. And maybe, if Jake was truly awful and intervened with his father, he would never have to see Molly again.

The trouble was, even Molly couldn't convince herself that the man she'd gotten to know in the last two weeks was anything but sweet and kind. Jake didn't come off like a schemer, not once you got to know him. She'd always trusted her gut before, but now she didn't know what to think. They obviously needed to talk about this, but Molly wasn't entirely sure she wanted to hear any of Jake's answers.

Chapter Twenty-Five

JAKE JOGGED THE whole way back to Ceecee's to get his car, so he could swing back and quickly pick up Molly and his sister. He wasn't sure why he hurried—they seemed like they were getting along well enough. Besides, the worst secret was out in the open now. There was really nothing else to tell, so it must be safe to leave them alone again. He just didn't want to prolong any awkwardness, that was all. Or have them wonder what happened to him.

As it was, Jake knew he was acting completely juvenile. First running off to the bathroom, and then fleeing the premises altogether. He'd panicked, plain and simple. Even though he'd done nothing to be ashamed of—and had never intended to keep the information from Molly in the first place—he sure was *acting* guilty.

Molly's expression had been difficult to read when Jake dropped his little bomb. She didn't *seem* mad, but who could tell? She could've been putting up a front because Healey was sitting right there.

Once he reached Ceecee's, Jake looked up at the house and thought about Molly's reaction to it. Now that his life was entering one heck of a growing pain, he couldn't quite believe the house was really going to be his—until the transfer of the deed was finalized, Jake was living in fear that Ceecee would renege and take it all back. So, when Molly started losing her mind over the house earlier, he'd hesitated to mention that it was going to be his. Jake had wanted to just sit back and enjoy the way her whole face went soft and yearning as she gazed at the place he planned to live in until he was old and gray.

He hadn't been able to hold it in, though. His excitement was too big, too uncontainable. Ceecee had finally given him the house, and by some stroke of provenance, Molly was already in love with it. If he could get Molly to fall in love with *him*, too—now that would be the ultimate victory.

He picked up the girls without incident, but the car ride to his sister's place was terrifyingly silent. Jake fretted over what else Healey might've told Molly, because Molly wouldn't look at him. Instead, she toyed with her hair and stared out the side window, way too quiet.

In the back seat, Healey texted furiously and ignored them both, as if Jake was a taxi driver and not her big brother. When he dropped his sister off at her place, Jake got out and walked her to the door. He was hoping for information on how it had gone with Molly, to arm himself for the next part of the drive. But when Healey finally opened her mouth, it wasn't to help—it was to spit venom at him.

Keeping her face averted from view of the car, Healey hissed, "You might have mentioned to Molly how *recently* Bess dumped your lying ass, you dog! What the hell were you thinking?"

"I did not lie," Jake protested hotly. "What're you talking about?"

"Molly seems nice," Healey complained. "I don't want you to hurt her."

"That is the exact opposite of what I want to do."

"Well then get your shit together, and start acting right!" Healey scolded. Then she swooped through her building's front door, and slammed it in Jake's face. He scrubbed a hand over his head and got back in the Audi.

BACK AT HIS place, Molly still hadn't said much, trailing after him through the foyer hand-in-hand, but deep in thought. Jake sank into his recliner in the living room, then pulled her to sit in his lap. She was pensive. Instead of cuddling up against his chest, she straddled his thighs and perched back on her heels—facing him, but still keeping her distance. Molly's back was ramrod straight, and she gazed down at Jake, looking concerned. He fiddled with the silky ends of her hair, where it fell below her breasts.

Why had Jake brought her to one of the most obvious high school make-out spots in town earlier? In retrospect, it seemed so dumb, but now that he considered it...Jake supposed he'd developed a heretofore unconscious need to start mixing the woman of his future with memories from his past.

Jake could almost pretend there had never been anyone in his life except Molly, and at the same time he could encourage her to grow some serious roots here. The more places he took her, the more places they made happy memories, the more Wilmington would feel like home to her.

Damn Bobby Palmer, though. That prick had been an obstructionist son-of-a-bitch back in high school, and clearly not much had changed. Jake suspected that Molly had been about to make his night vastly more interesting out there on that beach blanket—before Officer Bob showed up. Hell if that wouldn't have been a memory for the ages. Instead, Jake should probably be grateful Bobby hadn't tagged them with an indecency fine. The dude probably made a habit of driving by that spot, looking for kids to shine his flashlight on. Bob probably *loved* that part of his job.

"I'm sorry about the way everything turned out tonight. That whole thing with Bob…but also the way you had to find out about me and Blake," Jake began.

"I wish you would've just told me," Molly said. "So many things would've made a lot more sense the last two weeks."

"I know. I meant to tell you—"

She cut him off. "Why didn't you?"

"Well, it never seemed to be the right time," Jake admitted. "To be honest, when you and I are together…I'm not thinking of anything else but us."

"Oh." That got her thinking.

Duke padded over and rested his chin on the arm of the chair, blinking his huge liquid eyes at her. Molly stroked his nose.

"Yeah, *oh*," Jake echoed. He traced the outside of her arms with his fingers. "Stuff that happened before you feels like it belongs to a different life."

Molly shifted closer on his legs, and leaned forward to kiss him softly. A small offering, but Jake held onto it.

"I saw her, you know," she said.

That was unwelcome news. "Really? Where?" What must Molly have thought of Bess? Or of him, for being with her?

"At the coffee shop near the B&B."

Jake nodded. That made sense—Blake's parents lived near there.

"And…I think I saw you guys have a fight on the street one time," Molly admitted. She peeked at him from under her lashes, waiting to see how he reacted to that bit of information.

He couldn't stop the hot flush that hit his cheeks. "Well, that sucks," he complained. "I'm sorry you witnessed that."

"She's pretty, but she seems kind of mean," Molly confessed. "It's hard to understand what you saw in her."

The longer Jake was apart from Bess, the more difficult that question got to answer. He shrugged, knowing how lame he must sound. "There was a little bit of 'the evil you know,' I suppose." He stretched up and kissed Molly, longer this time, lingering. "Plus—even a weed can look pretty if you've never seen a rose," he murmured. Molly was *definitely* a rose. His cheeks heated again, and he wondered a little frantically where the hell *that* notion had come from. Not that he didn't mean it, but...if Tim, for example, were to hear Jake spouting poetry like that, he'd make Jake's life hell for the rest of his days.

Molly didn't look like she minded. Her eyes went soft, along with her body. Jake hugged her to his chest, and stood. He sent Duke to his doggie bed in the corner, and carried Molly off to his bedroom.

He thought he must have explained the Bess situation well enough, because Molly appeared to believe him. She wouldn't have fallen into bed with him again, otherwise. Jake hadn't even had to go into any details, other than why they broke up—Bess was temperamental, selfish, and controlling—and whether Jake was truly over her.

He was *so* over her. Hell, even his dog knew the difference between a bad woman and a good one. Duke had always tolerated Bess from afar—keeping a watchful eye on her from his bed in the corner, where she couldn't snap at him for muddying her skirts with his paws. But from the start, Duke had followed Molly all over Jake's condo, always tried to muscle his way onto her lap on the couch, and would've shimmied up to sleep next to her in the bed if Jake hadn't given him the stink eye for it.

Speaking of which, Jake had been mostly careful to leave the dog out of the bedroom, just in case. As attached as he was to Molly, who knew how he'd take her and Jake getting frisky? Except earlier, Jake had been so grateful that the Bess revelation was blowing over with hardly a ripple in the water, that he'd kind of…forgotten about Duke. Jake couldn't remember if he'd latched the door—and given the way his woman had her legs wrapped around him, he could hardly bring himself to care. But…

He felt his mutt jump up on the foot of the bed, though Molly didn't seem to notice. Jake wasn't exactly in a position to do much about it—he had Molly tucked under him and breathless, letting out little panting moans with his every thrust. If Jake stopped now, they'd both be left high and dry. Molly was so close, he could tell—just another minute or two and then she'd be soaring, and Jake could let himself go, too.

He heard snuffling around their feet and…was that a wet nose on Jake's knee? Molly's legs were pressed tight to Jake's hips—it was hard to tell. Jake tried to remain immune to the canine interference, intent on his end goal—and mercifully, he succeeded. Molly came with an agonized-sounding gasp, tensing all over beneath him. Jake growled at the exquisite sound of it, and rapidly followed her over the edge, like he always did. *Nothing* finished him off faster than Molly's bliss—she was absolutely incredible. Jake buried his face in her neck with one open-mouthed kiss. His breath felt hot, blowing across her damp skin.

And then—right there next to Molly's ear, there was a serious-sounding, very loud *bark*. Molly jumped, and Jake froze, clutching her tight against his chest. He turned his head to look at his dog.

"Down boy," he said carefully, keeping his voice even and firm.

Instead, Duke emitted a rolling growl that ended in another sharp bark. Moving slowly, Jake rolled to the side, gently pulled out of Molly's body, and put himself between her and the dog.

"Duke," he warned, nudging the animal away. "What's up with you?"

But his dog leapt adroitly over them both, landed on Molly's free side and belly-crawled close to her. Whining softly, Duke began sniffing frantically all up and down her side. He was obviously worried. But when his wet nose connected with her skin, Molly began to giggle. She tried to pull up the sheet—tangled down around her and Jake's legs—to cover herself. Her laugh seemed to be the sign of health the dog was looking for, because Duke launched himself at her—licking her face extravagantly, even for a 75-pound hound.

The dog was definitely relieved that his master hadn't murdered Molly. She gasped out loud shrieks of laughter, trying to extricate herself, but Duke wouldn't back off. Jake had to laugh, too. His dog had lost his damn marbles over the woman, just like every other red-blooded male in creation. He really couldn't blame the guy.

Jake stood and stepped into the bathroom, disposed of the condom and grabbed a towel. When he came back out, Duke stopped licking Molly only long enough to fix him with a baleful glare. Jake stopped laughing at the ridiculous sight, and frowned at his dog. The dog resumed his sloppy, overjoyed kisses.

"Naw," Jake said drily. "My dog doesn't like you at all."

"Oh God," Molly gasped wildly, trying to fend off the effusive mutt. "Make him stop!"

"Like he'd even let me," Jake muttered. The furry traitor. "Woman, I cannot even believe you turned my own dog against me." He chuckled, watching her. "You've got some nerve."

She had both hands raised now, blocking her face from Duke's efforts—but he only redirected, licking her palms and forearms into kingdom come.

"You're gonna have to do it, you know," Jake told her. "That dang beast thinks I was mauling you. If I try to touch you now, he's liable to take my whole hand off for messing with his mama."

He smirked as Molly attempted to take a firm tone with the animal through her giggles, guiding the mutt off the side of the bed to the floor. Duke parked it on his haunches right there on the rug, gazing up at her devotedly. He was clearly prepared to defend her honor again at the drop of a hat. Jake listened as she cooed at his erstwhile canine friend, and was struck suddenly by his thoughts.

Mama, he'd said. His throat closed. *Mama.* Abruptly, he wanted nothing more than to make this gorgeous woman a mother. With an utterly primal, bone-deep determination, he knew for a fact that *he'd* be the one putting a baby in her belly someday. Maybe not right away, but at some point in the future: Jake would be the man who made Molly's belly grow round with his child—he, and no one else. He tensed. If any other man even *thought* such a thing about her, he'd kill him dead where he stood. Molly was *his*, damn it.

She blinked at him, and Jake realized that he'd been scowling at her and the dog for way too long.

"Everything okay?" she asked warily. "I swear I didn't do it on purpose." He must look furious, Jake thought.

"Just perfect, darlin'," he assured her. Carefully, slowly, he slid into the bed and drew her back into his arms, keeping a watchful eye on his traitorous mutt all the while.

Moments later, Molly's phone started dinging on his nightstand, lit up with incoming texts. At first, she just groaned and rolled over, trying to ignore it. Eventually curiosity won out, because she reached for the cell and started to mutter grumpily.

"No. Oh, no. No, no, what is *wrong* with me?" Molly wailed. "What did I *do*?"

She battled out from under the twisted sheet and stared at the screen in disgust—and maybe a little horrified amazement.

"What's going on?" Jake asked.

"I—I can't believe…I'm usually so careful… but I think I screwed up bad."

Jake thought for a minute, trying to let his brain catch up. It was nighttime, so no way was she late for an interview or an appointment. This had to be personal.

"Not a work thing?" he confirmed.

"Nope this is much worse. The other night…"

His eyebrows shot up and his eyes themselves narrowed. She could not have any problem with how things went down either of the last two nights. *Heh*. Literally. Jake smirked.

"No! It's not *that*," Molly claimed. "But the other night I think I must have given out my real number to someone. Oh my God."

Jake had to smile. Lord, she was something else. "Anything but *that*."

"I *know*, right?" she murmured, agonized.

"Who'd you give it to?" Jake asked. She'd literally been *on* him—sitting on his lap—for half the night. Where'd the girl find the time?

"That DJ!" she cried. "He kept asking and asking, and I just blurted it out without thinking! I wasn't even that tipsy—I don't know what happened." Molly's phone had dinged twice more during her recitation, and Jake tried not to laugh. Dude was *committed*.

"Gimme your phone," he offered.

Molly looked a little wary, clutching it to her chest. "Why?"

"Because I'm gonna clean up your mess, that's why. Now hand it over." No need to fill her in on how pissed Jake was that some dickhead was macking on his girl—while she was *in his bed*—or that said perp was now neck-and-neck with his dog in ruining the lazy post-coital vibe Jake had been hoping to encourage. No, his motives were strictly based in goodwill, as far as Molly was concerned.

She unlocked the home screen and slowly extended her phone toward him. Jake snatched the device and scanned the flurry of "Hey baby" texts the guy had sent. Then Jake fired off one of his own.

WHO IS THIS?

Then, not liking the tone of the guy's reply, Jake tapped out another. DJ Dick's respect level was not improving, though, so Jake decided it was time to stop fucking around and *end* this. He called the guy.

"Hey baby," the DJ answered, creepy as a nightcrawler.

"You got the wrong number in a big way, asshole," Jake growled back, aggressive and nasty.

There was a loaded pause. "Are you—is this Molly's number?" the guy tried. Stupidly stubborn, if you asked Jake.

"Who the fuck is Molly?" Jake demanded, winking at her. Molly gave him a giddy thumbs-up, wreathed in smiles.

"Um…" The other dude hesitated, trying to suss out his next move.

"Stop texting me, or I will come and find you, mother—" The line went dead. Excellent. DJ Dick had finally found his tiny little brain—the one up top, anyway.

Molly was still kneeling in Jake's messed-up sheets. She'd put on his t-shirt from earlier, and had her hands clapped over her mouth. Her eyes were wide with admiration.

Jake blinked at her and held up her phone, the soul of innocence. "*Huh*," he said. "That's weird. He just hung up."

As he'd hoped, Molly pulled her hands away from her face and began cracking up.

"Problem solved," he grinned back.

"Oh my God, Jake! You were amazing!" she squealed, bouncing on her knees a little. She was laughing and gazing at him with such an expression of awe and fascination—eyes shining, hair tousled, shoulder tan where his shirt had slipped aside…Molly was so damn beautiful it hurt.

Jake raised her phone, and held down the camera icon, taking a whole burst of twenty or more photos of the glorious angel that had somehow landed smack in the middle of his life with no warning whatsoever. Molly grabbed for it once she realized, and Jake had to wrestle it away from her and hold it way over her head so he could text the pictures to himself. But he finally got it done, and set the cell on the nightstand behind him. When Molly came at him again Jake was ready, and let her tackle him flat.

He spread-eagled across his mattress, and let her straddle his stomach. He grinned up at her, just enjoying the view.

As usual, Molly gave as good as she got, though—she swiped her cell off the table and promptly aimed the camera straight at him, taking photo after photo while Jake kept smiling into her eyes.

He wondered though—would his feelings show through? Could the feelings inside a person's heart and mind actually be captured by that tiny little lens? Was there some sort of alchemy of recordation, in which a person's innermost thoughts were transmuted into photographic evidence?

He hoped not. Jake barely understood what was going on with himself—no need to frighten a commitment-phobe like Molly before he'd lined up his evidence and compiled his case. If Jake intended to win her over for good (and of course, he did) his case was going to have to be airtight…especially if he expected to overcome problems like Blake and Molly's dad.

THEY SLEPT IN the next morning. Jake hadn't shopped, though—so with apologies murmured into Molly's groggy ear, he clipped on Duke's leash and went out to get them some lunch. Something about the occasion was calling for big messy subs, layered in cold cuts.

When he noticed the touristy boutique next to the sandwich place, Jake decided to pop in there, too. He breezed through the aisles feeling shady as all-get-out in his wrinkled t-shirt and frayed ball cap—but he still left with a cute tank top, skirt, hat and pair of flip flops for Molly to wear when she left his apartment today. Mrs. Denson was sweet, but she was also the world's worst gossip. If she caught Jake returning Molly to the B&B wearing the same clothes she'd left in the night before...well, Jake may as well pack up and leave town right now, because the torches and pitchforks would not be far behind.

He hooked the bags of food and clothes on his arm and grinned the whole way home. Molly might be a city girl—and a Yankee to boot—but no way was she going to do the walk of shame home from Jake's house. He was about to feed her and dress her up in Tar Heel blue with a camo snapback—just like the Carolina boy he was. She was going to look *amazing*.

Chapter Twenty-Six

ON MONDAY, SHELBY Polk announced his imminent retirement in a late afternoon meeting at the firm, then invited everyone to join him at an impromptu party at his country club the next night to celebrate. The legal community's rumor mill had gotten the event right, it appeared—they'd merely connected it to the wrong partner. Jake and Maryanne had each called Molly separately to tell her the news and invite her to the party.

Molly hadn't expected to attend so many fancy parties—and definitely hadn't packed for them. At first, she'd cobbled together a new outfit from parts of other outfits she'd worn the week before—a ruffled cream shell from one day, a black pencil skirt from another. Some modest, black leather work pumps, benched in favor of her favorite lucky heels. Her hair hadn't been behaving, so she'd put it up. She'd been fairly confident in the results, too—Molly thought she'd looked polished and professional. At least, she did until she considered whether Tansy or Blake might wear that outfit to an evening soiree at a country club.

Instead, Molly had decided to recycle her dark violet dress from the bar association party, and hope for the best. She'd originally worn the dress as a bridesmaid in a friend's wedding years ago, before altering it into a cocktail gown for this trip. Now that she was at the club, though—and saw all the trendy pastel cocktail dresses the other women were sporting—Molly felt positively wintry in comparison. Dowdy and unfashionable.

Across the room, she spotted Jake's sister Healey in conversation with another woman. Molly made her way over, happy to see a friendly face in the throng. Except, Healey didn't look that happy to see her.

She said, "Hey, Molly." But then the woman she was standing with turned around, and Molly went stiff. "This is my friend Blake," Healey continued, introducing them like it was no big deal. "We went to school together."

Naturally, Blake looked fantastic. She was wearing a melon-colored chiffon confection—with a jeweled halter neck that bared her toned shoulders, and a full skirt that floated around her legs when she walked. Her hair was sleek and shining, like a halo. Her strappy, nude-colored wedges were the exact shade of her skin, and made her petite legs look feminine and pretty. Blake's manicured toenails matched her dress perfectly. Her fingernails were done in a paler version of the same color, beautifully setting off the huge diamond on her hand. Molly choked on her rosé. Diamond. On her *hand*.

Blake laughed. "Call me Bess," she said, shaking hands. Her left hand held a half-full glass of champagne in addition to the ring, but the tiny bubbles in the glass couldn't come close to competing with the flash of that stone. Molly blinked quickly, suddenly unsteady on her heels. Bess smirked at Healey, who looked brittle to say the least.

"At some point, you're going to have to start introducing me as your sister, you know," Blake drawled. There was an edge to it, though, as if she knew Healey would shank her, given half the chance. Like Blake might do the same. She turned back to Molly, not bothering to hide that she was sizing her up.

"Leelee's brother and I are engaged," Blake explained then. *Territory staked and claimed.*

"Were," Healey muttered. "And I go by Healey now."

Blake flicked angry eyes at Jake's sister, and then smiled a little ferociously back at Molly, waiting. Maybe she'd seen Molly and Jake enter together tonight, or maybe Blake was just guessing. Molly didn't think it mattered much, either way.

She forced words out through numb lips, since everyone clearly expected a response from her. "I'm in town interviewing with Mr. Alexander's firm," she explained, moving her mouth into what she hoped was a polite smile. Two weeks—she'd been falling for this shrew's man for over two flipping weeks. *Oh God.*

Bess emitted a pleasant little hum. "You must be the one Jackson has been chauffeuring all over town." She waved at another acquaintance nearby, already bored. By way of goodbye, she said, "It was so nice to meet you." Blake skipped over to a clutch of women near the bar. Confident. Unthreatened by a mere interloper.

"*So* nice," Healey growled as Blake left them. "Molly, listen to me," she insisted, facing Molly. Her face was urgent.

"How long?" Molly murmured, watching Bess.

"Molly—" Healey tried again.

"I said, how *long?*" Molly nearly shouted.

"How long what?"

"How long have they been back together?" She turned on Healey, another thought occurring to her. "Or did they ever split up to begin with? Were you just lying for him that night?"

"No! Oh my God, *no.* I swear to God they split up. And as far as I know, they haven't gotten back together again. Molly—"

"She's wearing a freaking ring, *Leelee*," Molly spat.

"I don't know why she has that on," Healey sputtered. "She's a lunatic."

"Has Jake been cheating on that woman with me this whole time?" Molly inquired. She needed to know. As much as it hurt, as much as that old, familiar pain sliced her in two, she had to know.

Healey's face was serious, intent. She shook her head and stared like she was trying to talk a maniac out of exploding. "*No*, Molly," she said. She'd been too loud, though, and a couple nearby shot them an inquisitive look. Healey smiled innocently at them, then lowered her voice. "Jake broke up with Bess before he ever laid a hand on you. He would never do that to you."

Molly noticed Healey's peculiar choice of words. Apparently, Jake *would* do that to Blake, though. The only problem was, Molly had been in Blake's shoes before. The distinction mattered to her—a lot.

The night's honoree, Mr. Polk, strolled up to them. Molly had to make small talk about his plans for retirement for a few excruciating minutes before she could excuse herself. Healey hurriedly broke away as well, and came charging after her. She caught up with Molly just outside the ladies' room.

Molly whirled on her. "Assuming you are telling the truth—and I'm not convinced you are—how long before I started sleeping with your brother did he dump his fiancée?"

Healey shrugged, but her eyes were shifty. "I'm not sure—"

"How. *Long?*"

"Um, maybe a day or two after you got here?" Healey tried. "But no way were you two getting busy that soon, right?" It was clear she wasn't sure of the timeline, and didn't want to get Jake in any more trouble than he already was. But that ship had sailed.

Molly knew exactly when the breakup was. "Blake threw that damn ring in his face, didn't she? Right on the street?" Who knew why she bothered, though—she'd seen it with her own eyes. Jake had called her that night, too, weird and out of sorts. The very next day, he'd kissed her in a garden full of flowers.

Healey stayed silent, but her expression was answer enough.

Molly nodded. What a fool she'd been. She strode into the ladies' room and locked herself in a stall, ignoring Healey's knocking and her hissed requests that Molly *open up*. At last, the voices of other women entered the room, and Healey was forced to relent. Her steps retreated, and Molly imagined that she was headed right for her reprobate brother. Much as she would've liked to stay in that stall for the rest of the night, though, Molly would have to break out of this den of vipers now.

She followed Healey out and took stock. Jake's sister was caught up in a conversation with her mother and another woman. Blake was holding court across the room. And Jake himself was right where Molly had left him—seated at a table of other attorneys talking shop. He rose when he spotted her, and sauntered her way.

Molly's heart pounded. She had to get away, but Jake had brought her here. Short of grand theft auto, she couldn't leave without making an enormous scene in front of her potential employer. So, she stayed where she was—rooted to the spot and forced to witness the way Healey grabbed Jake's arm when he passed, and the way his sister pulled him down to whisper urgently in his ear. Jake barely paused to listen—his steps didn't slow and his smile didn't waver as he approached Molly. Healey looked like she was waiting for catastrophe to erupt.

Jake sidled up beside Molly, where she stood on the side of the country club dining room. A small dance floor had been set up in the center. Earlier, Molly had discovered that she could watch the other invitees in relative anonymity by sticking to the shadows right where she now stood. Sadly, *some* guests had still noticed her.

"Are you trying to kill me with that dress?" Jake inquired.

Molly eyed him speculatively, smoothing her palms over the dark violet silk that covered her hips. She'd had enough champagne to realize that some courage was in order.

"Oh honey, if I wanted to kill you, you'd already be dead," she smiled. Yes, that was the tone she wanted. Implacable. Like he couldn't hurt her.

Jake watched her face a moment, looking wary, but then dragged his eyes down over her figure. He *laughed*, damn him. Someone else had been hitting the bubbly too, it seemed.

"Well you've got that right," he agreed, before plopping into one of the gold bamboo chairs at the abandoned table next to her. Molly looked at him—knees splayed wide, casually watching the dance floor. She was surprised that the delicate chair could hold his height and weight when he sprawled like that. Molly perched carefully in the chair next to his, curious to see what he'd say.

"Healey told me you just met Bess," he commented, but he didn't look at her. There hadn't been time for his sister to say much more than that. Molly wondered whether Jake could guess, whether he even realized that everything was over between them.

"What did you think of her?" he asked casually. He paused, then added nonsensically, "Would you believe that's her real hair color?"

Oh God. He was *drunk*. There was no other explanation for why he would say such a thing to her. Molly tried to order her thoughts before speaking. She gazed at his fiancée's sleek platinum bob across the room, then thought of her own long brown locks. Her hair had been unruly since she was at least thirteen, and the most unremarkable mud-brown in creation.

"No, I can't," she admitted. "But that's certainly not all I can't believe." Had that really just come out of her mouth? So much for playing it cool.

Jake snorted, not seeming to pick up on her message. Oblivious.

Molly turned to study his profile. "Does she make you happy?" She wondered, of course, but that didn't mean she had to ask him right then. The night was just full of surprises, though. Much like Jake.

He didn't answer right away, watching Blake dance with an older man who was expertly maneuvering her around the floor.

"Not anymore," Jake muttered quietly.

Molly fought for composure. She wanted to cry. She wanted to fight. Instead, she said quickly, "What I meant was—"

Jake held up a hand. "It's okay," he interrupted.

"Does she feel like home?" Molly asked softly, unable to hold the question in. Maybe he wouldn't hear her, though. The music was certainly loud enough, back there by the speakers.

But of course, she couldn't get off that easily. Jake turned to her, brow furrowed. "Home?"

Molly nodded, turning away so she didn't have to meet his eyes. "Presumably you'll be spending a lot of time with her. A lot of...years." She gagged a little on the words, but still barreled on. "Shouldn't Blake feel like home?" Molly would not think of the hours she and Jake had spent companionably together, in which he'd begun to feel like *her* home. She would *not*.

Jake contemplated this idea, then answered a little faintly, "It would've been fine. I guess."

Even Molly, with three hasty glasses of champagne under her belt, could see his uncertainty. *It would've been fine*—if Molly hadn't blown into town to tempt him.

"Good. Fine is good. Fine is—comfortable," she yammered. "That's a lot better than what I knew, anyway. Our home life sucked." She drew out the syllables of the last word for a beat or two, wondering if she was only talking about her childhood, or also this present conversation.

Molly couldn't bring herself to sing that woman's praises to Jake. She just...couldn't. So "fine" was what it would have to be. She glanced at him, and watched as he squeezed his eyes shut, exhaling sharply and shaking his head as if to clear it.

"What?" she asked, curious.

"It's only—" He stopped. Thought. "Only...aw, heck. I've completely lost my train of thought."

Molly raised an eyebrow at him. She hoped it was effective—she'd paid fifteen dollars to get the damn thing waxed before she came down here, and it damn well better look imperial.

"All I can think about is how to get you to say *sucked* like that again," Jake admitted, only a little sheepishly.

Molly felt a bitter smile playing at the corners of her mouth. Her eyes opened and closed in slow motion. The air rushed in and out of her lungs. This man was just too much.

"Oh, I know way better words than that," she murmured softly. If Jake was going to insist on flirting shamelessly with her—despite what she now knew—Molly was going to make him suffer for it.

He studied her face, nonplussed. "I'll just bet you do," he retorted. He coughed a little, then slapped his hands on his knees and hauled himself to his feet.

Molly knew words all right. Words like *Cheater*. Words like *Goodbye*.

"Well," Jake blurted, seeming to be at a loss for words. "Back at it, I guess." He gave her a little salute, then strolled off into the crowd. He glanced back at Molly once or twice, though, a measuring expression on his face.

Molly moved to intercept a white-jacketed waiter, who was passing by with a fresh tray of sparkling champagne flutes. Snagging a glass, she drank deeply, then muttered to herself, "Oh yeah, that went well."

She watched Jake's mother speak to him. Moments later, Jake was cutting in on Blake and her current partner. Molly watched how Jake spun her politely around the dance floor without ever making eye contact. Their mouths moved, but Jake looked wooden. Well, of course he did. His party was over, and he probably knew it.

Molly had finally exhausted her emotional reserves for the night. Her feet ached, her bra chafed, and a bone-deep weariness was dragging down her every move. So, she gathered up her wrap and her little sparkling clutch, then found Jake's father and Mr. Polk and said her farewells.

"God *damn* it," Molly grumbled on her way out of the dining room, and hoped she hadn't said it too loud. She made her way through the little knots of doyennes littering her path to the lobby of the club, where she hoped she could call a cab.

JAKE BEGAN TEXTING within minutes of her departure. Molly had only made it as far as the portico outside—the valet podium was empty, and cell service was lousy. She was trying to search for the number of a taxi company on her phone, when it began dinging.

> Where'd you go? I can't find u.

Molly scowled.

> I left.

Jake fired back:

> What? Why?

She didn't answer. Who had the time?

Jake didn't give up, though.

> Molly? Where r u?

Grudgingly, Molly tapped out her reply. The last thing she needed was him raising an alarm.

> I'm outside.

Unsurprisingly, Jake was ready for that.

> Wait there—I'm coming out.

Molly groaned. There was no justice in the world, none at all—and especially not for her.

Chapter Twenty-Seven

J AKE HURRIED OUTSIDE, waved away the cab Molly was trying to get into, and convinced her to come with him to his car. She got in the Audi readily enough, but she sighed heavily when he fumbled with his keys, trying to start the car and get the A/C running.

"Jake, *stop*," Molly insisted, exasperated. "You've had too much to drink. You can't drive right now." He knew that. Of course he knew that. But having Molly and Bess in the same room—unexpectedly—had done a number on him. Jake was all tied into knots, afraid of what his ex-fiancée might have done. Molly's expression was scaring the shit out of him right now—and Jake was regretting every beer he'd pounded while trying to calm down.

Desperate to convince himself that everything was still okay between them, Jake scanned her face. Jesus, he loved her. Before Molly could even blink, he lurched over and grabbed the woman. One hand behind her neck and the other snaking around her waist, Jake set his mouth on hers with ferocious intensity.

He couldn't help it. He wanted in: into her body, into her heart, into her life. He hadn't been this tipsy in years, and it was messing with his usual control. Jake felt unrestrained, without an ounce of his usual gentility. Usually it was glorious to be that way with Molly, like the two of them were capable of soaring, together. And at first, Molly didn't resist him—her bones melted against Jake and her kiss was just as fervent as his.

At the light touch of her hand on his cheek, Jake paused—and Molly pulled back. He leaned his forehead against hers while he caught his breath and gathered his wits. Molly was unnervingly quiet, so Jake rushed to fill the silence in the car.

"Why are you pulling away?" He glanced around the club's parking lot, then turned back to her and tried a smile. "I'd assure you that I don't bite, but that wouldn't be entirely true, now would it?" Normally, Molly liked him mischievous, but not now.

"C'mon, Jake," she groaned, shaking her head.

He tried again. "Girl," he breathed against her sweet rose lips. "I can't seem to get the taste of you off my mind."

Molly's lips quirked up, except...she was anything but happy. "Me either," she agreed. "But I wonder—why are you so desperate right now?" There was an edge there, along the underside of her words, and Jake's spine shivered to hear it.

His answer was the bald-faced, unvarnished truth. "Because I know you're leaving soon, and I don't want you to go. It scares me."

He wanted to get Molly to trust him and give him her heart. He'd been looking for a way to tie this woman to him, searching for the connection that would bind them together for longer than this short interlude they'd had. Jake hadn't found it and it was killing him. He'd been barreling down the track for weeks, giddy with possibility, but now he'd hit a wall. If Molly left before Jake could scale it, what then?

She bit her lip. "Well, I now know that you're getting married soon, and I don't want you to do that, either," she stated calmly, mirroring his tone. Not a word about fear, though.

Jake froze, and felt the blood drain from his face. He sat slowly, carefully upright. Oh, hell—was *that* what Healey had been trying to tell him? He hadn't understood at the time, but…

"Oops," Molly said dully. "I meant to say that a little more artfully."

"Molly—whatever you think you heard…it isn't…" Jake stuttered out, hating how fucking *guilty* he sounded.

"So, it's true," Molly decided. "You *are* still engaged." Her voice lacked all inflection, flat and horrifying.

Jake's mind whirled, trying to unravel what could have happened. What could Bess have possibly said to Molly? None of it made any *sense*. Besides, Molly knew him—knew he was head over heels for her. She wouldn't believe the word of a stranger over him, would she?

Jake gripped his knees and tried to explain. "No, of course not," he tried. "I don't know why you would think that."

"Oh, I don't know—maybe because your fiancée told me so. Why would she lie?" Molly asked. Her hand rested on the door handle, like she was contemplating bolting.

"It's kind of complicated," Jake answered. How to explain the mental and emotional debts—all the damn debts that Jake would never finish owing his father or the Suttons? How to explain how they wanted him to pay and pay forever?

"Complicated," Molly repeated.

Jake nodded, willing her to understand—or at the very least, give him a chance to explain. He hadn't meant for it to happen this way. He'd meant to find the words to defend his choices sooner, so that they made sense to Molly. Jake had wanted to talk about the way she'd taken over his heart and destroyed him for any other woman. The way she *was* his heart, now and forever. No one else—not Bess or any other woman—could possibly compare.

But then, like a bad dream, the Suttons had appeared at Polk's retirement party—and his father had warned him not to do anything stupid. Jake had slipped out to the club's bar for a few minutes, trying to decide how to handle it. With sickening certainty, he knew he couldn't trust Blake not to do or say something awful, but he'd left Molly with her future coworkers—he'd thought she was safe.

Jake had one too many beers, maybe. By the time he'd returned…man, had Bess ever screwed the pooch. Healey had tried to tell him that Bess had gotten to Molly, but Jake hadn't listened. Instead he'd bee-lined straight for Molly, and…the conversation had been weird. The details were fuzzy. Had he talked about Blake's *hair?*

Jake's mother had pulled him aside after that, to point out that not only was Blake wearing his god-forsaken ring again, but that she was flaunting it all over the party. His mama demanded that he speak to Bess immediately—to forestall any further awkwardness and arrange for an unequivocal end to things. Even though Jake had been putting that off, he knew it was necessary.

So, he'd asked Bess to dance, enabling them to have a quick private conversation without starting any unsavory gossip. In the middle of the dance floor, there was no way Bess would make a scene—especially not after her last public snit had gotten her in such hot water with her parents. Jake asked her to meet with him the next day, and butted up against Blake's stubborn streak.

Jake knew he had to be firm, or Bess would walk all over him as she always had. With Molly to fight for and the liquid courage coursing through his veins, it turned out to be easier than he expected. Jake stopped asking, and simply *told* Bess: *Take that ring off now, and don't even think about not showing up in the morning.* Blake had been so stunned that she'd agreed just as the song ended, and the dancers around them stopped moving.

She would meet Jake at his house the next day, and he would bury their relationship once and for all—thank the Lord. After that, Bess would finally understand that she and Jake were through, and no amount of scheming on her part was going to change that. Then, Jake could move forward with Molly, unfettered by the past. Unworried about ambushes around every corner.

As Jake had exited the makeshift parquet dance floor, though, two horrible things occurred. His sister had rapidly collared him to say that Molly was misunderstanding everything she had just witnessed. And Jake had seen Molly herself high-tailing it out of the party like her shoes were on fire.

Jake's window for explaining anything—for smoothing the path forward for him and Molly—had slammed shut with a deafening crack that made him want to vomit. Now he was on straight damage control—and based on Molly's demeanor, Jake was fucked six ways to Sunday.

"I need to go back to Mrs. Denson's now," Molly told him, turning away. "I'm going to go call another cab." She held her arms tightly around herself, and her face was as cold and remote as a grave.

"Molly," Jake started, not sure how to begin—only knowing he had to. "Whatever you think you know right now, it's probably wrong."

"Don't," was all she said. With dreadful assurance, Jake knew by her tone that anything he tried to say now would only make things worse.

"Okay, listen. We're both upset, but we need to talk about this," he said.

"Maybe tomorrow," Molly said grudgingly. He doubted mightily that she meant it.

"I'll be home all day," Jake persisted. "Whenever you want, okay? I can come to you, or you can come to me."

"Okay," Molly agreed, and then she slid from his car and walked away.

Jake sat there, sobering more by the second and feeling powerless. He tried not to freak out that the woman of his dreams was walking away with a distinct air of finality. No way would God gift him with a beautiful future like the one he'd glimpsed with Molly, and then...just wrench it away like this. Jake had to find his balls and clean house, because failure was not an option. Not this time.

HE DIDN'T SLEEP all night. Jake laid in his cold sheets with Duke nestled tight to his side, and stared up at the ceiling. Memories from the last couple years marched through Jake's head, torturing him with all the times he had a chance to right his ship—but didn't. At the crack of dawn, he'd risen and taken a run, going until he couldn't take one more step, until his lungs burned and his legs felt like jelly.

He'd showered and changed, choked down some coffee, and waited in his building's lobby for Blake to arrive. Hopefully, the whole thing would be over soon.

Bess had other ideas, though. She showed up at Jake's condo on time and dressed to kill. A woman on a mission. When she got out of her little white convertible, she launched herself right at Jake—and in seconds, Bess was wrapped around him like a weed, her tongue down his throat.

It took a minute to disentangle himself, but Jake was finally able to break free—to gently set Bess away from him. He didn't want to *actually* hurt the woman, and that was a real danger just then. The rage he felt about Bess pulling yet another selfish stunt, surprised even Jake with its ferocity. He hadn't thought anything could top the indignity of her rubbing Molly's nose in his diamond. But Blake trying to kiss him now, after everything, was too much to endure.

Jake should have expected her to attempt seduction, but he hadn't. It felt sordid. So once Jake extracted himself from Blake's clutches, he didn't let her in the building like he'd planned. Instead, he kept her outside, where he'd be reasonably safe from any further advances, and she couldn't spin their interaction into something bigger.

"C'mon Bess, knock it off," Jake grumbled, pissed.

"Seriously?" she demanded. "You don't feel *anything*? After all we've been through together?"

"Sorry. But this is really for the best," Jake confirmed.

"Unbelievable," Bess huffed. "It's because of that Milly woman, isn't it?"

"It's Molly," he corrected her. Jake sidestepped her accusation, then redirected: "You know, someday you're going to be, like, a governor's wife or something. And you'll be great at it. You don't need me, Bess."

Blake rolled her eyes. "Oh gee, thanks, Jackson."

"Don't mention it."

"Anyway—here's this." Blake flashed the ring on her hand in front of his face. Originally, Jake had expected she would keep it—locked in a safe deposit box somewhere, or reset into a necklace. Etiquette said she could, despite how expensive it had been. The good Lord knew Jake never wanted to see the damn thing again.

But after what Bess had pulled last night, the mothers had negotiated a deal in which Jake and his folks would pay off a couple of the deposits that had already been put down for the wedding, and Bess would hand over his engagement ring. It seemed fair enough—at least she wouldn't have it on her manicured little hand anymore, to mislead other people or blackmail Jake. Blake extended her hand, and made him slip it off her finger himself.

Jake did, and pocketed it. He felt nothing but a twinge of sorrow that he'd once thought marrying Bess was a good idea. The Jake of six months ago hadn't had the first clue what real love was, and that saddened him. So much time wasted, fumbling around clueless and in the dark. Now that Jake knew what love could be—what it was *supposed* to be—life was both immeasurably better…and much, much worse.

"Thanks," he said. "Oh, and you'd better take this." He handed over a different, less-flashy band.

"What's this?" Blake's nose wrinkled as she examined it.

"It's your grandmother's wedding ring. Your daddy gave it to me when I asked him for your hand. He thought I could surprise you with it at the wedding." Jake had accepted it, even knowing how much Blake would be annoyed to not have the band she'd picked out herself as part of the ceremony.

"Oh Lord. Good thing you remembered. Mama would never have let it rest if I came home without that." Blake stashed the antique deep in her handbag, and didn't seem the least bit troubled.

"I believe that," Jake said. Suddenly, he just wanted this woman gone—from his home, and from his life. "Okay. Well—I think that does it." He leaned in and forced himself to give Bess a chaste hug, like something out of a middle school dance. No need to encourage her. "I'll guess I'll see you around," he murmured.

Blake withdrew and patted him on the arm. "Yeah—I guess. Hopefully not for a while, though."

Jake smiled. With the way his luck was going, he'd be running into her all month and the next.

"Bye Bess," he told her, turning away. He'd watch from inside the lobby—just to make sure she didn't have car trouble or anything—but felt no need to make a production of it.

Blake sighed. "Are you sure about this, Jake? I mean…we could…"

Jake interrupted before she could gain any steam. "I am really, really sure. I think you are, too."

Bess nodded, gave him a little wave, then walked to her car and drove off.

Jake stood and let the emotions wash through him. Now that he really didn't have to marry her, he could allow himself to feel a small measure of sentimentality. Bess had been in his life for a long time, in one form or another. Jake truly didn't know if he'd have been able to pull himself out of his college spiral without her—maybe the spiral wouldn't have even happened without Blake. Either way, Jake could be happy now. With or without her version of "help," he had made it. And in her wake, Jake had been left with a clean, glowing slate. Perfect for starting anew.

All that was left was the damage control with Molly. But what Jake had with Molly was so good, so pure and true, that he had to believe it would all be fine. Now that her temper had had a chance to cool, Molly was certain to see that Jake loved her with all of his heart, and would be devoted to her for as long as she'd have him.

How could she not? She'd given him some trust and the run of her body. Once Jake explained what had truly happened last night, he'd get the rest of her trust—and then he figured they'd be good to go.

Then Jake could start looking toward a future brighter than anything he'd ever envisioned for himself. Someday, he was going to marry Molly. They could raise their babies in Ceecee's house, and maybe even open their own firm together. Jake smiled even bigger now, and entered his building. Life, at last, was going to be good.

Chapter Twenty-Eight

MOLLY HAD DRIVEN to Jake's place the morning after Polk's party, thinking she would give him his say away from prying eyes. Blake—and Blake's public fit of temper—were still fresh in her mind, and had been for most of the night. Now, anything Molly could do to distinguish herself from Jake and his tempestuous fiancée seemed especially important. She refused to be like them, either of them.

Besides, arriving in her own car gave her the ability to leave when and how she saw fit. Not like the night before, when she'd stood outside that stupid country club for an eternity, trying to get a cab to take her home while Jake sat in his car and stared off into space. Molly had finally been forced to accept a ride from Healey, who had—thankfully—forgone any further attempts to sway her. She'd only asked, twice, if Molly was okay.

Oh, Molly was okay. More than okay. She'd driven across town this morning, uncertain if Jake would have anything compelling to say. Instead, she saw him kissing his fiancée out in broad daylight and playing with the rock on her finger. He looked down at her beautiful upturned face, affectionate and wistful. He probably told Blake that Molly was just some chick who meant nothing to him—here today, gone tomorrow. Jake probably even *believed* that.

He hugged Blake goodbye and stood watching her drive off, and the smile on his two-timing lips grew even wider. It was the smile of a man who had just pulled off the world's biggest fraud. A smug smile—Jake thought he'd won. And maybe...maybe he had.

When his fiancée had grown inconvenient, Jake had managed to have Blake be the one to break things off, so he didn't have to. By taking her back, he now looked like the generous one—charitable and forgiving. Blake was probably falling all over herself with gratitude, since she thought she'd dodged a bullet of her own making.

Likewise, when Molly's presence in Jake's life proved too complicated, he had managed to set things up so she too, would do the dirty work—just like Bess. Jake wouldn't have to give Molly the "it's not working" talk, because he'd killed two birds with one stone. With chilling efficiency, he'd placated his fiancée and rid himself of his side piece, all by standing sedately on his front steps. Molly might have been impressed, if she weren't so furious with herself.

Despite her best intentions, she'd fallen for his spiel—hook, line and sinker. It rankled. When Jake finally went back inside his building, Molly didn't follow him. She refused to give him another audience for his lies. Instead, she drove too fast back to the B&B, then sat on her bed, shaking. Would she even get the job at his father's firm now?

Jake had convinced her to change her plane tickets, so she could stay another week with him. He'd even sweet-talked Mrs. Denson into letting her stay longer. Molly didn't see why she should bother staying the rest of the week now. She'd have to pay a fee, she supposed, to change her tickets a second time. But Molly needed to get back to Boston and move out of her room. She needed to get back to *real* life, not the fantasy Wilmington had woven around her.

Just in case, Molly should probably send out some more resumes when she returned, too. The idea of working at the legal aid office any longer depressed her—she'd been getting burned out for a while, and being teased with the *APF* position only made things worse. If she quit, though, how would she pay rent? What the heck was Molly going to *do*?

The answer was simple—anything that didn't involve Jake Alexander, or any other man. Molly could hustle with the best of them, and she would. This precarious feeling she had in her chest was only temporary. Soon, she'd be back to her determined, resolute self, and she'd never have to dwell on this embarrassing slip-up again. She could bury thoughts of Jake in the same hole she'd put the memory of Carter.

Jake, per the usual, refused to leave her to it. Right on cue, he texted her:

> You want to come here, or should I come to you?

Molly had no desire to prolong the inevitable, so she typed:

> Neither.

She could almost feel Jake's frown through her phone. He wrote:

> But we need to see each other.

Molly said,

> I've seen enough thx.

In seconds, his response popped up.

> What??

Molly rolled her eyes. There was no fixing stupid.

> Forget it. There's nothing to talk about anyway.

Her phone began ringing, vibrating right off the bed in its insistency.

"Molly?" Jake asked when she answered. "What's going on? Of course, we need to talk."

She sighed, weary to the bone. "Jake, please—just leave me alone."

"Why would I do that? I'm crazy about you, Molly. I *thought* you were crazy about me."

Molly sat in silence. She had thought that, too. It just went to show you how treacherous emotions could be. How they could trip you up and make you do the unthinkable.

"I'm coming to the B&B right now. Is that where you are?" Molly heard Jake's car door slam, heard the Audi's engine roar to life.

"Yeah," she admitted, resigned. Why did anyone ever think that phone breakups worked? It was impossible—they never succeeded the way they were supposed to. *Never.* It was so frustrating.

"Stay put, okay? I'll be right over," Jake begged.

"Fine." Molly hung up, and prepared for the worst. Nothing—*nothing*—was worse than a pathetic guy who just wouldn't get it.

JAKE ARRIVED WITH record speed. Molly didn't even have time to warn Mrs. Denson, who cheerfully let the bastard in and directed him right up the stairs. He sat across from her, in an armchair near hers, and leaned as far forward as he was able.

"Molly, I'm telling you the truth. I don't understand why you won't believe me. Even if you ignore everything else— everything I've said and done up to this point—how can you ignore *this?*" His hands motioned back and forth between them, manic and jerky. "Whatever this is between us, *means* something." Jake was growing frantic, his expression pleading and his tone desperate.

Molly, on the other hand, felt dull and calm, like she'd been wrapped in packing material and stored in a box. With sudden, awful clarity, she realized something. All this time, she'd blamed her mother: for moving them around too much, for being weak, for needing a man to take charge so she could feel whole. Molly had blamed her mother for infecting her teenage brain with that ethos, and for not only condoning, but urging, Molly's relationship with Carter.

Now, looking Carter 2.0 dead in the face, Molly understood that she was just as much to blame. Because by the time Carter Boatwright had extended his hand and asked for hers in return, Molly had been so damn tired of fending for herself that she'd accepted the promise of respite without even thinking twice. Molly, it seemed, was just as weak as her mother—just as much a silly romantic who needed a white knight to come to her rescue. If she wasn't, she would never have agreed to marry that asshole, never been taken in by his sweet words and fervent kisses—never envisioned a golden future as Mrs. Carter Boatwright.

It seemed impossible, given the way she'd steeled herself ever since, that Molly could have been taken in again, by *exactly* the same sort of devil. That was the hell of hubris—when you were so sure you could guard against the enemy, you never saw him coming. Molly hadn't seen Jake coming—at least, not like this.

"That's just it," Molly told Jake. "I know exactly what you are, what *this* is." She didn't bother trying to keep the sneer from her voice, though she wasn't sure whether it was meant more for her or for him. "I know, because I've seen it all before. I've been taken in by it before. It's my own fault I didn't catch on sooner."

Jake shook his head, denying it. His mask of innocent confusion was so real, so convincing, that Molly could almost forgive herself for believing it. Almost.

"This isn't a lie, Molly," he whispered, horrified. "You *know* it's not."

"No, I don't know that at all." Her voice was flat. She imagined that her expression must be, too. "Where's Blake right now, anyway? Where's *Bess*? What does *she* think is going on?" When Jake opened his mouth to reply, Molly held up both hands to forestall him.

"No. Don't tell me. I know," she said. "Bess is sitting somewhere thinking you are loyal and true, and that you still love her. She'll believe that, even when she is confronted with irrefutable evidence to the contrary. She will walk down an aisle someday—in a pretty white dress she picked out just for you—and she will lay in your bed at night thinking her place in your heart is safe. But it's not. It's *not*."

"It's not, because I don't love her," Jake replied. "I never did—not like I love you."

"Bullshit," Molly retorted. "You love yourself. *All of you* just love yourselves."

"All of who? Molly, who else are we talking about here?" Jake's eyes searched hers, trying to understand. His knuckles were white where he gripped the arms of the chair, as if he had to physically restrain himself from grabbing her. He'd better restrain himself—if Jake tried to touch her now, Molly was liable to punch him.

She'd probably said too much, but by now she couldn't work up any worry about it. Besides, with the way this was going, Molly knew she'd never get the job with his dad's firm. Not now, not after giving Mr. Alexander's liar son the boot. Molly would just have to find something else. And, really…if she wasn't going to be here in Wilmington, living in Jake's orbit, what did it matter if he knew the truth? If he knew what kind of woman she really was?

"Molly?" Jake prompted, eyes moving over her face. "Is this something about your dad? Who else are you talking about, exactly?"

"Why can't you just believe that I've met your kind before?" Molly muttered bitterly.

"Jesus, you've told me you know guys like me about a thousand times since I've met you. If I'm going to sink or swim on some other asshole's merits, don't you think I ought to at least know his name? Who the hell hurt you so badly?" Jake wanted to know.

Well, the time had come, hadn't it? Molly had known she would have to admit her past to this man at some point—she just hadn't expected it to be like this.

"I'm talking about my *husband*," she revealed, enunciating the words with deadly accuracy—letting the secret she had guarded so carefully fly free. "His name is Carter," she said, staring at her feet. "Carter Boatwright."

Jake didn't say anything to that. When Molly peeked up at him, his face was stony, immovable. No, not immovable—there was a small tic, there at the side of his jaw.

"His name is Carter," she repeated. "and I married him in secret when I was seventeen years old. We fucked like bunnies the whole summer after my junior year of high school, because we were soulmates and we were man and *wife*. And then, Carter went away to college, and I started my senior year. I never saw him, or heard from him again."

"*Ever?*" Jake exclaimed, seemingly stunned by that detail more than any of the others. "Wait, wait, wait. Start over," he said.

Steeling herself, Molly elaborated, "When I was sixteen, my mom met a man—a dentist, from New York—and got remarried. Rob moved us from Mystic back to his hometown."

"In New York," Jake clarified.

"Yeah. Rye, specifically. Pretty ritzy."

He looked like he was doing the math in his head. "And Mina was…?"

"Already married by then," Molly explained. "Had been for a year or so, I think."

"So…" Jake prompted her.

"Yeah, so, the dentist's kids were already grown and out of the house, and Rob had his new trophy wife. Having a teenage girl like me in the house, too, was a bit of an imposition—so they stashed me in prep school and basically forgot about me."

"I'm sorry," Jake said, and had the temerity to sound almost sincere about it. The bastard had probably spent his whole life in prep schools, and couldn't possibly understand what that had been like for Molly.

"Anyway, I was alone a lot, didn't really fit in, whatever." She swallowed. No big whoop. Happened years ago. Moving on. "When Carter eventually noticed me, it was…" A benediction, really.

"Oh yeah, Carter. Let's talk about him," Jake said acidly.

The poison in his voice, in his expression, almost stopped her. Molly hesitated, watching Jake—he was sprawled across his chair. Sprawled…trying to look relaxed but tense as could be. The minute those hateful words emerged from his lips, he looked regretful. A little sheepish. He ran a hand over his face, as if to wipe the dregs of that statement away, and Molly pushed on.

"I don't know why he picked me, but we spent every waking moment together. There was no one around to notice, or care," she told him. "But despite all the dysfunction in my life, all the moving around and what not…I was still pretty innocent. Naïve, I guess." The words were like cardboard in her mouth. She'd never told a living soul this story—not even her sister. Molly had, in theory, known that eventually she would, but the action felt alien nonetheless.

Jake, for his part, was beginning to look truly alarmed now. She could guess what he must be thinking. He had no idea.

"He wanted to…you know." Was she really going to be precious about this *now*? "He wanted to sleep together, but I was, um…reluctant."

Molly wondered, suddenly, if some part of her had guessed at Carter's true nature, even then. Even when she'd thought herself in love, maybe some tiny shred of self-preservation had been warning her—deep in her gut—to keep away. It wasn't like she'd been particularly prudish, or even religious, back then. There had been no real reason to withhold herself from Carter. So, why had she?

Jake's eyes squeezed shut. He'd been a seventeen-year-old boy once. He had to know. Except, there was no way he could.

"We got married in secret the summer after my junior year, then had sex every chance we got for months. I should probably be happy I never got pregnant." As expected, Jake's eyes had snapped wide open at the word *married*, and grown even wider at her bald-faced words. It was just as well. He needed to know, once and for all, what the hell he was up against.

Molly droned on, her voice deadening with each successive revelation. "Carter went off to college in September, and I started my senior year of high school. No one knew about us except my mom—who was so, so proud that I had snagged such a big fish. She had to sign off on the marriage—you know, because I was underage." Molly swallowed hard against the lump in her throat. What did it matter, what Jake thought of her, or her family? What did any of it matter anymore? Molly was older and much wiser now. And Jake was not for her—had never been for her.

Jake seemed to rouse himself in his chair. He cleared his throat, sat up, and asked, "What, uh…what happened?"

"Oh, well, that's where it gets so special," Molly smiled. "I never heard from my *husband* again."

"What?"

"You heard me. Never called. Never wrote. Never sent me flowers."

"But how—" A long pause. His forehead wrinkled in confusion. "Are you still *married* to that prick?"

"Thankfully no," Molly replied cheerfully. "You're right—I wasn't quite accurate. I did see him once," she said thoughtfully.

When Jake spread his hands and raised his eyebrows, she explained, "There was the one time I took the bus to the city to find him, and saw Carter in his fraternity house. His brothers took me right to him," Molly explained sweetly.

Her smirk must've been all Jake needed to see, though, because he sat back and rolled his eyes. "Oh, here we go. Lemme guess," he muttered.

"Yup," Molly agreed. "There Carter was, upstairs in bed—lording it over his pretty little Tri-Delt girlfriend. His brothers found that really, *really* funny. It was *epic*." Molly stared at Jake's face, determined to drive her point home while he gaped at her like a fish.

Jake inhaled through his mouth and held it, his chest expanded with the breath, nostrils flared. Finally, he released it in one disbelieving gust, and burst out, "Do you mean to tell me you never saw him again after *that*?"

"He waited a whole *year* before his next appearance," she told him. "My husband ignored every single attempt I made to contact him. At least until his father's attorney served me with divorce papers in my dorm cafeteria—just in time for Christmas of my freshman year. No one saw, so I guess I won that round. Carter didn't get to humiliate me quite like he must have hoped," Molly mused.

She had moved off campus six months later, just in case he ever wanted to try to embarrass her again. Besides, she couldn't afford to pay for both room and board, *and* her attorney's fees. Molly had to save money wherever she could, since Rob the dentist was pointedly unhelpful when it came to teenaged divorcées.

"And you will not get to humiliate me either," Molly told Jake. "Because I'm leaving, and I'm never going to think about you again." *Lie.*

Sometime during her recitation, Jake had slumped in his chair. He blinked at her in disbelief. "I can't believe he *married* you. Why did he marry you?"

Oh, his tone said it all, didn't it? Why would any well-bred young man buy the cow, when he could get the milk for free? The disgust, the disdain—it was all there, plain as day. Molly fought to keep the sting of it from her face. She held silent, waiting for the right words to come to her, the ones that would sink her dagger deep, and end this farce once and for all.

"Look, I know this is some kind of fucked-up joke to you," she said. "You and I got our rocks off, and now I'll head back to where I came from. You can go on with your sad, pathetic life—never standing up for yourself with your parents or your fiancée. You can sleep around behind her back as your one secret rebellion. Hell, your friends will probably all be doing the same thing. You can gloat about it on poker night," Molly jeered.

Jake looked positively chalk-white now, which Molly supposed was the only victory she was going to get. He asked, "And what will you be doing?"

"I will be busy not missing you."

In the ensuing silence, Molly had plenty of time to study the way the wallpaper was slightly faded on the wall opposite her bed, right where the sun streamed in every afternoon. She noticed the layer of dust along the windowsill. Naturally there'd be dust there—it was too hot here to ever open that window, wasn't it? She noticed the slow, steady ticking of the clock on the writing desk. Loud, like a disembodied heart.

Eventually, Jake broke the silence. "You do realize that I'm not Carter, right? Not even close. I wouldn't have laid a hand on you if Bess and I hadn't broken things off. Molly—you *have* to realize that."

For some reason, his use of Blake's nickname in that moment infuriated Molly. "I don't *have* to do anything," she retorted. "Because you are a liar. You never would've told me a damn thing if you hadn't been forced to."

Jake shook his head, kept shaking it as he tried to defend himself. "*No*, I never lied to you. Never."

"But you didn't exactly tell the truth, did you?" Abruptly, the room felt claustrophobic, and Molly hopped up, needing to move. Her chair jumped back on the rug, and a loud, stomach-churning crunch punctuated the air. Molly looked down and spotted her phone on the floor. The bright screen was shattered in a starburst, radiating around the claw foot of the Queen Anne chair.

"Shit," she stated, staring at it. Must have slipped out of her pocket as she sat there telling her tale of woe. Figured.

"Molly, everything I ever told you was the God's honest truth. I swear it," Jake tried again. He made a move to get down on the floor, to rescue her battered phone for her.

Molly darted back to grab it instead, and was rewarded for her effort with a vicious sliver of glass in her thumb. That was too much—it was all too much.

"God *damn* it," she sobbed, swiping at the tears beginning to streak down her cheeks. She was frustrated, enraged—but whether it was at Jake or herself, she wasn't sure. How could this be happening to her heart again? How could she have *let* this happen again?

It was unfathomable. Molly had guarded meticulously against heartbreak. She'd been wary and *ready*, and she'd never once slipped up. Despite all that, it had happened anyway—yet another snake had slithered into her soul, and bitten hard. The problem was, Molly didn't think Jake would be nearly as simple to get over as Carter had been.

She cried harder, hating her tears. Hating the show of weakness in front of him.

"Molly," Jake started, rising and taking one uncertain step in her direction. He hesitated when she glared at him. She held out two trembling hands, like she planned to hold off his advance with witchcraft, or maybe the Force.

Jake looked horrified, and faintly ill. "Listen," he whispered.

"No," Molly said. "No, you—you get out." Her ruined phone started ringing.

Jake closed his too-pretty eyes with their spiky black lashes, and shook his head. Then he opened his traitorous mouth to speak again.

"Get *out*," Molly shrieked at the top of her lungs, like a fishwife. Like the trashy, low-class *broad* she really was. In that moment, she didn't even care that Mrs. Denson could likely hear every word, and would probably be calling half the town already. Now that Jake had single-handedly destroyed any chance Molly had at the *Alexander, Polk* position, it wasn't like she was going to be living here long-term anyway.

Jake swallowed and backed away, never taking his wide, hurt eyes from her face.

"I love you," he whispered tragically.

"No. No, you're a horrible person and you're *lying*," Molly sniffled.

Molly's cell phone kept ringing. Finally, Jake seemed to notice. He exploded, "God *damn* it, Molly, will you just answer that damn thing?"

"I can't!" she yelled back, stabbing at the broken screen. "It won't work!" Her thumb was still oozing blood, and she picked out the sliver, flicking it into the trash can under the desk. She jammed her thumb in her mouth and shooed at Jake with her phone. "Just go," she insisted.

His back hit the door of her room, and Jake fumbled behind himself for the knob. When he pulled the door open and stepped backward however, Jake bumped right into Mrs. Denson, standing in the hall.

"I'm sorry," they both said, in unison.

Molly expected the other woman to be unhappy about the racket. Mrs. Denson's face was pallid, though—not angry.

"Molly, honey, you have a phone call," she said grimly.

Molly glanced down at her phone, then back at the B&B's proprietor. Mrs. Denson nodded, as if to encourage her. Jake may as well have been a lamp, for all the attention she paid him.

"Coming," Molly said, sidling past him and making sure that no part of her touched even an inch of Jake.

When she'd gotten halfway down the grand carpeted staircase, Jake stepped into the upper hallway and closed her door behind him with a devastating little click. Molly turned her back and flew the rest of the way down the stairs with her heart in her throat. Whatever had necessitated reaching her so badly, whatever had put that horrible expression on Mrs. Denson's face, couldn't be good. Jake trailed more slowly behind, and had the gall to look worried for her.

Molly had thought it would be okay to kiss him—to do *more* with him—as long as she kept her wits about her. If her eyes were wide open, what harm could come of a little messing around? A little passion? As long as Molly made Jake prove himself first, as long as she didn't do something stupid like actually *fall* for the bastard, then all was supposed to be well.

She'd underestimated them both. Jake—with his adorable dimples, cute grandmother, and endearing *dog* was far more dangerous than she'd given him credit for. More fool she.

And Molly, with her apparently limitless capacity for being a sucker, was far more gullible. She had avoided relationships all these years because she'd proven, beyond all shadow of a doubt, that she had no sense when it came to men. If she had ever been inclined to forget it, her stepdad had been ready and willing to remind her.

Everyone who mattered knew—irrefutably—that she couldn't be trusted. Molly could screw up even the most basic of social interactions with the males of the species. A family friend acting as her tour guide, for instance—that situation was fraught with misunderstanding and peril. It was a wonder that Molly herself hadn't asked Jake to marry her.

She grabbed for the receiver that Mrs. Denson was holding out to her.

"Hello?" she said.

Chapter Twenty-Nine

MOLLY'S FACE WENT sheet-white as she talked in monosyllables to whoever was calling. Jake felt his own face contort in a mixture of frustration at their impossible situation, at their ghastly interrupted conversation—he hadn't even had a chance to explain himself better—and concern for Molly as he watched the call unfold.

"What? What happened?" he asked when she finally disconnected the call. She'd made promises that she would be *there* as soon as possible—that she would call for flights as soon as she hung up. Molly was really, truly leaving him—not that Jake deserved her to begin with.

"It's my brother-in-law," she replied faintly.

"Grey?"

Molly nodded. Jake didn't even have to ask if he was dead, because the truth was written all over her face.

"What happened?"

Molly sagged onto a chair in the B&B kitchen and looked up at him, her face blank with disbelief. "Car accident. He uh—he died in a car accident this afternoon."

"*Shit*," Jake breathed, sinking into a crouch in front of her. Hesitantly, he reached for her knees, and it wasn't until she forced herself to meet his eyes that Molly seemed to remember—Jake knew Grey, too. Maybe even better than she did.

She brushed him off and jumped up, backing away to put some space between them.

"I'll help," Jake said. "I'll bring you up there, and we can…" The words backed up and clogged in his throat when he saw her expression.

"No," Molly told him. "You won't."

"Molly—" Jake began, wanting to argue.

"You should leave," she told him, though every word sounded torn from her like a half-healed scab. "I have to go help my sister, and I have a lot to do."

Before she even finished, he was already shaking his head—but Molly merely watched him with almost clinical detachment. Jake was still trying to fight the inevitable, and clearly—even in this—she thought would have to be the stronger one. Her tears were gone now.

She steeled herself, and uttered the words Jake least wanted to hear. "You need to go back to Blake and take care of your own life," Molly said coldly. She had wrapped herself in cold, actually, and used the force of it to back Jake toward the front door.

He wanted Molly to ask him to run interference with his father. He wanted to take care of everything for her, to envelop her in his arms and never let her go. But Jake could only do that if there was nothing and no one between them. And they both knew that wasn't the reality. If Molly didn't trust him more than her ex Carter, then the specter of Bess would continue to be a hurdle.

Jake let Molly shove him out the door. He stumbled a little on the threshold—which was odd, he supposed. Normally, he never tripped on anything.

Before she closed the door in his face, she added, "I'm sure you can find out the funeral arrangements from the Dekes."

Then it was over. Molly was left alone in the foyer, with only the whirring of the air conditioning for company—and Jake stood out on the front stoop like a stray dog.

Eventually, he made his way to his car, where he managed nothing more heroic than blinking out the windshield and trying to understand where he'd gone wrong. Mrs. Denson came out and shooed him away—so Jake went home, grabbed up Duke, and drove out to his aunt and uncle's beach house. He took a long walk on the sand with his dog, trying to outpace his own stupidity.

But he couldn't. As he plowed through the wet sand there at the edge of the surf, Jake reviewed everything that had occurred in the last forty-eight hours. With meticulous precision, he identified each and every place he'd gone wrong. Every misspoken word, every ham-handed effort to fix things, every failed attempt to staunch the flow of blood from his wounded heart. All of it might have been prevented, if Jake had just said something about Bess *sooner*.

Once they returned to the beach house, Jake tossed a frisbee for Duke to retrieve, over and over, while he sat in his shorts in the sand. He should be with Molly. He should be there, helping the woman he loved through this difficult time. Instead, he was *here*—sandy, pathetic, tired…and hugging on a smelly wet hound. Jake hadn't deserved Molly, and so she'd been taken away.

MOLLY *WANTED* TO cry some more. After she pushed Jake out the door, there was nothing she wanted more than to sink to her knees and sob about every wrenchingly unfair thing in the world. Every widowed sister. Every fatherless daughter. Every soul in love with someone they couldn't have, and every last broken heart. But she couldn't—because once she started, she suspected she wouldn't be able to stop. And Molly had to catch a plane.

She couldn't face her room again, not after what had just transpired there. Molly decided this was the perfect time to make an exit instead. She spun on her heel and left the foyer, then stepped right out the front door of Mrs. Denson's B&B. Molly hit the sidewalk and walked—past the pretty porches and potted plants, past the coffee shop and the market, until eventually she hit a small tidy park that she hadn't even known was there. She sat under a tree, not crying, batting away gnats and mosquitos and waiting. Molly waited until she was positive—sure in her soul—that Jake wouldn't turn around and come back. And then she waited some more.

Finally, she wandered back—lingering at the edge of the lot until she examined every last vehicle in the area to be certain that Jake's was not among them. When she finally went upstairs, Molly righted her chair and tried to ignore the lingering scent of Jake's cologne, hanging in the still, quiet air.

She would have to call the airline and arrange for a flight from Wilmington to Baltimore. She needed to rent a car for the drive to the shore. First, Molly used her room phone to call and check on her mom, to see if she needed any help getting to Maryland. And then, she called the offices of *Alexander, Polk & Futch* to tell them she was leaving.

It was after hours at the firm. Molly got a message instructing her that she'd be transferred to the on-call number, where she could leave a message for the appropriate employee. After some clicks and soothing music, Maryanne's brisk voice answered. Molly explained the situation as succinctly as she could.

As always, Maryanne was everything polite, but eventually she asked to put Molly on hold for a moment. Before long, though, the office manager was back on the line. Officiously, she intoned, "The partners have asked me to extend their deepest condolences for your loss. We'd like to assist. If you'll allow me, I will call the airline and get the next available flight out for you, and arrange for a car service to take you where you need to go once you get to Maryland. It will probably be easier that way, since I made the reservation to begin with."

Molly was flabbergasted. "I—thank you, but that's really not necessary. I can…"

Maryanne interjected. "Don't be silly, that's what I'm here for. Now, I just need to ask you a couple questions, and then I'll leave you to start packing."

Molly sat heavily on the side of the bed. "Thank you. That's very kind of you."

"It's what we do—we take care of our own. Best you learn that now, hon. I'll be sure to call you back when I have the details for you, all right?" the woman said.

"Okay, thanks. I'll, uh—I'll be here," Molly told her.

She rubbed her eyes, trying to wrap her head around what was happening. In the space of only a few hours, Molly had lost Jake, her sister had lost Grey, and the office manager of the firm she was interviewing at had referred to Molly as "one of their own." Had the whole world gone mad, or had Molly been dumped into some dreadful, alternate universe? As it was, the next several days promised to be bad. But if Molly did get the job at *APF* and had to live in Wilmington—had to actually run into Jake on a regular basis—that could very well destroy her in a way Carter had never been able to.

The awful truth was that Molly was in love with Jake— even after everything he'd done and said, she knew her heart was a mangled, tender muscle that still beat mercilessly for him. She was no teenager anymore, and had learned a thing or two along the way. But a broken heart could hurt you, even if you knew better. Molly had thought she was strong, had thought she could handle anything after surviving Carter—but falling for Jake Alexander was quite possibly going to be the worst mistake she'd ever made.

Chapter Thirty

H ER FLIGHT OUT of North Carolina was, thankfully, far less interesting than her flight into the state. Instead of fending off unwanted advances, Molly merely had to endure a repetitive internal litany of misery: *Oh God, she'd fallen for it again. Jake had screwed her over and she'd fallen for his lies. She was such an idiot. She shouldn't be allowed around men. She only fell for losers. Molly was a train wreck for whom there was no hope.* Why did she even try? She should just give up now.

In the baggage claim at BWI, Molly met up with her driver. Maryanne hadn't bothered with a rental car—instead, she had arranged for a beautiful black Lincoln Town Car to ferry Molly over the bridge to St. Michaels. Nestled in the back against the soft tan leather seat, Molly stared out the tinted window and tried to enjoy the view. But just as they were reaching the start of the Bay Bridge—and beginning the climb into the sweeping blue sky—her cell phone rang. Molly gazed out at the tiny white sailboats dotting the water and answered her mother's call. One more hour—Molly had hoped for just one more hour of peace, before an entirely new kind of heartache set in.

"How was your flight?" her mom asked. "Are you on your way here yet?"

"Yeah, we just got to the bridge," Molly told her. "Are you okay?"

"I'm only calling because Mina's not eating well. She's doing too much, and I can't get her to stop," Elaine whined.

Molly could imagine how that was going. "Well, who else is supposed to do everything?" she asked, as levelly as she could.

"Who knows? Someone in Grey's family could handle the arrangements. One of his brothers—or his father."

"Mom, Mina was Grey's *wife*," Molly explained. "It makes sense for her to do this."

"Well what about someone in the Navy? They must have some protocol to follow in cases like this," Elaine persisted.

Molly sighed. Sometimes you couldn't win. "I wouldn't know," she said.

"This is so, *so* terrible. I can't believe it—why is this happening? What is Mina going to *do*?" her mother wailed.

It was clear that their mother was being more of a nuisance than an actual help. No wonder Mina had been so anxious for Molly to arrive quickly. She was probably going crazy trying to prop up their mother and plan a funeral too, all while grieving her own husband.

After her sobbing subsided, Molly's mother refocused. "Anyway, at least you'll be here soon. You always were the most practical one—you can help us all get through this."

"I'll do my best," Molly said.

"I know you will. You always do."

Molly waited for her mother to ask how her interviews had gone. She could easily talk about those, and wouldn't need to say anything about Jake—no one needed to know what had happened with him. Mina might inquire, but all Molly needed to say was that she and Jake had lunch a couple times.

Naturally, their mom's antennae would be on high alert at the mention of a new man, but Molly was certain she could play it off. There was plenty of other drama swirling around to keep Elaine occupied. And if Molly shed a thousand tears, no one had to be the wiser about who the tears were for. It was a funeral, for Pete's sake. Everyone would be crying.

"You haven't called much lately," her mom said. Molly wondered if Elaine even *remembered* where she'd been. If her mother even cared.

I've been too busy hitting the sheets with the man destined to end me, Molly thought.

"Sorry," she said.

"And you never cashed the check we sent. No thank you note, either." Hurt lay heavy in Elaine's baby-doll voice.

After Molly's stepfather had mulishly refused to pay a single dime of her legal fees—despite his wife's pleading—Molly had begged her mother not to ask him again. Rob had claimed that Molly made her own bed, and she had to lie in it. At the time, he had no clue how good Molly was going to get at that. She scrimped and saved, and somehow kept everything afloat.

Last month, though, her mother had finally sent a check for the entire amount that Molly's divorce lawyer had charged her—five years to the day from when the motion had been finalized. Molly had ripped open the envelope, taken one look at the check, and jammed that blue paper rectangle right down the garbage disposal. Chew on *that* Doctor Rob.

"Too many strings attached. But thanks anyway," Molly managed to say.

If only that could be the end of it. In all likelihood, Elaine would keep trying to rub her ex's nose in her current husband's tardy munificence, and Rob would keep hating his white-trash stepdaughter. Molly would keep loving Jake—as asinine as that was—and Jake would keep developing unseemly liaisons with gullible women. The world would keep turning, and life would go on. And on. And on. Lonely. Empty. Sad.

MOLLY ARRIVED AT Mina's house to a flurry of activity. Mina came rushing out the front door to meet her, only to be overtaken by their mother— who collapsed in Molly's arms and began crying loudly again. Mina rolled her eyes, pulled the older woman away, and held Molly tight herself.

Into her ear, Mina whispered, "She's been like this since she got here. I'm ready to kill her. Possibly myself, but probably her. It won't be pretty, I swear to God."

"I'm so sorry, Minky," Molly murmured, using her childhood nickname for her big sister. "I got here as fast as I could." She stepped back to the driver and handed him a twenty for a tip. He pocketed it graciously, then retrieved her bags from the trunk. He set them carefully on Mina's porch before sliding behind the wheel of the Lincoln, waving, and pulling away.

"No worries. Everything go okay? The firm didn't mind that you had to leave?" Mina asked.

"No, they were great. They made all my reservations and everything. Even lined up that car for me," Molly told her.

"Good," her sister said. "Then come inside. We'll give Mama her meds and put her to bed, and then you and I can order a pizza and catch up."

Their mother accepted being bundled into bed like a toddler with no complaints. It was easier for everyone concerned, really. Elaine was no good at rising to the occasion, and was even worse without her husband to lean on. No one had yet mentioned where Rob might be, or even if he intended to come at all. Molly decided she could easily wait until the next day find out—with her mom out of the way, her shoulders were already less tense.

Molly parked herself on the couch with her sister and a large, greasy pepperoni pizza that had been delivered to the door. Mina opened a bottle of Shiraz that her neighbor had left in a basket on the porch that morning. The front parlor was littered with cloying flower arrangements, the kitchen counter was lined with baked goods, and the freezer stuffed to the gills with casseroles. Mina wouldn't have to cook for months, if she ever decided to eat again. Molly ate two big slices in the time it took for Mina to nibble away a third of one.

"Doing okay?" Molly inquired.

Mina finished off her wine and changed the channel a few times. "Oh, yeah. You know."

"Nope. I don't," Molly said. "Not in the least."

Mina blinked into space for a bit. "The truth is, we…hadn't been getting along. For a long time. It's so weird to still be so furious with Grey, when everyone expects me to be inconsolable. I mean—I just keep thinking what a crappy move it was for him to go get himself killed, right when we hit a rough patch, you know?" Mina massaged her forehead with her thumb and forefinger. "Never mind. I must sound like a horrible person."

Molly shook her head. "You've got to be in shock. I'm sure that when you have time to process all of this, of course you'll feel sad. It's not like it happens on some kind of schedule, right? Don't you have to work through all the stages of grief at your own pace, or something?"

Mina's eyes looked older than the ocean when she replied steadily. "Yeah, absolutely. I'm sure you're right." She refilled her wine glass.

Molly was getting to be something of an expert at recognizing a load of BS when it was being shoveled her way. She figured her sister had earned a break, though, so instead of calling her out, Molly merely squeezed Mina's knee.

"What still needs to get done? Give me some marching orders."

"Tomorrow. We can do all that tomorrow," Mina groaned, waving her off. "Trust me—I have lists out the wazoo. Now that you're here, I'll be able to actually accomplish some of it."

"Whatever you need," Molly said.

Her sister nodded thoughtfully, and studied Molly's face. "What do *you* need?" she asked.

Molly was startled. "Me? Nothing."

"You sure about that?"

"Yes. Why?" Molly's voice came out sounding guilty and shrill. She cleared her throat and gulped down some wine.

"A—I wasn't born yesterday, and B—my eyes still work," Mina snapped. "You look hideous. What happened down there?"

Molly wasn't going to tell her. She'd sworn to herself she wouldn't tell her. This week was supposed to be all about helping Mina. But Mina was frowning at her with eyes that saw too much, and Molly had downed a hair more Shiraz than was advisable for keeping secrets.

Before she knew it, her whole sorry tale came spilling out of her lips, from Carter to Jake and everything in between. Mina, her beloved big sister, hugged her tight and let her cry until she felt like she'd been turned inside out from it. Molly had missed her far more than she realized.

Then, Mina dried Molly's eyes and smiled sadly. "There. Now I think we're in the same boat. Get some sleep, and be ready to work in the morning. Tomorrow is a brand-new day, and the O'Connells are going to be kicking ass and taking names."

"You're pretty feisty for a new widow, you know that?" Molly laughed.

"Better than being a doormat," Mina retorted, jerking her chin at their mother's closed door. Molly winced.

And then Mina was gone, closing herself alone into the bedroom she'd shared with her husband only days before. Molly corked the wine bottle—though there was only an inch left in the bottom—then sagged sideways on the couch. She pulled the afghan off the back and slept fitfully in her clothes, the scent of pepperoni in her nose.

Chapter Thirty-One

J AKE, IN HIS effort to be the good, dutiful son that his parents deserved, had unwittingly hitched his wagon to a shrew—a selfish, controlling woman hiding behind an angel's face. Blake's over-involved parents had merely added insult to injury. But then Molly had come along, making Jake believe that things could be different. That *he* could be different. Jake had thought Molly believed in him, that she trusted him. And he wanted to keep being the good man she saw, because it felt amazing. Powerful. *Life-affirming.*

As it turned out, though, Molly wasn't good at trusting so much as giving one heck of a *performance* of trusting. All the time that Jake thought they had something special, she'd been secretly harboring doubts. Even Molly—a woman he'd known and loved for a paltry few weeks—had understood on a gut level that she couldn't count on him.

Jake was fated to be a disappointment to everyone he cared about, and he'd only been fooling himself to think that life had anything better in store for him. He might as well face it, making his own choices was not working out for him. The few times he'd attempted it, he'd only created messes.

HIS PARENTS HAD invited him over for dinner—reluctantly, Jake dragged ass over there. He couldn't face his bedroom upstairs, not without heartbreak stabbing him through his chest again. But hopefully, he wouldn't have to—his mama had informed him that they'd be dining outside on the screened-in porch, eating steaks that his father was grilling. If Jake planned well, he might not have to enter the house itself at all. Might not have to face the specter of what he'd lost.

Even Duke missed Molly. He'd nosed around in Jake's laundry to find the last t-shirt she'd worn, carried it to his dog bed, and slept on it like he was protecting a hoard of gold. He had the right idea, though—the longer Molly was gone, the less Jake's sheets smelled like her. He couldn't bring himself to wash them yet, and he supposed that made him pathetic. Jake didn't care—he missed her. He'd been carrying around one of her discarded hair ties, like a talisman, for days.

He fingered the black loop of elastic in his pocket now. His mother watched him over the table as he ate, making note of each bite he took, and each pass of his napkin over his lips. Jake chewed slowly, and looked between his parents. An ominous lull had settled over the table, and he realized he'd been summoned for a bigger reason than merely filling his stomach. Duke trotted in carrying a stuffed hedgehog the housekeeper kept for him in the laundry room, and laid down on Jake's feet under the table.

"Give him some steak," Jake's father instructed.

"Don't you dare," Stella warned. "He shouldn't be here while we're eating, to begin with."

Jake wasn't about to tell Duke to go. He suspected he'd need a wingman any minute now.

Sure enough, his mother composed herself and began. "I spoke with your grandmother yesterday," she said.

Jake forced down his mouthful. "How's she?" Grandma Faye and Ceecee had been laying low since his conversation with them. He'd assumed they were busy arranging Ceecee's upcoming move, but maybe he'd been a shade too optimistic. Maybe they'd only been waiting for the best moment to strike.

His mother poked at her salad. "You know she's perfectly fine."

There was that word again. *Fine.* Jake had only recently discovered that "fine" usually meant anything but. He'd been telling people he was *fine* for days now, when in fact his insides resembled something that washed up on the beach, in the seaweed after a big storm.

Stella set her fork down with a firm click and stared at Jake. "Does he know?" She nodded at her husband.

"Know what?" Jake's dad asked. He shoved another bite of steak into his mouth and began chewing.

"Dad," Jake said. "*Nothing.* I—"

His mother huffed with impatience. "Jake, stop," she insisted. "Just *tell* him."

Clay frowned and looked at his wife. "Tell me *what?*"

"*Tell* him!" Stella demanded, slapping the table beside her plate with her palms. She hadn't *quite* shouted, but it was as close as the woman was likely to get. Under the table, Duke whimpered and crowded closer to Jake's shins.

Jake and his father stared at each other, in the world's most uncomfortable standoff. Finally, Jake squeezed his eyes shut.

"Crap," he muttered, pinching the bridge of his nose. "Dad, I don't want to be a damn judge," he admitted. "Not even a little bit." He dropped his head back and stared at the ceiling. Maybe, if he glared daggers at it, it would fall in on him.

"Well, why didn't you say so?" his father asked, reasonable and calm.

"Clay," Stella began, warning weighing down her voice. Her husband looked from her to Jake, then back again, as some sort of silent communication passed between them.

At last, the man spoke again. "I probably don't need to ask this, but—"

"*Or* the States Attorney, Dad," Jake growled.

"Oh." His father folded his napkin carefully across his lap while he thought about what Jake had said.

Jake might have managed to render him speechless for the moment, but now what? What came after admitting you were too ungrateful for your parents' help to do what they wanted you to do? What did a selfish future even look like?

His father blinked, and looked at his wife once more. "This have something to do with my new legal recruit? Because I like her. I swear to God, if you messed things up—"

"No, Dad," Jake huffed, exasperated. "I mean…not really." Jake had always thought he might feel lighter, having the career discussion off his chest once and for all. Instead, he just felt hollowed-out. Numb. Without Molly, it felt meaningless.

Jake's parents watched him, and for the life of him he couldn't read their expressions. When his father spoke again, he inquired, "Well, then—what *do* you want to do?"

Jake hadn't really let himself consider that question, knowing how far-fetched it was. But now, he let himself dream.

"I guess…" Jake thought about sitting on the end of that dock with Molly at his side and Duke at his back. Swinging his feet back and forth, eating ice cream, it had been easy to tell her what he secretly wished for himself. So—keeping her beautiful face in mind—Jake spoke the words he kept locked inside him: "I guess I want to be an estate attorney. Maybe even…open my own firm," he confessed. He reached down and rubbed Duke's soft floppy ear between his fingers.

For the first time since Jake had gotten there, his mother's face softened and her shoulders relaxed. "Now we're getting somewhere," she murmured, satisfied.

Jake's father nodded, taking Jake's earth-shattering announcement in stride like they were discussing the weather. "How can I help?" he asked.

WHEN JAKE DROVE away that night, he navigated the winding lanes of his parents' development with his windows down, so Duke could hang his head out and let his ears flap in the breeze. Jake had learned several interesting things before leaving, courtesy of two stories his father had told after dinner.

In the first, Clay had driven hell-for-leather up to the Chapel Hill campus, determined to beg, borrow, or steal (or to make a sizeable donation to the endowment fund) to keep his son in college. Instead, he'd found himself dining at the home of one of the university's undergraduate deans— enjoying a meal of chicken cordon bleu and an amicable conversation about famous Tar Heel alumni. He'd learned all kinds of details about the dean's grandkids.

It wasn't until the very end—when Clay had begun to wonder if he'd made the trip in vain—that the man brought up Jake. He explained that sending Jake home for the rest of the semester was supposed to be a bit of a lesson, intended to scare a good, smart kid straight. He thought Jake seemed overwhelmed, and maybe just needed one little nudge to get him to embrace the responsibilities of adulthood. If Jake did well in a few summer classes, he'd be welcomed back into the UNC fold the following fall—and the man saw no reason to believe Jake wouldn't go on to make the Tar Heels proud someday.

Upon learning this, Jake had sputtered, "But…I thought you…"

"Actually did something?" his father laughed.

"Well, yeah."

"Nope," Clay chuckled. "You're the only one who did things—both bad and good."

"But why did you let me believe you had to pull strings to get me back in?" Jake asked, poleaxed.

His father was amused. "We thought the lesson might make more of an impression if it put the fear of God in you," he said. "We just didn't expect it to have quite the sticking power it did."

"I'm...stunned," Jake admitted.

His mother smiled and left, mumbling something about going to get them all some ice cream.

Jake's dad continued, "Jackson, you always cleaned up your own messes, even when you were a kid. That time sophomore year was no different, in the end."

Jake could only manage to nod his head and then mutely accept a bowl of butter pecan—his favorite—from his mother.

The second story his father told was shorter, but no less surprising. Once Jake had a few minutes to think about things, he decided to ask one more pertinent question. Had Mr. Sutton truly gone to bat for Jake at Wake Forest Law? Had the man really gotten Jake in, as he'd been alleging for years?

Jake's mother had gotten a pinched look about her, and his father had appeared nearly apoplectic. Neither were aware that Blake's father had been claiming it, and the truth was an unequivocal *no*—Sutton had done no such thing. Bess's daddy had been holding a lie over Jake's head for years—and because Jake's own guilt and embarrassment had kept him silent on the subject—no one had ever been the wiser. He wondered if even Bess knew. He wondered...what *had* gotten him in. At that point, a dark horse candidate unexpectedly entered the fray.

Meryl, his mother's long-time housekeeper, had stepped onto the screened porch and cleared her throat. "I didn't mean to listen in—I was just coming to get the bowls," she said. She had looked at his dad. When Clay nodded, she stepped over to Jake—her heavy clogs thumping loudly across the slate tiles of the floor.

"I was the one who called that school," Meryl admitted. "It just seemed so unfair, after how hard you worked to graduate on time and what not."

Stella's eyes welled up as she gazed fondly at the other woman—Jake realized, watching them, that the ladies were far better friends than he'd ever suspected. His mother reached up and squeezed Meryl's hand.

"But...what did you tell them?" Jake wondered.

The housekeeper shrugged. "I don't know, sugar. I didn't really have a plan. I guess I just told them what I knew about you—what kind of person you were, and so forth. How you were always such a helpful soul, and how you never looked down on others like they were less than you. I told them..." At this she paused, and for the first time, looked shy.

"What?" Jake prompted her.

"I told them that if they took a chance on you, they wouldn't be sorry," she said.

By that point, even Jake's dad looked a bit emotional. "Meryl, that was very kind of you," he told her.

"Oh, it was nothing," she scoffed, waving him off.

"But it worked," Jake said, in awe of her. "You got me in."

"Nonsense," Meryl said. "That was no more than what you deserved. You earned that spot at school yourself, fair and square," she insisted.

"Even so," Jake replied, rising and enfolding the squat little woman in his arms. "Thank you."

Meryl squeezed him back for the briefest moment before she wriggled away. Gathering up the empty dessert bowls, she beckoned for Duke to follow her back into the house, and ducked her head to hide her flaming cheeks.

Jake might have sat there dumbfounded, for the rest of the night if his father hadn't clapped his hands and shooed Jake on his way, reminding his son that he still had one mess left that needed fixing. Molly—the most important mess of all.

J AKE WALLOWED FOR days, waiting to hear news about Grey Whitney's funeral arrangements. He imagined he'd have to wait until kingdom come to hear any news about Molly herself. She hadn't responded to any texts, calls, or emails. Jake had given up for the time being, not wanting to seem like he was stalking her, but he was worried sick about how Molly might be holding up. Not just about Grey's sudden death, but about how things had been left between her and Jake.

He was even more worried that the longer Molly refused to talk to him, the less chance he had of ever winning her back. With time had come clarity—it was possible that Jake wasn't *quite* as undeserving as he'd convinced himself. And if that basic fact were true, then a future without Molly was a nightmare too awful to contemplate.

So, he'd made a deal with himself—let Molly get past the funeral, and then figure out if she was going to move to Wilmington for the job or not. Once that was decided, Jake would have a better idea of what his next play should be. In the meantime, he would hopefully get to see her when he flew up to Maryland to lay Grey to rest. A brief snapshot of Molly to hold close, until Jake had her in his arms again.

He didn't expect Blake to waste her time attending Grey Whitney's funeral, since they'd barely known each other at UNC—that was a rookie mistake. When Jake pulled into the church parking lot in his rented sedan, Bess was there. She stood chatting with a group of DKE brothers and their significant others like it was a damn brunch or something.

Jake was peeved to have to see her again so soon, and in such an unwelcome place. But he was out-and-out livid that Blake had chosen *this* place, in particular, to make her stand.

Jake needed this time with Molly—to see how she was, and to decide how to get her back. That task would be immeasurably complicated by Blake's presence. Bess could be vindictive, after all, and—if she decided that Molly was somehow to blame for the dissolution of their engagement—she'd be gunning for trouble.

Never mind the fact that Blake's own temper had been the straw that finally broke the camel's back—if she suspected that Molly had led Jake astray, Bess would want payback. She'd find a way to get it, too.

Jake shook out his neck and shoulders, trying to loosen the muscles tensing up there. Bess couldn't have picked a more inappropriate place for her games. It felt tawdry and small. Jake wished he could merely stay away from her, but he was terrified about what she might say or do. There would be no avoiding Blake here—not if he expected to shield Molly and her sister from any fallout. Jake would have to stay close and stay alert.

As soon as he was noticed, Jake was absorbed into the huddle of Dekes, some of whom he hadn't seen in years. Bess took full advantage of them being the only two unaccompanied guests—by latching onto Jake's arm when she grew suspiciously wobbly on her heels, and letting the other women assume they were still a couple.

It was excruciating, trying to remain a gentleman—while also wondering if Molly might be watching him from some hidden alcove or another. Jake knew that at any second, she might catch sight of Bess and assume the worst. But short of inflecting bodily harm on his erstwhile fiancée—inside a house of God—Jake was stuck.

So instead, he did what his grandfather would have wanted—he prayed. Jake got down on his knees, ignored everyone around him and begged God to let Molly be well, and to open her mind and heart to Jake. He prayed that his path be made clear, and that when the time came, he would find the right words to express what he felt. As Jake sat back in the pew and gazed at Grey's casket, and then at Grey's stone-faced widow, he sent one more plea heavenward— that Jake not have to meet his maker before he could love Molly O'Connell for a good long time.

Chapter Thirty-Two

MOLLY DIDN'T SPOT Jake until after the service was over. She sat for a full hour in the chapel, staring at the gleaming brass fittings of Grey's casket when they glinted from under the edge of the flag draping the top. An hour of the priest reading familiar words of comfort. An hour of Marine Corp dress uniforms rustling throughout the gathering, and of handing Mina dry tissues to replace her damp ones. Sixty minutes of dust motes drifting in that sanctified, stained-glass air.

At the end, Molly stood with Mina near the doors of the church, greeting the parade of pitying faces that trudged past them. Suddenly, Jake was there, looming up before her. He was impeccable in his charcoal gray suit, and looked impossibly handsome despite his melancholy. Jake stared right at Molly, trying to catch her eye.

For some reason there was apology in his expression, though it took another minute to understand why. But then Molly saw her. There on Jake's arm—in an absolute vision of Southern gentility and sorrow—stood Miss Blake Elizabeth Sutton. Cool, collected, composed. Appropriately somber, but not a single lowbrow blotch or tearstain on her smooth and perfect cheeks. Of course—yet another horror to add to the list.

Molly choked on the indignity of it. How could he? After all they had said to each other, how did Jake dare bring that woman to the site of Molly's family tragedy—to the place of their grief? How could he rub salt in the wound like this? It went beyond all bounds of decency. But really, Molly shouldn't be surprised. She'd learned the hard way exactly what kind of man Jake Alexander was.

As she struggled with herself, they moved closer in the line. Molly wanted to leave—to turn tail and flee—and she prayed that she could do it with squared shoulders and head held high.

She wanted that more than her next breath, but Mina had a death grip on her arm. If Molly deserted her sister now, she was afraid the woman would shatter into a thousand pieces—and Molly was determined to forestall that as long as possible. Certainly, as long as there were witnesses.

The O'Connell girls might be many things, but they never, ever showed weakness to the world—they rarely even showed it to each other. But that didn't mean it wasn't there, spider-webbing in fissures all across their insides, just waiting for the one great hammer blow that would break them. Standing there, hugging each mourner in turn, Molly was reasonably sure that neither she nor her sister would emerge from this day whole. Here, perhaps, was their hammer.

With dead eyes, she registered that Bess had reached Mina, and begun talking in her cultured, soft little drawl.

"Mrs. Whitney, I am so sorry for your loss," she was saying. "I'm Blake Sutton. I knew Grey at school. He was a senior in the Dekes when I rushed the Deltas my freshman year."

Jake stood next to his future bride, and would not look away from Molly. He seemed to be trying to convey a thousand words with his eyes, and Molly felt trapped by his intensity. Drowning, unable to save herself. She drifted back behind her sister's shoulder, wanting to make herself invisible.

Mina just nodded, weakly attempting some interest in the other woman's explanation. She'd already heard a hundred variations on the same theme, a hundred memories of the one Deke brother who'd been a married veteran before he even entered college. Not a soul seemed to remember Mina herself.

Blake continued smoothly, "I believe you already know my fiancé, Jake Alexander?" At this, Mina's attention focused swiftly, and she glanced back at Molly before nodding warily at Bess.

"We've spoken on the phone, I believe. Thank you for coming, Jake," Mina said, shaking his hand.

"Of course," he murmured, smoothly transferring his attention to Molly's sister. He gave her a small half hug, then inquired, "How are you holding up? Is there anything I can do?" His face was pale, but still a flawless mask of solicitousness and concern.

Good Lord, Molly thought. They were magnificent together. A picture-perfect magazine spread of all that was enviable in the world. Jake and Blake. Blake and Jake. Even their names were echoes of each other. She didn't know how she hadn't noticed it before. How had Molly thought she ever stood a chance?

"No, no, we're doing fine. Thanks for asking," Mina deflected.

Fine. *Fine.* There was that God-forsaken word again. No one here was doing *fine*, with the possible exception of unflappable Blake Sutton—soon to be Mrs. Jake Alexander. Molly snorted at that appalling thought, and all eyes turned to her.

"You know Molly, of course," Mina said sardonically. She pulled Molly to stand beside her again.

Blake said, "Nice to meet you," though they'd met in Wilmington—and extended her slender, manicured hand. Molly, ever the masochist, found herself looking instead for Blake's *other* hand, wanting to glimpse that sparkling diamond one more time.

Jake spoke over his companion, "It's good to see you again, Molly." He took Molly's hand in his before she could reach his fiancée's, then sandwiched it with his other palm, holding on tight. Jake refused to break eye contact, so Molly looked away—only to clash eyes with Blake, and Blake's pretty frown. She didn't look like she enjoyed being thwarted.

"Again?" Bess inquired, a false note of uncertainty creeping into her voice. She turned and smiled faintly at Mina, seeking explanation.

Mina was only too happy to oblige. "Jake was kind enough to show Molly around Wilmington when she was interviewing at his dad's firm a couple weeks ago," she explained. She pivoted toward Jake. "Thanks again for doing that, by the way. We really appreciated it."

Mina might be leveled by this day, and unable to actually say her dead husband's name out loud at the moment—but she was still a big sister to her core. There was an identifiable threat in the sound of her words. Molly could've kissed her.

If Jake was ruffled by the comment, he hid it well. "It was my pleasure," he claimed, giving Molly another bone-melting look. He squeezed her hand between his large warm ones. Oh, he was devastating, all right. Molly tugged on her hand, hating his bright blue eyes and those stupid long eyelashes of his.

Blake was good, but even she wasn't that good. There was irritation written all over her face before she managed to school her features into placidity again.

"Yes, of course," she managed. "Now I remember. If you come down again, we'll have to *all* get together." With that, she tugged on Jake's arm, forcing him to release Molly as she pulled him toward the church steps.

"You all take care, all right?" Bess called, dragging Jake behind her.

Molly and Mina smiled their polite smiles, then turned as a unit back to the re-forming receiving line.

"Fiancé?" Mina growled under her breath. The guests moved toward them.

"Did I forget to mention that?" Molly murmured behind her hand when she passed it over her face.

"Sure did," retorted Mina. Her game face was firmly back in place and she resumed the role of the grieving widow.

THERE WAS A reception after the service, at Mina and Grey's little cottage. Mourners filed in and out, bringing yet more flowers and muffins and casseroles. Elderly aunts produced old dog-eared pictures of Grey as a boy, smiling from backyard swing sets with clusters of his cousins. The Dekes drank beer and ate sandwiches in a corner of the living room, and periodically erupted into laughter at someone's reminiscing. Molly's mother was steadily working her way through a bottle of chardonnay, and telling anyone who would listen about the dental conference her husband was speaking at.

Despite all that, Molly felt it—the moment Jake stepped through the front door. His gaze was like a brand, burning between her shoulder blades. Without turning, she grabbed a handful of empty plates and cups, and made for the safety of the kitchen. But Jake was quicker than she hoped, and followed her smoothly. In moments, he had Molly cornered in the pantry, crowding her into the tiny space and blocking the door with his large body.

"Molly, God, how are you?" he asked.

"What are you doing?" she demanded, pushing at Jake's chest. "Let me *out* of here!"

"Stop, woman. Would you just stop? I have to talk to you." He looked forlorn, the rat.

All right, then. He wanted to talk? Great. Molly could talk. "How *could* you?" she hissed. "How could you bring that woman here?"

"I'm so sorry. I didn't want her to come."

"But you did it anyway!" she cried.

"First off, I didn't *bring* Blake—she came on her own. Secondly, she knew Grey, too," Jake explained. "It would've been a little tricky to exclude her."

"Really?" Molly squawked. "Or were you just too chicken—as usual—to stand up to her?"

Jake blinked, a little taken aback by her fury. "Molly, Bess came with other people. I had no say in it whatsoever. But listen, what's more important is that—"

Molly bristled, every nerve in her body sizzling into furious, avenging life. "*No*. I don't have to listen to a thing you say. All you do is *lie*."

"You still think that's what I did?" Jake replied, getting angry himself, now. "You think I *lied* to you?"

Molly nodded, desperately trying to choke back her tears. She wanted to cry about the weird relief she felt to *see* Jake, and about the agony she felt that he was *here*. She wanted to sob out her complete inability to explain why it was all so horrible and mixed-up in her heart.

"Molly, listen. Not one damn thing I ever said or did with you was a lie, do you hear me?" Jake croaked. "I'm gonna keep sayin' that until you *hear* me, damn it."

"Well, then it was a lie by omission," she sneered. "Because you certainly never mentioned your damn fiancée while you were making out with *me*."

"I…" he stopped. Opened his mouth, then shut it again. Started over, "Molly, I never expected what happened between us. It was a total surprise, and—"

She cut him off. "Oh, it was a surprise alright." *Sarcastic.* Yes, that was the way to go. Sarcastic was much, much better than pathetic.

"Listen, it took me by surprise, it's true—but it also made a lot of things clear to me. I just needed a little time to make things right, and then…"

"Make things right?" Molly asked, incredulous. "Make things *right*? How on earth is bringing Blake here *making things right*?" With that she gave another shove, pushing Jake into the shelves of soup cans so she could escape out the door.

But Jake had a long reach. He wrapped his hand around her bicep, then used it to swing her into his body in the middle of the kitchen. He wrapped his strong arms around her and held Molly in place. Not too close to his familiar frame—but close enough for Molly to remember everything they'd done together. Every moment and every inch of skin.

He ducked his head, and inches from her lips said roughly, "Molly I am *not here with Blake*. She grabbed my arm in the church when she saw you standing there, and then she called me her fiancé just to piss you off. We are *not* together, and have not *been* together since the moment you saw her toss that ring in my face."

"Yeah right," Molly whimpered.

"I'm dead serious, honey," Jake said. Sincerity was etched into his face, and poured off him in waves. If Jake was lying, he was very, very good at it.

Next thing Molly knew, he had pulled her tight against him. She stood stiffly, trying her damnedest not to melt into his embrace, not to notice his familiar comforting scent, or to let his warmth thaw her heart. He dropped one soft, tender kiss on her forehead, then another.

"God, Molly," he whispered. "I love you. Please stop fighting me."

"No," she refused. She had to stay numb—it was her only chance to survive. Jake would never love her the way she needed. He couldn't.

But when Molly looked up at him, defiance in her eyes and ready to tell him what she thought of his love, Jake did the worst, most unexpected thing he could do—the bastard kissed her. Gently at first, just a slight pressure of his lips against hers. In the next breath, he tilted his head, and everything changed.

Molly O'Connell stood in her sister's kitchen wearing her black mourning dress, and had the wits kissed out of her. Jake's lips and tongue waged war on hers, and won. She'd tried to be strong, she really had—but holy hell. No woman could resist this, and she had missed Jake so darn much.

Molly surrendered. She wrapped her arms around Jake's neck, pressed against him and gave herself up to it. To the fury and the grief and the love, and everything that festered in between. It was heaven and hell all wrapped into one. Until, suddenly, it wasn't.

Jake broke off on a sharp inhale, raising his head to look over her shoulder. Molly stared at his green and blue striped tie, inches from her face, while Blake's voice washed over her.

"Well, I suppose that's one way to comfort someone," she drawled. Bess leaned forward and placed her punch glass precisely on the counter next to Molly. "Not the way I might have chosen, but what do I know?"

"Lay off, Blake," Jake spat.

"You don't get to tell me what to do," she informed him. Then Blake turned on her heel and walked away, her delicate sling-back pumps clicking on the hardwood floor.

Jake looked down at Molly, his face intent. "Stay here," he instructed, moving her to the side with firm palms on her shoulders. "I will be right back and then you and I are going to finish this discussion." Then he took off, following his maybe-fiancée with steady, determined strides.

"No," Molly whispered into the empty air after he left. His dress shoes snapped against the wood too, Molly noticed, in almost the same measured way Blake's had. Yet another thing they shared in common.

She heard Blake's voice in the hall. "How much of a dope do you have to be, Jackson? You broke us up for some girl who doesn't even want you!"

"For crying out loud, Blake," he fired back. "They just buried her brother-in-law today—what the hell is wrong with you?"

"The only thing wrong with me was ever thinking you would change."

Jake snorted. "You know what? There wasn't a damn thing in my life I needed to change but *you.*"

Molly peeked into the hall and watched him steer Bess right out the front door. She darted into the guest bath across from the kitchen to repair her appearance, and then— satisfied that she could brave the room with dignity intact, she walked out to rejoin her sister.

Mina stood in the dining room, holding the same plate of food she hadn't touched for an hour, listening to yet another woman rhapsodize about wonderful, sainted Grey. Molly pushed all thought of treacherous Southerners aside, and tried to decide whether to insist that her sister eat something. She didn't know if she could do the same, in Mina's position. Before she made up her mind, though, a good-looking, dark-haired man sidled up behind Mina, and laid a tentative hand between her shoulder blades. He took the plate from her, set it on the sideboard, then replaced it in Mina's hand with a full wine glass.

"Mom, give her a break," he said to the other woman. "Mina's had a long day."

The woman got misty, and pressed her lips together. "I know, honey. I'm sorry." To Mina, she explained, "I just can't believe it, that's all."

Mina nodded, very understanding. "It's okay, Mrs. Bolton. None of us can." She gestured to Molly then. "You remember my little sister Molly?"

"Hi, Mrs. Bolton. Hey, Mack," Molly said. Mack was one of Grey's childhood friends from the Eastern Shore, she remembered. She'd met him once or twice, when she was still a teen and her sister was having a hasty wedding to a young Marine. That was back before Molly had gone to prep school—where she'd learned that *all* men were traitorous, lying jerks, and not just her own dad. While Mack *seemed* nice enough—both then and now—Molly knew that didn't mean a thing.

"Oh, honey, how are you?" Mrs. Bolton asked. "All the focus is on Mina of course, but you lost a brother, didn't you?" Tears began streaking down her face again.

Molly winced and peeked at her sister, but Mina had her wine glass tipped up and was taking a deep drink. She cast them all a brisk smile and made to leave, heading for the next cluster of people gathered to mourn Grey. Before she left the Boltons with Molly, though, Mina knocked her shoulder into her sister's. With a quick, imperceptible jerk of her chin, Mina indicated the big bay window at the front of the adjacent family room—through which Jake and Bess were clearly visible, their postures tense and voices raised.

Molly watched Jake hand her a car key he fished from his trouser pocket, and she watched the other woman stalk down the driveway all by herself. Blake couldn't be that mad, Molly surmised, since she hadn't tossed anything in Jake's face this time. Still, when he turned back to the house, Jake's expression was bleak. Why had he stayed here to torment her? Why couldn't he have just gone with Bess, and left Molly in peace?

"So," she chirped, spinning back to her companions. "Did you have any trouble getting over the bridge this morning? I heard the traffic was awful."

"Not at all," Mrs. Bolton demurred. "We left early enough. But it will probably be bad later, on the way home." She turned to Mack. "What time do you think we ought to leave, hon?"

Mack didn't reply. His eyes, Molly noticed, never wavered from her sister's back—glued to Mina as she made her way around the room and the clusters of family and friends gathered there. And wasn't *that* interesting?

"Mack?" his mother tried again.

Molly placed a hand on each of their arms. "I'm just going to…" she murmured, but she didn't bother finishing. She drifted away, and neither of them even noticed she had left.

MOLLY SPENT THE rest of the reception keeping busy—clearing plates, dumping trash, and refilling platters and coffee cups. She meticulously avoided any private corners or alcoves where Jake might get her alone. When she thought Mina had consumed enough wine to almost certainly be tipsy—if not outright hammered—she switched the wineglass in her hand back out for a fresh plate of food.

At her mother's request, Molly found Elaine's purse in the guest room, retrieved a pill, and cut it in half for her—so she could, as her mother put it, "Keep it together." Their mom had never been great in crowds, or with strong emotions. Molly wasn't surprised in the least that she was medicating, but she wondered whether her stepfather knew. He must, she decided—no way would her mother forgo the opportunity for more attention.

Molly toyed with whether to give the other half of the pill to Mina, but decided she'd had too much to drink to consider doing that. In the end, she fished it out of her pocket and swallowed it herself—gulping it down with the last of the punch before handing the huge bowl off to their mother to wash in the kitchen. After the week she'd had, Molly figured she could forgive herself for that one weakness, at least.

Jake eventually left with a man who had introduced himself as the president of the UNC Deke chapter where he, Jake, and Grey had all met. The man's wife was a leggy brunette with a glossy chignon. Molly thought she was named "Missy," or maybe "Misty."

Molly watched her from behind the edge of the front door. Missy slid gracefully into the back seat of the car and left the two men to sit up front. They continued their conversation while she scrolled absently through her phone.

For some reason, the sight of that woman complacently agreeing to be driven around like an afterthought irritated the hell out of Molly. She would never be able to explain why. It was only more evidence of a world and a life that she would never be a part of, she supposed.

Soon after, the last stragglers finally departed. Their mother and Mina retreated to their respective bedrooms, both wanting to be alone with their thoughts after the long and exhausting day. Molly slipped off her heels and finished cleaning up the house.

Then, she made her way into the home office—where she'd been camped out for the last three days on a fold-out couch. Molly fired up her laptop, and began looking for a flight back to Boston.

Between taking off from Wilmington so abruptly and her foolishness with a partner's son, it was possible she'd already lost the job at *Alexander, Polk & Futch*. But even if she hadn't, they would not be contacting her for at least a week. Molly needed to go home, pay some bills, and send out some more resumes. She had to find a place to live, at least temporarily.

And she had to pretend that life moved on—whether she was ready for it or not.

MEG AND HER future brother-in-law Charlie met Molly at the airport. She was relieved that Meg's fiancée Edward hadn't come, too—the very last thing she needed was to be confronted with all *that* love and happiness. Instead of bringing her to the house where she sublet her room, however, Charlie drove them right to a quiet side street in the Back Bay.

"Ready to see your new digs?" Meg smiled.

"What are you talking about?" Molly knew she'd had a rough couple of weeks, but she was pretty sure she'd remember getting a new apartment. Charlie, though, was already bouncing down a set of stone stairs and unlocking a freshly-painted red door at the bottom.

"It's George's old place," Meg explained, fishing Molly's bags out of the trunk. "When you had to go to the funeral, we figured we could at least help you out by getting your living situation squared away."

George was another one of Edward's brothers. "But where are George and Poppy staying?" Molly asked, completely confused. Inside the basement apartment, all of Molly's things appeared to have been unpacked and arranged—mixed in with some additional furniture that must have been George's. She stood and turned in a circle, utterly stunned.

"Poppy wanted to move into the place they bought on Beacon Hill," Charlie chuckled. "George is having a conniption, trying to live there while they do the renovations."

"That's the truth," Meg laughed. "Anyway, there are three months left on the lease here, so it seemed like the perfect solution for everyone."

Molly took in the sun slanting in the windows set high in the front wall, and the cute little kitchen off to the side. She stared at her two sweet friends standing in the middle of the room, gazing at her with hopeful looks on their faces. They had not only found her a place—but they had moved her *into* it.

"You guys. I...I can't believe you did this for me."

"Of course you can," Charlie scoffed. "Don't be ridiculous. You know we're fabulous."

Meg shrugged, and pointed at Charlie in agreement.

"How much rent does George want?" Molly asked. The apartment was a sizeable two-bedroom, in a nice part of town. Even the kitchen was updated and modern. It didn't look the least bit affordable.

Meg said, "He didn't want to take anything, but we told him you'd never agree to that."

No, Molly was no one's burden.

"We negotiated him up to a hundred bucks a month, but he refused to take a cent more. He's pretty pissed about it," Charlie said. "Which, naturally, I love."

A hundred dollars a month? For this place? It was unheard of in the city. Molly's dingy little bedroom in a scruffy part of Allston had cost her at least five hundred a month, and only that when all the other bedrooms had been sublet out.

Molly took a deep breath, then released it. She sank into a comfortable loveseat that she'd never laid eyes on before, blinked at Meg and Charlie, and opened her lips to thank them. Instead, she started bawling—big, messy, jagged sobs that horrified her and seemed like they'd never end.

Her friends knew her well, and had planned for even that occurrence. Charlie waltzed into the kitchen, procured a bottle-opener, and pulled the cork on a bottle of red. Meg retrieved three wine glasses from a cabinet near the sink, and brought them into the living room. They sat on either side of Molly, wrapped their arms around her, and let her weep.

Chapter Thirty-Three

HEARTBREAK HAD TURNED him into a lovelorn fool. Jake had spent weeks mooning around, listening to the same song over and over on his phone and not caring about much more than feeding his dog on time. Even Duke must be sick of "Hey There Darling" by now—Jake sure was.

Without Molly around, he had plenty of time to think, even though much of it was spent on a virtual hamster wheel of self-recrimination. If he'd only met Molly some other time—either before Blake, or long after. If only Jake had *said* something, anything, much sooner. If he had somehow managed to be a better man, then maybe—just maybe—he might have held onto the best thing that ever happened to him. He didn't know how he was supposed to even *look* at another woman now—as far as he was concerned, Molly was it for him. And since the only person Jake owed anything to anymore was himself, he thought maybe he'd earned some happiness with her.

But Molly wanted nothing to do with him. Instead of simply earning her heart and keeping her, Jake was now in the lousy position of having to win her back. While he planned what to do, he considered—at length—what he knew for a fact about Molly.

Her father had essentially taught her all about faithlessness, impermanence, and disloyalty, right at an age when she likely needed him the most.

Her mother was worse. Jake had met Elaine at the funeral, and she was the type who clearly needed a big, strong man to manage everything. Instead of using her own life choices to teach her daughters how to be women—how to demand the respect they were due—Elaine had doubled-down and expected them to do as she did.

Mina, it seemed, had learned that lesson well—hooking up with Grey as a teen and leaving her mother and sister behind without a backward glance.

Molly had to figure out how to be an independent adult all on her own. And she'd become so damn independent, that she thought she didn't need anything from anyone. Not help, not trust, and certainly not love—that asshole Carter she'd fallen prey to had made extra sure of that.

As Molly saw it, allowing herself to be vulnerable with a man would only ever be met with humiliation and betrayal. Was it any wonder she hadn't believed Jake? As much as he wanted to be angry with her for taking his stupid, fragile heart and running it through a meat-grinder, he simply couldn't bring himself to.

The question now was, how could he show Molly that she was wrong? Prove to her that he wasn't anything like those other people in her life? Jake supposed…by doing the exact *opposite* things that they had. He could show up. Be there. Not leave. Not change. Stay true.

Jake had some tentative ideas about how he could make a start, but first he *had* to see her. It looked like Jake would be taking his first trip up to Boston. With luck, it would also be his last.

HIS DECISION HADN'T been made for long by the time his mother managed to corner him. She'd called and asked to meet him at the courthouse—but Jake soon found himself escorting her to lunch. In a little bistro nearby, he learned her purpose.

With no preliminaries, Stella launched right in and demanded to know if Jake planned to send Molly a souvenir to commemorate her visit. Because Molly had left under such sad circumstances, Jake's mother was especially insistent that he find a gift to make it up to her.

Jake was confused, but of course his mama didn't quite know all the details of what went down before Molly left. At least, he *hoped* she didn't—it was definitely possible that Mrs. Denson had already leaked the details like a rusted old crab trap.

Jake tried to demur, to tell his mother that it wasn't necessary. Still, Stella kept insisting that it was the proper thing to do. She had barely even touched her pasta salad— with its tiny balls of mozzarella and sun-dried tomatoes— and Jake knew it was one of her favorites. He couldn't imagine why she was so worked up, why this had required a visit at work from her, unless...

He frowned. "Why, Mama, if I didn't know better, I'd say you actually liked that girl."

"I said nothing of the sort," she huffed, stabbing at her plate.

But she didn't *need* to say anything. Stella had made her point with a minimum of fuss, as usual. Another woman might have hollered at her boy—insisted that he go out and repair the mistakes he'd made or suffer the consequences. Not Stella Alexander, oh no. She merely pointed out one minor point of etiquette, sailed from the vicinity before matters had the chance to get heated, and that was that. It was up to Jake to take it from there.

He supposed, with a mother like her, he might have become extra perceptive when it came to women's moods. If only that skill had been remotely in evidence where Molly was concerned. But Jake was damned if Molly didn't upend every last shred of practicality he'd ever possessed—she made him crazy, and that was a fact. It was a good kind of crazy, though. A crazy he wanted to live a long time with.

When he thought about it, Jake decided that his mother's idea might tie in with his visit to Molly quite nicely. If he were to soften Molly up beforehand—send her a souvenir every day for a week, say—then maybe by the time he arrived up north, she might be willing to stay put long enough for Jake to say his piece. He'd have to make sure he cornered her in her lair, though, so Molly couldn't give him the slip before he had a chance to tell her everything he needed to.

His vague ideas began coming together into an actual plan of attack. It might be foolishness—and it might all come to naught—but at least Jake would know he tried.

Falling for Molly had maybe turned Jake ridiculous—and under normal circumstances, he couldn't imagine being grateful for such a thing. Except… he was. Loving her had given Jake the courage to break himself out of his horrible, self-imposed prison. While he'd been living in that cell, getting free had seemed impossible.

It was strange, that all it took to get out was unlocking the door and stepping away. Molly—Molly was the key that made everything else fall into place. If Jake didn't already love her for a thousand other reasons, he would've loved her for that fact alone.

And just like that, he knew what the first gift was that he'd send her: a tiny silver key pendant. Jake had noticed it in the jewelry case of that tourist shop—the day he'd brought Molly some clothes along with those deli sandwiches. It would look perfect on her, glinting in the sun and nestled into the hollow at the base of her neck. Jake's mind drifted, imagining taking it into his mouth when he kissed her neck there. He fantasized about her wearing that little key, and nothing else.

When he ventured out to pick the other gifts, though, he couldn't decide. Jake overdid it, and got too much of everything—a book from the plantation gift shop, and a flower from one of the shrubs that he snapped off and pressed inside. He bought t-shirts from bars and restaurants they had gone to, and one for the band "Damn Yankees," just because it made him smile. It was overkill, and in Molly's ass-backward view of things Jake would probably look like he was trying to buy back her affections. But he couldn't seem to stop.

Once he'd exhausted his ideas, he arranged his purchases into six piles—sorting them into boxes with ribbons, but no notes. Jake fished his old, beat-up Tar Heels hat out of his closet and dropped it in one box, because Molly had looked so cute in it the day she borrowed it at the beach.

Duke trotted up and dropped one of his toys in a box, too. Jake wondered if his dog had any idea what was happening, but figured he wouldn't fight it—it couldn't hurt for Molly to know that Jake's dog missed her, too.

When Jake bought his plane ticket for the following week, it was harder than he expected to decide on a one-way, or a round-trip. Should he get an extra one-way for the return, so that Molly could come back with him? What if sending a box a day—for a week straight before his visit—didn't work? What if Jake botched things up once he got there, and said all the wrong words again?

He couldn't think about that. He wouldn't. On the seventh day, Jake would present himself on Molly's doorstep, and offer her his heart as his final gift. It *had* to be enough. He had nothing else left to give.

THE WEEK PASSED, somehow. Jake couldn't have said how he spent it, other than making sure those boxes were sent out on time. Every evening, he took notes on what he wanted to say, and he devised the arguments that were sure to convince her. Jake didn't want to forget a single thought that might help his case. The pages piled up. He tried to speak Molly's language.

The night before his departure, he went to Healey's house to drop off Duke. Jake had considered actually bringing the poor mutt along, but in the end decided it was would be exercising an unfair advantage. Molly adored his dog, and having his sad puppy eyes blinking up at her might make her feel guilty for all the wrong reasons. If she was going to come back to Jake, he wanted it to be because she realized she could count on him—that it was safe to love him back.

Jake called up to Healey's apartment to let her know he was there. Before she could answer, though, his buddy Tim emerged from the elevator inside and came sashaying out the lobby door. A panicked, guilty expression crossed his face for half a second before he schooled it—and then Tim was knocking fists with Jake, and laughing about having a friend in the building. Another second, and Tim was taking off, claiming that he was late for work.

Tim's navy-blue uniform shirt was still untucked, flapping in the breeze as he trotted across the parking lot. He smelled freshly-showered. Jake frowned, wondering if the "friend" in question was more of a *flame*. Usually Tim told him about these things, but...Jake had been knotted up in his own head for a while. He could've missed something.

He asked his sister about it when he reached her apartment, but Healey looked blank and claimed ignorance. That seemed weird, too—usually she dove on the chance to gossip about Tim's conquests. It was probably Jake's imagination that he thought he smelled the same fresh scent on Healey. Probably a total coincidence that the ends of her hair were wet—like she, too, had just showered.

It would be total insanity if Jake's best friend were secretly involved with his little sister...wouldn't it? Jake couldn't spend time wondering about it. He had his own love life to worry about.

Chapter Thirty-Four

MOLLY LISTENED ABSENTMINDEDLY to her boss Wilda, talking on the phone extension across the office. When she applied to work part-time at the legal aid center during law school, Molly had mainly wanted something close to home—where she could do some good and build up her resume. The work had become so much more than that, with clients that tugged at her heart every day. And at the helm of the shabby storefront center, there was always Wilda.

She'd been the one to lobby for Molly's hire, right from the start. "We could use some more women around here," she'd told her then. Now, two of the three full-time attorneys were women, as well as several of the paralegals and student employees.

In a city of brusque Bostonians, Wilda insisted that her "chicks" be kind and compassionate to their downtrodden clients—for that, they universally adored her.

Most clients had simple cases, but some were poor immigrants with complicated visa issues, or women fleeing unhappy—or even abusive—marriages. Molly had never thought she'd get tired of helping all of them, but since she'd returned from Wilmington…things felt different. Losing Jake had turned her into something raw and unprotected, vulnerable to outside hurts.

Being worn out by her own emotions made helping the suffering aid clients a challenge. The work seemed hard and thankless and never-ending—and after years of toiling away at it, the many problems of their community felt too brutal for Molly's battered heart. She didn't think she'd last much longer there, as sad as that made her feel.

Most days, she found herself longing for a simple traffic case, maybe even a trust or a…will. Jake liked to draft wills. Maybe he had even quit his job and begun drafting wills already.

Molly heard the creak of Wilda's old leather desk chair, and hastily returned to the brief she was supposed to be working on. She'd been staring off into space, zoning out to the sound of her boss's voice, for who knew how long.

Wilda had probably noticed—she never missed a thing that happened inside the walls of her domain. Sure enough, the tall woman was leaning on Molly's desk within moments. Molly stopped and smiled up at her.

"What can I do for you?" she asked.

Wilda pulled up a plastic chair and sank into it. "I just had the most interesting phone call from a lovely woman named Maryanne. Apparently, she works for *Alexander, Polk & Futch* down in the great state of North Carolina."

Oh. Molly cleared her throat. "Did you?"

"Naturally I was obliged to tell her about your razor-sharp intellect and sparkling sense of humor," Wilda said, raising one sardonic eyebrow.

"I see." Molly frowned, trying to gauge her boss's mood.

"I also confirmed that you do actually work here," she laughed.

"Gee, thanks," Molly said, rolling her eyes.

"Molly...may I speak freely?" Wilda leaned back, crossing her arms against her chest. Her boxy blazer pleated up at her waist, and Molly figured she must have had an appearance in court that morning—Wilda wore suits only to appease the judges she practiced in front of. If it were up to her alone, she'd be wearing sneakers, jeans and hoodies all day.

When she wasn't in court, she often did. Molly thought that was probably why so many of their clients related to her so easily. Wilda was as approachable as an attorney was ever likely to get around there.

"Please do," Molly told her. Wilda looked like she wanted to drop some science on Molly, and that could either be very good, or very depressing.

"I know you aren't happy here. And the fact is...you don't *really* belong here. Which isn't to say you aren't great at the work you do—you are. I just don't get the sense that it's your calling, like it is mine. I truly love what I do here every day, but not everyone can stick with it long term. Not successfully, without getting burned out." She sighed, then continued, "You have a tender heart, kiddo, and this kind of work—it's already starting to wear on you. I really believe you would be happier working in a different kind of environment. Maybe around some more people your own age," Wilda told her.

Molly rubbed her eyes. "You might be right," she confessed.

"Besides, didn't you say you have family down there?" her boss inquired.

"My dad lives about forty-five minutes away from Wilmington," Molly found herself admitting. Her voice emerged smaller than she'd intended. Which was strange, because in the three years she'd worked there, Wilda had acted more like a parent to her than Molly's own ever had. Why should Molly care where Elaine or Skip chose to live?

What was also strange? The fact that Molly had no confidence whatsoever that her father would actually stay put in Holden Beach for more than six more months, at best. She hated that she *hoped* he'd stay. Still, even as old as Molly was, she couldn't *stop* hoping. But there you had it—more evidence that Jake had gone and turned her soft.

"It would be good for you to have some time with him," Wilda said. "That's one of the reasons I was so happy to be the person to field that phone call just now. You're going to be a wonderful attorney, but you should find a way to be happy personally, too."

"I will," Molly murmured. Somehow.

Wilda nodded, and sprang up. "I do wish you luck. If you don't get the job, it won't be because of me." With a wink, she sauntered toward the private area in the back, muttering about ditching her monkey suit.

Well, then, Molly thought. If Maryanne was calling around checking her references, that meant Molly was one step closer to getting the job she'd been pining for. One month ago, she was certain it would be the culmination of all her dreams. Now, she wasn't so sure. The dream had turned sour with Jake in the mix.

Three hours later, Molly left work and rode the T to her new, spacious apartment. She'd only been there a week, but she already loved the little historical details and the privacy of being separate from all the other units. As intense as she knew George to be, she found it funny that his former home was so serene. Molly thought that if she did end up staying in Boston, she would try to stay there—to sign a new lease if she landed a good-paying job in the city.

Except, every time she found an opening and got her resume together, she just couldn't bring herself to send it. Part of her was resisting giving up entirely on North Carolina. Part of her was still wishing for Jake.

She changed clothes quickly, then walked the few blocks to Meg and Edward's brownstone. Since she'd been back in Boston, Molly had avoided spending any time with them as a couple. She hated being confronted with everything she couldn't have, and Molly was beginning to suspect—more with each passing day—that if she couldn't have love with Jake, it wasn't going to be with anybody.

Her friends' latest dinner invitation had been unavoidable, though. They welcomed her into their home with warm hugs, then led her toward the family room in the back. Molly looked around—each time she visited, she noticed new layers of hominess. Another framed photo on a wall. Another little statue on a shelf. Each new item a talisman of the way these two dealt with each other and the world around them—with so much love to spare. With such gratitude for what they'd had to work so hard for.

By the time they all finished their cocktails and were seated in the dining room, Molly was wondering why she'd stayed away. Not only was Meg one of her dearest, most understanding friends, but her fiancée Edward was exactly the same.

Meg's seal of approval would have been all Edward needed to welcome Molly as a friend. But when he learned what Molly had done for the love of his life—when he wasn't there to do it himself—that really clinched the deal.

Edward had once informed Molly that he would feel eternally indebted to her for taking care of Meg, and Molly believed him. He'd put them all through the wringer, but now that he was well again it was impossible not to love him. If the two remaining single Hughes brothers weren't so unsuitable, Molly might try for one of them herself.

They'd barely finished with the salad when Edward brought up Jake. "Meg told me a little bit about what happened in North Carolina," he said.

"Ugh," Molly complained, glaring at Meg. "Let's not go there."

"Well…" Edward hedged.

"What?"

"I don't mean to stir the pot," he began.

Meg interjected, "But he wants to stir the pot."

"Seriously?" Molly groaned. "You lure me here with the promise of home-cooked food, and then you let your dude ambush me?"

"It's for your own good. You made *me* do lots of things I didn't want to do," Meg smiled.

Molly's eyes narrowed. "So, you're going to play the payback card?"

"Sure am," Meg smirked, taking a sip of her wine. "And I hear it's a bitch."

Molly turned to Edward, studying him. He was, at his core, a genuinely nice guy. Whatever he had to say to her, at least she knew he'd be gentle about it. She may as well get it over with.

"Alright, tough guy. Have at it," she snapped.

Edward chuckled. "For the sake of full disclosure, let's review the facts as you know them."

"Awesome. Now you're a lawyer?" Molly griped.

Edward shook his head. "Listen, did this bloke Jake *actually* cheat on his ex with you?"

Molly looked between Meg and Edward. "Well…"

"I mean, did he *literally* go from your bed to hers?" he prodded. "Just as an example."

Molly grudgingly had to admit the truth, "No. He would never do that. I doubt he'd have had the time anyway. We spent a lot of time together."

"Okay, that's good," Ed said. "Did he display any other signs of actively cheating? Like, only wanting to go to your place, or only taking you to places far away from his normal neighborhood? Did he ever introduce you to his friends or anything?"

Geez, Molly thought. Had these two been reading up on cheaters in the last couple weeks? "Not really," she explained. "I mean—we did hang out in the sticks a few times." At this, Meg's eyebrows rose, and she smiled slyly. Molly powered on, "But we went out downtown, too. Also, I met his parents and his sister and his best friend."

Edward nodded thoughtfully, and took a bite of his fish.

Meg mused, "That doesn't sound very sketchy to me."

"But you guys—" Molly protested. "You don't understand. Jake put the moves on me probably *twelve hours* after his fiancée dumped him. He didn't even wait a whole day! And he wasn't even the one to end it—*she* was."

"Did he explain why?" Edward wondered.

"Umm." Molly stared down at her plate, and poked at a spear of roasted asparagus.

Meg asked, "Molly?"

"I didn't exactly let him. He tried, but I was too pissed."

Edward took a deep breath and leaned back, but he didn't seem surprised. "The thing is—love doesn't exactly play by the rules. Sometimes it smacks you over the head when you aren't looking for it, or you aren't ready for it, or the timing is really awkward."

Meg laughed, "You think either of us went to the coffee shop that day expecting what happened to us?"

"With Poppy running that ship?" Molly smiled back. "Doubtful."

"Molly…listen," Edward continued. "Life is short. You never know what might happen in the space of a second. You can have everything you want, and have it snatched away in the blink of an eye. You have no control over it."

Molly knew Edward spoke from experience. She swallowed hard, willing herself not to start crying. Meg certainly was tearing up, damn her.

Edward said, "What we wanted to tell you was only this: if you and this Jake love each other—if that rare and mysterious chemistry is there between you—then you have to try to make it work. A happy life isn't always…just handed to you. You're going to argue about stupid stuff, and then have to find a way to apologize or forgive each other. You'll have to keep *choosing* each other—over and over, every day—if you want happiness."

"I know that," Molly complained reflexively. But the truth, the real truth, was that she didn't. Aside from Meg and Edward—and the rest of the Hughes family—Molly didn't know any other couples who operated that way.

She hadn't quite realized that she'd never learned any practical relationship tools before now. But here Meg and Edward were, giving her the handbook to happiness. It sounded so easy, so simple, that even a fool could do it.

But maybe Molly had been too much of a fool to even get that basic formula right. Maybe…she had gone and lost the best man in the world because she had screwed up worse than he had. Maybe Molly had declared Jake guilty without ever once considering the evidence—and maybe Molly had convicted an innocent man for the sins of someone else.

TWO DAYS LATER, Jake's first box arrived. There was a note inside, telling her to expect one thing a day for the whole week. Molly had received them as promised—and then some. One day, she also got flowers. Another day, a pizza had been delivered. On yet a third day, she'd opened a strange brown envelope to find a CD of "The Greatest Karaoke Hits of the 90's."

But now it was the seventh day, and Molly had come up empty. Nothing arrived at work, and nothing was in the mail. No packages were delivered during dinner, and she'd finally thrown in the towel. Molly showered and slumped in her pajamas on the couch—and admitted to herself that Jake's last gift really wasn't going to come. She didn't want to look forward to it. Didn't *want* to want it. But she did. She missed him. She loved Jake, and she was a reckless idiot who didn't deserve him.

She shuffled into the kitchen to make some tea, but then...there came a knock on her front door. Molly froze, hand on the mug sitting in her microwave. She stared at the thick wood panels. Another knock, and a faint cough that sounded so familiar. But it couldn't possibly be Jake—not several states away, and not through a Boston front door. It was wishful thinking, that was all. Molly padded carefully toward the door anyway.

She squinted through the peephole and there was Jake—staring right at her, a hopeful look on his face. Like he *knew* she was peering out at him.

"*Jake?*" Molly squeaked.

He must have heard her. A tentative smile curled up his lips. "Molly? Is that you?"

Molly ripped at the locks and threw open the door. "*JAKE?*"

"Hey girl." He hitched his hanging bag up on his shoulder and grinned, pulling the brim of his hat higher on his forehead. Jake's blue eyes sparkled in his tanned face—so out of place here in Boston, even in the middle of summer. He looked eager, but also a little wary, and if that didn't break Molly's heart all over again, nothing could.

"Jake, what are you doing here?" Molly cried, trying not to throw herself into his arms like a desperate trollop.

He shrugged. "Well, you know—I was in the area, and I thought I'd stop by."

"You were not, you big liar." She smacked him on the arm, because she *had* to touch him.

Jake's smile faded. "I'm not a liar, Molly."

"Yes, you are," she blurted out, and then she began to cry.

"Never," Jake disagreed, shaking his head sadly. "But especially not to you."

Molly gripped the edge of door and hung on, sloppy tears leaking from her eyes and dripping off her chin.

"Hey, don't cry," he whispered stepping closer. "It's going to be okay, I promise."

"You swear?" Molly demanded.

"Cross my heart," Jake said, hugging her tight and holding her close.

"I'm sorry I didn't believe you," she blubbered.

"I'm sorry I didn't tell you everything, right from the beginning," he retorted.

Molly pressed her face against his damp shoulder, "It's okay."

"I missed you so much," Jake murmured into her hair. "Did you get my packages?"

Molly nodded, crying harder. God—he was so, so wonderful. What had she done?

He leaned back and tried to catch her eye. "Molly?"

"What?" She squeezed Jake tighter.

"Do you think I could come in? People are looking at us kind of funny."

Molly laughed and backed into her apartment, dragging Jake in with her. She locked the door again, then turned and mopped off her cheeks.

"What are you really doing here?" she smiled.

Jake set his bags down near the door. "I, uh…" His eyes roamed around, taking in everything before settling back on her. "I come bearing your last gift, and also an offer from opposing counsel."

"Seriously?" Molly asked.

He nodded.

Molly dropped back onto the couch and stared as Jake unzipped the outer pocket of his bag, then carried over a legal folder. He sat cautiously next to her, handed her the folder—and swallowed, looking nervous.

Molly cracked the cover, and began skimming the legal brief inside. Jake's client acknowledged that errors were made and sought to pay restitution over a term of a hundred years. Said client proposed to love, honor, adore and spoil Molly's client, subject to the terms listed therein, signed by all applicable parties. The firm's letterhead listed *Jake Alexander, Attorney at Law,* as the sole proprietor.

Across from her, Jake was holding his breath and not moving a muscle. Molly blinked away the tears that began falling again, walked over to her kitchen counter to find a pen, then signed on the dotted line. The sound of it was loud in the quiet room. Walking to stand in front of Jake, she handed him back the folder and then the pen.

He accepted it with trembling hands. Molly watched him scrawl his name across the last page, and then he gripped the packet tight—like it was his new lease on life. Molly supposed, in a way, it was. For her, too.

"Oh, and also my dad wants to know how soon you can get back down to Carolina, because they already have your new office ready and they need to know what color you want it painted," he blurted out, smiling up at her.

"*What?*"

"Maryanne said she'd call tomorrow with the real offer, but she didn't want to steal my thunder." Jake laughed, "She's been trying to pick out furniture and pictures for the walls all week."

"You've got to be kidding," Molly said, trying to adjust to the change in topic.

"Now, what do you think?" he drawled.

Molly shook her head and sat beside him again. "You're not kidding."

"No. Oh, and they need you to schedule your bar exam, too. There's a prep class they want to register you for that starts in two weeks, but you have to tell them which exam you're taking before they can sign you up," he explained.

"Jake—was anyone even going to ask me if I wanted this job? Or did they just assume I was a foregone conclusion?"

"I think they were counting on my charm to tie up the case," he laughed. "I was warned not to screw it up."

"Oh God," Molly moaned. "I never stood a chance, did I?"

"To be fair…" Jake said, reaching for her, "Neither did I, darlin'."

Molly wrapped her arms around his neck and kissed him, pouring every ounce of longing and love she had into it. Jake gasped, knocked his ball cap off his head, then pulled Molly into his lap. He yanked free the elastic of her ponytail, and then wound his fingers tight into her hair. His tongue tangled with hers as Jake deepened the kiss, and his hands traveled over her back and rear, rough and desperate.

Molly breathed the scent of him in deep, inhaled the way he wanted her—and knew she was home. Whether it was here in Boston, or down in Wilmington, this man was home, and would be no matter where they were. *Home*—at last, Molly was home.

Chapter Thirty-Five

MOLLY STRADDLED HIM on her couch, kissing Jake back like her life depended on it. For a few minutes, that worked just fine for him. But she'd been gone for weeks, and Jake had been yearning rather abjectly for her. Suddenly, he needed to *see* her. *All* of her.

He grabbed the hem of her t-shirt and pulled, urging Molly's arms over her head with the gathered material until he could get the thing all the way off her. He dropped it somewhere behind him, then hooked his fingers in her bra straps and slid them off her shoulders. When her beautiful breasts were finally exposed, Jake set his lips against all that soft skin. He licked and sucked at her until Molly was taking in short little gasps of air—like bolts of electricity were shocking through her body with each flick of his tongue.

When she couldn't stand it anymore, Molly pulled away. Before Jake could blink, she slid to her knees on the carpet in front of him, working at the zipper of his jeans with nimble fingers. Jake was so hard that he could feel his pulse throbbing in his dick—before Molly could do him permanent damage, he batted her hands away and freed himself. Her movements were clumsy, needy. As much as he wanted to haul her off to the nearest bed and devour her on his own terms, Jake didn't dare refuse Molly now—she was liable to take a chunk out of his tender parts in her current condition.

Besides, nothing could have torn his eyes away from the sight of Molly taking him into her mouth. He watched, fascinated, as she moved her lips on him—one hand braced at the base, her tongue painting lines up the underside. Jake wrapped his hand around hers, tightening her grip. That felt so good that he couldn't resist helping Molly give him a stroke or two. She hummed in her throat, and he released her hand to gently cup the back of her head, trying not to flex his hips too hard.

Jake held out as long as he could endure it. But the headiness of being here with Molly at last—combined with the sweet heat of her talented mouth—made it impossible to last long. Gently, he eased her away and pulled her to her feet. Then Jake hauled Molly into his arms and carried her through her open bedroom door.

An oscillating fan was whirring on the top of the dresser. The breeze brushed over Jake's neck as he walked past and set Molly on the edge of the bed. She leaned back, propping herself on her elbows, and watched him with avid eyes. While he yanked off his t-shirt, Jake nudged her legs wide with his knees—and stared at the sight he'd been missing.

It was definitely his turn to hit the carpet and pay tribute to her body. Jake took Molly's pretty little feet in both hands, and set a kiss on the top of each set of toes.

"I love these," he told her.

He slid his palms up her legs to cup the curve of her calves. He kissed each ankle bone, then tickled the back of her knees, making Molly squirm.

"I missed these." Jake's breath feathered hot across the skin on the inside of her knees, and she shifted again. The smallest whimper escaped her lips, like she'd been trying to hold it in. With what he had in mind, Jake wanted to see Molly just try to keep quiet.

He smoothed his hands up the inside of Molly's toned thighs, spreading her even wider. He peeked up and saw that she was still watching, so Jake smiled as he nuzzled all that silky skin.

"I *really* love these," he said, his voice low and husky. As he kissed his way up her legs, Jake flicked his tongue out lightly, teasing her. Molly nearly jumped out of her skin, she was so tightly wound. He didn't have the heart or the patience to torment her, though—so when he reached her center, Jake didn't mess around. He simply opened his mouth and licked her, deep and hard. The shock of it streaked through Molly, bowing her back and turning her core to lava.

Jake growled, hungry and possessive. No one else could do this to Molly—could make her burn like he could. With every stroke of his tongue and his fingers, he transformed his woman into a vibrating, molten bundle of nerve-endings. He devoured her, tasting Molly's arousal until he heard her breathing change. When her hands drifted down to hold his head tightly against her, Jake knew she was close. He pinned her hips down with his hands and brought her right over the edge, exactly the way she liked best.

Then he stood up and said, "And I especially love that." Molly slumped deeper into the mattress and squeezed her eyes shut, a grin stretching her lips wide.

"Me too," she said.

Jake pulled out his wallet and extracted a couple of condoms, then tossed them on the bed next to her. He dropped his jeans and boxers where he stood, and kicked off his shoes.

"Scoot back," he murmured, loving the way the shaft of light from the high barred window fell across her stomach. Even though there was no lamp on in the room, the streetlights outside made it easy to see what he wanted. Jake couldn't get enough of seeing her.

He knelt between her legs and gazed down at her. Molly's arms were stretched over her head—her hands pressed to the wall and her breasts high and round on her chest. He leaned forward to taste one perfect nipple. Molly's hair was spread in a halo around her head. Her thighs were still trembling.

"Did you think about this when we were apart, Miss Molly?" Jake asked her.

She watched him. "Yes."

"Did you touch yourself, thinking of all the things we did together?"

She nodded mutely, arching her back toward him. Jake trailed a finger down her body, from the base of her throat all the way to her pubic bone.

"I did too, you know." He braced his hands beside her shoulders and leaned down to speak beside her ear, low and deep the way he knew made her shiver. "I got myself off every night in my bed, imagining taking you every which way I could think of."

"Oh," Molly squeaked, writhing in the most gratifying way.

Jake fumbled around for one of the condoms, ripped it open with his teeth, and then rolled it over himself. "But you know what I think?" he asked.

"What?" she whispered.

"This way will always be the best way." He guided himself into the tight, sweet heat of her body. *Home.* God, at last Jake was home.

"Why?"

"Because—" He kissed her, lingering over the taste of her mouth. "Watching your beautiful face when you come will never get old for me. Not in a million years."

With that, Jake withdrew and thrust deep again. Fast and hard, in a desperate rhythm like the beat of his heart.

"Come for me, Molly," Jake begged. "I missed you so damn much. Come again for me."

And bless her heart, but that woman did.

LATER, HE LAID in her bed and listened to the noise from the street outside, and to Molly's quiet breathing. Jake allowed himself to start making plans while the fan turned back and forth on the bureau, cooling the sweat on their skin.

Before he could say anything, Molly spoke. "How long are you staying?"

"Only a few days this time. But I'll come back soon, I promise."

"Oh good. I guess...I guess I could use a hand getting ready to move?" she said, her voice uncertain. "There's about two months left on the lease here, but your dad probably wants me to move down long before that, right?"

Jake smiled against her hair. "Not to mention me," he told her.

"Or me," she admitted, squeezing him tight.

Jake thought that was confirmation enough that Molly was well and truly his again. She'd come back home soon, and then all would be perfect. He'd do everything in his power to give her the best life he could, from here on out. Jake tilted up Molly's chin and kissed her long and hard, then gave voice to his idea.

"When you move down, I was thinking you won't really need to look for a place," he said, as casually as he could manage. "You could stay with me—or even move into my spare bedroom, if you wanted. That way you could have room to spread out, or your own space if you needed it..." Molly reached up and smothered the rest of his words with her hand.

"Did you just ask me to move in with you?"

Jake nodded, blinking at her.

Molly beamed, bright and sunny, even in the dark room. "I would love to," she said.

Jake had even more to offer, though. He pulled her hand away. "Then, when my aunt Ceecee moves out in a few months, we can start working on her house together. You know—take our time and make it exactly how we want it before we move in there."

Molly sighed, long and poignant. "You want to live there with *me*?"

"Of course. Who else would I want to live with? Molly...you and I—I want us to be together for a long, long time. I am never getting over you."

Molly contemplated that for an agonizingly long while. At last, she asked, "Jake?"

"Hmm?"

"So...someday—way, way in the future..."

He grinned, liking how that sounded. "Yeah, baby girl?"

"Do you think your grandpa's barn might be a good place to have a—a big party?"

"Naw..." Jake said. He flicked on the light beside her bed and chuckled at her crestfallen expression. "But it would be a great place for a wedding someday."

Molly went pink with happiness when he said it. "Really?"

"Absolutely. There's room for a dance floor in the middle, and tables all around the sides."

"And we could hang strings of lights from the rafters." She flopped back and gazed up at her ceiling, with that same expression of wonderment that she'd worn when they visited the barn the first time.

Jake watched her face, and saw how much she was hoping for it. Molly had no idea how much he was, too. A lazy grin tugged at his lips, and he drawled, "Yeah, we might could."

He laid on the hokey grammar and the Southern accent thick and deep, just to get her attention.

Molly's gaze snapped down and locked with his. Oh, she knew what he was doing, all right.

"What's it worth to you?" Jake asked softly.

"A lot. Why? What did you have in mind?"

"A lot."

"Really?"

"I should say 'more.' A lot *more*."

Molly smiled back, and then she was rolling toward him, bare and warm and happy. Jake was a lucky man—a grateful man. God, he'd never even guessed this kind of perfect happiness was out there waiting for him. He hadn't ever dared hope for it. Jake bent his head close to hers, absorbing her softness and the rightness of the moment, then suffused his kiss with every bit of his heart.

Chapter Thirty-Six

J AKE STAYED FOR three days, went home for two long
weeks, and then returned—exactly like he said he would.
Molly had packed up most of her things by then, so they
piled the boxes into George's truck, took them to the mailing
store, and had them shipped to Jake's condo. Once that was
done, they returned to the apartment—where only a few
suitcases, some paper plates and cups, and a mattress on the
floor remained.

Meg and Edward would drive them both to the airport
tomorrow, and Molly would start work at *Alexander, Polk &*
Futch the following Monday. Jake had already given his
notice at the States Attorney's Office, and had begun looking
for his own office space earlier that week.

They ate some sandwiches for dinner, played a round of
cards that was more strip than poker, and headed straight for
bed.

Now, though, Molly was too excited to fall asleep. She
still couldn't quite believe that it was all *really* happening.
Somehow, she'd gotten the job *and* the boy. She squealed a
little, kicking her feet.

Jake propped himself up on his elbow and grinned at her. "You know, honey," he teased, "I am not sure you are qualified to be a Southerner just yet." He toyed with her hair, spreading it across the pillow.

"Is that right?" Molly answered in her best southern accent. It wasn't terrible. Jake arched an eyebrow at her.

"That's right. I think maybe I ought to give you a little quiz to make sure we can let you in."

"A quiz."

"Yes. A quiz. I have authorization." Jake pasted his most professional expression on his face.

Molly stared him down, but Jake still nodded back, full of conviction.

"All right, cowboy, take your best shot," she told him. "But I'm warning you, I'm a sore loser." She narrowed her eyes at him and tried to look threatening.

"I *will* take my best shot. Thank you."

"And if I win?" she purred, pouring on the accent again.

"I will sacrifice my own body for the cause," Jake replied, hand over his heart.

"Very noble of you." Molly rolled her eyes, but he had a point. His muscled chest alone would make quite the prize.

"And if you *lose...*" he drawled, trying to nudge the sheet lower. His eyes followed his fingers.

"I won't lose." She yanked the sheet back up and held it there.

Jake feigned concern. "Don't you want to know what—"

"Nope. I intend to win." No accent needed. Molly was ready.

"I see." He eyed her expression warily.

"Mm-hm." She was firm. Resolute.

He swallowed, sizing her up. "Alright, girl. Let's get started. Who is the mascot of Texas A&M University?"

"Aggies," Molly said, all business.

"And UT?"

"Longhorns," she barked, giving Jake a "hook-em Horns" sign right in his grill.

"Nickname of the University of Mississippi?"

"That would be Ole Miss."

"What would one shout to root on the home team in Alabama?"

"Rolllllllll Tide," Molly smirked.

"Okay, now just one minute," Jake huffed, smelling a rat. "Are you cheating? Lemme see your hands." He grabbed her hands and made a show of looking for crib notes. Molly was naked as a jaybird, though, and grinned cheekily at him.

"Nothing up my sleeve," she said, smacking him on the arm. "Why don't you try to actually challenge me this time?"

"Fine. What trees do Georgia natives get nostalgic about?"

"Pine trees. Maybe peaches," Molly retorted.

"And in South Carolina?"

"Please! The magnolia. It *is* the Magnolia State, isn't it?"

"You appear to be a formidable contender," Jake muttered.

"Indeed, I am," she agreed, laying the accent on thick again. "But don't try to butter me up."

He eyed her speculatively. "Hmmm, butter. I—"

"Do not even go there," Molly warned. "I have a quiz to ace."

"Alright then. 'Chicken-fried' contains which meat—chicken, or other?" Jake leaned in to nip at her ear, as if she might be hiding something equally delicious there.

"Beef cutlet. Breaded and fried, and often served with grits and eggs for breakfast. Though personally, I prefer biscuits and gravy." Molly swatted away one of Jake's wandering hands.

"Fine—composition of grits?" he growled into her neck.

"Corn meal. And lots of cheese and butter if someone *really* loves you."

Jake snorted and sat up. "Are you sure you grew up in New England?"

"Here and there. Please proceed." Molly sat up herself, and plumped the pillows behind her, holding tight to the sheet across her chest.

"Okay, how about this? Name a southern town referenced in a beloved Johnny and June song."

"Jackson, Mississippi." Molly rolled her eyes again and hummed a bar or two.

"Name a favorite Carolina soft drink," Jake demanded.

"That would be Cheerwine. I believe it resembles Dr. Pepper. Maybe Mr. Pibb."

Jake was frowning mightily now. "Lowcountry soup loaded with sherry?"

"She-crab. You know, I'm beginning to think you *want* me to win," Molly told him.

"The heck I do," Jake protested. "What's a kind of booze people like to mix up in their yards?"

"Probably moonshine. But seriously—do people really do that?"

"You know what, sugar, I think I am just a teensy bit afraid of you. Remind me not to go up against you in a court of law." Jake backed away a little, but the mattress wasn't large. If he went too far, he'd end up on the floor.

"You are *not*. And you're a terrible liar," Molly smiled.

Jake flopped back on the bed to contemplate the ceiling. "I suppose it would be helpful to have you *with* me, rather than against me," he mused.

"You got that right. Also, *I win*—perfect score. Now pay up," Molly said.

Jake rolled to his side and gazed up at Molly, his beautiful blue eyes bright. "Just one more question, I think, for all the marbles."

"Lay it on me, hot stuff."

"What are you doing for the rest of your life?" he inquired softly.

Molly felt her face flush hot. "Oh, you know, this and that."

Jake shook his head, not letting her evade the question. "How about giving *us* a go?"

"Heck yes I will," Molly murmured, leaning in for his kiss.

"Right answer," Jake said, pulling her in tight. "And we both win."

Epilogue

I T HAD TAKEN many months, but with the small loan
Jake and Molly applied for and the gift from his parents,
they'd been able to replace the roof and the windows, gut
the kitchen and most of the bathrooms, and refinish all the
wood floors. Now, though, Molly refused to do a single
other thing before they moved into Ceecee's house. They'd
been ferrying car loads of possessions over to it all day,
before the moving truck brought their furniture tomorrow.

Soon, they'd go pick up a pizza and come back to sleep
on the pallet they set up in the bedroom. Jake figured it was
time to take care of one final piece of business—and Healey
had already dropped it off while Molly fussed around inside.

Eventually, Molly stepped back out, wiping her hands on
her gym shorts. He and Duke were in position—exceedingly
pleased with themselves and standing next to a big wicker
laundry basket on the floor of the porch. Molly frowned
down at it and pointed.

"What's that?"

Jake pulled back the blanket like a magician, produced the
wriggling little puppy from within, and handed her to Molly.
As he expected, Molly freaked out—cuddling the small

bundle of golden retriever to her chest and squealing like a school kid. The puppy started slobbering all over Molly's face.

"Oh my God! Jake! Where did you find it?" she cried.

"*It's* a she," he laughed, enjoying the scene. Duke barked once in agreement, panting up at the girls and wagging his tail.

"She! Where did you get her? Oh my God I want her!" Molly squeaked, kissing the ecstatic dog all over her fluffy face.

Jake chuckled. "Oh, well, if you want her, then I guess it's okay."

"*What's* okay?" Molly demanded.

"That I got her for you."

"Me? You got *me* a puppy?"

Jake should have known this would turn into an interrogation. "I sure did."

"But why?"

"Girl, I have never met a person who needed a dog more than you," Jake said. Duke barked again, quick and sharp, as if to say, *Duh.*

Molly just stared at him, not even registering that the puppy had hold of her braid and was giving it a tentative gnaw.

Jake cleared his throat, and stroked the puppy's soft back. "May I introduce 'Penelope's Sunshine Lollipop'?"

"Who now?"

He laughed. He'd had the same reaction. "That's just the breeder's name. You can call her Lolly, if you want."

"Lolly. Oh, Lolly, that's a perfect name for you, isn't it baby girl?" Molly cooed.

Jake rubbed a weary hand over his eyes. "Oh Lord. I just realized something."

"What?"

"I did not even plan this, but your names flipping *rhyme.*"

She paused, thought about it, and then laughed out loud—setting the puppy off into frantic, happy yips. "*Yes*! Yes, it's perfect!" Molly started dancing around the porch with the puppy, singing nonsense rhymes to her.

Jake looked down at Duke. "Oh, bud, what have we done? She's gonna have that poor dog tricked out in rhinestones and bows in about two seconds flat." His own dog huffed out an agreeable sounding breath, then flopped down on Jake's feet, watching the proceedings as contently as you please.

Jake sighed. "Well, it's going to be hard to top that dang puppy, but I think there might be one other thing in that basket."

Molly set the pup down and Lolly scampered curiously over like her back legs were faster than her front—then skidded to a stop on her pudgy little behind. She jammed her snuffling nose into the basket next Jake's hand, and rooted around with him. Unfortunately, Lolly found what Jake was searching for before he did. She yanked her little golden head free and began zipping crazily around the porch, the small box clamped in her jaws.

"Lolly, no!" Jake hollered. In response, the pup dropped the box under one of the rocking chairs, raced to the other side of the porch, and stood there panting expectantly.

Jake bent to retrieve the box, its handwritten note now sadly mangled and soggy.

Molly gasped, "Lolly, no!"

Jerking his head to the side, Jake watched the small dog squat in the corner next to the railing, and piddle right there on the boards of the porch floor. He and Molly both groaned, and even Duke dropped his head to his paws, a pained look on his face. At least they hadn't gotten around to sanding and painting the porch yet. Still, the smell was going to be the very devil to get rid of.

"Oh no," Molly moaned, looking worried. "Don't worry! I'll run in and get some water to rinse it off. And some paper towels."

Jake tried to shake off the distraction. Where Molly was concerned, all of his best-laid plans had a way of skidding sideways—but he was learning to adapt, day by day. When she returned, he was ready again. Jake knelt on the dry wood at the center of the porch, one dog on either side of him, and held the little box up to her.

"What's...what's that?" Molly squeaked, pointing at the gift.

"Why don't you read the note and find out?" Jake inquired, biting his lip.

Molly stood there blinking quickly. Finally, just as his knees were growing numb, she set the bucket and the paper towels down and reached for the box.

Slipping the little rolled-up piece of paper free, she read, "I'll want all of you, every day, forever—and if you want me back, I'll never leave you." Her voice hitched on the last word. When she met his eyes, Jake held up a new, untainted diamond ring that he'd agonized over—but picked out all by himself.

"Jake," she whispered.

"Marry me, Molly," he pleaded. "My world begins and ends with you and I can't wait any longer. Trust me...I tried." They might have both screwed up their first attempts at marriage, but they'd been given a second chance—and this time Jake knew he and Molly were going to get everything exactly right.

The dogs sat panting up at her, hanging on her every breath, waiting for her answer. "Look at them—these babies need some legitimate parents," Jake laughed, trying to defuse the almost unbearable nervousness he was feeling.

Molly shook her head, dislodging some of the tears beginning to streak down her face. Then she kneeled in front of Jake, spread her arms wide to include all of them, and cried, "Yes. Oh God, yes."

Review

Did you enjoy **Finding a Husband**? If so, please consider leaving a review at the retailer where you purchased this title.

Book reviews can be as simple or as detailed as you wish, but all of them help authors sell more books, and assist other readers in finding the stories they want to read.

Almost any book can be reviewed by simply logging into the website where you purchased the title, then scrolling to the bottom of the title's product page to find an area called "Leave a Review."

Up Next

Finding Forever

(Lost & Found, Book 4)

Twelve years is a long time to wait for the one you love.

Mina's husband Grey was a problem long before he died, but the realization that it's been two years since she buried him still startles her. She's been so busy learning to fend for herself—learning to leave Grey's ugly legacy behind—that Mina's barely noticed her efforts were turning her into an empty shell of a woman. However, when a sexy friend from her past comes to town, she can finally recognize that *she* isn't the one who died. There might be a lot of life left to live—if she's willing to look behind a door she's never dared to open.

Mack has always maintained a strict hands-off policy when it came to his buddy's delectable wife Mina. Sure, he *noticed* her—a guy would have to be dead not to notice Mina. That didn't mean Mack could do anything about it, though. For twelve long and painful years, he's had to sit on the sidelines, watching the lousy way Grey treated her. But now that Mina is free, Mack knows he won't pass up the chance to be with her himself. He wants it all—except there's a very real possibility that the woman he hungers for can't give him what he needs. Mack has no idea what happens then.

Can Mina and Mack seize their shot at forever, once and for all? Or will the demons Grey left behind sink them both?

Finding Forever

Chapter One

MINA PLOPPED A couple more cherries into the cocktail shaker and poked at them with a wooden spoon. She'd already smashed some mint leaves in the bottom of the shaker, as well as a little habanero chili. But now the recipe said to "muddle" the berries, and she wasn't entirely sure what that meant. She read ahead. The instruction to add ice and rum was easy—Mina could certainly manage that. However, to finish off the Porch Crawlers, she would need something called simple syrup, and she had *no* idea what that was.

She rifled through her sister-in-law's liquor cabinet. It was well-stocked, but it didn't seem to have anything resembling her mysterious drink ingredient. Mina re-checked the print-out she'd brought with her, looking for clues, and realized she'd also forgotten to bring club soda. *Rats*. She gnawed at her lip and tried to think of a work-around—maybe ginger ale would do the trick? She knew she'd seen a can or two of that in the pantry.

A car door slammed outside, and Mina cursed under her breath, "Damn it." Sadie and Trent had shown up too early.

She'd been hoping to greet her hosts with the cocktails right when they arrived, then shoo the couple out to the lawn chairs so they could watch the sunset together. Mina and her little nephew Monty could pop in a video for a while, and then she would get dinner started for all of them. It seemed the least she could do, since the Bly family had insisted she join them at their bay house, Winthrop Farm, for the long weekend. They hadn't wanted Mina to be alone for the anniversary of her husband's death. She supposed she couldn't blame them.

It didn't seem possible that Grey had been gone for two whole years already. In some ways, it was like he'd never existed—an unhappy dream that had happened to some other person. There were still days, though, when it felt like Grey Whitney's shade followed Mina around with a persistent, wolfish hunger. Never letting go, never letting up, always wanting to consume her. Those days were fewer and fewer, though. Mina had worked hard to get to this point, and she was so much better than she'd been.

She even thought she would be able to stay in this big old house with her dead husband's family, without any of them ever knowing what he'd put her through. His sister Sadie had always been kind to Mina, despite the way Mina and Grey had gotten together. And, if the extended Whitney family preferred to think that Mina's marriage to Grey had been a happy one, then so be it. They could have that illusion—they'd earned it. Mina would mark the anniversary of his death with them, and when she returned home in three days, she would raise a glass to herself for surviving it. *All* of it.

The screen door creaked opened, and she turned with a smile. "You're here!" she called. She planted her feet, getting ready for little Monty to charge her and leap up for a hug.

But it wasn't Sadie and Trent Bly and their toddler son, who stood in the front hall. It was Mack Bolton. Mina's heart began knocking haphazardly around in her chest, and her breathing didn't seem to be working quite right. She waited until she was sure her voice would be steady before she spoke.

"Well, well. Look what the cat dragged in," Mina finally drawled. Frantically, she glanced over his shoulder to the gravel drive beyond and spotted no minivan and no fancy

Volvo station wagon—just Mack's big white pickup truck and her little silver sedan. They were alone.

"Hey, kid," he said. He dropped a duffel near the bottom of the stairs which sure made it look like he planned to stay a while. "What's new?"

"Uh…" Mina shrugged, begging her brain to catch up with this new reality. "Sadie and Trent invited me out for the weekend," she explained. "Are you, uh…"

Mack jammed his hands in the pockets of his shorts and waited for her to finish. He looked amused by her discomfiture.

"Did they invite you, too?" she asked.

"As a matter of fact, they did. Sounds like Monty got sick and they couldn't make it."

"*What?*" Mina wouldn't panic. There was no need to panic about her and Mack Bolton staying alone in this house together. If things got too heavy, all she had to do was *leave*. It was that simple.

"They felt bad and didn't want to cancel," he explained. "So, they gave me a buzz and asked if I would come over and get things situated for you. Maybe take you out on the boat, that kind of thing."

Mina gaped. "Are you shitting me right now?" She had to remind herself that Sadie Bly did *not* know about her history with Mack. *No way* could she know. This was merely a crazy coincidence, that was all—not some devious master plan to get them to hook up.

"Nope." He lifted his chin at the big metal cocktail shaker in her hand. "What are you making?"

"I was trying to make them a drink called a Porch Crawler, but I'm missing a couple of ingredients." Mina huffed, "You'd think they would've let me know they weren't coming."

Right on cue, her cell began ringing on the kitchen counter. "Ten bucks says that's them," Mack laughed.

She turned, set the cocktail shaker precisely beside her, and picked up her phone. Sadie blasted her with a wall of words the moment Mina connected the call. She nodded at Mack—he was right.

"I'll go down to the basement and turn on the circuit breakers," he whispered.

Well, that certainly explained why the blender and the ceiling fan wouldn't work. Mina held the door for him and watched him trot down the stairs into the dark.

"Please don't go home because of us," Sadie pleaded in her ear. "Promise you'll stay."

"I—"

"There's a market right up the road. You remember where it is. Run up there now and then you won't have to leave for the rest of the weekend."

"Don't worry, I'll be fine," Mina assured her. She watched the basement door for Mack to reemerge again.

"One more thing," Sadie said in a rush. Mina could hear Monty crying in the background. "Trenton didn't want you to have to be alone. We sent—"

"—Mack Bolton to check on me?" Mina inquired.

Sadie groaned. "He's already there, isn't he?"

"Yep, he sure is."

"I'm so sorry! I meant to call earlier, but then Monty barfed all over his car seat and we got distracted. Is it going to be too weird having him there? You know him, right? He's a really good guy, I promise."

"It's okay, Sadie. Mack's cool—he and I have known each other for a very long time." Which was probably one of life's bigger understatements.

"I figured, since he and Grey were such good friends. So, you don't mind?"

Mack sauntered into the kitchen, washed his hands, then opened the cocktail shaker to take a sniff. He raised an eyebrow at Mina.

"No, I don't mind." *Much.*

Sadie asked, "Can I talk to him?"

Mina handed the phone over. "She wants to talk to you," she explained.

"Hey, Sadie," Mack grinned. He listened for a minute, then walked over to open a drawer in an antique sideboard. He lifted out a set of keys, jingled them at Mina and said, "Got 'em."

Mina could hear Sadie talking a mile a minute. Mack listened carefully before his eyes crinkled at the corners and he gave Mina a very obvious once-over.

"She seems fine to me," he said into her phone.

Mina rolled her eyes and gestured for him to hang up. He nodded, but then turned and stepped outside, cradling her cell against his shoulder as he pulled a couple grocery bags from the bed of his truck. At least *one* of them had been smart enough to stop at the store before arriving.

Mina wondered again if her sister-in-law could have arranged this on purpose. Would she actually try to throw her and Mack together? Sure, the Blys had encouraged her to start dating again, but a fix-up seemed unlikely—especially *this* weekend.

The spark between them had always been there, of course, but Mina had buried it deep and always hidden it from others. Sadie was pesky that way, though. She had an unnerving way of figuring stuff like that out.

Mack finished up and handed the phone back to her. She put it up to her ear, and immediately noticed the faint smell of his cologne. "Sadie?" she asked.

"She hung up," Mack said. "Are you sure you don't mind if I stay? I don't have to—I only live a few minutes away. If you wanted, I could just stop by if you needed anything."

"It's fine," Mina scoffed. "There's plenty of room for both of us."

Mack's amber eyes roved over her face. His hair was longer on top than the last time she'd seen him, and he'd grown a short, trim beard. He looked impossibly handsome.

"Tell you what," he said. He reached into one of the bags, extracted a bottle of margarita mix, and thunked it onto the counter. "Why don't you fire up that blender and make us a couple of these? I'll meet you out there," he pointed at the Adirondack chairs on the lawn facing the water, "Once I bring the rest of my stuff in."

Now that the electricity was on and the blender would actually work, whipping up some margaritas from a bottled mixer sounded way easier than unraveling the ambiguities of simple syrup. Besides, Mina was going to need every brain cell she had to figure out what to do about Mack. She dumped the contents of the cocktail shaker down the disposal, skimped on the tequila, and soon found herself staring down two glasses of icy-green liquid courage.

She could do this. Mack was a good, easy-going guy, who clearly didn't think anything crazy or life-changing was happening. They were old friends. Old friends hung out sometimes. Simple. Nothing to get worked up over.

Mina tucked her book under her arm, snagged the glasses, and headed for those lawn chairs. Mack's heavy tread was clumping around upstairs, and with any luck he'd take his time. Then she could have a couple minutes to take a few sips, read a few pages, and hopefully get her head straight before she had to make innocuous small talk with the man she'd had a raging crush on for twelve freaking years.

When Mack finally wandered out, he smiled down at Mina, sank into his chair and sighed happily. Other than thanking her for the drink, he didn't say much. Mina pretended to keep reading, and Mack lazily watched the boats sailing by.

The sun was setting—streaking the sky in sherbet colors over the water, which mirrored the colors right back again. Their glasses dripped condensation on the wooden armrests. Mina's hand and Mack's were inches apart, each holding onto their glass like a lifeline. Or...maybe that was just Mina.

She wondered how long he intended to stay quiet. He couldn't possibly think that she could still see well enough to read in the fading light, could he?

Finally, she broke the silence herself. "I think this may be the nicest place on earth."

"Agreed," he said. "I don't know how they found it. One of the perks of working in real estate, I guess." Sadie had sold houses for years, but as far as Mina knew, she had given it up once Monty was born.

"Hmm. No kidding," Mina agreed.

The slightest of touches feathered across her hand—the tip of Mack's little finger just grazing hers. Out of the corner of her eye, Mina looked down, but it was hard to tell if it was on purpose or not.

Mack said, "Maybe we should start thinking about dinner."

She dragged her eyes up from his hand to his face, but he was still looking at the water and made no move to acknowledge touching her.

"I hadn't really thought that far ahead," Mina admitted. She was talking too fast but couldn't seem to stop. "Sadie and Trent were going to bring the groceries when they came, so I can't vouch for what might be in there right now."

Mack shrugged. "That's okay, we can go out. What do you feel like?"

That was an easy one—even someone as distracted as Mina could figure it out. "It's fall on the bay, Mack," she beamed.

He grinned back. "Steamed crabs, it is. Smart girl."

Mina looked down again. Mack was *definitely* brushing her fingers with his. When he caught her eye, a faint laugh passed his lips and he jumped up.

"Come on, I'm starved. Let's eat," he said.

KING'S KRABS WAS right on a marina, a looming bright-blue structure with a boozy local clientele that was rabidly devoted. In a nod to the cool evening, the crab house had set up standing heaters around the perimeter of the covered patio. Coupled with the little flickering candles on the tables and the strings of twinkling lights zig-zagging overhead, they provided a welcoming aura of light in the dim dining area. The atmosphere was relaxed and happy, and Mina figured if she couldn't act normal there, she probably couldn't manage it anywhere.

They'd missed the big dinner rush, so the waitress was able to seat them at a table right next to the water. A line of sailboats and smaller yachting craft were docked a few feet away, and as they bobbed in the water, their fittings clanked softly. Thick brown paper covered the table, and the air smelled of seafood, beer, and bay water.

Mack sat across from her, slouching easily. Mina realized that she'd been trying so hard to play it cool that she hadn't really gotten a very good look at him yet. His worn-out gray T-shirt showed off his tan biceps, and his shoulders and chest looked broader and stronger than she remembered. He'd changed into an old pair of jeans and his hair was longer than usual, beginning to show just a hint of the glossy dark waves it would curl into if it wasn't trimmed regularly. Almost like a woman's hair, Mina thought, silky and thick.

Soft-looking. Usually, Mack's hair was cropped too short to notice anything other than the color, and the strong shape of his neck and skull—*not* that Mina had ever obsessed about *that*.

A few large tin lights hung from the ceiling, but their bulbs were so weak they didn't contribute much light. They swung a bit in the breeze, mimicking the motion of the sailboat masts, and their hazy spotlights moved in circles across the wooden floor.

Mina said, "This is great. The last time I was here was for a big 50th anniversary party. It was hard to enjoy myself."

Mack took a swig of his beer, and she noticed his neck again. Watched him swallow while he watched her. "Why?" he asked.

"I was usually a wreck at Whitney family get-togethers," Mina admitted. When Mack looked puzzled, she explained, "All those aunts always keeping an eagle-eye on me, waiting for me to screw up."

He nodded, unable to deny it. Mack probably knew Grey's family better than Mina did. "Luckily, this isn't a family get-together," he said.

In Mina's opinion, that was a good thing. So why did Mack sound faintly irritated? "You're right. I can smile at you—or even flirt with you—and no one here would even care."

Mack's eyes perked up at that and he grinned at her. He definitely liked that. "I will admit, I am partial to the idea."

It seemed she was still a sucker for his random little compliments, Mina thought ruefully. There'd been a time where she'd had to force herself to stop following him around at gatherings, like a stray dog hoping for another table scrap. It had gotten pathetic.

She drank another margarita, this one much stronger than the one she'd made at the house. The waitress delivered orders of hush puppies and dumped a pile of steamed and spiced blue crabs in the center of the table.

Mack mostly watched Mina eat as he drank his beer. It was a challenge to make eye contact when he had that seductive smolder aimed her way. Whenever she shoveled a piece of crab or hush puppy in her face, Mack got this little half smile that made Mina want to either smack him or kiss him—it was a bit of a toss-up.

"Will you knock it off?" she demanded. "I can't eat when you keep looking at me like that."

"Like what, kiddo?"

"Like I'm dinner."

Mack laughed out loud at that, and the sound of it just made the heat pooling low in her belly even worse.

"Come on. Help me out here," Mina begged. "You've hardly eaten any of these things."

Thankfully, he relented. "All right, you. Stand back and let a pro show you how it's done." He set about dismantling the crabs with efficiency and determination, and before long he had decimated the pile between them.

The waitress kept switching Mina's empty margaritas out for full ones, but Mina figured that was okay. Between the feast on the table and the way the tequila was keeping her nerves quiet, she wasn't about to complain. She had been on a few dates since she'd buried Grey two years ago, but not one had felt like *this*.

Could this even be considered a date, anyway? It seemed like one, but Mack was one of Grey's oldest friends. Maybe all his flirting over the years had been meaningless, and he'd never seen Mina as anything more than his buddy's wife.

Hah. And pigs could fly.

DESPITE STUFFING HER face, Mina ended up a little woozy when they finally decided to head out. The parking lot was dark, and a sandy, rocky mess—picking her way across the uneven ground in her thin flip-flops was more of a challenge than it had been before. Mina tried for dignity, but she still managed to turn her ankle on a hidden curb as they neared the truck. Unsurprisingly, Mack was quick to catch her.

He led Mina the last few steps to his truck with an arm around her waist. She propped herself against the passenger side to take the weight off her foot, giggling a little sheepishly while Mack dug his keys out of his pocket. He leaned toward Mina, trying to reach around for the door handle so he could open the door for her.

"Sorry," he murmured. "I just need to..." But when he got closer, he trailed off.

Mina's giggle died in her throat. Mack was so close now—she would only have to tilt out a couple of inches if she really wanted to close the distance between them.

As if he could read her mind, Mack froze in place and turned to look at her. His burning gaze at such close range wiped any last vestiges of humor from Mina's face. He was even more handsome up close, his eyes so dark they looked black, his jaw firm and scent tantalizing. Mina thought Mack was going to kiss her, and her heart kicked into overdrive at the notion—even with those dates a few months ago, she hadn't kissed another man besides Grey since she was nineteen years old.

Instead of going for it, though, Mack simply closed his eyes and grazed her cheek with his own. His beard was soft against her skin. The caress was tender and affectionate and totally unexpected. Mina's breath hitched, and she slid her hands under his soft t-shirt to keep him near. Along his waistband, Mack's skin was hot and hard and begging for closer exploration.

The contact seemed to jerk him awake. He took Mina's arm, guided her aside, then yanked the truck's passenger door open. He helped her hop up into the seat before shutting her in without a word. Mina might have imagined it, but it seemed to take Mack an awfully long time to cross behind the truck to the driver's side. *Someone* wasn't as cool a cucumber as he liked to pretend, and that made her feel better.

The ride back to the house, through the dark and quiet streets of town, felt awkward after their near miss. Mack's radio was playing soft country music but turning up the volume seemed wrong to Mina. Acknowledging that loaded moment back in the parking lot felt clumsy, too. Mina's head buzzed, and she tried to decide what to do. She wanted a taste of Mack Bolton—there was no denying that. But maybe she should discover if he felt the same first.

Mack glanced quickly at her, just as they left town behind and headed down the tree-lined road that led to the Bly property. He cleared his throat, then said, "It should be criminal how good you smell."

Mina snorted. It was the last thing she'd expected. "Like beer and crab carcasses?" she wondered.

Mack chuckled, but it sounded strained. "Yeah, that's it," he retorted.

Silence reigned for the rest of the drive.

MINA WATCHED MACK through the kitchen window. Once they'd gotten back, he'd gone out to sit on the back patio while she washed their glasses from earlier. He'd wanted to help, but Mina had needed a few minutes to herself. Mack only accepted being waved away when Mina finally directed him to Trent's humidor on the side table.

Now, puffs of cigar smoke were drifting around outside, and Mina couldn't find anything else to do in the kitchen. It had seemed like a good idea to dock her phone and play music while she cleaned up, but her playlist had shifted from pop and country to something far more sultry and dangerous.

Languid guitar and harmonica whined from the speakers and tangled mercilessly with the smoke and the night. Mina was hot and bothered, and pretty sure she wouldn't be able to prevent going outside to join the man out there. *Why* had she had so many margaritas at dinner? And how many had she had, anyway? Three? Usually one was more than enough for her, but now she had no impulse control left *at all.*

Mina tried to think. How outrageously had she been flirting with Mack over dinner? It had definitely been a while since she'd been around a man like him. As gorgeous as Mack was, no one could really fault her for it. Her moves were obviously pretty rusty—the inept moment in the parking lot and her complete failure to maintain a normal conversation on the ride back were evidence of that. Mack had probably been relieved to retreat out back by himself. That way, he could hide from Mina, so she wouldn't embarrass herself anymore.

With most of the windows closed, it was stuffy in the kitchen. Mina knew it would be so much cooler outside in the breeze. She fanned her face ineffectually with her hand and looked around for the ceiling fan switch but couldn't find it.

Mack really wouldn't mind a little company—would he? If Mina kept a decent distance away and didn't chatter nervously, it would be totally *fine* to go out there. Hell, she probably couldn't even enunciate well anyway—it was always the first thing to go when she'd been drinking. So, she would just be quiet and companionable, from a good, safe, neighborly distance. And Mina would *not* look at Mack Bolton's mouth, sucking on that cigar. Her face flushed. Nor should she even *think* about it, apparently.

Mina's feet carried her straight out the French doors and right to him. That's when the real trouble started.

To read more, please purchase *Finding Forever* from your favorite bookseller!

FREE BOOK

Get a glimpse of Morgan, Meg, Molly and Mina—*before* their happily ever afters take place!

Sign up for the author's Reader's List and get a free copy of the Lost & Found prequel novella "Girls Night Out."

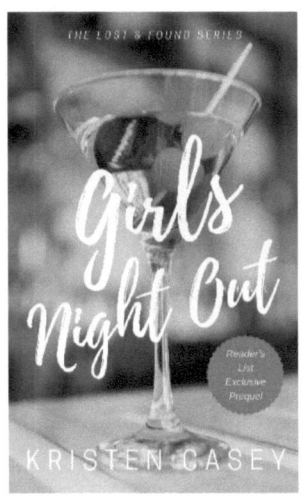

Visit Here to Get Started:

http://eepurl.com/ctGk1j

Also by Kristen Casey

The Triple Threat Series

The Titan Was Tall

The Doctor Was Dark

The Hero Was Handsome

The Masquerade was Magic

The Hero's Brother

The Triple Threat Box Set

The Black Watch Security Series

False Flag

Heat Seeking Missile

Brothers in Arms

Fight or Flight

Search and Destroy

Squared Away

Acknowledgements

Another book, another wave of gratitude. I'd like to thank my editor Helen, once again, for her stupendous efforts and great advice. Half the time, she works under totally unreasonable time constraints—through family responsibilities and through migraines (hers and mine!), to read and edit my manuscripts. For that, and so much more, I thank her. Her sharp eye and interesting questions made this book so much better. Her friendship makes *me* so much better.

As always, I want to thank Deborah at Tugboat Design for her lovely book cover design. Her expertise and professionalism are always on point, and I couldn't be more grateful.

Thank you to my readers, too! You never miss an opportunity to tell me how much you enjoy my books. You write me the *best* reviews online—and, you can't wait to tell me how much you look forward to my next story. All of that never fails to make my day, and makes this job such a happy one for me. Thanks!

Last, but never least, is my amazing family. My husband and children remain my most supportive, caring, fanatical fans—and that is a gift I will forever be grateful for. Thank you for creeping quietly around when I'm in the throes of a new story, and for always telling me I look cute in my new reading glasses. Love you guys!

About the Author

Kristen Casey writes the kind of heartfelt, steamy books she loves to read—full of relatable characters and delicious dialogue. She lives in Maryland with her husband, kids, and assorted cats, and in her free time, she enjoys all things crafty—especially projects she finds on Pinterest.

Sign up for her newsletter to receive exclusive free content and the inside scoop on sales and new releases—all emailed right to your inbox.

You can also follow her on social media for behind-the-scenes tales, character and setting inspiration, book reviews, and more:

Goodreads: Kristen_Casey
Facebook: AuthorKCasey
Twitter: AuthorKCasey
Pinterest: KristenCase0461
Instagram: Kristen.Casey.Books
BookBub: Kristen Casey
TikTok: KristenWritesRomance

Reading Order of Kristen's Books

The Lost & Found Series

Girls Night Out (Prequel exclusive to subscribers)

Finding Home (Book 1)

Finding Love (Book 2)

Lost in Love (Book 2.5 – Includes *Lucky in Love*)

The Flynn Sisters Box Set (Includes *Christmas in Cambridge*)

Finding a Husband (Book 3)

Finding Forever (Book 4)

Forever and a Day (Book 4.5 – Includes *Forever Starts Now*)

The O'Connell Sisters Box Set (Includes *Heroes & Husbands*)

The Triple Threat Series

The Titan was Tall (Book 1)

The Doctor was Dark (Book 2)

The Hero was Handsome (Book 3)

The Triple Threat Box Set (Includes *The Masquerade was Magic* and *The Hero's Brother*)

The Black Watch Security Series